The One To Watch

SHANE WATSON

The One To Watch

Quality Paperbacks Direct
London

This edition published 2002
by QPD
by arrangement with Macmillan Ltd
an imprint of Pan Macmillan Ltd

CN 108263

Typeset by Intype London Ltd
Printed and bound in Germany by
GGP Media, Pössneck

for Sophie

I would like to thank my agents and loyal friends Sarah, Felicity and Susannah, whose support goes way beyond the call of duty, my wonderful editor Imogen Taylor and all the team at Macmillan.

One

Transmission clock counts down the seconds.

A man wearing a velvet-collared Crombie coat stands in front of a large white house clutching a piece of paper which flaps, feebly, in the wind. He reads aloud from the paper into a microphone on a makeshift stand: 'On behalf of the Best family, it is my sad duty to confirm that Amber Best died at home, at 6 o'clock this morning, peacefully, after a brief illness.' He glances up with an expression of gravity before continuing, 'It is the fervent wish of Mr David Cross that his family should be allowed to grieve in peace and he asks that you respect their need for privacy at this difficult time.' There is a dull churning of motordrives. Camera pans to the figure of a man with cropped silver hair, wearing a long padded coat, making his way swiftly across the gravel towards the passenger side of a Land Rover. The driver of the Land Rover holds his right hand up to shield his face. Camera flashes ricochet off the windscreen. Camera follows the Land Rover as it accelerates at speed past the house and down the drive, taking in the photographers and camera crews ranged along the edge of the lawn, the cluster of policemen, the reporters, some of them talking animatedly into mikes, others crouched on the grass, drinking out of paper cups. Cut to close-up

1

of a young male reporter: 'That was David Cross, leaving the house, here near Kennet in Wiltshire, and we are informed that he will be staying with friends, locally, tonight. In a statement made via the family solicitor, earlier this morning, Mr Cross revealed that his wife, Amber Best, had been suffering from an incurable blood disease, diagnosed just two months ago, and that it had been her decision not to disclose her condition. Even those closest to the family are said to have been unaware of her illness. This morning, shocked friends and relatives are gathering on what would have been the eve of her forty-first birthday . . .' Voice fades out as The Rolling Stones' 'She's Like a Rainbow' fades up.' A series of images of a dark-haired woman appear on the screen, one after the other, apparently in no particular chronological order: an aerial shot of her lying spreadeagled on a lawn, naked but for arrangements of daisies; standing in a kitchen, tilting a mixing bowl for a gang of apron-clad, flour-coated children; on the cover of an album, smoky purple eyelids closed, glossy lips parted, with the words 'Pressed Flowers' painted in a silver arc across her collar bone; seated on a horse in a field, a fresh-faced girl in cinch-waisted black jacket, top hat and mud-spattered stock, gesturing with a whip in the direction of her mounted neighbour, just recognizable as the Prince of Wales . . .' Fade to black.

Jack gripped the sides of the basin and confronted her image in the mirror above it. Her skin was the colour of Caramac and there was a livid smudge along each cheekbone which had been 'peony blush' but was now 'peony blush' over an eczema base. Her shortish blonde hair looked yellow and parched and the glare of the television lights, combined with the effects of the make-up, had made her eyes crumple, giving her the look of a malevolent tortoise. She sat on the edge of the bath, pulled a mobile phone out of the breast pocket of her denim jacket and dialled Amanda's private line.

'Hello.' Amanda answered, as ever, like a woman professionally schooled in the arts of loving .

'It's me.' Jack was forced to whisper, being just a flimsy bathroom conversion away from the lights, cameras and entire production team of *The Real Amber Best*. She could hear Amanda's fingers pattering on her PC keys, could picture the giant moonstone and white-gold ring, the Camel Light smouldering in the ashtray.

'How's it going?' said Amanda.

'Very badly, thanks,' hissed Jack. 'Extremely poorly. They've made me put on a dress for a start, so it contrasts with yours and Lydia's "*image*".'

'What dress?'

She'd got Amanda's attention now. Amanda was the editor of *LaMode* and the appearance of her friends was a matter of professional concern to her. Particularly when the friend was also her contributing editor. Especially when there was every possibility that this friend would be seen by a viewing audience of ten million.

'Oh, you know, the red one.'

Amanda exhaled dramatically, 'What with? Not the cardigan . . .'

'Denim jacket . . . done up.'

'Shoes?'

'Listen. Forget the shoes. They're making me say

things I don't want to say. They keep asking questions about Amber and Dave, were they happy? Were we still close? . . . Oh, we were? Well, would it not have been normal, then, since she was your oldest friend, for her to tell you she was dying? I *knew* it would be like this. I don't know why we agreed to it. I can't believe we fell for that line about getting involved so we could "be in control". They couldn't care less about her or us, let alone the truth. They want "she was a slut, and I should know, and I've got the pictures to prove it".'

'Jack . . . Jack . . . whether or not they care, we do . . . and that's why we're doing it. Remember? Precisely because we're the only ones who know the real story. It's bound to feel a bit awkward to begin with, but it's only the start of weeks of filming, and most of it will end up on the cutting-room floor anyway. So . . . are you wearing the ankle boots?'

Jack's head was now under the basin, shrouded in a towel. 'Believe me, Amanda, they're not going to notice my feet. I am *covered* in eczema. I warned them not to touch me with that ginger muck but they knew best, and now they're out there, panicking, because suddenly they've got the Singing Detective slap bang in the middle of their glamorous documentary – Amanda? I can hear you tapping. Please concentrate.'

There was a long pause during which Jack could hear the fumbling sound of handset pressed against cashmere.

'OK. Jack? Mitzi's got hold of the production office, they'll have something on tape in a couple of weeks. We'll watch it together, darling. Dooon't worry. And, by the way, they're saying no problem if you want to bill them

for a haircut and colour. Only if you want . . . OK? Gotta
go . . .'

Needless to say, Amanda had not received the same offer
of a free cut and colour when she had met the Channel X
producer three weeks previously. Extending her moon-
stone-ring hand, she had given Janet Johns the split second
once-over – a quick downward flick of the eyes to check
the shoes, then dragging them up to meet Janet's with the
expression of absolute boredom and disdain that is the
fashion editor's speciality. The look said, 'Well there's only
one of us here who knows what's what, so let's get that
straight right away.' And it was very effective. Just like
that, Janet Johns forgot that she was Channel X's most
promising young producer, and became acutely conscious
of her two-year-old velvet-trimmed cardigan (Amanda
was wearing a cream leather motorcycle jacket) and
her square-toed shoes (pointy Jimmy Choo boots). They
exchanged pleasantries, went through the usual preliminaries, established the time frame for filming and all the
while Amanda (three O levels, struggling size 14, Botox
enhanced, forty-three) was conscious that Janet (first-class
degree, size 12, good skin, twenty-eight) was longing to
fling herself across the desk and beg Amanda to take her
shopping and make her cool. It was, Amanda had often
observed, fortunate that she had made her career in
fashion at a time when clever people lived in awe of those
who knew how to pick off the rail at Gucci. Which was
why she found herself in the offices of Channel X, nego-
tiating the details of a television programme, on behalf of

a group of friends who wanted nothing to do with the project.

That evening, after her meeting with Janet, Amanda had summoned them all together in a pub near her house in Shepherd's Bush.

'This isn't a pub, by the way, Amanda,' said Sam, rolling his eyes, 'it's a winebar stroke restaurant for people with live-in nannies.'

She ignored him, gesturing with a flapping hand for them to pack themselves into the corner booth. Sam shuffled along the seat first. Amanda pushed Nicholas in after him.

'Steady on, darling! No, not you, Riva . . .' Nicholas was on the mobile to their live-in nanny. 'Amanda, my love, Riva says we've got one hour precisely, and after that they're home alone.'

Lydia slithered in next and, with one eye on the pinstripe suit in the opposite booth, began twisting her red curls into coils, throwing her head back, shaking them out, and starting all over again. Jack hesitated, gripping her backpack to her chest, then bumped along the seat after Lydia, followed by Andrew who was glancing furtively between his wife's elaborate hairplay and the stranger, drinking it in. Finally Amanda tucked herself in on the far side, next to Sam, who was rubbing his spectacles on the sleeve of his fleece in preparation for cross-examining the waiter. 'Do you by any chance have a Peak District organic red?'

'Er . . . thank you, Sam.' Nicholas addressed the

waiter, 'Ignore my friend, he's an attention-seeking foodie . . . two bottles of the number three, please.'

'Right . . .' Amanda pulled a piece of paper out of a giant bag made from white varnished crocodile skin. 'Everyone paying attention? Lydia? OK. To recap. Last week Channel X contacted me to ask if we'd consider being involved in a programme about Amber.' She glanced round the circle of faces; Jack was staring at her lap. 'What they are proposing is a kind of collaboration between us – Amber's friends and family – and them. It'll be a documentary involving all the celebrity crowd, the various people she worked with, and so on. But the point is that they want input, and in return they're offering us a say in the way that Amber is portrayed.' Sam was trying to get a pen to work on the paper tablecloth. Amanda took a deep breath. 'Someone is going to make this programme. That much we know. The only question is who makes it first and how. And the Channel X line is that if we get involved now, the people who really knew Amber, we can at least ensure that it's accurate and tasteful, and a fitting tribute . . .'

'Are those your words or theirs?' said Jack, without looking up.

'Control is the word that matters here.' Amanda's chin tipped slightly indicating that she was not to be put off her stride. 'We either relinquish it and let some opportunist have a go, who'll dig up God knows who and what –' visions of some of the whos and whats flitted across the faces round the table, Andrew started to massage his temples ' – or, we take the bull by the horns. I don't want to be responsible for pushing this and getting you all into something you'll regret. But from where I'm standing we've got to get involved. If we don't, and they do some hatchet job, we'll never forgive ourselves.'

Andrew leant forward on his elbows revealing that under his waxed jacket he was still wearing a white lab coat. 'So, when you met them today, did they give you a clearer idea of exactly what they have in mind?'

'They want it based around interviews with us. They want it very personal . . . lots of anecdotes, access to photo albums and cinefilm, that kind of thing. They're very big on girlfriends' reminiscences. They love the fact that Jack was at boarding school with Amber . . .' Jack blew her nose. Amanda swallowed. Her voice, which normally carried like Maria Callas's, was slowly disappearing beneath the noisy clatter of the bar '. . . And Sam, having worked with her, would have a big role to play. Obviously they're hoping to hook a lot of A-list contributions – soundbites from the stars. From their point of view, there's no denying, this is a perfect excuse for a seventies and eighties retrospective with lots of archive pics and music clips and all that. But they also genuinely want it to be 'substantial', that's what they kept saying, and more *true* than all the stuff that came out straight after . . . afterwards. They, and I quote, Jack, "Don't want smut, they want soul" . . . And access to the memorial service.'

'Oh God,' said Jack.

'It does seem awful but, let's face it, it's hardly going to be private.' Amanda found herself, to her shame, picturing her entrance to the church wearing the Luigi e Luna skirt suit from the recent Sicilian widow campaign. With a shirt, of course. And much lower heels.

'Do we get a wardrobe allowance for this, Squidge?' Nicholas ran a finger round the inside of his striped collar.

'Nicholas, please.'

'Well, Andrew and I are reading, my darling. And you know how penetrating those close-ups were at the Crane memorial service. You could count the ply of the cashmere.' Nicholas was smiling at her, but he looked ill and worn. In the four weeks since Amber had died he had lost as many pounds and acquired dark purplish shadows under his eyes and a habit of waking in the night and going downstairs to read, or to walk in the garden. Suddenly she saw him standing at the graveside in the rain, head bowed, his back shaking, arms at attention by his sides.

'Well . . .' Amanda clasped her hands in front of her mouth to stop them trembling. 'Are we prepared to be the custodians of Amber's reputation? Are we ready for this?'

Jack was now slumped on the floor of the bathroom, cooling her fiery cheek against the white tiles and reflecting on how the others would perform for the Channel X team. She pictured Amanda, at home in Shepherd's Bush, checking with the cameraman that the copies of *LaMode* were in shot and the Scullin abstract above the fireplace was out ('we're not insured'), rearranging the books in the background so that a good cross-section of A-list contemporary authors would be in focus ('I think any lettering smaller than DeLillo just isn't going to show . . . am I right?') and making sure that the complimentary flowers from Earth (twisted willow and lilies) were somewhere prominent enough to justify their continuing support. To Amanda this was all part of the job. She'd have her own hairdresser there, absorbed in trimming hairs imperceptible to the human eye from the razor edges of her signature chestnut bob ('Branding, darling. In this line of work you need a distinctive style – look at Davina.'). She'd have canapés for the crew, celebrity gossip for the lighting boys and Riva, the Serbian nanny, manoeuvring ashtrays and coasters.

Jack imagined Lydia, varnished and buffed, ready for her close-up, knees together, calves elegantly poised on the diagonal. Would they film her in the kitchen extension with Clapham Common in the background? No, surely in the new bedroom, on the new chaise at the foot of the bed. She could see the tip of Lydia's tongue peeking between her teeth, her head tilted to one side, her shoulders drawing back and feet flexing as the cameras start to roll. She saw Andrew poke his head round the bedroom door, making an 'Urrr . . . scary . . . it's the telly face', waggling his fingers at Lydia as if she were far away, behind the plate glass of a departure lounge, and Lydia's expression of open hostility, 'Can't you see we're busy?' The irritable flick of the red curls indicating that her husband had compounded his offence by missing her warning and making her speak sharply in front of these people, shattering their impression of her as a sweet, easy going, attractive young woman.

Jack thought about Sam. Sam in his grubby leather coat with the paint stains and then the new Sam in the parka and beanie they bought him for his role as Amber's sidekick in *Garden, Kitchen, Bedroom: The Secrets of Family Life.* She could see him outdoors, spectacles misting up in the light drizzle, floppy brown curls swiping his face like lambs' tails, describing the vision for the series that they were three-quarters of the way through filming when Amber died. 'It was essentially a year in the life of a house and garden. But this was no ordinary house and garden, and of course, no ordinary woman . . .' She remembered Sam and Amber filming together at Hedlands: Sam ankle-deep in mud, hauling on a rope tied round the neck of a cow; Amber doubled over, laughing, the ear flaps of her rabbit hat quivering, a feed bucket upended at her feet. Jack felt a sudden twitch of something like anger at the memory of the carelessly discarded bucket.

There was a hesitant knock at the bathroom door. 'Everything all right in there?' asked a female voice. Jack shuffled along the floor on her knees and forced on both basin taps. 'Yes, coming,' she shouted above the roar of water, then counted to ten, turned off the taps and wandered out. 'I'm so sorry . . . I was . . . erm . . . washing.'

She picked her way across the eel's nest of cables covering the 12 × 15 living area of her flat and worked her way around the lights to the appointed chair, next to the photograph of herself, Amanda and Amber wearing bridesmaid's dresses.

'Well . . .' the director leant across her to stub out his cigarette in an ashtray at her side. 'At least we know the mike's working. Now, Sonja, can we do something about the rash?'

TWO

Transmission clock counts down the seconds.

A black limousine moves across the screen. There are children's faces, pink and blurry, at the window. Music, Elton John's 'Your Song' fades up. One of the children waves, she is wearing a Dalmatian-spotted hat with ears. The limousine comes to a standstill. Camera pulls back to reveal the arched doors of a church and scores of people congregating on the pavement outside. Music fades out. Voice over: '. . . family, friends and members of the celebrity community are gathering here, at St Margaret's in the Field, for the memorial service of Amber Best, who died exactly three months ago today, at the age of forty . . .' Voice fades out. Close-up of the designer, Martin Anderwurst, talking to the rock star Felix Ash, cut to close-up of the back of a high-collared black cloak, on which is stapled a blow-up print of Amber Best's face. Camera pans to focus on an old woman in a fur hat. Voice off: 'Can you give us some idea of how you are all feeling this morning?' The woman bats heavy eyelids, 'Well, still terribly shocked really, you know . . . it was so unexpected and Amber was so very . . . so full of life. She never seemed to grow any older . . .' Camera pans to intercept the path of a man with black collar-length hair, wearing sunglasses.

Voice off: 'Simon Best. Can you spare us a few words?'
The man stops and stands with his head on one side,
chewing something. Voice off: 'Perhaps you could describe
your role in today's memorial service, which I know has
been meticulously planned over several . . .' The man
raises a hand to stall the reporter. 'That'll be the brother
of the deceased,' he says, and turns briskly on his heel.
Camera tracks him as he moves off through the crowd,
plunging his hands deep in his pockets so that the back
vent of his coat flips open to reveal a flash of glittering
gold lining. Fade to black.

'Oh, my God! It's the Prada tweed. She's gone for the
Prada tweed. Oh, very good, Davina, very demure, very
British spirit of remembrance. And it's cream, of course,
so she can't fail to stand out like a bride at a . . . memorial.'
Amanda fanned herself frantically with the order of service, one French-manicured finger jabbing at the cluster of
people gathering on the pavement beyond the smoked-
glass windows of their limousine. They'd been in there for
the last half hour, Amanda and Jack and Lydia, parked up
opposite the church, watching the first of the congregation
arrive, fiddling with their make-up, regretting their outfits,
weeping quietly, clutching hands and dabbing at each
other with paper from the kitchen-roll bumper pack
wedged on the back shelf. None of them was quite ready
to step out onto the street and face their close-ups.

'Look! The cameras have spotted her already . . . Oh,
puurrleese. She's trying to get the bag in the picture, will
you look at that!' Amanda cupped her hands round her

mouth, 'No picture credits here, darling. It's a memorial, darling. M-E-M-O-R-I-A-L!'

'Amanda, I don't think this is appropriate.' Jack gave her a gentle smack on the knee.

'What, and that is? Attempting to upstage the . . . the dead person on their . . . I don't believe it. She's coming over.'

Davina was picking her way towards the car, planting her feet cautiously on the paving like a Lipizzaner in a minefield, gunmetal bob gleaming, fur tippet bouncing at her neck, eyes, as ever, concealed behind black wrap-around sunglasses. Amanda thought of that scene in *Rosemary's Baby* when Mia Farrow follows the sound of crying to the neighbour's apartment, looks into the black crêpe-draped crib with the upside-down cross, and screams, 'His eyes! What have you done to his eyes?' Davina knew they were in the limo. There was no way out.

'Fuck! Quick!' Jack and Lydia swept the Prêt à Manger wrappers, the half bottle of vodka, the paper cups and the carton of Silk Cut off the seats and onto the floor of the car. Amanda jammed on her sunglasses, yanked on her half veil and reached for the window button lowering it six inches precisely. Another two inches and Davina would have seen the Gap sale bags and the Prada tweed on the hanger (plan B).

'Amanda.' Davina always said 'Amanda,' with a hint of disbelief, as if she wasn't quite convinced that the name had stuck. As if she knew that Amanda was Mandy to Viv and Jim, her parents in Basildon, and Mandi with an i to everyone else she had known before she moved to London. 'Davina, hello . . . welcome.' The welcome was a mistake, of course. Amanda had panicked. She was attempting to establish the new memorial hierarchy in which Davina, for the first time in their acquaintance, would be several rows behind her and very much in her shadow. Instead, she'd given Davina cause to smile the little-people smile. Amanda felt her bowels churning. She could picture Davina, back behind her glass and Wenge wood desk in her 50 square foot office on the 110th floor of Bondi Sacs Publishers' New York HQ, recreating this scene for the amusement of the sleek ponytails in sleeveless tanks.

'So, there she was. "Welcome! Bienvenue! I am your host for the day! May I show you to your pew" . . . I guess it must have been all those years front of house.' Amanda could hear the tinkling, pearly toothed laughter.

'I am so sorry, Amanda. I know Amber was a very special friend to you. You must be distraught.' Davina had one of those three-to-one American accents: two thirds of the sentence was delivered in clipped upper-class tones and then a couple of words were given the Katharine Hepburn treatment, like surrey and distraaauught. She leant closer to the window opening so that the fur tippet fell away revealing the kind of collar bone that puts an acute angle in a necklace. Davina was the woman who once famously said 'It's all about *bones*. Without bones you can be pretty, but you can never be sensational. If you've got bones and only bones, you can always be chic.' Davina was in the only bones category. She was on a permanent raw-protein diet and had to chew on a nettle compress at night, so they said, to counteract the meaty breath.

'Very, very special,' Amanda heard herself say. 'Exceptionally special.' She thought she could feel the tension vibrating out of Lydia and Jack up through the leather limo seat.

'You know Ralph had just done a shoot with her.' Davina's lips twitched.

'Really?' said Amanda, widening her eyes to distract from the paralysis that had struck the lower part of her face. Ralph was *the* photographer, exclusive to American *LaMode*, naturally. Amanda pictured black and white, outside, somewhere like the Hamptons, white shirt, scuffed Levi's, bare feet. Amber, sleeves pushed up, tussling with a couple of naked, tow-headed children, maybe a retriever . . .

'We were soo lucky to be offered her last photo session. I assume you passed?'

'Oh yes. Too close.' Amanda could feel her cheeks reddening. Davina's were bone white and chiselled like the prow of a racing yacht.

'Well, I'll see you inside.' Davina raised a gloved hand. 'By the way, *love* the jawline. I hear you're the reason no one in London can get an appointment with Dr Magda . . . you clever girl.'

Amanda lunged for the window button and flung herself back on the seat, moaning, 'Shit, shit, shit.'

'Which part was worst for you?' said Jack, reaching for the vodka.

'Ralph! Shooting Amber!' Amanda yanked the bottle out of Jack's hand and swigged from the neck. 'You know what that means? She knew she was dying, so what does she do? She calls up Davina! Davina the devil's own spawn, my number-one rival and sworn enemy of many years standing, and offers her probably the most coveted photo session of the year. If not the decade. She thinks, "I could call up Amanda, my old and dear friend with whom I have worked on so many occasions, who, as a matter of fact, was single-handedly responsible for making my modelling career. Or . . . I know! I could give a boost to the woman who is the reason why Amanda started taking Perzocan in 1996 and has never fully kicked the habit; the woman who stepped over Amanda's broken body into her job five years ago. Great idea! I could choose Davina over Amanda and add a couple of noughts to the profits of US *LaMode* in the process, what with reprint fees and . . ." ' she gestured wildly for the bumper kitchen roll making small hiccupy noises.

'Well . . .' Lydia was giving them her sick Bambi look, eyes at maximum extension, mouth very slightly turning down at the corners, the standard prelude to a more than usually malicious observation. 'It does make you wonder, doesn't it? I mean we were supposed to be best friends and yet it's starting to look like we didn't know what was going on in her life, at all.' Amanda's and Jack's silence was invitation enough for Lydia to elaborate. 'First she doesn't tell us she's dying. Then we discover that Nicholas was there on the night she died.' Lydia paused to arch one eyebrow in Jack's direction. 'Meanwhile his wife,' she glanced at Amanda, 'is passed over in favour of her arch rival, behind her back, without so much as a murmur of explanation.' Lydia flexed her hand on her knee, admiring the nude nail polish. 'I mean, it's hardly the behaviour of the average band of loyal pals is it?'

Amanda heard herself speak and simultaneously had the strange sensation of trying to keep up with what was being said. 'I knew . . . Of course I knew where my husband was. He just happened to be at Hedlands, helping Dave sort out some legal things – music royalties or something . . .' she felt her chin tipping up '. . . and the deal with Davina is, if you give it a moment's thought, completely understandable.'

Lydia made a 'Who is this alien?' face.

'Of course it is. You want the ultimate set of photographs for your family to remember you by, you want Ralph. Simple as that. And Ralph is under contract to US *LaMode*. So, no Davina, no Ralph.'

'And the reason she didn't tell you?' Lydia had dropped the Bambi look. There was a tap at the limousine window. It was Nicholas. 'Darling, hurry up, nearly everyone's seated. God it's a tip in there. Jack, have you moved in? It looks like your flat.' He flung open the door and one by one they emerged, blinking, into the cold November light, smoothing down their coats and checking their chests for fragments of crisp. Nicholas took Amanda's arm and led the way. 'You'll never guess what, Squidge. Davina's wearing that suit of yours. Phew, eh? It looks *completely* different. I didn't even make the connection until we started talking and she said it was a gift from Miuccia and I told her about all the palaver you had getting hold of yours, all those phone calls and flowers, and then, in the end, having to get one specially made up in your size. She seemed frightfully impressed. Anyway. Very lucky escape.' He tapped the side of his nose. 'I know what you lot are like.'

Amanda walked crisply at his side. But for the white knuckles gripping her clutchbag the very picture of the confident editor and wife.

Nicholas delivered Amanda to her place and then

returned to the front of the church to help with the last of the seating, giving her time to gather herself. She thought back to that Thursday in August. She was in the bedroom, laying out her clothes for a trip to New York the following week, weighing up the pros and cons of four pairs of black trousers with Riva huffing and pouting in the background, 'How can it be so different? Who can see the difference?' Ludo wandered in, with his hamster wedged in the crook of his arm, wearing his incredible conundrum face. 'If you did *Millionaire*, Mummy, would we get a robot?' She decided on the wide-leg Ann Demeulemeester and the Helmut Langs. 'If you did *Millionaire* would we get a ice-cream make it? Are you going to a party, mummy?'

'No, darling.'

'Where's Daddy?'

'At work, darling.' The phone rang and Amanda picked it up. It was Nicholas, on his mobile. His meeting in Manchester had run over and he'd decided to stay the night.

'Again?'

'Afraid so. It's just one of those things.' There was music playing in the background. She noticed because it was noisy, the kind of level that Nicholas complained about in restaurants. 'And it looks like we'll be at it until late tomorrow night as well . . . just to warn you.' She could hear that he was tired, willing her to make it easy on him. She decided not to tell him how much the awning outside the kitchen was going to cost, or that Riva had asked for a pay rise, the third this year, and a double bed.

'All right then, darling.'

She spent another half hour or so honing her outfits for the weekend, ten minutes shooting down Ludo's argument for a bigger hamster cage and then the phone rang again.

'Manda? John.' John worked with Nicholas at Dudley Polk Solicitors, she wasn't sure in what capacity but Nicholas was more senior. 'Sorry to disturb you at home, just hoping for a very quick word with Nick.'

'He's in Manchester, John.' There was a pause, during which she and John realized that John should have known that. She waited. 'You could get him on his mobile.'

'Yes . . .' Another pause. 'Of course, I am sorry . . . my mistake.'

When she got off the phone she went to look for Riva and told her that Mr Nicholas would like to talk to her about the money, and he didn't sound very happy. While delivering this information she held her hands clasped in front of her like the Mother Superior in *The Sound of Music* and assumed a hurt look intended to remind Riva that she was practically a refugee whom they had welcomed into their home and this was all the thanks they got.

'I hear you,' said Riva, 'you are two minutes on the phone to Nicholas. You don't speak about me.'

'Well, that was Mr Nicholas again,' said Amanda, 'and I can assure you that is his position. And he is very unhappy. Very.'

'OK,' said Riva, and Amanda burst into tears.

The next evening Nicholas rang and Ludo asked to speak to him, or rather to clutch the phone and stare into the middle distance, nodding occasionally, as if receiving orders from an alien species. 'Mummy,' he said when he finally replaced the receiver with a solemn goodbye,

'Daddy says he has to work so much so you can buy new clothes every day.'

'Daddy's just being funny, darling,' Amanda said, looking up just in time to catch Ludo and Riva exchanging the same look she and her sister used to give each other when their mother protested she never stayed out after midnight before she was married. 'Mummy has a job, Ludo, so mummy pays for mummy's clothes.'

'Jeremy says that mummies with jobs are selfinch.'

'Does he? That sounds like Jeremy's mummy to me.'

'His mummy makes cakes and takes them to swimming . . . and gets in.'

That night Amanda ate two bars of Green & Black chocolate and sat up until three highlighting things in catalogues that would transform the kitchen and dining area.

The next day was Saturday and she had spent the early part in bed phoning in her catalogue orders and booking herself a few treatments, including the one with the hot stones that cost £150. The television was on at the end of the bed, Ludo, Cass and Poppy were engrossed in making a hamster chute out on the landing and Riva was hoovering the stairs in a deliberate effort to avoid cleaning the kitchen. When the news came on Amanda automatically changed channels, but there was news on the other side too, and there was a picture of Hedlands, with a reporter mouthing something. Her first thought was that Dave had been given the arts fundraising job that there'd been whispers of since last year. She turned up the volume. There was Dave coming out of the house, striding across the drive, there was the new Land Rover and . . . the driver had his hand up to the side of his face, it was just a

split-second shot, but long enough for her to notice that
Nicholas was wearing the amethyst cufflinks she had given
him for his birthday. The reporter was speaking in a
solemn tone '. . . incurable blood disease, diagnosed just
two months ago, and that it had been her decision not to
disclose her condition. Even those closest to the family . . .'
She remembered the exact words. The phone had been
ringing all morning, but she and Riva had agreed not
to answer it because Riva was being hounded by some
American boy. Now it rang again. She picked it up. It was
Jack, crying uncontrollably, her words jagged and buried
in phlegm, 'Why . . .? Oh G . . . od . . . why . . . didn't
she . . . tell us? . . . It . . . can't . . .'

'I'm coming round,' said Amanda. She put down the
phone, went into the bathroom and was sick.

Nicholas edged into the pew next to her and clasped her
hands which were gripped in her lap. 'Just about ready I
think . . . Won't be long now.'

The day that Amber died he had rung several times
and eventually they'd spoken.

'You were there?' she said.

'Yes,' he said, 'just tying up a few knots.'

'I thought she used Dave's lawyer.'

'Well . . . there you go.'

'Couldn't you have told me, Nicholas?'

'Darling, it was work and, as such, confidential. I'm
sorry . . .'

To begin with it had astonished her that he could keep
such a secret so well. And then, at the funeral, when
they all saw the effort it must have taken to disguise his

emotions, when he stood alone at the graveside, detached from the group, hunched and stiff, then she was scared. 'I hope Jack's all right where she is.' Nicholas swivelled to look over his shoulder. 'She's taking care of my mother, bless her.'

Jack was kneeling, tucked in at the end of a pew, four rows back. Between her fingers she could make out a hat in the form of a vertical unicorn horn beneath which had to be Raschenda, Amanda's editor 'at large'. There was Roger, distinguishable by the stump of grey ponytail, and his wife Lady Milly, her long swoop of neck as creamy white as the lilies attached to the ends of the pews. She could see Andrew, to the left, crushed between Lydia and Felix Cat's girlfriend. They were leaning across him, flirting, thrusting at each other with their latest achievements and observations, forcing him to arch his back and look up at the ceiling. In the front pew, almost obscured from her view by a pillar, Dave Cross and Sam sat side by side, motionless, a small pair of Dalmatian ears just visible in the narrow chink between them. At the end of their pew, Otis, Dave's son by his first marriage, cradled a camcorder against his cheek, turning his head now and then to check for filming opportunities. Straight ahead of her, Amanda was surreptitiously signalling to the Channel X boys set up in the gallery. One impatient forefinger beckoned and pointed at the back of a head (Davina's), waggled furiously from left to right, then swung along the row and lined up like the barrel of a gun on another head (Raschenda's). Next to Amanda, Nicholas's blond head was bobbing gently as he read and re-read his address, memorizing the rhythm of the lines. And, just across the aisle from her, was Simon Best.

Jack's eyes lingered on the contour of his jaw, the lean fingers that raked his hair and then came to rest, drumming, on a velvet-covered thigh. The cuff of his shirt flopped open at the end of his velvet sleeve, lolling out into the aisle. It looked like silk, biscuit-coloured silk. Twenty-seven years ago, when Simon had tired of a shirt, Amber would add it to his pile of discards – loons, jean jackets complete with cigarette burns and biro graffiti, old cashmere jerseys – lay them out on the polished wooden floor of the dormitory and the girls would barter for them.

To most of them Simon's cast-offs represented a piece of Amber's world, something that was guaranteed cool, that would, even though you were only thirteen, attract admiring glances from the sly goddesses in the sixth form. But to Jack, they were pieces of Simon, and Simon was both who it was all for and everything you wanted to be. Occasionally his photograph appeared on the social pages of magazines and Jack would snip out the black and white picture of him squinting through a sticky fringe, his half smile revealing teeth that looked like he'd been eating liquorice. When the girls smoked, on the roof outside the bathroom window, they smoked the way he smoked, holding the cigarette between forefinger and thumb or right down in the cleft between the fingers and making a big deal of inhaling. Simon told Amber that you could tell what a girl was like in bed from the way she smoked. There was a whole code of smoke blowing and cigarette lighting that you had to know. Every inhalation and exhalation became to them like part of an elaborate seduction ritual, although their understanding of what lay beyond the end of the packet of ten Number Six was hazy.

Simon was the monitor of their transition from girlhood to adolescence. Under his tutelage – passed down through Amber – they learnt the answers to those most urgent questions that no teacher or parent or even sister could answer. Amber would announce 'Simon says he thinks it's time we started shaving our legs, all the girls in our form at Heythrop are already' or, 'Simon says we should all be using Tampax, STs are for grannies. And boys can smell them.' It was Simon who explained the art of the French kiss, Simon who broke the news about the male loathing of white tights, what contact was required at a school dance, and what was considered frigid. Simon knew why the boy who had a torch in his pocket on the dance floor had left so abruptly when Henrietta drew attention to it and it was Simon who explained the concept of the prick tease (although the torch was not a measure of that. The torch could happen if you were just riding on a bus, and that was called 'convoy cock'). They learnt that men liked girls with 'aura' who didn't talk too much; girls who didn't wear knickers under their jeans; small girls, with long hair. They were told, to the month, when to throw away their stretchy Smiley underwear sets and when to substitute their blue and silver tubes of Rive Gauche for Diorella.

Sometimes Jack would go home to Amber's house for the weekend and Simon would be there with a girl, the most excellent student of his perfect woman philosophy, long-haired and lazy, with eyes that were flashing and hungry for drama, even at breakfast. Simon would stroke her and call her babe and she would shrug him off and return to reading her colour supplement leaving Jack incredulous. 'Why would Simon go out with someone so . . . grumpy?' she would say to Amber. 'God, she's horrible to him. And she's not even that pretty.' And Amber would say, 'Because she's good in bed. Probably. Anyway they love all that. Men don't go out with nice girls, Jack. They're friends with nice girls.'

Between them, Simon and Amber taught Jack that there were people who put bread out for the birds, and watched *Steptoe and Son* with their supper on trays on their knees and then there were people for whom life was like a Rolling Stones' lyric, who smoked at breakfast and drank fresh coffee and had wine at lunchtime and went on skiing holidays every year. At Amber and Simon's house the grown-ups said 'fuck' as casually as if it were margarine and there seemed to be not so much friendship between them as a kind of compelling friction. None of the women had husbands and none of the men had wives, although they'd all had at least one at some point. The men were 'amusing', even if one or two of them were 'shits' and they wore several buttons of their shirts undone and cashmere jerseys in unfatherly colours, like lemon yellow, draped across their shoulders. The women were either 'sweet' or 'a handful' but always 'in beautiful condition' and fabulously interested in Amber. Everything she said made them crinkle their noses and clutch at her arms and then give Amber's father a heaving musky look which she and Jack referred to as 'fruity loins'. If one of them seemed particularly persistent then Amber would conduct an impromptu candlelit vigil in front of the portrait of her dead mother, while Jack read poetry aloud embellishing it here and there according to a prearranged plan: 'Earth in beauty dressed/Awaits returning spring/All true love must die/Alter at the best/Into some lesser thing/Prove that I lie . . . Oh dear mother prove that I lie . . . pray remind us (mother) that there is no replacing you, hard as we may try.' It never failed.

Amber's mother had died three years before Jack and Amber were sent to Northanger House School for Girls. She had been killed in a car crash, and for several months after Marc Bolan's fatal accident Amber became obsessed with finding the particular tree trunk against which her mother's white E-Type had buckled and burst into flames, so that they could festoon it with ribbons and photographs, just like his. It was hard to gauge how the death had affected Amber because she didn't talk about her mother much, but you could tell that she wasn't the sort of mother who tucked your hair behind your ears and made you sandwiches for school. When she died she was wearing an Ossie Clark mini dress and white boots and there was a young man in the passenger seat, who was said to be a friend of Simon's. Everything about the Bests' lives, even the untimely ending, against a tree in Windsor, seemed exotic and frightening, ricocheting with uncontrollable adult forces that Jack never experienced at home.

Simon was standing up, removing his sunglasses, and stepping out into the aisle. He had a slight swagger, a way of shifting his weight snappily from hip to hip, which seemed insolent in these surroundings, but when he stepped up to the lectern and adjusted the marker in the open Bible you could see that his hands were shaking. His head remained bowed for a moment, and then he looked up and started to speak and Jack saw that he was staring straight at her. Even at this distance, through the hanks of inky fringe, even now, in church, his eyes were impossible to meet.

They were blue, icebreaker blue . . . she could see them

glittering in the half darkness of the dance floor, smell the heavy citrus tang of his Eau Sauvage. She was staring down at their feet, watching them padding in between each other, softly, like monks shuffling to prayer, not daring to look at his face. Glancing up through her eye-lashes she could see the half smile stretching into something more like a grin, she felt his hand in the small of her back pressing her closer in. 'No torch,' she mumbled, still looking at the floor, and his lips split apart and she felt the vibration in his chest and his other hand sliding under her chin, tipping her head to make her look into those eyes.

'I can't,' she said, 'they're too . . . I don't know why.'

He was so close to her face. His body was hot and dry and his throat molasses brown in the ultraviolet light. She could feel his chest rising and falling.

'Then shut your eyes,' he said, 'and stop talking for a minute so I can kiss you.'

Kiss. The word sounded like pure sin. Jungle sin. She shut her eyes. She felt like she was floating in hot oil. She was fourteen.

'I don't think we should,' she said. It wasn't the fact that Simon's girlfriend was dancing next to them, or the fear of what Amber would say ('Oh God, Jack, not Simon. He's a monster, don't you know that? An adorable monster.') It wasn't that there was a chance that her mother was there already, a bit early, craning her neck over the swaying pairs of adolescents, wondering if Jack was all right, if the straps of her gold sandals had held out. It was simply because she knew that if he kissed her, the boy she'd loved since the first time she saw him, the most beautiful and desirable of the species, she would never, ever be the same again.

Outside the church Jack found herself standing next to Sam.

'Lift?' said Sam. 'Or would you rather wrestle for the passenger seat of Simon's Luurve Poorsssche?'

Jack eyed him warily. 'I'm sorry?'

'You were blushing. When he was doing his Richard Burton impersonation, you were somewhere else, weren't you, somewhere . . . rather hot?'

She could see Simon out of the corner of her eye, leading a girl by the hand who was moulting tufts of marabou with every tiny, hesitant step. 'Stop it, Sam. Come on, let's go,' she said, bending to check her heel and catch a last glimpse of him, now cupping the marabou girl around the waist, making her curve and sway like a tipsy dancer.

When Jack and Sam reached the van there was the usual struggle to convert it from mobile conservatory to motor vehicle. Sam launched himself full length into the back in an effort to compress the branches of trees and shrubs enough to make room for the seedlings, watering cans, bucket of lavender and small Christmas tree wedged on the passenger seat. Jack crawled in next to him on her hands and knees and started stacking bags of soil against the sides.

'Jack. JACK!' Amanda was gesturing from the other side of the church wall. 'What are you doing? Sam, get her out of there!'

'Radiation leak?' Sam was on all fours now, with his head poking out of the back.

'*That* is a Donna Karan suit.' Amanda flipped up her veil and whipped off her sunglasses using the arm of them to indicate Jack, now gingerly sliding out onto the pavement. 'Have you gone out of your mind? There's a perfectly good limo sitting ten yards away. Look at you.'

'I can't go in the limo again,' said Jack, vigorously rubbing the hem of her skirt with what looked like an old sock, 'there's too much tension, and it's a two-hour journey.'

'Well, sweetheart, this isn't exactly a tension-free situation, all right. If you ask me, I think you two are exhibiting all the signs of extreme denial. Rolling around in . . . foliage . . . when we're about to be filmed at one of the most high-profile par . . . gatherings of the year.'

'Whoops,' said Jack.

'You know what I mean. We are on show. Like it or not. *Everyone* is here. Bloody Ralph is here, apparently. I don't know why you won't just have one of my pills.'

Sam was bouncing up and down on top of the pile of branches. There was a sound of cracking and splintering and the scrunch of stone on metal. 'I'm listening,' he mouthed through the window. Amanda replaced her sunglasses in one deft, practised movement, like a barrister about to quote from a legal precedent.

'There's a toad in there, Sam. Look! Right there, uuuurggh, it's disgusting.'

'Is he mooning at you?' Sam shouted. 'I am sorry. I've told him about that.'

Amanda had the same expression she wore when she realized that money wasn't going to solve something. She

30

tucked her bag under her armpit and strode off in the direction of the limo.

'I'll deal with it,' Sam called after her. 'I know all about turning frogs into princes.'

Jack noticed a tea-coloured copy of the *Evening Standard* on the floor of the van, picked it up and spread it across the passenger seat. A small photograph of Amber stared up at her from the diary page alongside details of the memorial service:

> . . . after which the congregation are invited to follow the family back to Kennet in Wiltshire to drink her health at Hedlands, the house she shared for nine years with her husband, Dave Cross of The Perfect Fixture. London's premier chauffeur-driven car service, Blade Runs, is said to be struggling to meet the demand for group-A vehicles . . .

She flipped the paper onto the floor and sighed as she plonked herself down on the seat, glancing across at Sam who was now bent under the steering wheel scrabbling between the pedals.

'What if I'm no different from the average person out there who was dazzled by the wonderful life and times of Amber Best? Sam? What if I was just another fan blindly soaking it all up without really seeing . . . well, anything?'

'Gotcha!' Sam brandished a croaking fist in Jack's face, then leant out of the door and let the toad plop onto the pavement. He turned the key in the ignition.

'I mean, maybe it isn't possible to really be friends with someone like that. Maybe if you live in that kind of world, where you can have anything, have anyone, maybe friendship with civilians is just a sort of amusing diversion. When I was feeling closeness and trust and all of that, she was probably just feeling . . . curiosity.' She heard her voice closing down.

'Jack. Come on now. You know how it was. Maybe you did idealize her. Maybe she did enjoy being the living embodiment of all your fantasies. Who wouldn't? But so what? You both got a lot out of it. She adored you.' Jack was staring hard at him. 'Of course it's going to be different being friends with "someone like that". She was a star, or an ex-star anyway. She was a TV personality and a famously beautiful woman – ' he paused to wipe the windscreen in front of him with something that left whorls of smeared wet mud in its wake – 'but it worked, didn't it? Why are we having this conversation anyway?'

'Because she didn't tell us she was dying and she was supposed to be our best friend. Because it turns out she had a lot of secrets. It's like, in the last three months I'm just starting to find out who Amber Best was. And . . . and it feels like the Amber I've known, from the age of eleven, wasn't the real Amber, but the Amber I wanted her to be, which is very . . . distressing . . . and humiliating. It's just too much to take on board all at once. There are too many possibilities that I don't . . . well, that I don't like . . . which just goes to show that I'm used to only seeing what I want to see. I just . . .' If she pressed her nails hard into the palms of her hands there was still a pretty good chance that she could hold back the tears and stabilize at the dull ache in the chest stage. She wanted to say what she'd wanted to say for weeks but she knew it would come out wrong. She wanted it to sound light, teasing, something like, 'But you would know all about her secrets . . . I don't have to tell you, Sam, about Amber's secrets . . . But, hey, what about your little secret then?' She'd gone over and over it in her head, but when she practised the words out loud they sounded bitter, angry.

'Have a mint.' Sam swerved to send a packet of Polos shooting over to her side of the dashboard.

'Sam? Why do you think I haven't got a boyfriend?' Sam leant his elbows on the steering wheel and stared dead ahead. 'Do you think if I were more the kind of girl who wore . . . you know, marabou stoles and those bras that proffer your bosoms like a tray of goodies . . . more of a forearm stroker, do you think that would make a difference?' She paused to drag the reserve half bottle of vodka out of her bag and took a gulp. 'I don't put out.' Sam raised his eyebrows. 'Apparently I don't. I don't flirt in the necessary manner. Everything's changed you know. Men are desensitized. You've really got to lay it on the table these days. You've got to point your knees in their direction and stroke your collar bone and stick your finger in your mouth and when you're dancing you've got to hook on like a pole dancer.' Sam glanced at the vodka bottle. 'Thank you, yes, I am pacing myself. And then you've got to have the kind of underwear you handwash. And luxurious Oscar-presenting worthy nightwear. And absolutely no body hair except for a neat little Brazilian runway.' Jack traced a spaghetti-width strip in the air. 'So you can pretend we're Lolitas . . . or boys if you prefer.' Sam put a hand out for the Polos, keeping his eyes firmly on the road. 'And you don't get any points for unsurgically enhanced anything these days. Oh, no. In fact the more tamperage the better. The faker the more fabulous to you lot.' Jack clutched her 34a cup bosoms, one under each

33

hand. 'Do you think if I was more like that . . .' She paused as a Mercedes overtook them carrying a cargo of memorial attendees. In the front passenger seat was a girl resting her Afghan blonde head on a bent wrist too slim to fill out the platinum strap of her Rolex. 'Do you think I'd be, you know, fighting on an even playing field?' Sam sucked his Polo at her and adjusted the rearview mirror. 'But then again, does a girl like me want the kind of man who falls for a forearm stroker before he even notices . . .'

'The quirky character in the corner?'

She glared at him.

'I'm serious, Sam. I have to know, so I can make an informed choice. I have to know, once and for all, whether it's all that stuff that makes the difference between—'

'Yes, I know. The marabou girl and you. You want to know if you played the marabou girl's game would Slime-on step over all the other identical marabou girls to get to you. And then would the combination of your sparkling personality and their marabou machinations be irresistible to him.'

Jack could see herself, long ironed blonde hair, Manolo Blahnik mules, those shiny high-polish legs stretching up into a cloud of thigh-skimming marabou baby doll, standing on tiptoe, her arms around Simon's bare brown neck . . .

'What did you call him?'

'Why don't you test your theory, Jack? Why don't you ask Slime-on out? Take him to dinner. Point your knees. Lick your lips, give him the works . . . and see what happens.' Sam fished in his pocket for a cigarette. 'And then we might just find out, once and for all, whether or not they're contact lenses.'

34

She was conscious of sitting very still and stiffly, like a child on the way to her first day at school. She suddenly felt a wave of panic that Sam, her friend and protector, should have suggested delivering her, as it were, into the lion's jaws.

He put a hand out to pat her knee. '*That man* is why you haven't got a boyfriend, Jack. It's one of the reasons anyway.'

Three

Transmission clock counts down the seconds.

A middle-aged man in a light-coloured suit, shirt buttoned to the neck, sits behind a glass desk with a view of the Thames in the background. Caption reads: Jeff Clarke, manager of The Perfect Fixture, 1970 to 1986. 'Dave first went down to look at Hedlands, with Amber, and Otis, Dave's son, in the summer of ninety-two. I remember it very clearly cos he rang me and said, "Whaderyerthink? Bloody Hedlands. Be a bit of a laugh woudnit?" And I was like, "Too right! I'm there!" Because what you've got to remember is for us, for our generation, Hedlands was like, iconic. It was like this temple to rock 'n' roll living and if you were anybody in that world all roads led to Hedlands. This house was part of rock 'n' roll history: you had Jed Beck of the Word living there all through the early seventies; Badly Done made all their best stuff in the studio there . . . you remember those pictures? All the groupies were starkers all the time, floatin' about on the lake. And of course Amber had lived there, off and on, over the years . . . with Felix, or whoever was the rock stud of the hour. So, for Dave, buying Hedlands was like cementing his status, in a way. And at the same time by marrying Amber (who was y'know – *the* girl of that era –

they were either sleeping with her or writing songs about her) and installing her at Hedlands, he was like announcing that the big f*(bleep) guns of the rockocracy had arrived. And it was a power base. A lot of things went on there . . .' Fade to black.

Amanda stood in the middle of the flagstoned hall looking up at the gallery, and there she was, leaning over the banisters, jet-black hair piled up like a turban, Chinese dressing gown hanging open to reveal Union Jack Y-fronts and a pair of almost breasts, the eighteen-year-old girl everyone was talking about. 'She'll do,' the photographer mumbled giving Amanda an exaggerated wink and raising his hand in a salute. 'Hi Amber! Stuart Groves, your photographer. Nice knickers!'

Amber giggled. 'They're Dylan's,' her voice was husky, childish and gravelly at the same time, 'he was the *last* photographer.' She giggled again and then squealed as a young man grabbed her from behind and lifted her feet off the floor. He was wearing red high heels and a pair of stripey bikini briefs. 'Isn't he just like Tim Curry? This is Norman, everyone, but we don't like the name Norman, do we, so we call him Fred.' Amber wagged a finger at Fred and then trailed it along the banister. 'So, everybody. How do we want me today?'

'Amanda?' Amanda looked down at the pale hand resting on her arm and smiled blearily, not quite rooted back in the present. 'Amanda, it's Milly.' Now she saw, exactly, Lady Milly married to Roger Marsh, neighbours of Amber and Dave's and fellow rock royalty. 'You were very far away.' Milly's eyes were gentle. 'Shall we have a look round together, share some happy memories?' She leant closer and lowered her voice. 'Get away from all these *fabulous* people.'

Amanda glanced around and saw that in the few moments she'd been standing there the hall had filled with statement-making people, all of them moving purposefully as if urgently needed at the other end of the house, all of them affecting the impatient, long-suffering expression of the perennially watched.

'Come on.' Milly took her by the elbow and steered her across the hall through a doorway into a white room swimming in the pink afternoon light flooding through floor to ceiling sash windows.

'The sun room!' said Milly triumphantly. 'The first of her many small victories. Oh, I remember it so well, don't you?' She cast her eyes about with a satisfied smile. 'Dave was determined, wasn't he, to have his bar and snooker table and what not in here? He had it all planned: big screen in the study, that mechanical massage chair, all his gold discs framed and hung around the fireplace and then in *here* upholstered leather, beer on tap, flock wallpaper.' She grimaced. '*Where* he'd got it all from. Anyway, she was desperate, wasn't she? Don't you remember? She managed to intercept that frightful leather designer and gave him some brilliant story about Dave being a compulsive fetishist who was always ringing up leather people, just for the thrill of saying the word!' Milly clapped her hands in front of her mouth delightedly. 'And then, clever girl, she persuaded Dave to let her do the whole thing in *white* leather, and make it like a "homage" to John.' She tipped her head on one side waiting for a reaction. 'You know . . . Chevening . . . in the *Imagine* video? With Yoko swanning about opening all the shutters? Yes, you do. Anyway, only of course Amber didn't mention that she was going to use the leather to upholster a lot of painted French furniture, and sneak in the odd Aubusson rug while she was at it.' She spread her arms wide to indicate the results. 'Not absolutely ideal, but inspired, as ever.'

Milly melted onto one of the sofas, beckoning to Amanda who perched gingerly at the other end, calves entwined, handbag locked under her armpit. 'Oh, we had some fun! She was such an ally. We were both in much the same situation, of course, both married to ageing rock princes who had got tired of being working-class heroes and wanted to join the upper classes, with solid gold knobs on, naturally.' Amanda gave her a suitably knowing look. 'And for that they needed more than mere millions – enter Camilla and Amber,' Milly winked, 'the Aristo Cats as we used to call ourselves. I had the title, she had the style, they wrote the cheques!' Milly held an imaginary pen in the air and traced a row of noughts, stretching her legs luxuriously, as if she were poolside in the Riviera, drinking in the sun. They were wonderful, bendable legs, the legs of a dancer, the legs of an ex-bunny actually. Lady Milly was a good fifteen years older than she looked. 'But my God, we earned it, I tell you. Amber used to say that she had made it her life's work to discover exactly what was required of the rock legend's wife – the last wife that is – the wife they were looking for when they'd had enough of the drugs and the booze and the girls on the road, and she certainly had the right CV for it. "You need to be able to ride like the wind," she'd say, "look hot in a miniskirt at fifty, flirt, keep ducks, make jam, give a passable shiatsu massage, and you want their number-one rival to have written you a love song, at some point." Ha!' Milly took a glug of her drink and waved her hand to indicate that she was on a roll and there was no stopping her. 'As far as darling Dave was concerned all that marmalade they've been eating since ninety-seven was lovingly prepared by Ambs, at the Aga, in a copper vat, wearing nothing but a pair of skimpy shorts and a bikini top. As if! It was all dear Judy in the village who practically had to leave her husband when she became the daily here, there were so many earth motherly things to be delegated. The curtains Amber was supposed to have run up one afternoon; the little lacy things in the downstairs loo; the children's fancy dress . . . all that. Ambs was a *lousy* cook and a worse housekeeper but she knew that nothing becomes a rock legend's wife more than a bit of a steam up in the kitchen, a bit of a dewy cleavage. "Really," she would say' – Milly planted her hands on her hips for emphasis ' – "Do you think I wake up and decide I'm just *dying* to wear one size too small leather trousers to take the kids to school? Or could that be the RLW's top survival tip, number ten?" ' Milly widened her eyes conspiratorially. 'Sooooo clever. She'd wander up and down the hill, right outside Dave's office window, wearing a long velvet coat, leading her band of raggle-taggle fairytale children, knowing the whole scene was like something straight off the cover of one of The Perfect Fixture's early albums. Dave would be just *pathetic* for days afterwards, gushing about how they were two halves of the same spirit, that she was his inspir-ation, Amber with her thumb up behind her back. And she did have terrific style with it, she was so good at pitching it just right, wasn't she?' Milly stretched out her hand and patted Amanda's knee. 'But you know only too well, she must have turned to you for advice endlessly. I remember when you found her that wonderful fabric for the kitchen. Perfect.'

Amanda remembered it too, as if it were yesterday. She was standing in the hangar-sized kitchen at Hedlands watching Amber up a ladder dabbing paint colours from miniature tins onto the flaking peach-coloured wall while her friends, three or four of them, flopped at the table, flicking through paint charts with the lazy fingers of those who just know it when they see it and never have to agonize or check to see if someone else might give away a preference. She could picture Amber applying the paint, one neat downward lick of the brush and on to the next pot. And then, suddenly, as if by a prearranged signal all the girls were shouting, 'That's the one! Perfect, not too red. Definitely IT,' while she, mystified, like a child caught in the crossfire of an argument, tried to memorize with all her strength the superior qualities of this one colour, knowing that strength was never going to be enough, that there were too many colours and words and things to be memorized. And then Amber had swung around and pointed at her with the dripping tip of the brush. 'Now we've got the colour, you, Amanda darling, are going to find the perfect curtains. Would you do that for me?' Amanda felt a tightening in her stomach as she recalled those weeks of searching, knowing it was such a small thing and yet being so anxious to please Amber, so fearful of misjudging it. She could see her assistant, Henrietta, a child straight out of school yet genetically programmed to get it right, breezing in one day with the swatch of fabric and fixing her with that flat, confident, unbothered expression that Amanda could now pull off better than any of them.

'Come on.' Milly was on her feet extending the pale fingers towards her. 'Let's go and look in the library.'

The library adjoined the sun room and was lined not only with books but with hundreds of framed photographs: the children piled into a pony and trap; Amber sitting at a dressing table wearing a towel and a long white veil; Dave on stage, eyes screwed tight shut, teeth bared, both hands clamped around the head of a microphone. And there, in a red lacquer frame, was the cover of the September 1978 issue of the *Look*, photographed on the lawn outside these very windows on that June morning when she and Amber had first met. In the end they had gone for a three-quarter length shot of Amber in an emerald-green ball dress, a million pounds' worth of diamonds draped around the crown of her head, Swarovski crystals glued along the line of each eyelash and the cover line in red one-inch lettering (it should have been bigger, and ranged left), *The One to Watch, Amber Best . . . model, actress, rock star, babe.* If you looked closely you could just make out the pools of water on the lawn where Stuart had doused her with the garden hose to get that 'Lady of the Lake vibe'. And, if you knew her, you could tell that Amber's eyelids were unusually heavy, dragged to half-mast by Stuart's Moroccan black. What you couldn't see were the bulldog clips hauling in the back of the dress, the wellington boots on Amber's feet, the wind machine filling out the skirt, the wad of sponge packed at the back of her head to hold the necklace at the right height, the tear in the hem of the dress, or Stuart's dog, Charles Manson, attempting to mount a duck in the background.

'That was one of yours, wasn't it?' Milly was over by the window. 'I remember it well. And the coverline still sums it up, doesn't it – the way she was always the only girl in the room you noticed, always ahead of the game. She never let us down on that score did she? She had to be first to try everything – even – ' Milly rummaged in her bag for something to dab her eyes with – 'Well,' she drew back her shoulders and took a deep breath, 'you've got to hand it to her. Unpredictable, right to the very end.'

Amanda stretched out her hand and stroked the glass covering a narrow black and white photo of Amber and Dave lying side by side in a hammock. Dave had his lips planted cartoon style against her cheek. 'They were so happy weren't they?' She kept her back to Milly, tracing the line of the driftwood frame with her finger, breathed in deeply and tried again, 'At least they always seemed terribly happy.' She heard the clunk of a Zippo lighter flipping open, the hiss as Milly lit a cigarette, and then the long drawn out exhalation.

'Oh yes. Well, Amber had Dave taped didn't she, right from the word go? I mean she knew what she wanted and she went looking for it, in the Chelsea Rooms of AA.' Amanda turned around to see if Milly was joking. 'Well, quite. What was Amber doing in AA?' Milly paused and cocked her head on one side. 'Much the same as half the other notably unraddled and gorgeous young girls who used to turn up there. It was well known that at any one of the meetings there'd be a multi-millionaire rock star, the son of a recently deceased big financier, the heir to a publishing fortune, that kind of thing, and they were all lovely boys. Just the sort one wanted to settle down with. Amber used to say, "I want a reformed rogue like yours", and there was only one place you were guaranteed to find that. The fact that she'd never had a problem with alcohol wasn't going to put her off.' Milly screwed up her eyes. 'I won't say David was fully aware of the situation at the time. Because of the kind of life Amber had led everyone had sort of assumed she'd come unstuck at some point. But he put two and two together pretty quickly when she was toasting their marriage with half pints of Bollinger.' She laughed. 'He didn't mind a bit, why should he? They're all terribly non-judgmental that lot, you know. It's all, "whatever does it for you". Oh, it worked, all right. Mainly because they gave each other a lot of rope: Dave did his thing; she did hers. I think if you can manage it that's absolutely the answer, don't you? Especially for two such well-developed egos as theirs. Roger would *love* it.' She glanced over and must have seen the anxiety in Amanda's face. 'Oh, I was never worried about *Roger*. Besides, the last thing Amber would have wanted was another ageing rocker. No, I think, if anything, she'd have gone for someone more conventional; the smooth, edu-cated type, you know, pinstriped, competent, smelling of Trumper's Limes. I got the feeling she missed all that a bit.'

Amanda pictured Nicholas dressing for work in the morning, crouching to check his hair in the mirror, splashing cologne onto his palms, rubbing his hands together and then slapping them against his cheeks while making hollow, howler-monkey noises, checking his cuffs, slipping on the jacket of his pinstripe suit over the shirt he had re-ironed to get the collar just right.

'Who knows?' Milly shrugged. 'But it all happens in the country, Amanda, let me tell you.' She laughed. 'Everywhere apart from at our house that is. You won't catch me taking off my thermals for anyone between November and March. I'm far too lazy to have an affair, all that waxing in months with an R, all that suggestive underwear, *such* a waste of one's energy. And Rog, although he's always imagining women coming onto him at bridge parties – ' she rolled her eyes ' – if it came down to it he'd be scared witless. *Terrified.* He's been with me for the last ten years and rightly senses that the ladies out there looking for action now expect a little more than the seven-minute special with breaks for puffs on the Ventolin inhaler.' She winked, took one last long drag of her cigarette and crushed it in an ice rink of an ashtray. 'No, unfortunately our plan for counteracting the tedium of monogamy is (thanks to Felix Cat, I might add) bloody tantric sex.'

Amanda managed a feeble laugh.

'Have you tried it?' Milly closed her eyes theatrically and put a hand in front of her open mouth. 'I tell you, Amanda, whoever thought that one up had a real sense of humour. It's like putting a forkful of steak in your mouth at about the time you feel like eating, leaving it in there, and then, when it's cold and you've gone right off the whole idea, having to swallow. Ahhhhhh,' she turned her head towards the door and raised her glass, 'the lovely man who read so beautifully in church – you must be Andrew. Amanda and I have, quite inappropriately, been discussing the many and various ways of keeping one's sex life on the boil.' Andrew looked confused, Milly sniggered and gave him an affectionate wink. 'You're quite right.

Enough! I'm going to get us all another drink.' She swept her pashmina over one shoulder and moved like a dancer across the rug, raising her arm and tickling the air as she slipped through the doors to the sun room.

Andrew's shoulders sagged and he slumped onto the sofa by the fireplace. 'That's a relief.' He smiled sheepishly. 'I don't think I'm up to talking about sex, I'm afraid.'

He seemed so vulnerable, for a quarterback of a man, cowed almost. There was a tightness around his eyes, that made him look as if he was permanently struggling to retain one of his chemical formulas, and he had a way of clasping his hands between his knees, as if preparing to resist arrest. Watching him, Amanda suddenly found herself a voyeur in Andrew's home, looking down from above on the marital bed as he pumped away bravely, having been called home from the laboratory by a thermometer wielding Lydia while Lydia, her head turned flat against the pillow, stared blankly at the wall. She saw Andrew collapse, exhausted, on his elbows and Lydia prise herself out from underneath him, snatch her satin robe from the end of the bed and make for the sanctuary of the bathroom. Then, minutes later, mindful of the counsellor's words ('remember only you can provide the support each of you needs'), Andrew follows Lydia into the bathroom where she stands motionless at the basin. He tries to rest his cheek against her shoulder and she pulls away, sobbing between gritted teeth, 'Don't touch me, don't try and pretend you want to be here. Don't try and make out this is perfectly bloody normal. Why? You're the bloody scientist! Why can't you do something? It's so – *humiliating.*'

How long had it been? Four years? Four years during

which Andrew had gone from being an easy-going man
with a booming laugh to a quiet, preoccupied figure who
smiled infrequently, and then guiltily, as if he had forfeited
his right to happiness. She could see Lydia's mouth coated
in the pale, glossy lipstick she preferred, forming the
words, 'Thoughtless and selfish . . . know how I feel . . .
your friends . . . care less . . .' Two summers ago Amanda
and Nicholas had thrown a party at Belstone Road and
Amanda had found Andrew on his own at the end of the
garden, on the rotten bench. She'd laid down some tissues
and edged onto the seat next to him and he'd said, without
any warning, 'I've let her down, Amanda. She married me
to have children, and I've let her down.'

'You'll have them, darling,' she'd said. 'Of course you
will. There's plenty of time. Now, tell me, who's her gynae-
cologist?'

In the days that followed she'd bombarded Andrew
with details of result specialists in the field. 'Mention my
name, don't say no to triplets, it sounds uncommitted.
You'll want a nutritionist too. Call this reflexologist,
mention my name.'

They'd never spoken about it since, but nonetheless
Lydia's biological rhythms, her fertile days and false
alarms were broadcast in the tense lines around Andrew's
mouth and in Lydia's fidgety, water-gulping presence.

Today was not one of those days. Amanda looked up
to see Lydia backing into the room, a man's arm clamped
underneath her own, around her waist. She glanced over
at them, raising a Martini glass to her lips while visibly
tightening her grip on the man's arm.

'Well, well. Slipped away from the crowd have we?'
She took another sip without removing her eyes from

Andrew. '*We* are toasting our dead friend in Ambertinis, speciality of the house.' The man looked trapped. 'Vodka, vermouth and a little dash of bitters. Very intoxicating, naturally, and it leaves that all important slightly nasty taste in the mouth. Doesn't it, Sergei? Have you met my husband, Sergei? He doesn't drink vodka although I expect he would make an exception for an Ambertini. Anything with a hint of Amber about it.'

Andrew shifted on the sofa. Amanda managed to catch the eye of the unfortunate Sergei and gave him one of her paint-stripping looks.

'I'll get more,' he mumbled snatching Lydia's glass out of her hand and bolting for the door.

'Amanda,' Lydia was staring at the floor, hands on hips, 'I'll thank you not to terrify my new friends with your evil eye. Not all of us wish to spend the afternoon huddled up with "the gang" reminiscing and getting morbid. Even if it is Andrew's special subject. My husband's awfully good at being sad, have you noticed?'

Amanda touched Andrew's arm to indicate that she was passing the baton, she'd done her bit and now it was up to him. She stood up and started to move across the room. 'I should go and find Nicholas.'

'Oooh yes,' said Lydia earnestly, her eyes bloodshot at this range. 'He won't have the *faintest* idea how to find his way around this house, will he?'

Amanda slipped past her and into the hall. She saw Nicholas straight away, sitting halfway up the stairs with Otis, apparently having the intricacies of camcorder focusing explained in detail. Standing at his side, a slender arm hooked awkwardly around his neck, was Amber's eldest child, Zelda. Otis, in his dark suit and flower-print shirt – he must have been fifteen now – was hovering in the limbo between the rock 'n' roll circus of his childhood and the anonymous cool of his schoolfriends; but the eight-year-old Zelda was a sherbet-burst expression of Amber's style, in rainbow-striped wellingtons, long satin slip and duckdown hairband. She had the blank expression and watchful eyes of children who have seen quite a lot and who have learnt that they must affect a certain silent poise in order to be allowed to see more.

Each of the children was a little testament to Amber, wild and wilful and photogenic. Every zigzag fringe and flamboyant tantrum spoke of Amber's 'It' history and a life unencumbered by the usual practicalities and routines. There were no special shoes or clothes for outdoors, nothing best that couldn't be dragged through the mud, no fingers too sticky to be trailed along the Zoffany wall-paper. Amanda had quickly learnt that to notice such trifles, let alone worry about them, was suburban, and that a kind of de-luxe gypsy approach to life was the hallmark of real breeding. What summed it all up was the hairbrush, or lack of it. In Amber's world you didn't brush. Children had matted, paint-splattered locks and adults the flattering equivalent. The principle of *not* in its place was the key and it applied to everything, from the wearing of pale suede trousers for riding, to allowing the unhouse-trained puppies the run of Hedlands. It was about effort too: the perfect set of luggage, the carefully chosen, exquisitely wrapped present, the good as new cream rug was somehow laughable. For Amanda, who saw her hairdresser twice weekly, kept her cashmere inter-leaved with lavender sachets and her trainers in a shoebag, some of this was a lesson too far. She tried. She learnt to do without a butter knife, or rubber gloves for washing-up, or a tissue box in the car. But the strain of reversing her natural instincts occasionally made her feel like the escaping prisoner of war in that black and white film, who is trained to think and dream in German and then, just as he's boarding the bus to freedom, is tricked into saying 'thanks' in English. All that effort, all that anxiety and one slip witnessed by the wrong person could land you right back where you started.

But for Nicholas of course it was completely different. He was in his element here at Hedlands where everything just came together in a wonderfully spontaneous good-looking way, and there was no fuss, no pre-laid, carefully decorated table, with seating plan and salad plates and coasters for both glasses. His own childhood was not exactly bohemian but they had lived on a farm, and his mother was certainly no perfectionist. It was the kind of house where the dogs were given the dirty plates to lick and where all the chairs were covered in a coating of little white hairs. You had to dry-clean absolutely everything, even if she so much as gave you a lift. And whenever they left the children there they came back unwashed, with half their things missing. Once, Poppy's ultrasuede coat was actually used for purchase under the rear wheel of her grandmother's car when it got stuck on the hill, in the absence of anything more suitable than brand-new Christa children's wear, presumably. But to Nicholas, that was how life should be. He loved the way Amber's children were so wild and unrestricted, like little Mowglis, eating their food on the hoof and sleeping in treehouses, even when rain was forecast. Her children were vegetarian, and organic as far as was possible, but Amber's were gnawing beef on the bone right the way through the ban. She watched Nicholas now with Zelda, Bacci baby as they called her, the accidental bonus of that disastrous holiday in Tuscany when she and Dave had spent most of the time in bed.

'Isn't she lovely?' Nicholas's mother, Bridget, was pressing at her side appropriating her line of view. 'That golden hair and those dark eyes, quite unlike the others. Y'know who she looks like, of course – picture in the spare room at home?' She gave Amanda a jab in the ribs. 'Gabby! Your husband's sister, when she was zactly that age. Abslute spitting image. Well, Amanda, immaculate as ever.' Bridget took a step back to give her daughter-in-law the once over, a favourite routine of hers. 'Oooh. Heavens! How do you get around in those – what do we call them now? Are they the pussy heels, or something new?'

Amanda managed a faint, queasy smile. She was looking at Zelda tucking Nicholas's faded blond hair behind his ears, watching his brown eyes scrunch up with laughter. She was thinking she needed to find the bathroom.

Glancing over Raschenda's shoulder, Jack saw Amanda sidestep Bridget, stiffly and unsteadily like someone who knew the route but was wearing a blindfold. She watched as Amanda slowly picked her way across the flagstones, head up, shoulders back, mouth crashing at the edges, and calculated that she was feeling a little the worse for wear, one too many pills on a habitually empty stomach.

'She's just *ex*-quisite, like a milkmaid who's lived on a diet of curds and butter.'

Raschenda was elaborating on the merits of the news-just-breaking model Diana, her 'discovery' and clearly something of a bacon-saver since Raschenda was employed to sniff out new talent and deliver it fresh off the street into the hands of *LaMode*, but hadn't had a big find since Martin Anderwurst, two and a half years ago.

'There she was – lying on the pavement outside some hairdresser's, sobbing her eyes out – this voluptuous creature. I wanted to *eat* her there and then. So I said, "Whatever is it?" And she said, "They won't do me cos they say I 'aven't got the money," and I said, "Thank God! A gorgeous thing like you shouldn't be having your hair cut in Tongers or Cutz U Like, or whatever. You are *devine*." Raschenda's hat extended like a chocolate mould all the way down over her right eye, finishing in a mousetail flourish underneath her chin. She dragged on her cigarette, reducing a third of it to ash. 'It's totally like – you know.'

'*Pygmalion*?'

'No, no, no . . . erm,' Raschenda snapped her fingers irritably, 'the Audrey Hepburn one – *My Fair Lady*. We're talking huge huge potential. She is so right for now and the whole ultra thing, all big breasts and full hips. Of course *nothing* fits her. Not a thing.' She gave Jack an 'I told you so' look with her one, beady, peacock-painted eye. 'It's the timing that's the problem, getting the pieces made up specially for the shows and then it's selling it to the industry, of course, convincing the photographers that it's a good look.' Raschenda tipped back her head and drained her Martini, leaving a poison-purple smear on the rim of the glass. She twiddled the stem between her fingers.

'So, how big is she?' Jack was picturing Ricki Lake, pre chat show.

'Large fourteen.' Jack did a double take. 'I know. I

know. Unbelievable. Do you know, she had never tasted mineral water before? Tap only. But wonderful skin. Amazing really.' Raschenda switched her empty glass for a replacement passing by on the flat palm of a waiter in starched white livery. Following behind him was a girl in a red velvet Nehru jacket carrying a moss nest of quails' eggs arranged around a little pond of caviar.

'But you know fat is the only thing that looks fresh, there's nowhere else to go.'

Jack watched as the waitress moved through the crowd, offering the nest to the left and the right. She saw a velvet sleeve and a lean brown hand stretch out across the nest and Simon's raven head tilt towards the waitress, watched as her pale skin scorched and her head drooped to let her hair fall across the unruly cheeks. When Simon finally took an egg, dipped it in the caviar and raised it to his lips it was like watching him swallow the girl's innocence.

'Now *he* is doing really amazing things with Tiziana.' Raschenda's heavy lidded eye blinked once, slowly, for emphasis. 'Pity to waste the opportunity.'

She grabbed Jack's hand and tripped over to where Simon was collecting exotically packaged women. Most were affecting sensuality overload, watching him through eyelashes with drowsy, drugged smiles, but a few were tensed like cats, poised, waiting for the split-second slip that would allow them to seize him from under the claws of the other predators.

'Simon,' breathed Raschenda, sliding her head either side of his and then clasping him to her chest and holding him there as if she'd long since given him up for lost in the jungle. He winked at Jack over her shoulder. 'Darling, faaantastic story in Italian *LaMode*. You are unstoppable.' She shot the pack a look that said, 'Back off girls this is grown-ups time' and placed a proprietorial hand on Simon's lapel. 'We absolutely must – talk.'

Jack turned to slip away but felt a hand close firmly around her wrist.

'Let's do lunch.' Simon was addressing Raschenda, then he turned to Jack, tightening his grip, pulling her towards him. 'And you and me are having dinner, Friday week.' He lowered his voice, 'I'm in New York or I'd make it sooner, we've got a lot to discuss.'

Jack stared at her shoes. Out of the corner of her eye she could see the big cats stirring, shaking their manes and running their pointy pink tongues along their shiny white teeth.

'Great,' she said, looked him straight in the eye, and held it for a count of three.

Four

Transmission clock counts down the seconds.

Amber Best, wearing a floor-length fur coat, walks down the pavement, towards the camera, on the arm of a tall man, just out of shot. The coat flicks open to reveal long bare legs and hotpants. As she draws closer to the lens she bows her head to protect her face. She is smiling. The camera judders and lurches, recovers and zooms in on the windows of a limousine as it moves off, just glimpsing the bare legs stretched out in the back and a man's hand laid across them. Cut to a man wearing a snakeskin jacket, sitting in a wing-back chair, caption reads, Felix Cat. 'I think the point about Amber is that she really was wherever it was happening. She was a top model right at the end of the seventies which was the last moment when models were really the business, crazy party girls, smart girls with a lot of style, not just kids, y'know.' He grins and takes a drag of his roll-up. 'They were totally in control, those chicks. Where they went we followed. They were at all the parties, making out, not just with guys in rock bands but with like the hottest artists, actors, racing drivers, you name it . . . That was when it all peaked and that was when Amber was the number-one girl.'

Cut to a sweep of stone steps covered in red carpet,

lined with photographers. Camera zooms in on the melee at the top of the steps, a crowd dressed in black tie including the Prince of Wales, and Amber Best wearing a dress made of sequins that dazzles in the light of the flashbulbs. Cut to Wimbledon, centre court. Camera pans the court, Borg and Connors are playing out a point, Borg slams the ball home, the crowd erupts. Cut to close-up of the crowd just below the royal box. Camera lingers on a wide-brimmed straw hat for several seconds, in the background the umpire's commentary can be heard 'change balls please', the hat lifts and turns revealing Amber Best and a dark-skinned man with an Afro and big-fly sunglasses.

Cut to Felix Cat. Close-up: 'She was a favourite up at the palace. They'd send cars for her and she'd keep them waiting for two, three hours while she was getting ready in that Kensington mews flat of hers. There'd be like feather boas hanging out of the windows, shoes spilling out of the door. She'd always say "He wants Amber Darling, and she takes one hour forty-five, plus Martini mixing time".' He laughs and starts to cough uncontrollably. 'Then she was a backing singer for us for a bit, about as long as we lasted, her and me, which was close on three years I guess . . . Yeah, I was supposed to have written "Daddy's Money" for her. But you know the funny thing is . . . she didn't have any money.' He appears to share a joke with someone off camera. 'But yeah . . . sure' (adopts serious analytical voice) 'there's a lot in the song that is based on a character not dissimilar to Amber Best.'

Cut to clip of Felix Cat video, Felix Cat sings: 'She wants Boy and she wants Crolla/ She wants to be a punk and rock in the Roller/ She's got an attitude problem and a laundry deficit/ She can't choose between Manolos and a powder hit/ Oh yes she can.' Close-up of Amber Best singing solo: 'Give me marks or, give me yen, make it francs or dollars ten, but gimme money, casssshhhh money.' Fade out.

'OK. I think you need to take a deep breath and relax.' Sam was lying on the beanbag in Jack's flat and Jack was tucked up at one end of the sofa, in the small space that wasn't occupied by John Lewis carrier bags, Boots carrier bags, Harvey Nichols carrier bags and two cardboard boxes with handles. She was wearing the expression of someone who has opened all their Christmas presents and just realized that the one thing they asked for isn't there. 'Right . . .' Sam was wriggling and making backstroke motions with his arms in an effort to get more centred on the bag. 'The thing is, you are approaching this all the wrong way. A bit of preparation is good. Definitely. You want to feel comfortable and in control, up to a point. But to try and turn yourself into the ideal date, at a week's notice, is not a good idea.' Jack shredded the Peter Jones receipt in her hands, glaring at the raft of bags. 'Now, let's just take it slowly. What have you got in all these? Probably a couple of things that could be very useful, and one or two not so essential . . . shall we have a little look?' Sam scrambled to his feet and delved into the nearest bag. Jack kept her eyes fixed on the wall behind him. 'Here we go! One double duvet, for the use of, two sets sheets, duvet covers, etc. . . . mmmm.'

'I've still got that single duvet I had at university – if it's any of your business.'

'Fair enough. I can see that the single duvet doesn't instantly say Miss Love Machine. Good decision to make the switch. Big white towels, all right. Diptyque candles, lovely. Four may be optimistic but, whatever. What do we have here – several CDs?'

'That's one of the first ways a man gauges if you are a soulmate or not. And since I was in the shop I thought, What if David Bowie drops dead, or Mick Jagger, and I have to join the queues of people buying *Ziggy Stardust* and *Beggars Banquet* for the first time, just because I never got round to getting them on CD? Imagine the humiliation.' Jack sighed and rested her head on the arm of the sofa.

'So, we've got – quite a few seventies classics.' Sam stacked the CDs one on top of the other, feigning shock every time he found yet another in the bag. 'Led Zeppelin . . . aaaah . . . and a . . . oooh! smattering of up to the minute chart breakers. Some mouthwash. Good. Dental floss. Yes. Deodorant. Yes. Body moisturizing jojoba whatnot. Good. Now, moving on. Books! Will there be much time for reading?'

'He worships Hemingway.'

'OK. For the bedside table then. Undies . . .'

'I needed some new ones, anyway.'

'Of course you did. Copies of one, two, five . . . eight glossy magazines. Plus Photo 100, Camera . . . and something Japanese . . .'

'He's done a story for them. He's a *photographer*.'

'Right, so, necessary research materials. Three bags clothes, I take it?'

'Yes.'

'Is there an opportunity for an outfit change, do we think, or should we narrow it down to just the one?'

'But you don't . . .' Jack sighed noisily. 'I mean you won't necessarily know what he likes.'

Sam drew back his shoulders and puffed out his chest. 'Jacqueline, I am a *man* and as such ideally equipped to select your big-date outfit. Who else were you going to ask? *Amanda?*' Jack chewed on her thumbnail. 'Will you lot never learn? She who decrees what you're all going to be wearing this season may have her finger on the pulse of the designer community's little white wrist but the last thing your fashion insider has the first idea about is what men want.' He extracted an item from one of the bags, shook the leaves of tissue from its folds and held up a lurex polo neck, glancing at Jack and then back to the polo neck. 'I mean Nicholas, poor bloke, hasn't seen his wife look halfway palatable since their wedding day.' Jack's eyes widened. 'No man wants to see a woman in a caramel leather bomber jacket and tweed trousers – what's all that about? She looks like a second-hand car salesman to anyone outside the fashion bubble. And those shoes! One minute it's the Nurse Ratchett lesbian surgical look, the next Minnie Mouse on acid—'

'What's Nicholas said?'

'Nothing. He doesn't have to, it's the way he looks so longingly at anything in a nice pink top or a little skirt or a tight pair of Levis. The only jeans Amanda would ever wear are ones that have been ergonomically reconceived by a team of Japanese technicians, twisted on the body at an angle of forty-five degrees, plastic coated, buried with iron filings'

'Oh, shut up!'

'You know I'm right, Jack.' Sam was doing his sing-song game-show-host voice. 'This isn't the time to flaunt your fashion credentials. It's the time to look *hot*.' He was holding up, between forefinger and thumb, a pair of men's cut, black flannel trousers and peering at her over the top of his glasses. 'You should have asked. I could have lent you some of these, you didn't need to go out and spend – ' Jack dived for the trousers and snatched them from him just as he'd located the price tag – 'a lot more than you can afford, evidently. Listen, save me some time here will you? Is there anything at all in these bags that could be described as "obviously female apparel"?' The next exhibit was an emerald-green chiffon blouse which Sam laid against the back of the sofa and proceeded to carefully fold.

'What's wrong with that? It's see through.'

'Maybe. But my mother's got one.'

'Look, Sam, seriously. Simon isn't like you. I mean he's not like the average man, he's a fashion photographer, he understands serious fashion, all right? He isn't reduced to helpless giggles by anything that isn't a flowery, strappy slip dress. This isn't going to work. Your ideal woman is Cherry in Pan's People for heaven's sake.'

Sam smiled and waggled his eyebrows.

'I know what you're trying to do Jack, but forget it. I will not be deterred by your snottiness, young lady. I'm here to help, whether you like it or not.'

'Why are you so keen to help?'

'Because . . .' he turned his back to her and continued folding the shirt 'I'm with you. I believe you've got to get this out of your system because you're not living in the moment. You're living in your head with Slime-on. And it's not healthy.'

'Yes, but why do you want it to work so badly, when you think he's a total arse?'

'I never said I wanted it to work, I said I wanted you to give it your best shot. Because that's the only way to guarantee that the outcome is conclusive. Now. Stop distracting me. Let's try some tips for how to behave on a date.'

'What sort of tips?'

'Good tips, useful ones. For example, do not hover by estate agents' windows, focusing on properties in roughly the range of your combined incomes. That's number one. Number two, do not mention football. Don't look at me like that. That whole post-*Fever Pitch* thing of finding it quite cute when women took an interest is over. End of story. Number three, smile and laugh a lot. Appear to be mesmerized by anything and everything he says. No subject is too insignificant to warrant your absolute, jaw-dropping awe. And do not, Jack, on any account be tempted to put him straight on European integration, or whatever it is you've got the hump about this week.'

'I beg your pardon?'

'I mean, by all means mention it, if you have to, but don't have a frenzied debate and if you should enter into a short discussion, just let him be right.'

Jack made a duuuur face. 'I'm not allowed to have an opinion that conflicts with his? Perhaps I just shouldn't speak at all, that's obviously the ultimate super-date state we're working towards.'

'Weeelll . . .'

'You're serious aren't you?'

'Well, I just – it's surprising how off-putting it can be to a man, in the initial stages, if he's having his ear bent.

And you do like to chew over the topics of the hour, Jack, and I'm just warning you that, basically, men do not want to be put through their paces, especially when they're worrying about whether their breath smells and if they remembered to change the sheets.'

'I get it! Caring about issues, strong opinions – no-opinions, full stop, are unfeminine! I see now. If you're not emanating tinkling laughter and scrunching up your little buttony nose you're a bit butch. So – hang on – if you must talk about something serious you should do so either in a Meg Ryany I'm-so-kooky-and-crosspatchy-and-mad-you-could-just-confuse-me-with-a-little-puppydog way, or, alternatively, in a sort of smouldering passionate, Mediterranean style, so that—'

'Jack!'

'Waaait – I'm catching on here – so that he thinks, "Mmmm bit of a mouth on her but could be a wildcat in the sack." Am I right?'

'There you go you see, spiky, spiky. That kind of attitude is all right in the movies but in reality it is going to really put him off. There's no point fighting it. It's very simple. Take two images: image A, Vinnie Jones, hands firmly round your testicles; image B, lovely nurse with cool hands soothing your fever in a very short blue dress and black stockings. You, at present, are conjuring up image A feelings and what we have to work towards is image B. We can do it.'

Jack frowned.

'Hah!' Sam jabbed a finger at her. 'Botox! I knew there was something we'd forgotten.'

*

Lydia was curled up on the sofa in Clapham, flicking through the papers while glancing every so often at the cookery book on the seat beside her and the Magnum photography book, open on the floor. She thought about pumpkin risotto, but then men weren't convinced by risotto. If you wanted to please a man like Mark Harman you'd give him . . . osso bucco or a tagine. They could have risotto to start, maybe. She wished Andrew hadn't asked Sam and Jack. Without them they were the perfect little group: Mark's girlfriend was a kind of saint and was very easily dealt with, Ros and Martin were the quick-fit-in Americans from next door, and with just the six of them there was no possibility of Mark being diverted from the business of them getting to know each other better. Celia, Mark's girlfriend, had been wonderfully accommodating. She'd told Lydia how she and Mark were planning to move in together but that Mark was worried they were rushing it. ('I don't feel it's too quick,' Celia had said, a deep furrow between her eyebrows somewhat clashing with her bright, friendly smile, 'but then I couldn't bear for him to feel trapped.' 'Don't you worry,' Lydia had reassured her. 'You take a strong line, men respond to that.') Celia had even volunteered Mark's promotion prospects – timing and salary – his favourite hobbies and his secret passion in life, photography, particularly the Magnum photographers. Lydia sighed and snuggled down among the cushions. She had another hour all to herself before Andrew made it back from Sainsbury's.

*

'Did you notice how much thinner I was last week?' Jack was smoothing down the front of a dress that the assistant had described as charmeuse and Sam had identified as 'super slime, perfect for you know who'. It was black, with cap sleeves and covered her like an oil slick as far as the hips, where it started to flare out slightly so that, incredibly, knickers were still an option. There was no doubt that it was a result dress, but one that came from the American new wave section of the designer floor, which meant that you could feel cutting-edge rather than like bait wriggling on the hook if you actually bought it.

'Jesus,' said Sam, 'you really need to talk your way into buying a dress that makes you look *soo sexy* you're almost unrecognizable?'

'What about the arms?' Jack was flattening her upper arms against her sides. 'They don't remind you of hams?' But her eyes were following Sam, who had just called her sexy not in the flat, objective, some-might-say kind of way. He waved at her from the rails in the middle of the room and held up a little sequin cape, flicking it, matador style, in her direction. She shook her head and turned away but carried on watching him in the mirror. Two teenage girls at a next door rail had recognized him; they were snatching looks in his direction and then collapsing, giggling, on each other's shoulders. He looked up, saw them and smiled broadly, making them claw at their arms and cross their legs as if they were desperate to pee.

She could see him in profile now, the same old Sam she'd known since she was nineteen and had met in her first week at university, same longish curly hair, same strong jaw, same boxer's nose, same round dirty spectacles, only from this angle he didn't look quite the same any more. The pillar in the centre of the designer room sliced through her view of him, right down the middle, so that she was seeing him again exactly as she had that day, through the half-open doors of the library at Hedlands. There were the hands, rifling through the rails, feeling the fabric, resting on Amber's shoulders, stroking the silk of her shirt. There was the mouth, on her mouth, her hands in his hair, his lips on her neck, both of them scrambling and laughing as they lurched out of view behind the door, where there was a sofa, big enough for two to stretch out on. She wished she hadn't seen them. It had been two months before Amber's death, and in those remaining weeks Jack had been cold towards her, and never got the chance to tell her why. It wasn't that it was Sam, it didn't matter who it was, it was still betraying Dave. But why did it have to be Sam? Why did it have to be the one man who wasn't susceptible to Amber's charm, who always said he didn't get what all the fuss was about? Jack had relied on him to be less predictable. They all had. And it felt so unfamiliar. Of course Sam had sex, of course he had girlfriends, but it wasn't something you ever thought about. They weren't those kind of couples: they were always on bicycles or walking dogs or salvaging things from skips. But with Amber everything was about sex, every minute of the day was bristling with sexual possibility, every innocuous domestic activity was like one of those sensuality exercises they give to couples with marriage problems. And it was just so strange to think of him in that context, like discovering a stash of porn in your father's bottom drawer. Sam was cuddly and you could fall asleep on his shoulder in the car or share a room with him, in a bed and breakfast, without sex coming into it at all. He just wasn't that . . . basic. That was the whole point about Sam, he was different. And now, suddenly, he wasn't so different, just another man for whom the epitome of womanhood was Amber Best. They must have had sex all the time. They must have been . . . desperate for each other, for them to have risked her seeing them. And they must have been in love. Well, he would have to have been, he couldn't have done it otherwise. Unless, of course, she'd got that wrong too. Watching him studying the rail, the tip of his tongue curled up over his front lip, glasses perched on the end of his nose, hair falling in his eyes, it was hard to believe that this was the same man she had seen seducing a legendary sex kitten under her husband's roof. She shivered, although the department was heated for the benefit of the bikini triers-on.

Behind Sam, she could see two women approaching the cash desk. One was small and tired-looking with bleached hair, the other was about six foot three with a lantern jaw and a shiny, conker-brown pageboy. When they reached the desk the smaller one spoke, 'Excuse me, we have an appointment to see the personal shopper. My name is Margaret Wilson, and this is my sister.' The assistant stared at Margaret for what must have been five or six seconds before her colleague leant across her and said in a firm, lilting East European accent, 'I am Darva. I am the personal shopper who will be helpink you this mornink, Mrs Wilson, and it is my great pleasure. Will you step this way please?' The group of seats to which they retired was just to the right of Jack's mirror. Jack kept smoothing the black dress and watching Margaret's sister. Darva sat in the middle, holding a clipboard, and turned her head to left and right at regular intervals, even though Margaret was doing all the talking. 'Today we'd like to concentrate on my sister, who is hoping to find some evening wear, mid-market in terms of price, not black, we think, and we like spaghetti straps and diamante.' Margaret indicated where the spaghetti straps might fall, on the shoulders of her Danimac. 'Possibly long, we thought.'

'Your name please?' Darva smiled broadly at Margaret's sister.

'Sylvia.'

Darva's smile never faltered. 'Sizing please?'

'Eighteen.'

Darva kept scribbling on her clipboard. 'And shoes?'

'Eleven.'

'Sooo, Sylvia. You are loooking for something rather formal or maybe a little glamoroos, a bit sexy perhaps?'

Margaret gave Sylvia the look mothers give their children when they are being offered something so unbe lievably good that they become confused and need confirmation from the one they trust. It was hard to see Sylvia's reaction behind her giant, lilac-tinted glasses but nonetheless it was Darva's job to make lightning assess- ments of people's requirements and desires and then to marry up the two as best she could, given the merchandise available. She leant across and placed a hand on Sylvia's powerful thigh. 'I think definitely sexy an' a bit special is good for you.' Darva wrinkled up her nose. 'I have just the things.'

Jack watched them disappear in the direction of the 'After Dark' section, Sylvia, shoulders hunched, taking small shuffling steps as if her knicker elastic had gone, Margaret with her arm hooked through Sylvia's, Darva pirouetting ahead of them, gesturing to right and left like a dancer taking her bow.

Sam was suddenly by her shoulder, tapping his watch. 'Show's over, ladies,' he said. 'Time, please.'

Jack felt tears welling: 'That's real love isn't it? Imagine caring so much about someone that nothing else matters, nothing but the other person's happiness.' She turned back to the mirror and in it saw Sam looking at her hard, his face set in an expression of grim resignation. The long day's shopping had obviously taken its toll.

'Yes,' he said, 'that's love all right. But that doesn't mean to say that Margaret's happy.'

Lydia was standing in front of the bedroom mirror holding a flesh-coloured crochet dress up against her, making her sucked-in-cheeks face that was a reflex response to any trying-on situation, when she heard the front door slam. The pert girl in the mirror dissolved and was replaced by a tight-lipped woman with a grievance. What exactly the grievance was Lydia hadn't decided yet. She met her own eyes in the mirror and paused, for a moment, to reflect on her best course of action. The question was, would a guilty, chastised Andrew, or a hopeful Andrew be more useful to her this evening? The advantage of the cowed Andrew was that he wouldn't interfere, but then again the misery he would radiate might just taint the whole proceedings. On the other hand, Andrew in eager mode could be equally damaging, clasping her around the shoulders, praising her every action and generally contradicting with his every loyal word the picture that she had been carefully piecing together for Mark Harman. There were the bouts of heavy drinking, the times Andrew never came home – 'What man doesn't go crazy and stay out once in a while?' she'd said with a sweet, hurt smile; the late nights working at the lab; his total lack of interest in her, in *that* way, a combination she supposed of the drink and the work. Poor Andrew, she'd said and she could feel Mark falter, almost see the adrenalin pumping, the muscles flicker and tense as his cocktail lubricated brain considered the possibility of touching her hand, or taking her in his arms and kissing her.

As she leant into the cupboard to pull out another possible dress Andrew padded into the bedroom behind her.

'Well,' he sighed, making for the bed, 'that was exhausting!'

'Don't!' snapped Lydia. 'Don't you dare. I'll want to show Celia around later.' The bed was a triumph, a white-painted four-poster smothered in white quilted and lace cushions.

'Not much room for a man here,' Sam had said when he'd first seen it. God how she wished those two weren't coming.

'What possessed you to ask Sam and Jack tonight?' she said accusingly. 'They'll have nothing in common with the others and they're so . . . scruffy. Sam will come in that frightful cord suit which I know brought moth into this house. Every time I try and introduce someone new into our lives, try and get away for one moment from the good old gang, you panic and have to reel in a couple of them for support.' She wheeled round for emphasis. Andrew started to lower himself cautiously onto a delicate silk upholstered dressing-table seat. 'Andrew – ' she jabbed a finger at the seat ' – I don't think so.' He straightened up and leant against the windowsill instead.

'It isn't like that, darling. They were just – there, and I thought they'd add to the mix.'

'They're always bloody there. That's the point.' She caught a glimpse of herself in the mirror; there was a thin lilac vein standing out on her temple. 'Anyway, the most important thing is that our new friends, Mark and Celia, have as nice a time as possible, and you like Celia don't you?'

'Of course.'

'So, she's your responsibility, she's very shy you know.' Lydia smiled her wedding photograph smile, her good Lydia smile. 'And Andrew, you're so good with shy people.' She could see the tension in his face melt away, she never used his name these days, so lately that was enough to do it. 'I just want it to be perfect for everyone,' she said, and she crossed the room and kissed him very lightly on the lips, slipping past him and out of the door before he had a chance to capitalize on this irregular bounty of affection.

Andrew perched on the chaise. He longed to lie down, just for ten minutes, but that would mean folding up the linen bedspread, and the quilt thing and stacking all the pillows – pillows or cushions? – on the chair by the window and taking off his shoes and socks. Even at night the prospect was intimidating. Lydia's first allegiance was to the bed. The bed was like a female lover who, in the name of open-mindedness, Andrew was expected to accommodate, even enjoy. Usually, when they had sex, they had it on top of the bed because, once between the sheets, Lydia was already taken. Her side was another country: the pillows were square with antique satin cases and she had a lavender-filled bolster and little cushions smelling of eucalyptus that formed a protective horseshoe around her. They never drew the muslin drapes, but he knew Lydia sometimes did when she was alone. She'd got the room just the way she wanted it – friends of hers literally gasped with delight when she pushed open the double doors and stepped back to reveal its contents – it was amazing really. But everything about it made him feel oafish and clumsy, even his jeans and sweaters, neatly folded on the boudoir chair on his side of the bed, looked like burglars at a bridge party. He'd taken to leaving his shoes in the little room next door (the bedroom was carpeted in an almost-white colour called Swedish parchment) but really it wasn't just the shoes that weren't welcome. Nothing of his had a place in that room.

He thought of the bed in her old flat in Islington. He could see both of them sprawled across it, with the Sunday papers, a tray of coffee and old toast, towels (my God, *wet towels* even). Mess. Nudity. He couldn't recall anything about that bed at all whereas this bed sat at the centre of his world like a greedy, pearly skinned odalisque. He gave it a kick and cupped his head in his hands. Lydia was right about Sam and Jack. He did need them there but not, as she thought, for support. He didn't need anyone's support in his own home, even now. He just needed people who had known Lydia before: before they were married, before they moved here and had the garden landscaped and bought the bed and made their life into something that bore scarcely any relation to the people they had been just a few years before. He needed them there to remind him of how he had got here in the first place.

Five

'I feel like that Replicant in *Bladerunner*.'

Jack and Sam were standing on the doorstep of Andrew and Lydia's house. Jack was wearing the dress, which they'd decided that she should test run in a neutral situation, with red lipstick and heels. Amanda had said both were 'a must . . . anything less is going to look feeble. And watch the bra.'

'You can't be a Replicant,' said Sam, 'without the sausage-roll hair. Anyway, she was all right, that Replicant. No heart, but cute.'

'Hiiiiii.' Lydia was arranged in the open doorway, hip jutting to one side, arm raised in the air, cocktail glass clasped between forefinger and thumb. 'Well, Jacqueline, goodness gracious me. All got up for little old us. Everyone,' she called back over her shoulder, 'it's Jack and Sam!'

'Result!' hissed Sam. 'You've been promoted to threat.'

'Ohmigod!' Lydia was pulling Jack into the sitting room, peeling off her coat as she ran the gamut of astonished expressions, appealing to her audience with saucer-like 'whaddayknow?' eyes. 'Now Mark, this is little Jackie, and Celia this is Jack. You will have lots to talk to each other about because Jack is a journalist, a contributing editor for *LaMode*, no less, and you work for the BBC, albeit not at quite the same level. And Marti and Ros, you know each other, of course. Well . . .'

All eyes were still on Jack who was gulping the glass of wine Andrew had handed her. Sam was reminded of an exchange he had recently witnessed at a party. A couple, not long an item judging from their level of attentiveness, had been approached by a woman who appeared to be very excited. 'I can't believe it, Bill,' she shrieked. 'You have lost *so much weight*! How long has it been? A year? My God, you must have lost three stone!' The man had attempted to shrug off her protestations, accusing her of wildly exaggerating, but she was having none of it, gripping the new girlfriend's forearm and assuring her that she wouldn't have recognized the old Bill in a million years. By the time she moved on the girlfriend had stepped back, out of reach of Bill's newly honed arms, and was looking at him in quite a different way.

'For those of you who haven't met Jack before,' Sam grinned at the assembled company, 'she's normally a dead ringer for John Prescott.'

Lydia shrieked with laughter. 'And this naughty man is Sammy, our very own landscape gardener, or is it architect? Oh I prefer architect.' She looped both arms around Sam's neck and in that instant he knew that she was already drunk, that she wasn't wearing a bra and was determined that should not go unnoticed, and that he was to be her stooge flirt for the night. Her warm-up man. She was wearing a chiffon halterneck dress and her long, curly red hair was loose around her shoulders. She should have looked great. Lydia took Sam's arm and belted it around her hips. 'Sammy, hand round the jug of caipirinha will you, Andrew's being so mean with them.' She wasn't wearing knickers either.

'Oh, not for me,' said Celia. 'Wine is perfect.'

'So,' Mark was sliding over in the direction of Jack, 'we're to take it that this is a new dress, and very lovely it is too.'

'Thank you.' Jack glanced at Sam. 'You probably gathered it isn't really my sort of thing.' She rolled her eyes. 'I mean I like it, but . . .'

'You mean it's a woman's dress, sweetie, and you're one of life's eternal girls.' Lydia saluted Jack with her glass. 'Here's to that very important distinction, without which we'd all be at each other's throats! Which one are you then, Celia, girl or woman?'

'Oh, I'd have to say woman, I think,' said Celia. 'I mean there's nothing I like more than pottering about the kitchen or baking a cake—'

'Oh?' Lydia dragged on her cigarette. 'Bit of a Delia, Celia? No, more of a Nigella, an all-round domestic goddess I should think.'

'Oh, hardly!' Celia giggled. 'No, and I'm terrible at all that style and grooming. I should be ashamed really. I'm still a quick up and down with the razor once in a while and that's me done!'

Lydia squinted at her through the smoke from her cigarette and smiled, extending her glass in Sam's direction.

'Relax while you can is my advice.' Ros had one of those soft, unidentifiable American accents that made her sound rich and witty, whatever she said. 'You're going the

US way, like it or not. Give it a month and it'll be a sin not to wax your thighs, just the way it is in New York.'

'Well, it suits me.' Lydia had moved so that she was within earshot of Mark. 'I think it's so important for a woman to take care of herself. It's a measure of your self-respect – and a gift to the man in your life.'

Ros glanced from Celia to Lydia and back and gave a high, fluttering laugh. 'Oh, who needs it? My philosophy is if the neighbours are coming over then tidy up the parlour, otherwise let it go.' There was a crash and Andrew appeared, pink faced, in the doorway of the kitchen, wearing an apron. 'I think we should eat, darling, soufflé's risen.'

The placement was exactly as Sam had predicted. Mark was on Lydia's right, Celia was next to Andrew, at the opposite end of the table, and the newly troublesome Jack was safely tucked away between Andrew and Martin. Lydia was still brandishing a caipirinha and, having waved away her own portion of soufflé, was leaning across the table dipping into Mark's, as if it were melting Häagen Dazs.

'I only wanted a little taste,' she explained to the table, each of whom was keeping up a semblance of conversation while soaking in every nuance of Mark and Lydia's exchanges. 'It tastes better somehow, doesn't it, food from someone else's plate?'

Now and then Mark would turn to speak to Ros, and Lydia would place a restraining hand on his forearm, or gasp as she remembered something terrifically important that she had neglected to share with him. From his end of the table Sam could hear snatches of her world view being delivered in a sultry voice, with a trace of an accent that, to someone unaware of her Esher roots, might have suggested that English was her second language.

'I have to get out in open country,' she murmured. 'Some women can't see beyond making a nest. It makes me so sad to watch the way they push and push, denying their men the space to breathe.'

Sam battled to keep Celia, on his right, occupied, while keeping one ear on Lydia and one eye on Andrew, conscious that in distracting them he was playing into Lydia's hands.

'Isn't she amazing,' said Celia. 'Mark hates people eating his food normally! But Lydia could get away with anything. I understand she could have been a top model but she just turned her back on it.'

Andrew seemed preoccupied with the dinner itself. Even when Lydia got down on the floor to demonstrate a yoga position to Mark, with a lot of elaborate tucking-in of her skirt and shrieking, 'You know why, Sammy!' he continued to bustle to and fro with plates of carved lamb and bowls of vegetables, apparently oblivious. Sam wanted to help but he couldn't tear himself away. He had the feeling that something big was about to happen, something he might be able to avert or should be there to witness, he wasn't sure which.

'So, are you and Jack a couple then?' Celia was helping Sam to potatoes.

'No.'

'Oh. Just great friends then, how lovely. I have a few close male friends but Mark doesn't really have any girlfriends. He doesn't believe in platonic friendship you see. He absolutely loved *When Harry Met Sally* because it vindicated everything he'd ever said about men and women being just good friends. He says that what people call platonic friendships are, in fact, one-sided crushes based on each party's accepting that they are in different leagues, sexually . . .'

Sam could hear Lydia in the background 'Not the Magnum photographers? No! You're just saying that! Well forever! I'm absolutely obsessed.'

' . . . Mark doesn't even believe that men and women can work together without, you know, sex rearing its ugly head. Half the people in his office are having affairs, apparently. I'm hopeless at picking up on the signals of course. Everyone in my department could be at it and I'd be the last to know. But then it's always the ones you least expect, isn't it.'

'Sam, Sam – we're talking about our programme.' Lydia was waving from the other end of the table. 'Tell us all how it's going, darling.' Lydia swooped towards Mark's ear. 'Did you know we're all going to be television stars? It's true! And Sammy, because he's Channel X's golden boy and' – she spread her arms billboard wide – 'the It Boy of gardening, has actually seen one of the finished tapes.'

'It's only rough,' said Sam, 'and it's not about us, Lydia.'

'Well, rough or not, it is *us*, and I can't wait.' She lowered her voice to a confidential murmur, a level that everyone around the table was by now attuned to. 'They tell me I'm the best, because I have natural camera presence.' Lydia waved her cigarette at Mark, who didn't seem to be quite as intrigued as he should have been. 'And you know what else? Because I tell it like it is.'

The table fell silent.

'What do you mean?' said Jack.

'I mean that I am the one person involved in this programme who isn't a paid-up member of the Amber Best Unconditional Adoration Society. I mean that what they are getting from all of you is a load of sentimental whitewash and blah blah blah but what they're getting from me is the perspective of someone who has some perspective. Who isn't an acolyte, or a lover or a—'

'Lydia,' Jack flicked a look of panic at Sam, 'what have you been saying to them?'

Andrew stood motionless beside the table clutching a carving knife and fork.

Lydia shrugged. 'Nuuttthing. God, see what I mean?' She nudged Mark. 'Talk about On Message or Else. And to my left,' she gestured towards Jack, 'meet Alastair Campbell. No prizes for guessing who Tony is.' She raised her glass at Andrew.

'I must say,' said Celia stumbling blindly into the enemy encampment, 'she always seemed like such an extraordinary person. Amber. I mean to those of us on the outside, who didn't know her personally.'

Lydia raised her eyebrows in mock interest. 'And did you by any chance believe that Tom and Nicole had a magical marriage, Celia? Yes, I thought so.'

Sam sensed Lydia subliminally vibrating, like a tuning fork; he knew that if cornered now, she would blow. He shook his head at Jack and tried to get Andrew's attention, but too late.

'Lydia! Stop.' Andrew slammed the handle of the knife down on the table. 'You are talking about someone very close to us all who has died suddenly, in tragic circumstances, you must have some respect for—'

'Oh, please. Just because she died doesn't mean we

have to rewrite history. That's what I mean. You are unreliable sources, all of you, because you feel safer regurgitating the same old goddess line, the same old diamond-girl-cut-off-in-her-prime crap, than in facing up to what she was really like.' Lydia cast her eye around the table checking to see if she had their full attention. 'I mean, for a start, the woman was a tart.' Her tone was pained now, as if the observation hurt her more than it would hurt them. 'Men were her hobby. So she took a little time out with Dave, and persuaded you that she was a changed woman with nothing on her mind but jam making and *pleaching*. So what? I saw right through that little charade. She had her eye on Nicholas from the start. They were having an *affair*. Can't you get it into your thick skulls? Why else was he at Hedlands, on his own, without Amanda? What else was he doing there the night she died? Playing Scrabble? I mean, I can see why Amanda doesn't want to face up to it but I draw the line at ignoring the facts so that you lot can preserve this perfect friendship myth. Get over it. She was probably doing that other local rock dinosaur too—'

'Lydia!' Andrew sounded more anguished than angry.

'What's the matter, darling, jealous?' She turned to address Mark. 'I am so sorry, it's just' – she dipped her head and looked up coyly through her eyelashes – 'there were three of us in this marriage, you see. Not that my husband was doing anything untoward.' She snorted and took another slug from her glass. 'Fat chance. Just worshipping from afar, you understand, ready to do her bidding whenever she clicked her fingers. The fact that she used him like an errand boy was neither here nor there—'

Jack scrambled up from her chair. 'I'm going. Lydia, how can you be such a bitch?'

'Darling, don't shoot the messenger. I'm not the one who was betraying my very best friends, I'm just the only one who could see it. And I'm quite sure I only saw the half of it.' Sam rose from his seat to follow Jack. 'Sammy? You afraid of the truth too? Well, what a surprise.'

Within minutes all the guests were in their coats jostling for position on the doorstep, saying their goodbyes to Andrew with promises of calling him tomorrow.

'I'm sorry,' he kept repeating, 'my wife has had far too much to drink. I do apologize.'

Sam, realizing at the last minute that he'd left his jacket on his chair, told Jack to wait and headed back to the dining room where he found Lydia alone at the head of the table, smoking another cigarette and hiccuping softly.

'Fuck,' she said. 'Well, that's put paid to my new friend.'

Six

Jack was woken by the telephone at 8 a.m. It took her longer than usual to reach it, what with not having anything on and none of the curtains in the flat being drawn. She had to make her approach doubled up and weaving, as if evading sniper fire, using first the kitchen door and then the chair for cover, finally squatting behind the sofa, reaching up with one arm and dragging the handset off the table and onto the floor. It was Amanda. Only Amanda rang her at this hour and persisted in ringing her despite her protestations that the longer lie-in was the outstanding perk of the single and childless girl's existence.

'Come on, Jack, the rest of the world has been up and at it for several hours. I've got something for you to do,' she would say. 'No hurry. The interview's not until ten.' If Jack didn't answer Amanda would simply hail her on the answer machine. 'Coooeee. Know you're there, up you get.'

'I could have been – out. I might not have come home last night,' Jack had tried, on one occasion.

'Yes,' Amanda had said, 'but the odds of you being holed up in a love nest with someone you met last night versus flat out, wearing your Virgin Airways eye mask, are just not high enough to put me off. Besides, you'd have rung me by now to give me all the details.'

'Hello?' Jack tried to sound bright and efficient, as if she'd just finished blow-drying her hair.

'Oooh, dear,' said Amanda.

'What?'

'You sound like Lee Marvin. Where's the dress?'

'I'm sorry?'

'When you took it off last night. What did you do with it?'

'Nothing.'

'Go and have a look. I'll hang on.'

Jack did her commando shuffle back to the bedroom. No sign of the dress. She checked the bathroom, including the laundry basket. Nothing. Looked in the cupboard, just in case. No. And then, acting on a hunch, she flung back the bed cover and there, crushed up and wedged like a draft excluder between the bed and the wall was the dress.

'Where was it?' Amanda sounded as if she were looking at her nails.

'Oh, draped across the chair.'

'Liar.'

'OK, across the bed.'

'I can imagine. You'll have to get it dry-cleaned before Friday. How was it?'

'A disaster.'

' No! Even with the heels?'

'Not the dress! The dinner party. Lydia's finally lost it and is threatening to tell her version of events to Channel X.'

'What version?'

'Oh, you know, just any horrible thing she can make up.'

There was a pause. Jack waited, chewing on her bottom lip, eyes shut.

'Well,' Amanda said finally, 'however thrilling Lydia's revelations might be, Channel X still need our co-operation if they want this programme to work. I'll speak to them today. But first we need to get you sorted out for this date. What are you doing now?'

'Oh. I was just about to—'

'Have a bath, don't bother to get dressed. I'm coming over for a flick through.'

A flick through was a kind of Jack and Amanda ritual that dated back to Jack's first interview commission for *LaMode* when Amanda had taken it upon herself to supervise a clear-out of Jack's wardrobe or, as she put it, 'do an edit'. Jack had only met Amanda on a couple of occasions but in the fashion world, as Jack was to discover, there was nothing personal about clothes. Amanda offering to separate her ins from her outs was just like a plumber of your acquaintance offering to repair your dripping tap so there was none of the walking on eggshells diplomacy that ordinary women practise when advising each other on their appearance.

Usually, among female friends, there is a strict code of changing-room behaviour. For example, if friend A tries on a pair of trousers that do her no favours at all, friend B does not double up laughing but looks quizzical, appears to give the matter a few seconds deliberation, and then adopts the 'It's not you, it's them' strategy ('I think they're cut a bit funny at the back'). In Amanda's world such pussyfooting was not only surplus to requirements, it was the sign of a style ditherer, a fashion incompetent. In her world everything was either a convincing yes or a resounding no, unless it was an eeeeeurch expression followed by a glare, as in, 'I can do so much, but boy you had better start helping yourself.' The first flick through had been a bit of a shock partly because of the speed at which Amanda separated the outs from the ins, but mainly because Jack's most recent and funky purchases hadn't slowed her down for a second. 'I've only just bought that,' Jack would say, 'it's great – look,' and she'd wriggle into it and stand there at the end of the bed, arms spread wide, and Amanda would give her the intense Colin Firth stare and say, 'I know what you think you look like, Jack, but you don't,' which, since she had guessed it was Jane Fonda in *Klute*, you had to respect.

In later years Amanda would accompany Jack shopping where the same rules applied: no flannel, no compromise, no what ifs. What If was, apparently, Jack's biggest problem. It wasn't so much that she had terrible taste, as that she couldn't restrict herself to buying clothes that she would have some opportunity of wearing, so that her wardrobe consisted of a few things she looked good in and a lot of things that she might look good in were she ever asked to, for example: a ball in a very hot climate having lost a stone (sequinned, orange, diaphanous, size-too-small dress); very cold après-ski do (chunky thousand-ply cashmere polo neck, not possible to wear indoors at any time of year). She had pairs of shoes she couldn't walk in, skirts she couldn't sit down in (could work for a drinks party, at her flat, had been her reasoning). But the What If condition was more serious than the occasional impractical purchase. An acute attack of What Ifs was when you looked in the changing-room mirror and instead of seeing yourself in the dress you saw the dress on some olive-skinned creature, spinning around a flare-lit pool in Marrakesh. The screaming What Ifs was when you bought the dress because it had the same effect on your senses as sniffing patchouli – because it reeked of another time and another place, and another person.

Amanda had given up a few Saturday mornings to conquering Jack's What If condition. She would accompany Jack on 'returned goods' missions and stand there drumming her fingers on the counter while the assistant ran through the routine: 'Receipt, madam? Lovely. Any particular problem with the article?' at which point Amanda would hiss in Jack's ear, 'Go on, tell her you bought it while under the impression that you were Marianne Faithfull circa 1967, but that in the cold light of day, after consultation with your friend, you recognize that a kaftan, on you, today, is more Born Again Christian.'

The doorbell went. Jack, who had gone back to bed as soon as she put the phone down, buzzed Amanda in and set about reviving her face which was now criss-crossed with those creases you mysteriously only get in the period between waking up and the time you actually get up. Amanda pushed open the door to the flat and paused on the threshold. She was wearing a blanket-stitched beige suede skirt with a Japanese-style, assymetric rose print top and talking into a mobile phone: '. . . card should read: congratulations, fabulous news, we want you on the cover *now*, exclamation mark. Yeeeees, the long tall thing with the dot on the bottom. And get Raschenda to call me, I'll be in at about eleven.' She snapped the phone shut and walked stiffly into the sitting room, glancing around distractedly. 'Christa got the job at Louis Louis. Absolute disaster for us. Where can I sit?'

'Chair? Sofa? Floor if you prefer.'

'You know what I mean, where can I sit in my *skirt*.'

'Aaah. Safest on the bed, probably. I mean you could risk the far end of the sofa but Sam slept there the other night and might have had some of that pointy peaks, greasy stuff in his hair. Couldn't say for sure.'

Amanda looked at the sofa and back at Jack and blinked once very slowly. 'You put on the outfit, I'll look through the make-up.'

Ten minutes later she was perched on the bed and Jack was, once again, standing at the foot of it wearing the dress, the shoes, the red lipstick, the almost fishnet tights that Amanda had salvaged from the back of a drawer, a silver necklace and quite a lot of a hairstyling product which gave you that cartoon urchin look as perfected by LuLu. But Amanda's faraway expression and the way she was jiggling one foot suggested that they were far from done.

'Should I try it with the cardigan?' said Jack. Amanda's lips twitched. 'What then? I'm not wearing that bra, if that's what you're thinking, it's like wearing falsies.'

'No, no, everything's great. It's you we've got to work on now.'

'Hmmm?'

'It's all there, Jack, but you're not *working* it. You've got to enjoy it – stick everything out a bit, loosen up. You look like you've just got out of a swimming pool in the dead of winter and someone's run off with your towel.'

Jack furrowed her brow and folded her arms.

'There you go, you see? You don't fold your arms in a

dress like that. Shoulders back – shoulders *back*. Undo the front a bit.' Amanda settled back on the pillows and squinted at Jack, her head tilted to one side. 'Now, if you can just keep that up.'

'It feels unnatural.'

'Darling, no offence, but natural is not going to get you anywhere. Natural is great for nineteen-year-old babes, but it has never been a suitable ambition for the over-thirties. Now, let's just brush up a little bit on how to play the actual date.' She raised her eyebrows, apparently expecting Jack to volunteer some ideas. 'All right then – first of all you want to be late, ten or fifteen minutes. Secondly you want to be in demand, your mobile might ring a few times during the course of the evening or you might bump into a few people you know, possibly a gorgeous man.'

Jack looked perplexed and then suspicious.

'Next, you need to put a sensual spin on everything – eating, drinking, taking your coat off – everything you do you've got to think sex, or specifically Juliette Binoche, if that makes it easier.' Amanda dragged on her cigarette and screwed up her eyes. 'And the same applies conversationally. Everything you talk about should have a kind of sexy subtext. So, for example, not global warming but, yes, your wonderful hot holiday in Brazil; not how stressed you are at work but, yes, how much you love yoga and how proficient you are at the climbing lotus, or whatever it's called . . . what's the matter?'

Jack was looking overburdened, literally, her shoulders had slumped forwards again and she was sort of sagging in the middle.

'I just – you know – it isn't so simple when half of you

wants something but the other half would rather stay at home and watch *Frasier*.'

'You'll be fine when you get going.'

'But the last person I kissed was that bloke at the Smirnoff party, and I just don't feel up to it, necessarily.'

'Well, nothing's changed in eighteen months, sweetheart. Same old rules apply. You've got to make them feel like gods but let them think that you have quite a few gods to choose from.'

'This is *Simon*! This is the man who was voted *Herald* magazine's most desirable man in Britain. Twice. He *knows* he's a god, he's got the certificates to prove it.' Amanda yawned. 'Well,' said Jack, 'I'd like to know how you'd cope if you were about to go on a date with the man who was recently engaged to Monica K.'

Monica K was a model who had recently appeared in a film called *Go Go Girls*, during which there was a sequence that had been described in the *Guardian* as, 'dirty dancing that surpasses the physical range of most professional gymnasts'. Jack and Amanda both fleetingly pictured the scene in question before Amanda swatted aside the image with a wave of her cigarette.

'This is no time for bottling,' she said briskly. 'He's probably fed up with all that Houdini stuff, anyway. Tight bodies and gymnastics in the bedroom can get boring, just like anything else you know. He probably fantasizes about real girls with cellulite and bad teeth.' Jack's eyes widened. 'It's the Charles and Camilla thing, isn't it? They get to a point where great tits and miles of leg just aren't enough any more. They want ... personality, actually, someone who stimulates them in other ways. A mate.'

Jack had a mental flash of the front page of a tabloid

newspaper featuring her pictured arm in arm with Simon under the banner headline: The Camilla Effect, Simon Best Trades Babes and Glamour for Comfort of Old Friend.

'I'm only saying' said Amanda, watching the Camilla Effect register on Jack's face 'that you are every bit as attractive, in your own way, as any Monica K.'

'It's not just the Monica K thing.' Jack was slumped on the floor now, picking at the stitching of her hem. 'I've lost my womanly wiles. I don't have what it takes, any more, I've been . . . Effeminated by years of doing my own DIY, and never being sent flowers, and not having anyone to care about what underwear I'm wearing. The thing nobody understands is that if you're single for long enough you turn full circle and you forget all your womanly training and experience and gradually regress until you become a virgin all over again. Simon thinks he's going to dinner with a mature experienced woman, when in fact he's getting a fourteen-year-old in a rude dress.'

'Well, nothing that can't be remedied with a Martini, I'm sure.' Amanda's mobile rang. 'Riva? Yes. What d'you mean? Well, what is she, if she isn't a woman of influence? . . . Who? . . . I know but we'd have needed a lot more than a Miss Piggy wig and a Versace top for Queen Elizabeth the first, wouldn't we Riva? . . . Besides, I think you should be backing me up in front of Mrs Elsworthy, thank you so much . . . No, backing, supporting . . . Oh, forget it. Tell Mrs Elsworthy that I'll sort it out with her after school.' The mobile was snapped shut and Amanda rolled her eyes heavenward. 'Just what I need. Apparently Donatella Versace is not who Pinton Prep had in mind at all for their dress up as a woman of influence day. Well, better get going.' She slipped off the bed and smoothed down the suede skirt. 'You're all set Jack, the rest is just fine tuning. Only, if you are going to bring him back here afterwards do try and make it look a little less like the set of *Men Behaving Badly*. You want him to walk in and think womb or bordello or, failing that, mummy, but not medical students' digs. Call me later.'

And with that she let herself out of the flat leaving Jack to contemplate which, given the materials she had to work with, was the easier call.

At 3.30 Amanda pulled up outside Pinton Prep. She liked to pick the children up once a week, usually on a Thursday. It made absolutely no difference to them who ferried them around town to their various engagements but Amanda enjoyed a certain reputation at PP and the antipathy radiating off the other mothers, plus the occasional craven act of homage, was, she had to admit, a bit of a pick-me-up. Sweeping up to the gates in her biscuit-coloured Mercedes she felt like Cruella DeVille at a PETA fundraising event, the car alone was like a badge of negligent mothering by comparison with the armoured tanks the other mothers arrived in. Hers, with its oyster-coloured leather seats and polished maple interior, said 'Strictly Adult Entertainment'; their mobile playrooms-cum-fortresses equipped with special anti-reflect screens, holders for Thomas the Tank Engine mugs, containers full of educational tapes and built-in first aid kits said, 'Prosperous child-centred family. Make way'.

The mothers were similarly practical and power driven. They looked like members of one extended family

– Afghan blonde hair, manageable high-heeled boots worn under tight jeans, year-round tans. All of them wanted exactly the same things: a lot more money, a bigger house in the country, a nanny who knew her place. They extracted jewellery from their husbands to mark occasions such as the birth of a child, with the poker-faced cool of debt collectors and ran their homes and skeleton staff with the same efficiency that they had organized their brief working lives in PR/city sandwich delivery. A large part of what got them out of bed in the morning was the drive to compete with each other, but they looked at Amanda and saw someone living outside their jurisdiction, who was therefore beneath contempt.

'Amanda! How are you?' One of them was tapping her fingers on the window of the Merc, Amanda couldn't remember which one exactly. She lowered the window, releasing a volume-seven blast of gangsta rap, and the Afghan, who was checking Amanda's outfit as best she could from that angle, leant into the car eagerly. 'LOVE your skirt,' she breathed. Clearly she was one of the break-away worshipful contingent as opposed to the lot who treated Amanda like Joan Crawford in her *Mommie Dearest* moment. 'Donna . . . Karan,' said Amanda, depressing the car lighter and rummaging in her bag for a cigarette. Just to the right of the friendly Afghan she could see the mermaid blonde wig bobbing towards them, and her silk jersey top snagged under the straps of Cass's knapsack. 'Excuse me–' she leant out of the window '–Darling, mind the strappy bits on mummy's top.' Cass stopped in her tracks, tugged at the batwing sleeves for a moment, and then carried on walking, the wig now slightly lopsided and the top gathered up around her shoulders like ruched blinds, so you could see her knickers. 'Never mind.' Amanda drew in her head and settled back against the oyster leather with a shrug. 'What can you do?' she said, branding her cigarette with the lighter. The Afghan watched Cass plod past on her pink platforms and make her way round to the other side of the Merc. As she opened the passenger door she waved gaily to a child in a passing car who was wearing a wimple and full habit.

'Bye-bye, Cassy,' said the Afghan, adopting a poor-baby tone.

'Bye, Mrs von Hoppenmeir.' Cass raised a regal hand and then set about belting herself in.

'Darling, knapsack off first, sweetheart. So who was that?' Amanda glanced in the direction of the retreating glove-fit leather trousers.

'Emily's mummy.'

'Emily?'

Cass rolled her eyes. 'Emily, yooo knoow. Her daddy's in gardening prison.'

'Aaah, that's it. I thought I recognized her. So,' Amanda leant across and yanked down the jersey top, 'what happened to your scary eyes, my darling?'

'Mrs Elsworthy took them off.'

'Oh dear. What did she say?'

'She said, your mummy had better see me after school,' Cass grinned. 'Oh, look! She's coming now.'

Amanda looked and there was Mrs Elsworthy, bearing down on the Merc. She stuffed the cigarette in the ashtray, yanked a scent bottle out of her bag and squirted a fine mist of L'eau d'Hadrien around the car. Cass watched her with big, traces of kohl-rimmed eyes.

'She knows you smoke, Mummy,' she said, matter of factly.

'How does she?'

'Because of Poppy's picture.'

Oh yes. One of Poppy's first class projects at Pinton Prep had been 'make a picture of your mummy'. The picture had consisted of a large, blue, potato-shaped head with one long horizontal eye and, in place of the mouth, a giant cigarette with a glowing red and amber tissue tip.

'Knocks Bob Marley's efforts into touch,' said Nicholas when she brought it home.

'Mrs Worth.' Mrs Elsworthy was tapping at the window, 'I thought I'd save you the trouble of coming in.' Amanda sprang out of the car and slammed the door making a flapping motion behind her bottom, the signal for Cass not to fiddle with the handbrake or similar.

'Thank you, Mrs Elsworthy,' she said. 'I am sorry, I understand there was a problem with Cass's – outfit.'

Mrs Elsworthy clasped her hands in front of her and smiled a smile that reminded Amanda of the one they make you do in yoga when you're at maximum straining point, and being encouraged to breathe through the pain.

'We felt that it wasn't quite appropriate for a seven-year-old,' Mrs Elsworthy said, glancing past Amanda to where Cass was carefully emptying the contents of the glove compartment onto the passenger seat. You could see she was thinking that a proper mother would have had a wipeable book or tupperware-contained energy snack to keep the child occupied. You could tell she was making an inventory of the contents of the glove compartment: 1 pr tights, bottle Listerine Mouthwash, 1 pkt Nurofen, 1 biro, 2 pr sunglasses, 1 bottle Bacardi Breezer. 'While we are aware that your job makes the world of high fashion very real to Cassandra' – sears its vulgar imprint on her vulnerable little mind, was what she meant – 'we were hoping for educational role models. Women of influence such as Joan of Arc, Elizabeth I, Mother Teresa, Cherie Blair.'

Amanda frowned hard, or as best she could given the effect of the Botox. 'Quite tricky to do Cherie Blair, I'd have thought,' she said dreamily, wondering if she had anything that could pass for Ronit Zilkha in her wardrobe, 'would Madonna have been any better? Cass was very determined to be Madonna at one point.' Mrs Elsworthy stared at her. 'She does live here now, after all. Madonna. In Britain, I mean. And she's a friend of the Prince of Wales, and Paul McCartney, quite a pillar of the—' Mrs Elsworthy was doing the yoga smile again. 'Well, I've got the message, thank you, Mrs Elsworthy.'

Amanda turned towards the car and whisked open the door. 'YO BITCH OUTTA MY FACE, GET OUTTA . . .' The sound of the car radio hit her and Mrs Elsworthy thwonk in the chest. Amanda dived for the volume button.

'Mrs Elsworthy?' Cass was peering out between the mermaid curtains of her hair. 'What's a condom?'

Amanda and Mrs Elsworthy exchanged looks like hot potatoes. 'Ask Mummy, darling,' said Amanda turning her back to Mrs Elsworthy and making frantic cartoon-desperate faces at Cass.

'But you spelt tomato wrong.' Cass was enjoying this.

Amanda turned back to face the teacher. 'Does this one come up much?' she said in her most buddy buddy, women's shared issues tone.

'Not in my experience,' said Mrs Elsworthy flatly.

'Once or twice among the children with teenage brothers and sisters.'

'Ah.'

'But we tend to find that when these questions do arise, the truth, framed in the context of a loving relationship, is the best way to proceed.'

'Thank you again,' said Amanda, stepping into the car and leaning on the window-closing button. 'Wave to Mrs Elsworthy,' she said as they drove off at the recommended 7 mph, 'wave, wave – Boy, are you in trouble.'

'What is it, then?' said Cass

'It's something men put on their heads when they are being silly, or sometimes on the exhaust pipe of cars.'

'Can we have "My Friend Flicka"?'

'No we cannot. We're going to have Heart. You like that. It's "Tie a Yellow Ribbon" and "Sailing".'

'OK.'

Amanda pressed the radio tuner, sat back, and suddenly they were immersed in the cracked, bronchial tones of Felix Cat. 'Yeah, that was what they always said' – he was making a kind of hissing noise – 'but, see, I don't think people realize quite how much influence she had at that point. "I'm Not in Love", 10CC. The "Big boys don't cry" echo throughout the song? Yeah? That was Amber: her voice, her idea. The Rolling Stones' "Angie". Written for her. Originally it was called Amber, right? Only Merlin threatened to break someone's legs, so they had to change the name to Angie. There was a lot of stuff like that. She had that power to like, inspire. She turned a lot of people's heads inside out. And that, to me, is what it's all about.'

'Would you agree, Alexander Whitley?' The presenter was female, edgy-sounding, intense.

'Well, no, I would have to disagree.' This new voice was deep and treacly, the voice of a fat man who liked his pleasures. 'Personally, I think to call Amber Best one of the significant muses of the twentieth century, even in the area of popular music, is grossly overstating it. But she was certainly *charismatic*. And there is no question that she was capable of making strong men throw in the towel and do exactly what she said, as Felix can no doubt testify.' In the background Felix was hissing quietly again. 'But now someone like Geraldine *Sharp*, in the thirties . . .'

'That's Zelda's mummy, isn't it?' Cass's voice made Amanda start and grip the steering wheel.

She leant across and flicked off the radio. 'Yes,' she said.

'Why are they talking about her?'

'Because she was on the television.'

'What's kerisma?'

'It's when people can't resist you.'

Cass stared at her as if she suspected that was a sanit-ized version of the actual meaning.

'Zelda's mummy and daddy don't have one bed. Zelda says they have lots of beds, in all different rooms, and her daddy sometimes sleeps downstairs, in a chair, or in the hammock.' Cass kept her eyes fixed on Amanda, waiting for a suitably amazed response.

Amanda said nothing.

'Daddy says that's because mummies and daddies sometimes need to get away from each other, or else they throw plates.' Her eyes were like saucers. 'Is that why Daddy was staying at Zelda's house? Mummy, why are you sad?'

Amanda realized there were tears streaming down her cheeks.

'I'm thinking about Zelda's mummy, that's all.'

'Cos she's dead?'

'Yes.'

'Daddy says people never die in your head, if you love them enough. They are just the same as alive human beings.'

'Well, Daddy knows best,' said Amanda. 'He certainly does.' And the tyres screeched as she pulled up outside their front door.

Seven

As a rule, Thursday after school was home improvements time. Over the last two years or so Amanda had gradually transformed the faded bohemian ambience of their four-bedroom Shepherd's Bush house to give it more of the fairytale feel that was, according to *LaMode*, the new shabby chic. *LaMode* had named the look Magic Realism; Nicholas called it the gilded-gingerbread look. It was a very labour-intensive decorative style. Not only did everything from fireplaces to loo-roll holders have to be touched by the magic wand but the sugar-almond colour spectrum and the silver leafing and the pale painted floors throughout made upkeep very time consuming. Nicholas was always saying, 'Why can't we just have a nice, clean, minimal house like everyone else?' But what he meant was, 'It'll be a lot easier for you to pull off,' and Amanda was determined to prove him wrong. Which was why you could find her, most Thursdays, daubing silver drops onto bathroom tiles, tacking candy-striped ticking to curtain pelmets and flinging patchwork quilts over bits of furniture. But not today. Today she had set aside for scrutinizing the evidence.

For this she needed photo albums, pencil and notepad and a bright-green paperback book entitled *Is He Having an Affair?* The latter was surplus to requirements, but she found it strangely comforting with its solid, bold type questions: **Has he been working late/travelling more than usual lately? Does he seem evasive or preoccupied? Do you have concrete evidence that he has lied to you?** At the end of each section was a line in italics: *Before you read on ask yourself 'is there any possibility that you have been mistaken?'* If the answer was yes you returned to Chapter One, 'The Nature of Suspicion'. Amanda hadn't turned back yet. She drew a thick pencil line down the middle of the notepad and on the left wrote 'Hedland', and underneath that, 'August, Manchester meetings'. These were her two cast-iron pieces of evidence: Nicholas captured on film, at Hedlands, the morning of Amber's death and those stay-over meetings that Dudley Polk had known nothing about. Now she had to establish a timescale. She drew a line across the page and under it, in the left-hand column wrote 'Wedding?', and next to that, in brackets '(Or Earlier, Tuscany?)'.

Their wedding album was white goatskin embossed with the initials A. & N.W. and the date, 18 April 1993. On the inside cover in big spidery ink letters were written the words, 'Darling Amanda and Nick, to your fabulous life, with love, your Best Amber' and underneath Amanda had glued a photograph of the three of them, her sandwiched in the middle, her veil trailing upwards in the wind like the gauzy tail of a kite, Amber waving the bridal bouquet aloft in mock triumph and Nicholas shouting something at the camera. 'The wife and I wouldn't mind a drink!' was what he'd said, and Sam had brought them each a miniature bottle of Moët with a straw in the neck – her idea – and then the band on her mother-in-law's lawn had struck up 'Mandy', by Barry Manilow, and at the 'Oh Mandy!' part everyone had joined in.

Most women say that their wedding day passed in a warm, fuzzy blur but Amanda could remember every second of hers in saturated technicolor and surround sound: every fragment of conversation carried on the breeze, every clatter of spoons on plates, every hot cheek and unwieldy hat bent backwards in greeting, every velvety glance and champagne-wet smile. Looking back she couldn't say if she had experienced the same heightened awareness throughout the day or if it had kicked in like an adrenalin jag to the heart, at the moment when she rounded the corner of the marquee and saw Nicholas bending towards Amber, her head in its strawberry cloche tipped back like a tulip waiting to be pollinated. Somewhere a car was revving, so that at first she couldn't hear what they were saying, and then there was the slamming of her heart, as if it knew something she didn't. She watched as Nicholas clasped Amber's hands to his chest. 'You just know what's right for us, without me even having to put it into words,' he said. 'I'm the luckiest man in the world.' And he leant forward and kissed her on the forehead.

After that Amanda had drifted, as brides do, isolated in their spotlight, observed at a strategic distance like a despot among nervous courtiers, trained to bob and smile but fearing to presume to come too close. Her special day. Occasionally she would wander into a group whose ranks melted apart, everyone smiling at her, laughing with her, all possibility of normal interraction suspended while they focused on the bride, nodding wildly when she made any observation. It felt as if no one could see her, only the veil and the dress and the borrowed tiara, and that those had tripped some reflex, unleashing a barrage of rehearsed responses: 'beautiful' and 'radiant', 'the garden looking so lovely' and 'what a day for it'. Though she was aware that you couldn't expect to know everyone at your wedding, looking around she felt she knew no one at all.

'Manda.' It wasn't her nickname, it was just the way her mother-in-law, Bridget spoke, everything longer than two syllables was reduced to a more manageable double, as in Man-da, Mar-vlus, Ab-sley. 'Manda, I've been thinking about tea.' She had one hand on top of her hat though there wasn't a breath of wind. 'We thought, lay it all out during the speeches and let everyone help themselves from the orchard end.' Amanda tried not to look blank, she was never sure which of the gnarled and dead-looking trees that surrounded the farm were fruit trees and which were – the others. 'Sooo, just wondering,' Bridget peered intently at Amanda as if preparing herself for the reception of some new information that she was determined to remember for future reference, 'will your friends be expecting milk with their tea? I mean, it is Earl Grey, of course, but' – she grimaced – 'you never know.'

'Perhaps it would be nice to have it as an option,' said Amanda. 'Thank you, Bridget.'

'Oh, not a bit. I'd rather know what to expect. And I had a little word with – Martin, is it? About his speech. We don't want it to go on for too long, do we? I'm 'fraid I told him rather firmly that we're not 'specting any bawdy tales.' She leant in confidentially. 'A lot of friends have come up to me today and remarked on how absley marvlus you are.' She patted Amanda's arm vigorously. 'Be a shame to spoil all the hard work.'

Strictly speaking it had been Amanda's decision to have the wedding at Bridget's. Nicholas had always said that he'd assumed they'd be getting married at her parents' ('Darling, I've been counting on a Basildon thrash'), but then Nicholas had never actually set foot at 28, The Glebe. On the one occasion he had met Viv and Jim, on their own ground, Amanda had organized a private dining room at the Runnymede Hotel in town.

'Wouldn't he like to see the house where you was born?' Viv had said, when Amanda rang to give her the instructions. 'It seems a shame. Your father's been out and bought a lovely new three-piece suite off of Ted.'

'I thought it would be a treat for you, mother,' Amanda snapped.

'Well, it would love, but what'll I do about the photographs? And will your father be able to get a pint there?'

In the event, Viv had bought one of those zip-up wallets containing concertina strips of plastic photo holders, and simply transferred her favourites from around the house. Jim had arrived wearing a loud tweed jacket and slacks, fresh off the peg from the gents' hire shop, and proceeded to order a spritzer.

'Excellent people, your parents,' Nicholas had said afterwards, 'though you might have told me your father had a thing about drinkers, he was giving me the most frightful looks when I went for that third pint.'

When she rang to tell them that Nicholas had proposed, her mother got her father on the extension and they asked her what she'd like for a wedding present. 'Well . . .'

'We know what we'd like to give you and Nicky,' said Viv.

Amanda pictured the birdbath at the garden centre

that they had once picked out as being 'perfect for a special occasion'.

'We may not have a garden in the new house,' she said.

'No dear, and that's why we want to give you your reception here, at home, so you can spill out if you want to. Your father's been making some improvements as it is. We could open the gate into next door's if you'd like – Geoff wouldn't mind a bit, would he Jim?'

'Not at all,' said Jim. 'We'd make it nice for you, love.'

Amanda couldn't speak.

'You could tell us,' said Viv, 'just how you wanted it. Eh? We could get all little night lights like the Boltons did for their Sandra's twenty-first. You loved that. What d'you think, Jim?'

'The thing is, Mummy,' Amanda heard herself saying, 'Nicholas has sort of set his heart on it being a country wedding, and we thought we might do it in Dorset.'

'Oh yes?'

'At his mother's . . . farm.'

'Oh . . . well then. That'll be lovely.'

'Yes . . .'

'D'you hear that Jim? Dorset. Your father's never been to Dorset. Well. You'll let us know then, what we can do. We've been looking – we've got a bit put aside for it, anyway – you just let us know, Mandy love.'

Amanda said goodbye, put down the phone and cried until she couldn't cry any more.

Nicholas had found her, eventually, helping the catering staff to pack up the champagne flutes in their plastic punnets. 'Well,' he said, snuggling up behind her and wrapping his arms around her waist, 'they say marriage changes everything, but ballbreaker to domestic drudge in three hours flat – not bad!'

'I don't know anyone.'

'Anyone where?'

'You don't know me, Nicholas, not really – ' she turned around to face him, her fists bunched against his chest ' – and I don't know you, do I?'

Nicholas snorted with laughter and then, registering her anguish, pulled a stern face. 'My darling . . .' He paused, head on one side, debating whether or not to humour her all together or tease her a bit. 'Squidgy, sweetheart, we read about this together in *Cosmo*, remember? "Wedding Day Blues, Ten Symptoms To Watch Out For?" You've got the screaming commitment nerves hormone thing. You are possessed by the wicked husband-doubting fairy and, I think you'll find, "testing your man's resolve". Well, test away! Because I've sussed it! Only darling, hurry it up, will you? I came to tell you Bridget's determined to get on with the speeches.'

'We don't know anything about each other.' Amanda felt as if she was reading a speech off an indistinct autocue. 'I'm a . . . Basildon hairdresser made good, and you're a . . . a posh bloke with a penchant for fashion parties who happens to have been momentarily sidetracked. And, whatever we might like to think, that stuff is what counts and, in the long run, the gulf is insur . . . unsupr . . .'

'Unbridgeable?'

'Unbridgeable. In the end. You belong with people like – like all these people here.'

Nicholas glanced around with one eyebrow cocked. 'Auntie Nell? Raschenda? Ahh . . .' He raised his glass to someone. 'Martin Anderwurst – of course.'

'You know what I mean,' she said. 'You know what you really want.'

'What?'

'A posh girl.'

Nicholas wrinkled his nose.

'What? Like Lulu?' Lulu was the last of the uncompromised Sloanes. That day she was wearing a substantial diamond brooch in the form of a fox being ridden by a jockey and a confetti-dispensing belt.

'Well . . . or Penny . . . or Amber.'

Nicholas looked like he'd swallowed a fly and then made a tremendous spluttering noise. 'Are you completely off your trolley? I suppose you haven't noticed that Penny has already been behind the hedge, throwing up, and that Amber is your very best friend.' She held her breath. '*Please*', the voice in her head shouted, 'please don't stop there.' 'Not to mention the last person on earth one would want to actually *marry*.'

'Actually marry. Actually marry' – the voice filed the words for easy access during future surges of emotional insecurity: actually marry, suggesting openness to a range of other possibilities, most notably actual affair, possibly lasting a lifetime, actually lust after, actually love, actually long to be with but nothing so mundane, nothing so limiting, as actually *marry*.

'Why not?' Amanda's voice was surprisingly steady. 'Why not actually marry?'

'You know. Too wild, I suppose. Lovely, and all that, but not what you'd call a solid bet.'

'Solid bet', the voice was filing again under low self-esteem: solid bet, suggesting strong work ethic, driven personality, salary and perks which represent significant bonus to husband's lifestyle etc., brackets fat ankles, child-bearing hips. Amanda had a sudden split-screen vision of Nicholas: in the left-hand section he was knotting his tie in the mirror, while she perched on a chair beside him, gigantic diary in hand, going through their commitments for the coming week; in the right-hand section Nicholas and Amber were writhing on a bed, the tie was wrapped around her wrists tethering her to the headboard, the Hilditch & Key shirt lay in tatters on the floor.

'So that's it. I'm solid?'

'Dar-ling. No.' Nicholas tightened his grip around her waist. 'But I didn't just want to marry you because of your fabulous tits and magnificent temper. I wanted to marry you because I knew you would be a lovely wife and mother. Because you pretend to be an utter bitch in a leather skirt, but actually you are sweet and homey. And then there was the small matter of loving you, which I had to take into consideration. But the question of your skill involving the ice cubes, I have to say probably swayed it.' He held up his hands in a guilty-as-charged gesture, sneaking a quick glimpse at his watch on the way.

'So there's no one else you'd rather be married to?'

'Yes.' Amanda froze. '*You*, before you went raving mad and accused me of lusting after all the inbred guests.' He gave her a hug and rubbed his nose against hers. 'Mind you, now that you mention it, I wouldn't mind you putting on a bit of posh, now and again, when we're alone. Perhaps some lovely tight white jodhpurs and a Husky waistcoat – maybe a bridle.'

She looked up at him and he was gazing back at her with a grin so big and guileless it made her feel sure of everything.

The other albums had all been plundered by Channel X. There were gaps on every third page, pale rectangles flagged with Nicholas's neat script: 'New Year's Day '93'; 'Mary Sullivan, Amber, Self, Budcaster opening meet, November '94', but they had left the four pages devoted to 'Villa Arlecco, Arezzo, Italy, May 1992', untouched. It wasn't surprising, on reflection. Channel X were looking for slices of Amber's social scene and there had only been the four of them on that particular holiday. She slid back the transparent paper and gazed at the shiny prints, regular holiday snaps, like anyone else's: smiling faces and bare brown arms round a candlelit table; women stretched out on stripey sun loungers, their costumes strategically hitched and undone; couples posing awkwardly in the shadow of monumental treasures. But now she saw them differently. She noticed Nicholas squeezed shoulder to shoulder with Amber, at a table big enough for ten. In the only group shot, she and Dave stared straight into the lens, tensed up waiting for the automatic timer, but Amber was laughing helplessly, leaning against Nicholas for support while he gazed into her eyes, smiling. Amanda dragged over the wedding album and flicked quickly to the photographs of the speeches, the ones taken from behind her head, as if through her eyes, looking into Nicholas's smiling, adoring face. She ran her hands through her hair and turned back to the Tuscan pages, gripping the edges of the book. Next to the team photo there was a picture of Nicholas and Amber leaning against the side of a fountain, the caption read 'Lucca, day five of the bug'. She remembered the day. They had come back in the early evening and Nicholas had brought her a lemon sorbet and sat with her on the end of the bed. 'Thank God you're on the mend,' he'd said, 'there's only so much sightseeing a man can take before he goes Tonto.' Behind him Amber had stood in the light of the window lifting her hair off her neck, twirling it into an ice-cream flourish, swaying to the sound of music floating up from the village. She remembered saying, 'You both look remarkably fresh after five hours in the hot spots of Lucca,' and Amber had smiled and turned to leave the room letting her brown fingers trail down the sleeve of Nicholas's shirt as she went.

There was another picture, of her and Amber, lingering on the steps of the swimming pool, Amber in an old-fashioned halterneck one-piece, her in a turquoise high-leg bikini. She'd managed to wear a towelling robe for most of the time but then Nicholas had teased her about looking like Michael Winner, and the one journey she had made, unprotected, from sun lounger to shallow end, he had snapped with glee, shouting 'Gorgeous! Gorgeous!' She had felt like those turtles in the Galapagos that make the dash from hatching place to the safety of the sea, knowing that at any moment they could be flipped and skewered by the birds hovering in wait. Side by side she and Amber looked like different breeds, the pit pony and the Arab charger. The caption underneath read 'Squidge and Amber'.

Amanda grabbed the pencil and notepad and scribbled down Zelda's date of birth, 23 January '93, a little over eight months from the date of their holiday. Just as they had always said, the Bacci baby had been conceived at Arlecco. She jabbed at the pad as she calculated the time Dave and Amber had spent together there. Dave had been detained by work and had arrived three days late. She and Dave had both fallen ill later that same night and were in bed for the rest of their stay. That gave them, by her calculations, a window of opportunity of roughly half an hour before dinner the night he arrived. Her hands were clammy. She rubbed them on the carpet, then smoothed down her suede skirt, the sides of her hair. She flicked forward, to the end of the book, and the children's party at Hedlands, scouring the pages, up and down, for the image she was looking for. There it was: Zelda and Cass squashed together on the swing. She used the transparent interleaving to cover up their features, comparing them strip by strip, and then her eyes wandered to the adjoining picture and she saw it at once. All her children were spread out, cross-legged on the grass, Cass, Ludo, Poppy at the back, and in the middle of them was Zelda with Amber's youngest, Melly, on her knee. All of them were squinting into the midday sun, their left eyes drooping, brows clenched, noses wrinkled. All of them except for Melly. She took the notepad, scored out the question mark after Tuscany and underneath wrote, Zelda.

Amanda had skimmed *Is He Having an Affair?* up to the last chapter, What Happens Next? This was particularly reassuring, with it's (a) to (d) multiple choice that managed to almost obscure the basic – leave him or live with it, either way you lose – reality of the situation. She turned to section two and read: 'If you have established beyond reasonable doubt that he is having an affair then you must ask yourself do I a) want revenge, or b) want a marriage. If the answer is b) then your best strategy is what we call **considered confrontation** (CC).' Amanda made a retching face and turned the page. 'You should acknowledge, if you have read this far, that the chances are you do want a marriage more than you want revenge.

The principle behind CC,' continued the author, 'is that by preparing the ground you will reduce the trauma experienced by both parties when it comes to the moment of confrontation, and establish a solid base from which to rebuild the relationship. Step one, plan ahead: make an arrangement with your partner that demonstrates your commitment to a shared future.' Amanda fumbled for a cigarette. 'Step two, inform those who need to know of your decision: for the marriage to thrive it is important that anyone who has knowledge of your problems is made aware that **you have chosen to forgive** (see Chapter Twelve).' 'You have chosen to forgive,' Amanda mouthed, pursing her lips and waggling her head from side to side in the manner of Shirley Temple singing 'Animal Crackers'. 'Furthermore,' said the book, 'you will gain their respect for putting your relationship before personal pride.'

Amanda pictured Davina sidling up to her at a fashion show, placing a bony, diamond-loaded hand lightly on her arm. 'Darling, how brave you are,' her voice just low enough to give the appearance of discretion while allowing anyone that mattered to catch every word. 'Your husband fathers a child with your best friend, continues to . . . see her throughout your marriage, hurries to her bedside for her final moments while all the time not exactly helping with those self-esteem issues of yours. The weight – who knows – maybe even the skin was down to that?' At this point she licks her teeth, a well-known Davina tic signifying her arousal at moments such as signing up a photographer like Ralph, or watching an adversary squirm. 'And you, Amanda, have chosen to . . . what was the phrase again? That's it. Chosen to forgive. Well, I'm sure you'll get your reward in heaven.'

There was the muffled thud of the front door slamming followed by the familiar sounds of keys being deposited in the bowl on the hall table, briefcase skidding over the wooden floor and the grinding of stool legs on tiles as Cass and Poppy ran to show their father some new discovery or work of art. Their father, who for months she had suspected of betrayal and now knew, beyond reasonable doubt, had loved another woman for almost as long as she had known him.

Because, of course, she had to introduce him to Amber the moment they were officially an item. The pleasure of presenting Nicholas – tall, immaculate, Etonian Nicholas – not just to the world but to Amber in particular was, if she was honest, one of the best things about the whole affair. She had quivered with excitement and fear and hope as Amber and Nicholas sniffed around each other, teasing out one another's social DNA. 'Yes, my brother was there . . . Dorset . . . he's my godfather . . . Glenrothes, exactly . . . never miss it . . . we go for August.' They had never met, but they had lived the same life, on different sides of the same hill, with much the same view from the windows, and what it would take Amanda years to discover about her husband, Amber had known automatically. It thrilled her, nonetheless. It thrilled her, that she had a friend like Amber to show off to her new boyfriend and that Amber now had proof, incontrovertible evidence, that Amanda passed in her world. When Nicholas hugged her and told her he loved her it was wonderful, but it was even more wonderful when he showed her affection in front of the people who wouldn't have imagined such a thing possible, and it was the purest pleasure she had ever known if they were Amber's immediate circle, the girls for whom Nicholas and his kind were exclusively reserved. He was her trophy and her security, her rubber stamp that guaranteed she was no longer who she had been. By choosing her, Nicholas had buried Mandy White and given life to Amanda Worth.

She was prepared for him to be dazzled by Amber, of course. She'd have been disappointed if he'd been immune to her charms, it would have somehow diminished her moment of triumph, and made him seem dull. But she had never considered that Amber might be interested in him. He was the opposite of everything Amber wanted – straight, predictable, employed in a suit-wearing nine-to-five job – 'a seat belt' as Amanda called them, never failing to clunk clink for every trip and firmly secured in his place in life. She heard Lady Milly's voice, again, echoing in the library at Hedlands, 'I think, if anything, she'd have gone for something more conventional: the smooth, educated type – you know, pin-striped, competent, smelling of Trumper's Limes. I got the feeling she missed all that a bit.' Amanda simply hadn't seen it. She couldn't have seen it, she was too flushed with new-found confidence, too excited watching the ease with which they bonded, the mutual understanding that demonstrated that she was part of their club, spoke their language.

Maybe it had started that very first day in Amber's flat in Kensington, when Amanda had slipped out to fill the parking meter. Maybe Amber had asked Nicholas for a light, covering his hand with hers, looking up at him through her too-long fringe, those moss-green eyes making the colour flood to his cheeks. Amanda could see her laughing, shaking her hair out of her eyes, arching her neck back and exhaling the smoke up to the ceiling in a long teased-out stream. 'I can tell we're going to be such friends,' she'd have said. 'Will you bring Amanda down to stay this weekend? Oh, please. I don't think I can bear to be separated from you both. You'll like it, we could go riding, we can do anything you want, anything you want.' On the way home in the car, Nicholas had held Amanda's fingers, changing gear awkwardly with his right hand, the steering wheel wedged against his legs in their beige corduroy trousers.

'What did you think of her?' Amanda had asked.

'Frightfully pretty,' he'd said, 'absolutely lovely. But a bit full on for me . . . quite a handful I'd say.' He made his Cripes! face, and squeezed her fingers tighter. 'Give me my easy Squidgy any day.'

Amber had called her later that afternoon. 'Darling!' she'd said, her voice raised to carry over the hairdryer whirring in the background. 'What an adorable man! I *loved* him. I made him promise he wasn't going to waste our time by letting us get to know him really well and then slithering off to join someone else's gang. But he says not to worry. He is definitely the One.'

'You *didn't*!' Amanda remembered how her heart raced though she was smiling, and Amber was laughing.

'Amanda, he's not the type you have to *trick*, silly. He's heaven and he's mad about you, so why waste time? I'm having you both down for the weekend to get to know my new best friend.'

If Nicholas had been having an affair with Amber from the beginning then all Amanda had ever been to him was a kind of practical back-up, the sum of all those dreary things that Amber would never have deigned to be. And if Nicholas hadn't chosen her after all, then the proof that she had been accepted as one of them had just been an illusion. What was more, it meant that Amanda Worth was lower than Mandy White had ever been.

'Darling,' Nicholas was beside her bending over the albums, 'what are you up to? I'm disappointed not to find you silver-leafing one of granny's heirlooms.' He crouched down beside her, resting his elbows on his knees. 'Am I mistaken or is that a chandelier that's appeared in the kitchen? Darling?' He was leaning forward, peering into her face. 'I thought the children must have done the paper-butterfly things hanging all over it, but apparently not! Riva tells me they were ordered from a shop in Sweden,' he was inches from her face now, eyes creased and sparkling, 'and that they cost the equivalent of her monthly salary.'

Amanda stared at him. She was so intent on seeing her husband for the first time, recataloguing his details, peeling away the layers of assumptions connected with every tic and gesture, that she hardly heard what he was saying. Those gentle, honest eyes – not honest at all, but deceiving, manipulative, fake. The big strong hands, father's hands, provider's hands – now seducer's hands with knowing, practised fingers. That guileless smile – she narrowed her eyes in concentration – she could see now was, in fact, lascivious, greedy, the mouth of a sex fiend.

'Amanda? Are you feeling all right? You look most peculiar.' Nicholas had his hands on her shoulders. 'What have you been doing here anyway? Not more Channel X legwork I hope? Haven't they had enough yet?'

'Apparently not,' said Amanda. 'Apparently they've only just started.'

'Sounds ominous. When's my slot anyway? Squidgy,

you must help me with what I'm going to wear. I thought maybe smart casual, cashmere jumper and Todds sort of thing . . .'

I have chosen to forgive, Amanda said to herself, I have chosen to forgive, I have chosen to forgive. Step one: plan ahead.

'Nicholas,' she said, 'I want to have a fortieth birthday party . . . together.'

Nicholas sighed heavily, tossing the olive branch to the floor and grinding it into the carpet with the tip of his polished brogue. There was no provision for this in the book, the partner who shows contempt in the face of your magnanimity. Amanda felt her throat constrict. 'I am demonstrating a commitment to our future, actually,' she said, slamming the albums shut and scrabbling to gather up her research materials. 'To our *shared* future, thank you.'

Nicholas's head was cocked on one side, his eyebrows sloping up to a point in the middle of his forehead, like a dog waiting for a ball to be thrown. 'Because I have chosen my family!' She spun around to face him, her lower lip trembling.

Nicholas glanced to left and right as if checking that he hadn't stumbled into the middle of an amateur dramatics rehearsal. 'I'm sorry, my darling. I had no idea you wanted a party so much. I thought the whole – he cupped his hands round his mouth and lowered his voice to a whisper ' – *fortieth* business, was a bit of a no-go area for you girls. I assumed you wanted to keep quiet about it. After all, it was three years ago, Squidge.'

She stuffed the copy of *Is He Having an Affair?* under

her arm, pushed past him, and was almost at the door when the telephone rang.

Nicholas picked it up. 'Hello? Hellooo Viv! How are you?' Amanda paused and turned to gesticulate that she would take the call in the kitchen, Nicholas gave her the thumbs up. 'Yeeees . . . Well, no, filthy mood actually. Yes. No she's tried the herbal thing . . . and the cream on the stomach . . . Yes . . . Well, I'm not allowed to say that, Viv, you have a go by all means . . . Well, actually we do have some news, as of one minute ago. We're going to have a party for her fortieth . . .' he winked at Amanda ' . . . Well, I am too . . . No, of course it was, yes . . . You did, you sent that lovely soap thing . . . Not a bit of it, absolutely determined to have you all here. I choose to be with my family, were her exact words . . . Yup . . . Well, it may be a first, but I think it's terrific . . . All right . . . I'll just hand you over to the boss now and let her give you all the details.'

When Nicholas looked up Amanda was slumped in the chair by the door with her head in her hands, rocking.

Eight

Transmission clock counts down the seconds.

Bird's eye shot of an animated watercolour representation of Hedlands. Camera swoops over the grounds, across the lake and maze, gliding steadily downwards, skimming the walled garden, moving lower, weaving in and out of stands of sweet peas, racing along rows of lettuces and strawberries, finally coming to rest inside the head of a poppy. The words Garden, Kitchen, Bedroom: The Secrets of Family Life, fill the screen. Cut to Amber Best standing at a kitchen table pounding the contents of a large bucket. She turns to smile at the camera. Bottom of screen reads: With Amber Best. Camera tracks through the kitchen window to focus on Sam Curtis, digging the garden, bottom of screen reads: And Sam Curtis. Theme tune fades. Cut to Sam, one foot resting on a garden fork, he removes his hood and wipes his forehead with the sleeve of his parka: 'This may seem like an unusual time to be digging the garden but not if you're planning on planting a Moroccan spice garden.' He widens his eyes to camera. Cut to Amber coming out of the back door wearing a floral dress, apron and wellington boots. She walks towards the camera. Voiceover: 'Amber Best's highly successful series for Channel X was averaging eight million viewers, midway through the series, and the big American networks were already showing interest in bringing her, and her sidekick, Sam Curtis, over to the States to replicate the formula . . .' Cut to close-up of Amber. 'What exactly are we growing, Sammy?' She rests a wrist on Sam's shoulder as he unrolls a sheet of newspaper on top of a low garden wall and spreads seeds out along it. 'Well this one is a pepper from the Atlas that thrives in colder climates . . . it's name translates as "hot devil".' He rolls the seeds in his fingers. 'Mmmm,' says Amber, leaning into his shoulder. 'I thought you'd like that,' says Sam. He winks at her and she laughs.

Cut to interior of a modern apartment, camera closes in on a man wearing an open-necked shirt. Caption reads: Brian Connor, Channel X Commissioning Editor. 'At the outset we were focusing on the Amber Best . . . mythology, if you like. The It girl goes to the country, rock'n'roll meets *The Good Life*, etc. But then, as the series progressed, we realized that what people were really tuning in for was the relationship between Amber and Sam . . . the gorgeous society girl and the scruffy gardener. So we switched the focus and, without much conscious effort on our part, they evolved into this very original odd couple, who were apparently totally mismatched – he was quite intense about the gardening bit, she was a bit away with the fairies – yet had this terrific rapport. And it worked.' Voice off: 'A modern-day Lady Chatterley and Mellors?' 'Well,' Connor laughs, 'I don't know about that. But, yeah, let's just say there was enough chemistry there to get us in the top ratings.' Fade to black.

The weekend Jack had got herself and Sam invited down to Hedlands so that Sam and Amber could discuss the possibility of working together, had been the same weekend he decided to declare himself. The timing seemed just right. It was six months since Jack had broken up with Christopher with the lisp, four months since Sam's career as a landscape gardener had really taken off and Jack's thirty-eighth birthday was looming on the horizon which, if Jenny, Sam's sister, was anything to go by, was a very receptive time for single females.

In Jenny's case, the catalyst for change came when Susan, her best friend, suddenly started seeing, and then equally suddenly got engaged to, a man they had hitherto both referred to as The Drip. And it was true, you could have wrung this bloke out. But Susan's point – Sam happened to have been there when she came round to break the news to Jenny – was that all this elimination – of the drips and the squares and the gauche and anyone under five foot eight – had got her precisely nowhere. There simply weren't enough available men who matched up to Jenny's and Susan's requirements. Plus, as Susan put it, they were writing them off before they'd even had the interview, so to speak. They had all these criteria that must be met before they would even consider a bloke and a long, detailed list of disqualifiers – Sam, who was seven years younger than his sister, was very anxious to get his hands on that particular list – and, as Susan said, 'At the end of the day, what it all adds up to is single for another year.'

Marrying The Drip was definitely taking the resolution to give more men a chance that bit too far, but they could all see Susan had a point, especially Sam's mother, who had been making it herself for some years now, though only to Sam. 'In my day you didn't have time to fanny around waiting for Mr Exceptional,' she'd say. 'That's the problem with your sister and her friends, they want everything, the all-singing, all-dancing, romance and money and what have you. No man is up to it, Samuel.' And Sam's dad would clear his throat and ruffle his newspaper

With Jack, the wobbly thirty-sevens were just beginning. All the signs were there: those apparently innocent conversation openers, 'What do you think makes a good relationship?' or, 'I wonder where we'll all be in a year's time?' The mooning around Baby Gap months away from Christmas; the talking to ugly but interesting men at parties. All were evidence of a woman wrestling with her priorities, experiencing the first, nagging suspicion that love might not come in the package she's been waiting for. Basically Jack just wasn't sure any more. And that was a start.

Before he embarked on the declaration weekend Sam decided to get some input from Andrew. It wasn't so much that he valued his advice, more that he wanted to tell someone who knew both him and Jack how he really felt, so that they could then say: 'We've all been hoping for this for years. You're made for each other, we've always said so.' And there was no one who knew them better than Andrew. They had lived together at university, they'd been on holiday; shared parties, and, once, a Triumph Herald; and Sam and Jack had been co-best 'persons' at Andrew's wedding. Plus Andrew was married, so he had the edge in terms of experience, even if you did get the impression that he wasn't altogether sure how he'd got there.

They met in the pub at the end of Andrew's road. It was warm, so they sat outside at a trestle table, a ripped-open bag of dry-roasted peanuts spread out between them.

'God, I hate these,' said Sam. 'You know, if you feed these to mice, constantly for two weeks, it kills them stone dead.'

Andrew took a handful. 'What's up?' he said.

'Well, not much. Work's all right . . . good actually.'

'Is it?'

'Yeah. Jack's taking me down to Amber's at the weekend, to sort of find out if we still get on and talk about maybe doing some work together.' Sam inhaled deeply, as if preparing to attempt an underwater length. 'And I thought I might . . . finally make a move on Jack. Whatdyouthink?' Andrew stopped chewing. 'When I say "make a move", I don't mean anything . . . hasty. I just mean I thought I'd get it off my chest . . . lay my cards on the table.'

'You and Jack?'

'Well. No. Me, at the moment, and with any luck, Jack, when I've told her how I feel.'

'I thought you were mates?'

'We are. But I've always— are you saying you can't conceive of there being a me and Jack situation?'

'Well, give me a chance. You've only just hit me with it.'

'*Hit* you with it! What happened to "Perfect! My two best friends!"'

Andrew took a long, slow draught of his pint while Sam watched him intently, one hand supporting his chin, the other flipping a box of matches over and over.

'So you never thought there might be a bit more than

friendship there – with Jack, I mean. You've never seen a glimmer of something else under the surface.'

Andrew put his glass down on the table, very carefully, as if afraid it might crack. 'Dunno . . .' Sam was not so much hanging on his words as pegged out, spreadeagled in front of them, stark naked, hands tied. 'I suppose I'd assumed that if there had been more to it something would have happened by now. You've had one or two opportunities, Sam, over the last twenty years.'

'That's just it! There's never been a good moment. Either she's been with someone, or I've been with someone, or we've been living in the same house, or it's been the perfect time and she's started going on about the joys of having such a close male friend.' Sam raked his matted curls with both hands. 'And then there's always been that Simon Best tosser lurking in the background.'

'So what's happened to him, then?'

'Nothing. But I'm figuring that time is moving on, she's not getting any younger, he's not getting any more available and I'm a much more eligible prospect when you think about it.' Andrew raised his eyebrows. 'Well, compared with a couple of years ago when I didn't even have a place to live.' Sam put his elbows on the table and leant towards Andrew. 'I mean we get on so well, we're best friends, she's – she relies on me.'

'She definitely likes you. It's just a bit of a leap, isn't it?'

'Andrew, please – this is a big thing for me.'

'OK. Sorry.' Andrew grinned. 'It'll be great!' He reached over and slapped Sam hard on the back 'You'll be great. Bit nerve-racking though? Seriously. What if she just laughs?' Sam rolled his eyes. 'No – OK – Sorry. So, what are you going to say to her?'

'What d'you mean?'

'Well, have you thought about how you're going to put it? "Jack, I've loved you since the moment we met? Jack, I can no longer trust myself to behave like a friend towards you?" I mean it's a tricky one, you've got to admit.'

'Look, for all we know she's been feeling the same way for as long as I have.'

'Which is how long, exactly?'

'Oh, you know . . .'

'Dear oh dear,' said Andrew. 'I had no idea it was that serious.'

By closing time they were agreed that Sam should borrow Andrew's two-seater for the job and that Andrew and Lydia would get themselves asked for the weekend too, just in case Sam needed back-up.

'What kind of back-up?' said Sam

'You know. Feeding you lines. "Tell us the story about the time you wrestled the shark", that kind of thing.'

'But she knows all the stories. She's been there for most of them . . . Oh Christ.' Sam slumped on his arms and muttered into the crack between the boards of the table. 'I wish I hadn't started this. I really do. It's going to be like a cross between seducing Madonna and my sister.'

When Sam drew up outside Jack's flat in the red MG, two days later, his leather coat smelling of Tusk aftershave, teeth glinting in the morning sun, he felt like David Hemmings in *Blow Up*, without the confidence. He sat for a while, stroking the walnut steering wheel, ruminating on the great changes that were about to take place in his life. If he closed his eyes he could picture himself standing on the lawn of a garden in midsummer, pointing out features of interest to a group of faceless, erudite figures. Jack was at his side, wearing that denim dress with the tight top, gently massaging the back of his neck as he explained his plans for a sculpture garden, '. . . which will be dedicated to my wife Jack . . . And . . .' The fantasy reel stalled, momentarily, blank film spooling through the projector, the screen crackling white, then recovered with a judder '. . . and . . . to little Samuel Curtis.' Jack placed a hand on her stomach and turned her smiling face towards his, lips slightly parted and—

'Ouch!' Sam held his hand up to his throbbing earlobe. 'What was that?'

Jack was leaning into the car snapping her forefinger and thumb together like a pair of pincers. 'You were in a trance. I've been watching you from the window. Very creepy. Wherever you were, you were obviously showing off big time.' She wedged her overnight bag behind the seats and opened the passenger door of the MG. 'What's this anyway?'

Sam was suddenly preoccupied with stowing the bag securely. 'It's Andrew's,' he said.

'I know *that*.'

'The van's off the road.'

'Since yesterday?'

'Yes, it's got a burst, something or other. What?'

Jack was staring at him. 'Ahhh. I get it. You want to impress Amber.'

'Not at all.'

She winked at him. 'It's perfectly natural, you haven't seen her for ages.'

Shit! David Hemmings to Sad Pseud in 0.5 seconds.

'Look, forget about the car. How have you been? You look *great*.' Jack was tugging on a corduroy peaked cap, she was wearing a green suede coat and a stripey scarf and the freckles were coming out on her nose. The thing about Jack was that she wasn't so dazzlingly pretty but, with the freckles and the gap between her front teeth and the mop of cropped blonde hair and the *Dr Who* wardrobe she looked bright and youthful and alive, like those girls at Beatles concerts.

'Fine, thanks.' Jack looked faintly suspicious.

He could just lean over and kiss her, at some point, but when had that ever worked, with both parties stone cold sober?

'D'you want a drink?'

'It's 10.30.'

'No, but I mean, I could stop and get you a couple of those pre-mixed things, for later on.'

She stared at him. 'No thanks, and you're not having one, if that's what you mean.'

Aaargh, Sad Pseud to Old Soak.

'Listen, I'm a responsible bloke you know, not some louche It Boy.'

He didn't dare look at her. She frowned for a moment and then started raking through Andrew's tapes looking for an alternative to Blockbuster Hits 1980–3 – brackets the university years – which Sam had selected after much deliberation, and then fast forwarded to halfway through the track that was playing when they first met, so it didn't look as if he'd set it up. He drummed on the steering wheel and adjusted the wing mirror. Christ. He had to get this over with quickly now that he'd made the decision, before he turned into person I think you want me to be, the single most common trap for the very keen suitor, not to mention person wearing compatible love interest CV ('Hi! I haven't booked my summer holiday yet, and I really like windsurfing, and I think you do too!'). He'd known her for twenty-one years. He'd seen her naked, at least once, and yet here he was wearing a pint of Tusk and a new set of underwear, with a mouth scorched from the full ten-minute Listerine gargle, behaving like the kind of man you might get fixed up with by a well-meaning brother-in-law. In short he was displaying all the symptoms of Date Man.

Every male knew the perils of Date Man. Date Man happened when you cared too much, or you didn't care much at all but the girl in question was somewhat intimidating, or you were just pretty young. He did things like lighting the filter end of his cigarette, he walked slightly differently from you, his conversation segued from humorous stories about his time in New York to caring, sharing stories about helping out at the donkey sanctuary during his school holidays. Date Man forgot how to park, or rather knew how to park but tried to park looking like Steve McQueen and ended up grinding the exhaust into the pavement. He initiated conversations about fashion designers. He gave girls long, lingering looks that suggested depth and hurt and a possible sideline in the secret services. He interracted with music, wherever, whenever, doing the tortoise-head extension, or the shoulder shimmy, and had a tendency to chew phantom gum. If you ran into him yourself you would undoubtedly think he was ripe for a kicking. And the really horrible thing about Date Man was that even as he was taking over you knew it was a disaster and you could do nothing to stop it, nothing. It was like being wide awake on the operating table.

'There's a funny smell in here,' said Jack. 'I know what it is, it's that Fahrenheit muck. You haven't splashed that on since you had the date with Charlotte the Harlot.' She raised one eyebrow. Uh oh . . . lush to Predatory Married Friend Fancier.

'I just had a bit left so I thought I'd get rid of it,' he said.

'Liar. You finished the bottle that night. I was there, remember? You've gone out and bought a whole new one.' She shook her head and smiled.

Was that unbridled affection, or pity? Could it have been jealousy, disguised as amused disbelief? No. Actually it was straightforward incredulity based on Jack's absolute conviction that he didn't have a hope in hell with her friend, with or without a husband, because he didn't have what it took. Not enough height, not enough ironic clothes, nothing like enough of that panther-packing-an-Uzi body language that meant certain men lighting a cigarette could do for a woman what Pamela Anderson soaping-up in the shower did for men. In fact, a chronic deficit of suavery and savoir-faire, generally.

It was funny that friendship was the worst possible basis for romantic involvement. That crucial honeymoon period of self-revelation, when you offer up pieces of the jigsaw and they are received with a mixture of awe and gratitude, that key component of the falling in love feeling was eradicated by long-standing friendship. Without it you were like the eunuch in the harem: valued, trusted, maybe even loved, but unable to generate the necessary spark of interest. Plus both of you knew too much. There was no room for the usual editing, airbrushing and rewrites. For example, Jack knew all about the Charlotte date, the panic Sam was in before the Charlotte date, the decision about how many shirt buttons he should leave undone (Hugh Grant or Colin Firth?), the precise manner in which Charlotte had turned him down, her comment to her friend about Sam being too grubby for her, the fact that he had then got the friend into bed, on a sympathy trip, and, in the event, been unable to get it up. All that stuff meant that he did not enjoy the same level of respect from Jack that he could reasonably expect from a woman he was meeting for the first time. Similarly Jack couldn't see him as Sam the glamorous landscape gardener with the 'scarecrow charm', as she presumably would have done if she'd only heard of him in the past few months. Instead, she thought of him as a kind of lovable twit who had managed to wing it this far, and that was purely down to unlimited access. The moral of the story was that female friends were terrific, just so long as there was absolutely no possibility of anything developing in the future.

'Did you see the *Sunday Times* mag at the weekend?' Sam rested his elbow on the door of the car. 'The profile – of me.'

'Yes! God. Yes!' Jack clapped her hands together delightedly. Sam felt himself inflating very slowly like a life-raft, he shifted in his seat and threw her a wry, experienced sort of smile. 'Wasn't it fantastic?' Jack was bobbing up and down. 'That picture of you, lying in the flowerbed. You know what it reminded me of?'

Jim Morrison? thought Sam. That's what the photographer had said, 'Take your shirt off, it'll be very Jim Morrison. You've got that look . . . ruffle the hair a bit . . . that's it . . . eyes over here.'

'That magician! You know, who was always taking his top off, the one with the leopard-skin trousers. Not that you looked remotely fat – just slightly – ' she was giggling now ' – uncomfortable! But the best bit was all that stuff about you being Byronic and equating different styles of gardening with styles of poetry!'

Ah good, the Pretentious Git.

Jack was beside herself now, remembering passages of the interview and then collapsing with laughter. Sam drifted back to the fantasy projector. He and Jack were perched side by side on a white modular sofa in a vast, minimal room, Jack was doing the talking. 'Our relation-ship works rather differently from the average. I can't take Sam seriously sexually, or in the context of his career, in fact, not in any sense at all. But I do find his media image wildly entertaining, and that works for us.' At this point Sam rises from the white sofa, produces a black cane from behind his back, holds it at arm's length in front of him and starts to tap dance vigorously while singing, 'Make 'em laugh, Make 'em laugh . . .'

'But, hey . . . You know who saw it and thought you looked absolutely gorgeous?' Jack gave his knee a squeeze. 'The lovely Alice *Clarke*! You're in there, definitely.'

Sam glanced at Jack, who nodded and wrinkled her nose in encouragement. Didn't the fact that a woman like Alice was interested in him give her pause for thought at all? Alice Clarke was, by any standards, above averagely pretty. She had notably good tits and a very generous attitude to showing them off. Plus she was photographed at society parties, had a big, centrally located flat and a trust fund.

'You know I'd never go for *her*,' said Sam, sounding hurt. 'What makes you think I'd go for her?'

'Oh, come on. All this celebrity stuff. It's all about impressing those girls isn't it?' Jack grinned at him, conspiratorially.

No, it's all about impressing you, you stupid cow. It always has been. At every party, every time I hit the dance floor, I willed you to be looking and thinking 'Wait a minute . . . I see it now. He is dynamite!' I wanted you to see every girlfriend at breakfast and think, 'She's not having him, why should she have him? I want him.' Every shared holiday was a chance to show you how great I was outside the environment you took me for granted in: all that diving off eighty foot rocks in Greece, all that wrestling with station officials, all of that you were supposed to notice and file away in your memordex of things that separate the men from the boys, the flings from the stayers. Whenever I got a job or a promotion, I always wanted to tell you first because it felt like it was for both of us, even when we were nineteen, a step along the road to what we'd have together at some distant moment in the future when you'd got all your Simons out of your system. Christ. Hadn't she picked up on any of it?

Of course, there had been whole chunks of time, months at a stretch, when he'd barely thought about Jack. Once or twice he'd been in love and so distracted that seeing Jack had seemed like an inconvenient interruption. 'Tell her I'll ring her back,' he'd shout from the bedroom and then sometimes he just wouldn't. On a couple of occasions he'd really felt as if they'd moved on and Jack had just become that girl that every man has crouching somewhere in the locked cupboards of his past, the one that might have been, but then almost certainly wasn't for a good reason. And sometimes, at the beginning of a new relationship, Jack would annoy him more than he could say – firstly for not having her breath taken away by this fresh, sexy, enviable thing happening under her nose, and then for not playing the game. There was an unspoken rule, wasn't there, that you treated your friends in new relationships like gods? If you saw the difficult, potentially exposing question coming out of the dark, you flung yourself in front of it, took it right in the chest to save them. There was a guaranteed period of grace when you laughed at all their old jokes, set them up for all their best stories, crowed about their achievements on their behalf, generally entered into the spirit of, 'Wow!' To think you have been chosen by this unbelievably special person.' But Jack was exactly the same as she ever was. Worse, if she liked the new girl she would befriend her, so that after a couple of hours they were nudging each other and giggling like they were both members of the Humour Sam Society rather than the Lucky To Be Even Seen With Sam Elite and that, in fact, this was just a cover for them to get together because they had sooooo much in common. Dinners that he had pictured as dreamy retrospectives of his life thus far, with the three of them laughing into their brandy balloons as they shared observations about his qualities into the small hours, became animated two-way conversations about hair colourists and celebrities' eating disorders with him left scribbling on the tablecloth, unmissed. There were also times when Jack had looked really, truly, unfanciable: that phase she went through of wearing clown dungarees covered in badges and ten kinds of Bozo scarves in her hair to name one.

But the feeling would always return at some point, that subtly-more-than-friendship feeling that fluctuated between a warm fraternal fuzziness and intense sexual jealousy. He'd never really got used to seeing her with men. Once he had accosted her between the bookstacks in the university library and accused her of making reckless choices. 'Jack, I need to talk to you about Mark Blower,' he'd said, hands stuffed in the pockets of his brown cord jacket.

'What is it?' she'd said, eyes wide, her beret making her seem vulnerable and noble, an SOE on the alert for downed airmen.

'Well he's ... We all think he's bad news.' Sam removed his hands from his pockets at this point and tried to slouch a bit, to counteract the headmasterly tone. 'He's just not right for you, Jack.'

'Why not?' she'd said, sounding genuinely interested. Why not? Because he looked like the fucking sixth Rolling Stone, that was why.

'Because, for a start, he drinks a hell of a lot.' Sam had a sudden flashback of Jack trying to drag him over the doorstep of their house where he had collapsed semi-conscious after the Reptiles' annual vodka challenge. 'And he has no respect for women.' There he was again, in the Cat and Whistle, with a pair of fake breasts strapped over his ACDC T-shirt.

'Anything else?' said Jack.

'Well, he's just a bit of an arsehole and ... the fact is – ' he'd closed his eyes at this point to suggest that this was harder for him than for her ' – the fact is that when you're involved it's very difficult to see people for what they really are.' Jack looked interested now. 'I would have been grateful for advice like this myself on a couple of occasions, Jack. You – one – is always the last to see it.'

'This wouldn't have anything to do with Mark being taken on by the Glass Band would it?' The Glass Band had been offered a recording contract that week and, yes, it most certainly would.

'Whaaaat? Oh, come on. Give me a break.' Sam shook his head from side to side extra slowly, trying to shrug off her gaze. 'Look, if I'd thought you were going to take it like this I wouldn't have bothered. I just don't want to see you hurt – OK?'

'Thanks, Sam,' she'd said. 'I'll be careful. And by the way, since you've been so honest with me, I think you should know that Josephine's nickname is Never Says No Jo and you're the last person on your football team to have asked. See you . . .'

His mother hadn't helped. Right from the start she'd taken the line that Jack was far, far too good for him and from the moment they met she, his own mother, had signed up to the Humouring Sam Society, saying things like, 'Oh, ignore him, Jacqueline, he's always pretending he's a great rebel, but he had to come home from that outdoor concert early because his ears were hurting.' Once she was peeling potatoes at the sink listening to Jimmy Young and she'd suddenly said, 'Wouldn't it have been lovely if Jacqueline had been interested in you,' which was disturbing on several levels. One, that she should assume that slim possibility had long since expired, two, that she should be so confident Jacqueline had no feelings for her son whatsoever, and three, that she, the state-of-the-art bullshit detector, had spotted Jack's potential.

'Thanks, Mum,' he had said.

'Oh, never mind, Samuel,' she'd said. 'We all have our own level. Probably for the best in the end. She's not what you'd call domesticated.'

Shifting Jack's perspective was the key. Getting her drunk would be good, in theory, but then he'd have to wait until tonight and fix it so they were alone together, and besides they had been there so many times, and it had never worked out yet. The difficulty was timing it so that she'd got past the everything-is-so-funny stage and was hovering on the cusp of the warm, fuzzy stage, but catching it before the warmth tipped over into tears and recrimination, nausea, hostility or all of the above. Anyway, he couldn't face going through all that and then her not remembering a thing in the morning. No, the car was definitely the best place to do it. Driving along side by side, no need for embarrassing eye contact, him at the wheel, confident, powerful, in control of both their destinies, surging down the motorway into open country in the first green days of spring, buds on the trees, warm wind ruffling the cleavage of her top. It was a metaphor for their new beginning.

'*Watcccch* – Sam! We were nearly in the ditch then.'

Fuck, fuck, fuck. 'Noooo . . . relax, don't be so jumpy.'

'And watch those sheep up ahead. Don't roar up on them.'

'Jack, if you don't mind, I do not need to be reminded of the country code, thanks.' As they drew alongside he waved to the bloke in the wellingtons chivvying the flock along with the aid of a worn-out-looking dog and a small girl wearing plastic Barbie-doll mules.

'In a hurry are we?' said the farmer, or was he a shepherd, and then, twitching his head to indicate that this was intended for the lady in the passenger seat, 'You wanna teach 'im some manners.'

The next leg of the journey passed in silence.

'Hey,' he said twenty or so miles later, when the urge to gnaw the steering wheel had almost passed.

'What?'

'I was thinking, if this comes off, I might get somewhere. A little place.'

'You?'

'Why not? I'll be earning enough and I'd like to, you know – '

'Turn the music up to volume ten, throw your old food out of the window, keep a cow in the bedroom to save you the trouble of going to the shop for milk, grow an acre of weed in the garden—'

'Jacqueline. It's a very long time since we lived together.'

'Mmmm?'

'And this would be different.'

'Yep. The difference is I won't be hosing it down with Dettol at the end of term.'

Shit. The maggots incident dredged up out of the blue. 'You might actually like it, Jack. You could write there. At weekends. Don't you ever envy our married friends?' Jack looked perplexed. 'You know, with their weekend cottages and all that?' She wrinkled her nose.

'All right – Dave and Amber then.'

'Well, they have a lovely life.'

'Exactly! What man wouldn't want to be Dave, in a beautiful house with a beautiful wife.' Whoops! Married Friend Predator again. 'Looking out over your own fields, lambs gambolling, fruit ripening, children playing – I could get used to that.'

She glanced at him. What was she thinking? Gold-digger? Fotherington Thomas?

'It's not the lifestyle so much, it's the – ' Sam cleared his throat ' – the commitment to something. I just think we're all getting on and this is when you start to look at other people's choices and – you know – wonder about getting stuck into some of life's big challenges yourself.'

Life's big challenges! Life's big challenges! Now he sounded like Baby on Board Man; Holding Hands with Wife at Cocktail Party Man, Matching Sweaters Couple Man, the kind of creep that made Date Man look like a terrific guy. He grimaced at himself in the mirror.

'That's OK.' Jack was smiling. 'You've just got a dose of the shivering thirty-somethings. Welcome to the club.'

'Do you feel like you're ready then?'

'Yes, but there's . . . it's a tricky one.'

She looked at him almost bashfully. He thought of Andrew, in the pub. 'What if she laughs?' But the mood had shifted, there was going to be no laughter. They were slipping easily into that quiet, direct, confessional mode that only happens once in a while and relies on both parties being equally ready, supporting each other's groping attempts to go further than they've been before, foothold for foothold, resisting the temptation to lunge for the safety cord.

He took a deep breath. 'But isn't that what it's all about? Taking a risk, trusting your instincts and saying this isn't easy, it's not perfect, but still – it feels right.' Jack was frowning and nodding. 'And that's when it all falls into place.' Jeepers, he'd impressed himself, and Jack – Jack was knocked out, she was really thinking now, you could tell. He rummaged in his pocket for a Trebor mint, just in case.

'I don't know.' She pulled at a stray chunk of straw-blonde hair, trying to get it to touch her nose. 'It's just, you wait so long, and then when it comes to it – it just seems so daunting.'

You bet, daunting. He couldn't even picture it. If he did a quick controlled test, and imagined himself undressing the most intimidating prospect imaginable – say Amber – and then undressing Jack, there was no contest. Average to chronic anxiety levels for the first scenario, right off the scale for the second. His hands were sweating on the wheel. Would she talk throughout? Would she do that staring thing? He remembered a friend of his, a doctor, describing the first time he had to examine a female patient, apply his bare hands to her bare flesh, the terrible head-pounding, stomach-churning build-up to planting them on her chest, firmly, confidently, without hesitation or lingering. 'You just have to slap them down on there,' he'd said, 'it's like putting your hand in the fire, but once you've made that contact the panic subsides pretty quickly.'

'I mean we don't have to rush it.' Sam glanced surreptitiously at Jack's chest area. 'It's just making the decision to take it to another level.' Ooooh dear, that was a bit perched on a high stool, brandishing a mike, satin shirt slashed to the waist.

'You're right,' she said, 'we just need to make the leap.'

She turned to him and grinned. It was all going to be OK. He squeezed her hand, more tenderly than would have been appropriate between friends and considered spitting the mint out over the side of the door, but they were coming up to a roundabout, and she'd turned away. She had a dreamy look that he didn't recognize. This was it. They'd crossed a boundary and from now on he would see things in Jack that she had never revealed to him before: bleary morning moods, fiery jungle-woman tantrums, little-girl phobias. She'd have cute habits like sleeping with her hands tucked under the pillow or wearing his Steppenwolf T-shirt in bed. He'd always wanted that, one of those American jock's girlfriend types who hangs out in your boxer shorts and sports socks, making all your stuff look like it belongs to a great testosterone pumping brute. Jack let out a small sigh and nestled down in her seat, chewing absentmindedly on her thumbnail. He felt protective, responsible for her, hungry for the responsibility. They were as close as it was possible for friends to be but now he had travelled beyond her, and he felt stronger, wiser, manly, distanced from her by his vision of their future. He rolled up the sleeves on his shirt to reveal his brown forearms tensed on the wheel. He was an Amish husband about to build the homestead barn, he was an expectant father racing her to the hospital delivery room, he was omnipotent and generous . . .'

'So,' he said, sucking in his stomach, 'have you made any plans for your birthday at all?'

'Sort of.' There was the trippy smile. Maybe she'd never smile at him any other way again.

'What d'you want to do then?' Sam ejected the tape and went for a second attempt with the eighties compilation. It was all about timing, and now was definitely the right time for The Specials.

'Actually, Amber's brother is in town and he's going to organize something.'

'Hmmm?' Shit, shit, where did he come from? 'What do you mean?' What did she mean? What did she mean bringing him up now, when everything was . . .

'I dunno, he's going to do dinner, I think.' Was she blushing? She was actually blushing

'Dinner you think?'

'I don't knnnnnoooooow . . .'

Jack had shifted into that excrutiating behavioural mode that women select for announcing news of the new boyfriend: we-are-engaged variety, sort of feckless and girly, drunk on their own femininity – 'I suppose a party basically. He's just come back from Russia and he's got all this vodka and caviar to offload.' Oh, now she was talking Slime-on – 'offload, like lose.'

'When did you decide all this, exactly?'

'Last night.'

'Last night?' What was he going to say? It wasn't illegal. 'It's a bit sudden isn't it? What's the rush? *We* could give you a party. We've got all your friends' numbers.'

'It's fine, Sam, really. It's just going to be small.'

'Well, am I asked?' Jesus.

'Of course.'

Sam jabbed at the tape ejector button and went straight into some elaborate high-revving overtaking.

'What's the matter, Sam?'

The matter is we were talking about us, about our future together, and now we're talking about you and Slime-on and, worse, you've turned into a Cadbury's

140

Caramel bunny at the mention of his name, shamelessly, in the passenger seat of the car I borrowed to seduce you in. You disgust me.

'I just think it's a bit sad the way you drop everything when he turns up.' Sam scratched his head vigorously.

'I haven't got anything to drop.'

'You know what I mean.' He rings, you jump, he goes back to one of the Champion Pedigree girlfriends. Something stopped him from saying it out loud, something warned him that if she had to choose, right now, her loyalties would not necessarily lie with him.

'I know what you mean about knowing when it feels right.' She couldn't . . . Hang on! Wait a minute! 'Like you said, he isn't the ideal choice, it's not perfect by any means. But if one of you is so sure that you can't imagine there ever being anyone else then you've got to give it try. Right?'

Sam stared at her. How could this be happening? How could she twist his words?

'I know,' she said. 'I know you don't like him, and I love you for caring enough about what happens to me to put that to one side. I love you for seeing it all so clearly.' And she had slipped her hand round his neck, pulled off her corduroy cap and kissed him hard on the cheek.

Nine

Transmission clock counts down the seconds.

Sound of Super Eight running in the background. Camera pans across a group of young men and women in various states of undress, stretched out on a grassy bank beside a river. They shade their eyes from the glare of the sun, squinting and waving. Camera pans right to zoom in on a girl with her back to the lens, paddling in the shallows. Her long black hair reaches to a few inches above her bikini bottoms. She turns suddenly, as if she's been called, skips out of the water and runs towards the camera laughing, hand outstretched. The picture lurches, there's a sideways glimpse of river and tree and sky before it comes to rest on something grey and fuzzy then pulls back to reveal teeth, a grin, the freckled face of Andrew Norton. He waggles a finger at the camera as it focuses shakily on his bare chest before veering off again, skidding over faces and limbs, then stealing up on a redhead lying on her front, head tilted to one side. Camera zooms in on the sunbather's profile. Her closed eyelids flicker. Cut to the same face in the present, hair scraped back, eyes wide, looking straight at the camera. Caption reads: Lydia Norton. 'I was at university with Jacqueline Farmer in the early eighties, and that's when I first met Amber. She used

to come down during the summer, when exams were over
and the parties had started. I wasn't part of that group,
but our paths crossed on a few occasions. She was definitely the star attraction, but you had to see it for what it
was, which was essentially a lot of hype.' She lowers her
chin and looks up at the camera. 'Amber was really the
queen of spinners. People thought she was this gifted
beauty – ' she shrugs, ' – what they forget is that there
were a lot of talented contemporaries of Amber's who
didn't have the advantages that she had, who couldn't just
fix it with a phone call to some friend of their father's.' She
shifts in her seat and crosses her legs. 'It's a habit in this
country to make out that girls like Amber have this kind
of rare blood that makes them automatically extraordinary, and everything they do fabulous. They look
bored and they're described as enigmatic; they dress like
bag ladies and they're held up as paragons of eccentric
British style; they sleep around and that's party-girl spirit
whereas for everyone else it's plain old promiscuous.
There was this total acceptance that Amber was born to
be celebrated and who cares if she had anything going for
her, or who she used to get there.' Cut.

'Excellent, really nice, Lydia.' Mike, the director, strolled
over to where Lydia was sitting and hunkered down beside
her chair. 'You were really . . . electric in that last part.'

Lydia uncrossed her legs and reached for a cigarette.
Four days of filming and she was already warming to the
Bette Davis role. She knew she was good and she knew she
had power. 'It's your call,' Mike had said, 'but then you're
not the kind of woman who's going to shrink from the

truth.' He'd told her, at the start, that she was the natural of the group. 'You've done this before? No? Really? You amaze me.' When she admitted that she had tried a bit of modelling in the past, he'd asked to see her book, poring over it, making a frame with his fingers and holding it up to her face every now and then. OK, he had a vested interest in keeping her sweet, but she did feel good in front of the camera and she liked having her hair teased and the neckline of her dress adjusted while Mike nodded admiringly in the shadows. This was how Amber must have felt most days of her life; important, stroked, beautiful.

'I don't know if it wasn't a bit overdone,' she said with a little pout, tapping the cigarette absent-mindedly. 'I don't want you getting me into trouble.'

'Hey, Lydia. Remember you are not telling us anything that we don't already know, or strongly suspect. The public is ahead of us, they know when they're being fed a line.' Mike stretched up and pushed a strand of hair off her face. 'What I want you to do now is condense that; get away from the generalizations, start putting some facts in there.'

Lydia turned her head to one side and stared out of the window, parting her lips and very slightly tilting her chin. Mike had insisted on filming her from the right the whole of yesterday, which apparently was unusual for this kind of programme, generally it looked too staged. But Mike had said, 'I won't let some other guy have the pleasure of being the first to capture that profile.'

'Where do you want me to start?' she said.

At the beginning of filming, Mike had suggested that it might help to structure her thoughts on paper. 'We're getting a lot here,' he'd said, pouring her a third glass of Andrew's Chablis. 'But when all is said and done I want you,' he pointed both forefingers at her like a couple of Colt 45s, 'to feel that you've got what you wanted out of this. So, what I'm proposing is that you get down a few points, just as a guideline, so you know exactly where you're going. For example, men. Where did she draw the line, if anywhere? How much did her friends turn a blind eye? Reinvention? . . .' He hunched his shoulders and spread his hands wide. 'Could be a point? The whole earth-mother bit. What was really going on behind the scenes? Yeah?' He paused, eyebrows raised. 'Just some pointers, so we can really sharpen the focus. Are you with me?'

She started at the beginning, at Mike's suggestion, from her first encounter with Amber. ('What did you see, what did you think? Take us back there.') It was at a student birthday party, given by two boys in some dilapidated cottage, and the fact that Lydia turned up was the best present they could have hoped for. That's just how it was. She was seen to be different, wholesome and exotic at the same time. She swam naked in the sea most mornings, and danced weirdly, like some Left Bank poet's troubled girlfriend, letting her head loll and her arms swing free. Other girls' rooms were knee deep in cigarette ends, old coffee cups and dirty black clothes, hers was filled with flowers and fifties' cotton dresses. The dancing was an affectation, but the rest wasn't. She was different, maybe because she knew that all she wanted was romance and attention and the good things in life and wasn't interested in being a boy like the others. Women liked her well enough. Men picked her up and spun her around and fell in love with her as a matter of course.

This night was no exception. Lydia first saw Amber upside down, as she was being fireman-lifted out of the cottage in the direction of a motorbike, flailing and giggling and congratulating herself on having bagged the most desirable of the first-year intake, right from under the nose of his pink-cheeked escorts. Amber was standing in the gateway, even from this angle and after several snakebites, a skewed vision of something very out of the ordinary. 'What a pretty thing,' Amber had said as they brushed past, and the first year had agreed, patting Lydia on the bottom as they swung off across the street. Lydia craned her neck to catch another glimpse of the stranger, in the light from the open door of the cottage. What did she see? Long black shiny hair, a silver coat, an extra long, extra white cigarette. Money. There was an E-type Jaguar parked in the street that had to belong to Amber, or to her boyfriend, a tall, beaky man in a fur-collared coat. But it was more the way they held themselves, as if their joints had been soaked in molasses, or the air they breathed was subtly heavier. Lydia saw unassailable confidence shivering off them both like heat off a fire, and such worldliness in the lazy eyes of the man, for whom this was an amusing palate-refresher in between rich and rare experiences.

What did she think? At first she felt threatened and then, in the next instant, she saw Amber as an ambassador from a parallel universe carrying a banner that read, 'If you think this is it, then this will be it.' There was this life, her life, in which she was destined to glow if not to shine, to work at something amusing for a while and then to marry comfortably, have a family, a lovely house, maybe horses, the de luxe version of her own upbringing in fact. And then there was this other, alternative life, where all those aspirations were an evolutionary stage in the past, where material luxury was a given and life's journey started with the resources and the attitude and the imagination to be anything you wanted. In that moment, as they came to the bend in the road and the silver coat was swallowed up in the dark, she thought, 'I want that. I can be that.' And she asked the boy to put her down and take her home.

The second time she met Amber was six months later, at a picnic. She hadn't seen much of Jack and Sam that year. Andrew had been pursuing her and she found it easier to avoid them all. He was unlike any man who'd shown interest in her before. The others charmed her and then wound her in on silk ribbons, or claimed her like a dog claims a bone, with two heavy paws and warning snarls over their shoulder. But Andrew watched from a distance and only approached when he had a reason to. 'I found you a second-hand bicycle,' he would say, or, 'If you want, I'll take you to that.' There was something flattering about his devotion. As Jack said, 'He's so sure, I can't believe you won't give him a chance.' But Andrew was so far from being the kind of man Lydia was interested in, especially now. She couldn't say it to Jack but, in the natural order of things, she and Andrew were literally leagues apart.

The leagues, the way Lydia saw it, were clearly demarcated – Gold, Silver and Also Ran – and even at the age of nineteen no one was in any doubt as to which they belonged to. Later on, of course, the categories would get shuffled about. Men who were Gold League in their twenties would drop two places, overnight, after some business scandal while Gold League women, specifically thirty-something unmarried ones, slipped slowly down the scale until they found themselves looking quite favourably on life's Also Rans – men they wouldn't have taken a lift from five years previously. But, at nineteen, Lydia was categorically Gold League and Andrew just wasn't in the picture.

He was at the picnic, of course, as were Sam and Jack and two men who came with Amber, one of them an artist, the other the heir to a publishing fortune, called Gus. They lay on the banks of the river, soaking up the end of term sun, drinking Pimms and smoking joints, and that afternoon Lydia left with Gus and never came back to finish her degree. At the time it hadn't seemed like any choice at all, she was taking the best opportunity she could hope for and anyone could see it was the right thing to do, except for Amber. As Lydia was pulling on her jeans over her bikini bottoms, getting ready to head off to London in Gus's sleek little white sports car, Amber had drawn her to one side. 'I hardly know you,' she'd said, 'but listen. Gus is a fast liver. I just thought you should know. It doesn't suit everyone.' Lydia thought of how Amber had been skinny-dipping in the river, cavorting with Andrew, transparently for the benefit of Gus, the one eligible man there. 'I'm sorry I've ruined your plans, Amber,' she'd said, 'but really it was a mistake to assume that a little college girl like me would be no competition.' The funny thing was Amber had seemed shocked, and Lydia had felt an inexplicable twinge of panic, the same feeling she'd had as an adolescent defying her parents, shouting louder and louder, knowing all the time that they were only trying to help. She could still see Andrew's face as they'd driven off. 'Dear, oh dear,' Gus had said, pulling her towards him with a skinny, cashmere-covered arm, his reflective aviator sunglasses glinting blank above a hard wall of teeth. 'Anyone would think I was stealing off with the school virgin.'

'OK,' said Mike, 'let's see what you've got, starting from the top.'

Lydia drew back her shoulders and glanced at her notes. 'Just as if the camera was running?'

'As if the camera was running.'

'So . . .' Lydia cleared her throat, 'the first time I met Amber she was surrounded, as ever, by a group of her cronies—'

'Where? Give us a picture.'

'It was at a party, a student party at university in 1981, she used to come down every so often. I think it was a break for her, refreshingly simple fare compared to what she was used to – ' she glanced at Mike, he made an O with his forefinger and thumb ' – and I thought then, this is a very controlling woman. Well, of course my initial reaction was that she was beautiful, but at the same time I sensed that there was something manipulative about her. From the way people reacted to her I could tell that she was used to having her own way. Later on that became a problem, the fact that I wasn't prepared to stay in my proscribed place. In particular, she was very territorial about men and you were not expected to compete with her on that level. But, unfortunately, Amber wasn't always the one they wanted.' Lydia smiled and folded her hands in her lap. 'She just couldn't accept that other people, other women, that is, could have what she had, be all the things that she was.'

Gus didn't want her to get a job, he wanted her to manage the house in Cheyne Walk – by which he meant watch the cleaner and order the takeaways – and there didn't seem to be much point in her working since his father was number sixty-three on the *Sunday Times* rich list. Besides, she didn't have any qualifications. She wasn't happy, exactly; she was bored a lot of the time and she missed the daylight. Gus didn't get up until noon, and then he liked to spend a few hours behaving like Ray Liotta in *Goodfellas*, hanging out in a dressing gown, watching TV, fixing up deals on the phone and generally making himself feel like a hotshot. He'd say, 'Drape, baby, drape,' and she'd go and sit on his knee while he talked to 'business associates', for which read friends from school with similarly big plans, unlimited supplies of daddy's money and a taste for instant gratification that prevented them from making a start at anything. But then most of her friends were slaving away for a pittance and living in hell holes – whereas they had an American washer and dryer in their own utility room, to put things in perspective. And Gus took her everywhere and gave her everything she wanted, the only condition being that she 'turned on the fizz', as he put it.

Everyone Gus knew got their fizz in powder form. It didn't agree with Lydia which meant she was naive when it came to matters of narcotics, though not so naive that when she found him half naked in the lavatory with a

Russian model she didn't recognize that his habit was affecting her life. So she went out with his friend, Rex, and then Rex's friend, Costi, and then Costi's friend, Michael. She was engaged to Michael for a year, but then Michael got made redundant, so Lydia started making men's boxer shorts, which she sold desk to desk in the city, and within a month she'd met Richard. Richard was twenty-seven, ambitious and plain speaking, a futures trader determined to make his first million before he was thirty and 'wipe the floor with the pansies you've been hanging out with'. She moved in with him on condition that he bought her a ring and they started to look for somewhere to buy, north of the river. One night they were in a bar and Richard was buying tequila shots for everyone and calling for assistance with setting up some limbo dancing. 'Get us a fucking *pole*, you have got to see this,' he roared at the assembled group of men, winking and wiping his beer-soggy mouth on the back of his sleeve. This was his party piece, and she was happy to oblige. Being game on, scantily dressed and ready to limbo was part of the deal, and she liked the applause and the way the men looked at her as if she were some forbidden fruit. The pole was being hauled into position between two chairs when she saw Jack and Amanda and Amber, staring like Sunday school teachers who'd wandered into a strip bar in Patpong.

'What's the matter with you?' She said the first words she had spoken to any of them in three or was it four, years.

'Nothing,' Jack said. 'Nothing. Are you all right?'

Amber was gazing over at the bar, watching Richard do the bump with a girl from the office.

'Great. I'm running Sixteen Minute Sandwiches – you

know? Richard – that's Richard – set me up in it. And he's doing really, really well.'

They all looked in the direction of the bar.

'The one in the belted trousers?' said Amanda.

Jack was watching Lydia, hawklike, the way old friends of reformed junkies look at them in the early days, dwelling for too long on the eyes, searching their faces for clues.

'I'm engaged, actually.' Lydia clapped her hands together, as an afterthought. 'We haven't set a date but it's definitely going to be before my thirty-sixth, I'm determined about that!'

Jack looked at the floor.

'Why don't you come out with us one night?' said Amber. Her eyelashes were beating slowly against her cheeks, as if in time to the music. 'We never see you now.' Something about her reminded Lydia of Andrew, waving her off on the day of the picnic.

'Hey, who are the girls?' Richard threw an arm across Lydia's shoulders and leant into her like a prop forward in a scrum. 'Don't keep them to yerself, babe. Any frienda yours . . .'

'We're just passing through,' said Amanda. 'Really, we're meant to be somewhere else.' And the three of them shuffled like penguins and edged towards the door.

'Bye,' said Amber.

'See you,' said Jack.

Lydia watched them as they passed the front window of the bar, arms linked, hair bouncing, made invincible by their friendship. Two men recognized Amber, gripped each other's arms to seal their mutual mind-reading, and ran after them, shouting.

'Whoa.' Richard was nuzzling her ear in what he would have described as a super horny move. 'Well, you scared that lot off pretty quick.'

'Actually,' said Lydia, 'they are very good friends of mine – you slobbering oaf.'

'Much stronger,' said Mike. 'Keep going . . .'

'Amber had a very tight circle of girlfriends: Jacqueline Farmer, Amanda Worth and myself. It was regarded as a great honour to be one of the chosen inner circle, of course, but you had to be prepared to give and give. If you didn't, as I did, take a stand then there was no cut-off, no limit to the amount that could be asked of you.' Mike jabbed his head and made rolling motions with his hands. 'It wasn't just us, but our husbands, too, who had to be at Amber's disposal day and night. Nicholas, Amanda's husband, is a member of the legal profession and he was away from home, dealing with her affairs, for longer and longer periods. So, effectively, one was asked to put Amber's happiness before one's own marriage.'

'Great! We'll come in there with the Hedlands footage of Worth leaving the house, tears at the memorial, etc.' Mike crossed his arms, tucking his fingers under his armpits. 'OK. Great. Carry on Lydia.'

'Amber found it very hard not to see people, but especially men, as objects to be manipulated.' Lydia paused to take a sip of water. 'She knew exactly what she wanted out of everyone and she knew what she had to do to get it. I don't think she had a relationship that wasn't based on some kind of manipulation, sexual or otherwise, and, of course, she was very good at showing people what they wanted to see. So, to some she was this "groovy" London girl, and to others she was the earthy, green-fingered, mother provider.'

'OK, so this is the point where we get into Hedlands – Dave, the children, the dream life. Keep it coming, this is good.' Lydia closed her eyes and breathed deeply, placing both hands on her ribs. 'Everything all right?' Mike was leaning back in a kitchen chair, elbows propped against the new French dresser. 'You look a bit pale.'

'I'm fine. I'm just trying to get it all straight in my head.' She took another sip of water.

'How about something to lead us into the videotape of the kids, babe? Some examples of how eccentric she was with them.' Lydia glared at him. 'Well OK, bad mother – whatever – how about some of that?'

It had been Lydia's suggestion to use some of her video footage in *The Real Amber Best*. 'I think you should look at this,' she'd said to Mike. 'You might find it useful.' They'd watched, side by side on the sofa in the dark, as the red MG sputtered up the drive of Hedlands that warm spring weekend, coming to a stop in a fog of gravel dust. Jack and Sam wrestled with seat belts, waved to the camera, flung open the doors of the car and stepped onto the drive as Amber walked into the picture, bare brown back tied up like a present with a pink string bow, hair cascading from a topknot. She and Jack hugged, the crushing, rocking from side to side hug of as good as sisters, and then Amber turned towards Sam, each placed a hand on the other's shoulder and stretched across the distance decided by their feet, to peck each other lightly on both cheeks.

'So, not particularly intimate at this point then?' said Mike.

'No. This is three years ago. They hadn't seen each other for quite a while. But look at this.' Lydia fast-forwarded the tape – jabbering heads round a table, bobbing and jittering, small pink bodies writhing in a bath, more jabbering heads. 'Here . . .' The tape slowed and Jack was standing with her back to the camera, a croquet mallet discarded at her feet, waving a piece of wood in the air.

'What's she doing?' Mike stretched his arm out across the back of the sofa and shifted his weight so that his body was turned towards Lydia's.

'Throwing a stick for the dog. Now look.'

The camera swung left and came to rest on Sam and Amber, standing, hipbone to hipbone, a paper's width between them. The sound of the Super Eight whirred in the background as the picture slid down their silhouettes, taking in her frayed jean hotpants, his long navy shorts, and then stopped dead as Sam's hand snaked around Amber's bare thigh and her hand met his. Their fingers locked for a moment, a few precious seconds, before they backed away from each other, leaving the camera gaping into a blur of green woods.

'Well, that's pretty conclusive, I'd say.' Mike was grinning. 'Clever girl. Any more?'

'There's a bit of the children's bedtime – if you want the chaos behind the scenes.' Lydia leant a little to her right so that he could comfortably curve his arm around her shoulders. 'Here we go, it's coming up in a few seconds.'

*

'Yaaaaaaaabbbbbb!'

The screen was crammed with little faces, tongues out, mouths open wide like hungry chicks, then the focus drifted and sharpened again on a long wooden table and sitting round it Sam, Jack, Lydia, Dave, Amber, Milly and Roger. A skein of cigarette smoke hung between the table and the iron candelabra chained to the ceiling.

'Andy mate,' Dave was at the head of the table, his hand cupped round his mouth, 'don't film the little buggers, Andrew. Pick 'em up, they should be in bed, it's ten thirty.' Dave rolled his eyes and put two fingers to his temple.

Amber stood up from the table and smiled at the camera. 'All right,' she said, her voice was creamy and hoarse at the same time. 'Andrew, you take Zelda and I'll take Melly and Max.'

'Naaaaaaaaahhhhhhhh . . .'

The camera followed as the three children set off, turning the corner of the table tightly, as a pack, then disintegrating as they debated whether to make the full circuit or turn back, finally linking hands and running to the fireplace at the end of the room where they har-rumphed and stamped like miniature Rumpelstiltskins. Melly picked a cigarette up off a side table and pretended to smoke it, expertly flourishing the Gauloise in her hand and screwing up her eyes when she took a puff.

'All of you up NOW!' roared Dave, wheeling round in his chair. 'If you're not up those stairs— Bayyyyyb!' The camera followed Dave's eyeline, left, to where Amber was leaning against the bookcase, calmly lighting a cigarette. She walked over to him, and gave his shoulder an affec-tionate squeeze. 'All right, monkeys, do as daddy says, or you know who's coming to get you!' And picking up a riding crop from the table she flicked the air as they ran from the room squealing, 'Misswhiplash, Misswhiplash, Misswhiplash and her terribell CROP!'

Dave plunged his head into his hands in mock exasperation. 'Andy, do us a favour and turn that fuckin' thing off.' He reached across the table for a bottle of mineral water. 'Can you imagine if the social got hold of that – I'd have some explaining to do. Channel effin X wouldn't much like it either. It's not quite the picture of Hedlands family life that you see on the box, is it? I say to Amber, "Whose kids are those then, the little cuties with the aprons helping with the brownie mix?" They're not the ones I fish out of my games room where they've been – get this – trying to get in the back of the jukie looking for money! Unfuckin' believable . . .' He chuckled and sat back in his farmhouse chair with a huge grin. 'They get it from their mother – the old cash Hoover . . .'

'Superb.' Mike reached for another glass of wine. 'You haven't got anything of her going for them, have you?'

Lydia smiled and pressed the fast-forward button on the remote control. The film stopped and Amber's face was perfectly centred in the middle of the screen, her eyes as big as a bushbaby's. 'Andrew, you are not helping,' she whispered directly into the mike. The camera panned right to Zelda, jumping up and down on a brass bed. 'Zelda,' Amber's voice sounded muffled, 'settle down now, that's it. Be good for Andrew and Lydia, I'm going to deal with the others.'

Zelda stopped bouncing and plopped down on the pillow, tucking her feet under the top of the sheet. 'Will you read me a story, Lydia? Mummy said you would, and it could be this long . . .' she waved a copy of *The Water Babies* in the air as a blood-curdling howl emanated from the next-door room and the camera spun around just in time to catch a small naked body hurtling past the door. Zelda folded her arms as if to suggest they were all in for a long night.

'All right?' shouted Andrew.

'Yep.' Amber's voice was faint, drowned out by the rumbling of feet coming back along the corridor, and then a small pink bottom was proffered in the doorway. 'Sticky picky lug bug skug pooooh!' Max shouted, haring off in the direction of Amber's raised voice and loud, crashing sounds. The camera followed rapidly down a dark corridor, eventually swinging into a huge room with two small beds at the far end, tucked in so tightly the mattresses were buckled like hammocks.

'Oh, what a tartan rug can do,' said Amber, stubbing her cigarette out in a Beatrix Potter dish. 'Houdini couldn't get out of those. The thing is,' she wagged a finger at the camera, 'we only ever have these battles when my husband is trying to impress our friends with what a disciplinarian he is.' She turned her back to the beds and whispered, 'they're not used to it, poor darlings. Right – lights off. Any more out of you two and you're sleeping in the spooky room with the bats.' She loomed towards the camera and winked.

*

158

'That's it,' said Lydia, reaching for the remote control, 'there isn't any more.'

'No, go on.' Mike put his hand over hers. 'Let's see the rest. It's interesting.' The camera was back in the doorway of Zelda's room, focusing in on the bed.

'Lydia?' Zelda took her thumb out of her mouth, resting it on her bottom lip. 'Do you like me best?'

Lydia fidgeted on the sofa. 'Come on, Mike.' She rubbed the back of his neck. 'Why d'you want to see this?'

'Ssssh . . .' said Mike, 'I'm missing it.'

The focus narrowed in more tightly on the bed.

'I like you all the same,' said Lydia, without looking up from the book, her head shifting from side to side as she examined each of the pictures on the page thoroughly.

Zelda let the thumb slot back in for a few quick, throbbing gulps. 'Because Mummy says you are special. She says you an' Uncle Andrew are special to me.'

Lydia withdrew her hand from the top of the sheet where it had been resting, and turned the page.

'Are you sad?' Zelda twiddled a lock of blonde hair around her fingers and dusted her face with the blunt ends. 'Mummy said you was sad and I should be nice to you.' The thumb was half in half out now, the eyelashes blinking. 'But anyway, I would have.' Lydia shifted on the bed as if she was about to get up. 'I wish you lived with us, Lydia. We've got lots and lots of spares rooms, and then you could have lots of children too.' Zelda wriggled out from under the sheets and flung her arms around Lydia's neck. 'I love you Lydia,' she said.

Lydia visibly sagged, as if she'd been winded, then gently removed the child's arms from round her neck and placed them down by her sides. 'Well, I lo—' She paused and stood up from the bed. 'I love you *too*, Zelda,' she said briskly, as if correcting her grammar. As she bent down to pick up the book from the bed she noticed the camera in the doorway and slowly turned to face it, her eyes glistening in the light from the bedside table. 'Well . . . I bet you enjoyed that little scene,' she whispered, her voice stiff and gritted, like a novice ventriloquist's. Then she turned her back to the camera, bowed her head and the screen went black.

Mike sat in silence with his arms folded. 'You're right,' he said eventually. 'Nothing much there for us. She's a character though, isn't she, the kid? She's eight now, she must have been what, five, when you filmed that?' Lydia didn't answer him. 'The only thing I don't quite get,' Mike paused and glanced at her, 'and don't get me wrong, but I don't see why you – personally – hated Amber so much. Dyouknowwhadimean?'

Lydia took a sip of wine. She pushed her hair out of her eyes and stretched her neck as if composing herself. 'I have spent days demonstrating to you my reasons for – "hating her", as you put it.' She spoke softly and slowly, looking straight ahead at the blank television screen. 'I have talked you through every detail, shown you that she was sleeping with at least two men other than her husband, that she was a negligent mother and a less than desirable friend. It may not have had an impact on me *personally*, but I don't think that makes her behaviour any less – damaging.' She took a deep breath and tried to smile. 'I suppose, I didn't like to see her get away with it, that's all.'

She kept staring at the screen, even when Mike shifted forward on the sofa to get a better look at her face.

'Yes,' he said, 'but that's not all, is it?' He put a hand up to her chin and turned her face towards him. 'I've seen revenge before, Lydia, and this, sweetheart, is revenge.'

Ten

Amanda was lying in the bath reading her copy of *Yes, He Is Having an Affair* ('For a friend,' she'd said to the girl behind the desk in Waterstone's, lifting her sunglasses and giving her the eye shrug, 'isn't it just too bad?'). She hadn't felt comfortable until she'd got it home and covered it in two layers of brown paper. The idea had come to her after finding Riva absentmindedly flicking through *Is He Having an Affair?* with one of her suspiciously immaculately manicured fingers.

'Don't touch, thank you, Riva. It's a present,' she'd said, scooping the book up into her handbag.

'Oooooh, shame. Who is for?' said Riva, eyeing the handbag wistfully.

'Mrs . . . thing. At number . . . thirty-something.' Amanda gestured vaguely in the direction of the street.

'Reeeelly?' Riva looked gutted. 'The one wiz the blonde hair? But she is so preeeety, so younk, so energy always—'

'Er . . . Helloooo!' Amanda yanked a teacloth off the back of Riva's chair, tipping her forward on the seat. 'How old are you, Riva?'

'Seventenk.'

Amanda blinked.

'Well, it is not the case that all women who are betrayed by their husbands are old, ugly and faded.' Riva's lips thrust forward. 'Quite the reverse, often. Now, where is the brown paper?'

Tonight, two hours away from the British Glamour and Style Awards, at which Amanda was hosting a table, and was quite likely to collect an award herself, was not the best of all possible times to be reading *Yes, He Is Having an Affair*. But, in the introduction to the book, it specified very clearly that the programme – Saving This Marriage – had to be worked on daily, and this was her first opportunity. 'Exercise Three,' she read.

In this chapter we have dealt with time and learning new habits. For this week's task we would like you to either:

a) cook a meal at home and share it with your partner, alone

b) take on a task that your partner would normally automatically undertake, such as mowing the lawn, and ask him to do the same in return

c) get ready for bed an hour or so earlier than you would normally, and spend that extra time talking to each other. Note: resist the temptation to have sex on this night. It is important not to confuse the new emotional intimacy we are aiming for in the programme with acts of physical intimacy.

Amanda looked frantically around the bathroom, appealing to the sanity of the loofahs and potions and candy-pink painted shelves stacked with loo paper.

'Uuuurrrrrrrgh,' she moaned, screwing up her nose and turning the page as if it were covered with something irritating to the skin.

> If you are in employment ask yourself if your work is getting in the way of your relationship. Maybe your partner's work is causing the strain; but for now, let's concentrate on you.

Amanda eyed a litre bottle of jojoba nectar, propped on the back of the lavatory cistern. She glared at it Carrie-style, eyes bulging, willing it to shatter, and then, with a sigh, returned to the page.

> You are already aware that work pressures are one of the most common causes of stress within a relationship and that it is this stress, and the underlying depression that frequently accompanies it, that leads to one or other partner straying.

Straying. *Straying.*

> Take a moment to look at your weekly schedule. Ask yourself, is there time allocated for you and your partner, for you and your family? Or are you operating as separate units sharing the same house?

'Riva . . . Riva!!!' Amanda sat up in the bath and opened her lungs. 'RiiiiVaaaaaa!'

'She's not here.' Ludo's muffled voice was just audible through the keyhole. 'She makin' my supper.'

'Oh. Lovely, darling! How are you my sweet boy?'

'Carn hear.'

'Are you all right, my darling?'

'You neber cook me supper.'

'That is not true.'

'Carn hear.'

'I cooked you spaghetti on MONDAY – when Hector came.'

'That's *ages* ago.'

'Well, no. Three days, Ludi.'

There was the squeaking of rubber-soled slippers on wood as Ludo, tired of the debate, wandered off down the corridor. Amanda yanked her handbag off the stool by the bath and rummaged in it for her mobile phone. She dialled her own number. 'Riva? It's me – I'm in the bath . . . Upstairs! God help us. Listen. Tell Mr Nicholas when he comes in that Cass is doing a project for school and it's called What My Father Does, so I'm afraid he has to get involved . . . tonight. And Riva, I'm going to give Ludo and Cass their supper tomorrow . . . Oh, God! So it is . . . On Monday then. OK. Bye.' She put down the mobile and returned to *Yes, He Is Having An Affair.*

'Hi.' Nicholas was in the bathroom.

'AAAhh! What are you doing?'

'Might ask you the same question, telephoning downstairs and leaving me messages. It's Thursday, remember? Thursday when I get home early, and do homework and whatnot, and then watch a video, on my own, because you are going to the launch of a new pair of tights.' Nicholas settled himself on the edge of the bath. 'A book, Squidgy? I don't think I've ever seen you read an actual book before, unless it was called *Calvin Klein's Dirty Underwear.* Looks like one of Cass's school books.'

'It is.'

Nicholas did his Marty Feldman eyes. 'Reeeaaaaly? What's it called, *Tudors and Stuarts Style Wars*?' He flicked at the foam peaks. 'So what is it tonight?'

'Glamour and Style Awards.'

'Will you be on the telly?'

'Might be ... And you're doing What My Father Does.'

'Don't worry, we've started already. I'm a god in my daughter's eyes now, but she does seem to be morbidly preoccupied with the divorce side of my work. Do I help daddies leave home? Do I say it's all right for daddies to see their children only at weekends?'

'She talks to Zelda. Evidently Amber didn't bother to disguise the facts quite as much as some of us.'

'Hmmm ...' Nicholas gazed out of the window. 'Still, not very happy topics for a seven-year-old to be contemplating.'

'Perhaps you should have thought about that sooner.'

'What? And specialized in tax, so I never had to answer uncomfortable questions for the class-three school project? I think that's taking good parenting a little too far.'

'Hand me a towel, please.' Amanda tossed the book onto the bath mat and grabbed at the towel Nicholas was dangling just out of reach. Once it was wrapped around her and neatly turned over at the top, she pulled herself up to her full height, five foot five, and delivered her proposal. 'Tomorrow, we are going to have supper together, alone, and before that I am going to – watch Sky Sport and you are going to – I don't know – do my yoga class with Liani. Then we are going to bed early.' She stepped out of the bath, flip-flopped her way across the cream rug and out into the corridor. 'We're doing the concentrated version for fast results because I can't take much more of this,' she said to no one in particular, and then, over her shoulder, 'And *no sex.*'

The British Glamour and Style Awards were held in a huge tent in the middle of a London park and consisted of an awards ceremony and dinner or, as the presenter put it, 'stuff that gets greeted all round the room with the same, do they really-expect-me-to-eat-this? expression, "This is *carbohydrate.*"' Everyone laughed knowingly – there were cameras balanced on the knees of crouching men pointed at most of the tables – but it was reported the next day in the press that of the 600 salmon en croûte served, just thirty were eaten in their entirety. Amanda's never even reached the table, she waved it on, as she'd waved on the little round anchovy toast things, the vegetable terrine and the choice of rolls, everything, in fact, apart from the Chablis and the mineral water. Like everyone seated in the tent Amanda drank water as if it were fat burner. She had 1.5-litre bottles posted all over the house, cash and carry trays of them stacked to waist height in the larder, and one of those water filter jugs, the latter purely to appease Nicholas, who had estimated that they spent £30 a week on Evian. 'On *Evian,*' he told his friends who came for dinner, 'it's not even fizzy.' Tonight she was wearing the chocolate jersey Martin Anderwurst dress featured on the cover of this month's *LaMode*, which meant she hadn't consumed anything but Evian all day and only mini-rice cakes in the preceding week. 'Darling, why not just unzip the beanbag and guzzle away at the stuffing,'

Nicholas had said, 'or crack into a bowl of those lovely polystyrene S-shaped things that all your mail order kitchen stuff comes in?'

Martin Anderwurst was seated on the *LaMode* table, as was Lily Lister, both of them tipped to pick up the big awards of the evening: Most Stylish Designer and Most Stylish Accessories Designer, respectively. Then there was Martin's boyfriend, Ignacio, Raschenda, of course, Diana (Most Stylish Model, possibly), Peace (Most Stylish Model, almost certainly), Mark Blumfeld, CEO of Bondi Sacs Publishing UK (Most Necessary to Keep Sweet), his wife Moira and a Welsh popstar called Stiffie, who Raschenda was courting with a view to getting him to feature in her 'Bad Vibrations' fashion story. 'It's about the really out there fringes of the surfer scene,' is how she'd explained the idea to Amanda at the run through. 'Neon colours . . . boys with body paint . . . girls with bone white hair and piercings. It's all based around this customized surf board of Tiziana's.'

'And the model?'

'Peace. She's just had that rodent cut and looks er-may-zing. And then Tiziana wants some rough-looking boys on the scene, like maybe Stiffie and Wet Reg.'

'How rough is rough?' Amanda had asked.

'Bad hair, bad skin, you know. It's not the Beach Boys,' Raschenda had said, giving her that 'why did I ever leave the *Fusion* to come and work for a glossy' look.

'*The* glossy,' Amanda had said, 'and I want to see them, in the flesh, first.'

She glanced across the table to where Stiffie was assuming the 'boy at the back of the class' position, arms folded, body sagging dangerously to the left, tea-cosy hat pulled down so far he had to tip his head back to see. Occasionally he would raise one arm and flick his wrist violently, or move his head rhythmically, forwards and backwards, like a nodding dog. Peace was flirting outrageously with him, staring sulkily into the middle distance, getting him to light her cigarettes without shifting her gaze from the far marquee wall, flashing her winsome smile randomly at passers-by and becoming exaggeratedly animated whenever a man approached the table. It was working like a dream. 'What's she on?' Amanda saw Stiffie mouthing into Raschenda's vulture-feather epaulettes. 'Charisma!' shouted back Raschenda, making the fibre optics attached to her headpiece dance like sea anemones. Stiffie looked confused for a moment and then formed an O with his forefinger and thumb.

Mark Blumfeld, who had asked to be seated between Peace and Diana ('I think you'll agree that I should have my finger on the pulse, Amanda'), was, nonetheless, looking like a tourist who had been stranded in a non-English-speaking country. He raised a glistening hand in Amanda's direction, her cue to bob up and scuttle round to his place in the semi-crouched position people adopt when moving between tables at functions. Blumfeld rose from his seat as she approached, arms extended, and they touched cheeks and elbows, as he murmured complimentary nothings into her hairline, while covering her in the smell of sweet aftershave. Amanda could clearly remember the day when the elbows were first introduced. The transition from cheek brushing to cheek brushing plus elbow cup was a crucial rite of passage; it indicated that you were a trusted and valued employee, rather than on trial, position still, unofficially, open. In her world elbows were what the palm tickle was to the Masons.

'I'm counting on you to introduce me to the hip and happening crowd,' gurgled Blumfeld as she turned to make her way back to her place. 'Don't let me down, Amanda.'

A moment later the tent reverberated with a general murmur as the presenter asked for the lights to be dimmed in preparation for a series of short films, introducing the nominees for Most Stylish Designer of the Year. Ignacio bristled and stretched his neck as if he were standing under a refreshing shower and one of Martin's people approached the table carrying Butch, Martin's bull terrier, wearing an Anderwurst-designed harness and lead. An enthusiastic burst of applause greeted the end of the first short and then it was Martin's turn to be profiled. They saw him sketching at a drawing board in his Hoxton studio, walking between fabric stalls in a market ('As if,' mouthed Ignacio, rolling his eyes and patting his breastbone to indicate who it was who really knew their colourways), pinning a dress on a model, and then backstage at a show in among a cluster of women dressed in black and wearing earpieces. In the background was a board covered in bold lettering: You Are a Bitch! You Don't Need Men but they ADORE You. You are STRUTTING YOUR STUFF on Miami Beach. You Just Left Your THIRD Husband. YOU THINK maybe you are an EAST END GANGSTER in a Babe's body. The camera moved in for Martin's close-up. 'I dress women who know their style not their labels. I don't want people to look at the women I dress and think "That is Martin Anderwurst".'

There was a burst of applause, somewhat more

enthusiastic than the first, principally on account of Ignacio's contribution which stopped just short of whooping.

'Mango and passion fruit slice?' Amanda activated her fanning-on hand. 'Mango and passion fruit slice?' The waitress leant closer to Amanda and manoeuvred her serving tongs into position.

'No!' Amanda glared at the fruit slice now half on the tongs. 'Thank you, no.' The waitress stayed where she was. Amanda's eyes were fixed on the screen in front of her where Visible Destruction (Leisure Wear) were rapping for the camera.

'You're not on a diet, are yer?'

Amanda's eyes fluttered, she turned her head mechanically and, for the first time, looked directly at the waitress.

'You was always on a bloody diet.' The waitress's eyes were like saucers; her mouth wide open, she swung at Amanda with the tongs. 'Yeaaaahs! It's mee, Jewlee. My God. Wouldjer believe it? Wot are the chances of this, eh? I'm not even wiv my lot, they just drafted a bunch of us in at the lars minute ter make up the numbers. Look at yer! What you doin' 'ere then?'

This must be, Amanda thought, what it's like to have an out of body experience: the physical Amanda was gazing up at Julie, Julie Elder her best friend from Basildon days, while Amanda's mental faculties were off somewhere on the other side of the room, regrouping, sizing up the scale of the problem, intermittently sending messages back to base ('Smile – Turn your Back to Blumfeld and Cover her – Get her to bend down').

'Magazine editor,' she whispered. She had swivelled round, turning her back to the table, and dipping her head as low as it would go, so that Julie had to crouch down behind the chair balancing the plate of fruit slices on her knee.

Julie gawped in appreciation. 'Reeelly?' She was looking up into Amanda's face with an expression that was both expectant and anxious, like a mother in the process of persuading her small daughter to forget about the bullies and get back in the playground fray. 'You look like a fashion editor.' She nodded at the Martin Anderwurst dress as if to say, you wouldn't be wearing that otherwise, would you? 'Which magazine is it then, Mandi?'

'*LaMode*.' Amanda was barely audible above the hoots and whistles for Visible Destruction, but Julie managed to lip read.

'Naaaaoooooow! *Larmowed*!' She punched Amanda's shoulder, her mouth hanging open in disbelief. 'Inthatamazin? Mindjew, I'd 'ave put my money on you settin' up yer own 'airdressin' business.' Julie sank her teeth into her bottom lip and shook her head slowly. 'You were that good. I was a liability, d'yer 'member my Rod Stewarts?' She slapped a hand over her mouth, and deposited the fruit slices on the floor, settling back on her heels. 'Still, vis is glamorous innit?' Julie's eyes roved around the table and, even in her preoccupied state, Amanda couldn't help but notice that there wasn't a flicker of either recognition or wonder on her smiley, moon-shaped face. ('Act – Explain – Quickly – Middle of awards ceremony'), Amanda's mind was radioing her body with increasing urgency now ('Will get in touch – Busy – Important guests').

'What's going on here?' Amanda looked up to see Mark Blumfeld, his bulging eyes locked onto Julie's

Hawaiian Tropic cleavage, and in that instant her mind's rapid reaction facility short-circuited. She could feel the fizzing and numbness creeping down the back of her neck as he loomed closer, the sensation that everything was happening in slow motion. There was a lapse of three or four seconds before the emergency back-up response finally kicked in ('Remove him – Stand up now – Take him by the arm . . .'). Amanda's legs started to lift her off the chair just as Blumfeld squeezed himself onto the edge of her seat and gave her knee a sticky, lingering pat. Then he shifted, turning the blackboard of his back to face her, the better to focus on his new quarry. 'I don't think I've had the pleasure?'

'You know you 'aven't!' Julie shook her nutmeg-blonde with ginger highlights mane and gave him a big wink. 'We know 'is sort, don't we, Mand?'

'Mark.' Amanda placed a firm hand on Blumfeld's arm. 'I think we should get ready, Martin's award is going to be announced at any moment and—'

'I'm aware of that, thank you, Amanda, but first of all who is this enchanting young lady?'

'Whas 'e like?' Julie was up and waggling gently on her white leather mules, hands on hips, coral-pink nails spread like fans. Amanda was suddenly struck by how little she had changed since they were senior stylists and colour consultants at the Final Cut: same unfeasibly col-oured, layered hair, same mid-thigh skirt and heels combination – now worn with a tight black waistcoat, whereas then it would have been denim, probably patch-work – same tangle of gold chains and dexterity inhibiting manicure. It wasn't that she was surprised at the lack of development in the course of twenty years, rather that the look that had marked Julie out as a bona fide Essex Slapper for most of her adult life was currently the last word in what was called Cortina Chic. All around the marquee there were girls doing a version of the Martin Anderwurst 'original' and, if it weren't for the slightly crêpey cleavage, the rum tan, and the jaunty, gregarious manner, Julie Elder could have been just another middle-aged fashion victim determinedly strutting her credentials. In some ways she had the edge over them. For one thing she had the bandy legs and brick-shaped calf muscles that everyone was mad for at the moment, and her hair was just that bit more brittle and synthetic than most of them were prepared to go. It dawned on Amanda that Blumfeld, particularly in this light, with his penchant for booze and sketchy grasp of the subtleties of trends, would have every reason to assume that Julie was a scion of the fashion community. What is more, the combination of Amanda's willingness to dive into an intimate huddle with her, and Julie's apparent lack of interest in schmoozing him, would have suggested major league to the CEO, someone really influential, Italian *LaMode* at the very least. ('Move,' the brain was back, more insistent now, 'Get in between them . . . Do it . . .') Amanda shifted, just as Blumfeld grabbed for Julie's hand, or was it her hip?

'I pride myself on knowing exactly who's who in our business,' he said, beads of perspiration collecting in the pale lagoons on either side of his remaining spit of hair, 'and I am quite appalled that I haven't come across someone so obviously talented and—'

'Well!' Amanda interposed herself between the two of them and briskly set about regaining control of the situation. 'Er . . . Julie has got to be backstage in two minutes,' *Make-up*, she mouthed at Blumfeld, *works with Kristof* 'so there it is, no time to waste I'm afraid. Off we go.' And she pushed Julie away from the table in the direction of the stage.

'Wot abat my fruit slice!' Julie looked back over her shoulder to where Blumfeld was craning his neck, pressing an imaginary telephone to his ear with one hand while pointing, repeatedly, to the centre of his chest with the other. 'Mandi, you'll get us sacked – Wot you up toooo?' She was giggling now, holding her wrists together in front of her as if she were being taken prisoner.

Amanda gave her a jab in the ribs. 'Just keep going,' she hissed, 'we're not in the clear yet.'

Suddenly there was a roar and a hammering and scraping of chairs and seconds later Amanda found herself enveloped in leather and stubble and the smell of Acqua Freeze. Evidently Martin had won the award for Most Stylish Designer and was making his way towards the stage, grabbing at the bodies in his path as he went.

'Brilliant, darling,' Amanda managed to mumble into the side of his Dracula-span collar as he cast her to one side and yanked Julie towards him, planting a kiss on her mocha and damson lip-lined mouth.

'Love the way yer wear it,' he growled, giving them both the thumbs up as he strode off in the manner of someone who had been in the saddle for several days.

'Who the 'ell does 'e think 'e is?' said Julie, aiming a coral talon in Anderwurst's direction. 'Look, enough's enough, Mand. I need those effin' fruit slices. I got firty tables of sorbets after—'

'I'll sort it out, for God's sake. Let's just get round the side of the stage.' Amanda placed her hands on Julie's shoulders and twisted her to face in the right direction as the sound of Martin's voice, cracked and whispery, echoed all around them. 'And this, *this*, is what it's all about – ' Amanda looked up to see Martin pointing the silver base of the award directly at her and Julie ' – the women who wear the clothes, who make them *real*!' A white spotlight washed over them and the two women froze like prisoners on the wire, Amanda's hands still on Julie's shoulders. 'That's the editor of *LaMode*, Amanda Worth, giving one of my all time favourites an extra *ton* of class, as only she can' – there was a ripple of applause from the direction of Amanda's table – 'and one cool lady taking Cortina Chic to places I could only have dreamt of!' More catcalls and whistles and cries of, 'Go, girl! Go!' Martin raised the award high over his head with one hand and gave Amanda and Julie a victory sign with the other. 'That's fashion workin'! Big up. God Bless!'

Within seconds Amanda and Julie had been surrounded by cameras and photographers, pressing them together, shouting instructions: 'That's it, hands on her shoulders, as you were, now arm around her waist, this way Amanda, can you come forward a bit? Right leg – that's it, lovely. Look at each other – How about cheek to cheek? Great. And again.'

'Whoa! Hi, girls!' Martin was wriggling in between them, stretching an arm across each of their shoulders, hands dangling limp from the wrists. 'I want you for the campaign girl,' he shouted at the cameras, managing to keep his lips off his teeth. 'Baby, baby, baby, yer in a job! I said, baby – Hey, Alex,' he was addressing a bearded photographer with a notebook, 'get that in the daily grovel. This fabulous Cortina Chic babe is my new Diana.'

In the spirit of celebration Martin had removed his 'neo tattoo' jacket and was bare chested, but for a light spritz of body oil. He shimmied in between Amanda and Julie like a glamour model, his mousey dreadlocks lashing their faces with every triumphant toss of his head.

'So what's her name, Martin?' The photographer waited patiently, pencil poised, Amanda stared straight ahead.

'Her name is Rio, and she . . . hey, hey.' Martin was licking his lips as if they were on fire, and jigging up and down wildly. 'Get the DJ to play it. *Ignacio*. Get the DJ to play it.'

Out of the corner of her eye Amanda could see Julie craning her neck round Martin's bouncing chest, her arm stretched out, palm upwards, in a request for information.

'Where did you find her?' Martin was crushing Amanda against his side, pressing his lips to her ear. 'I love that kind of worn-out, but still funky and diggin' it, look. God, I'm so over big.' He reeled back as if he'd been struck. 'I mean Diana is *fat*! Jesus! What was that all about? This is *real*, this is like alley sex, visible panty line, fancy a cocktail, Ratner's tat, but like really in the Moment, Living It.' He snapped his fingers together, one, two, three.

'She's a waitress,' hissed Amanda.

'Yeah, right. She's a waitress, she's a shop-girl, she's a *hairdresser* . . . I'm seeing like those boxer dogs, horrible glossy boxer dogs with like, *drool*, and like sun loungers in some scary back garden with a whirly clothes line, and skinhead kids. Or her in the back of a Cortina, heels out the window, fag on, dog in the driving seat, wearing six inches – *whole neckfuls* – of the rhinestone collars.' He paused for a moment as the room was swamped with the sound of Duran Duran's 'Her Name is Rio' and then joined in, singing along in a strange falsetto.

Amanda seized the moment, slipped out from under his arm and grabbed Julie by the elbow, dragging her into the shadows over by the sound system.

'Wooooh! So wot's next?' Julie was enjoying herself, it was important to wrap up this little interlude without delay.

'Julie.' Amanda slipped easily into I'm-sorry-it's-not-working-out mode, her tone was upbeat yet firm, to avoid any risk of misinterpretation or any hope of a reprieve. 'Julie, I'm going to square all this with the catering company, make sure they completely understand the situation and then—'

'D'yer mind explaining it to me first?'

'Martin thinks you're wearing his clothes.'

'Come again?'

'His designs, from his latest collection. He's taken you for something you're not – obviously – and I think, for your sake, it's better if we nip this misunderstanding in the bud right away and spirit you out of sight. Forget any of this ever happened. Because he is a maniac, actually . . . and besides you've got a very important job to get back to.'

'D'you keep that voice up all the time then?'

'Julie,' Amanda breathed hard through her nose, as if it wasn't the easiest option open to her but, nonetheless, she was determined, 'I am not who you think I am.'

Julie looked unimpressed. 'I know egg-zackly who you are: Mandi White, Basildon's top stylist and colourist,

1975 to 1977   well, maybe top equal with Troy – now Ar-marn-dar wotever, lording it up on planet fashion an—'

Julie's words were drowned out by the presenter's voice, booming out of the speaker above their heads, spotlights strafed the ceiling of the tent like searchlights '. . . and the award for Style Leader goes to Amanda Worth, editor of *LaMode*.'

Amanda and Julie's eyes met.

'Fuck!' said Amanda. 'Fuck!'

'That's you, all right.' Julie grinned. 'Better get up there, I'll wait 'ere.'

Heralded by kidney-vibrating rap, buzzed by needles of white light, Amanda stalked across the floor, stomach sucked in, shoulders thrust back, a long, thin smile branded across her face. As she ascended the steps to the stage the presenter stood to one side, clapping hands raised in front of his nose, wearing an expression of utter solemnity and reverence.

'Thank you.' Amanda swooped at the microphone, clinging onto the base with one hand. 'I hate to say the obvious, when *LaMode* prides itself on being always unpredictable . . .' she paused to accommodate the few gentle titters. 'But this is a team job and this is a team award. And thanks to Martin for designing this beautiful dress,' mild flutter of applause, 'and for proving that we thirty-somethings can do cutting edge for ever . . . just as long as the cut is right.' Amanda's giant, honeycomb-pored double, mouthed the words on the screen behind her while, out in front, six hundred of her peers were soaking in the drape of the dress, the choice of shoes, the contours of her upper arms. She could see their eyes flashing in the half light, their mouths dipping towards each other. ('You wish, dear.' ... 'Oh, *please*, she edits the magazine from Dr Magda's surgery.' ... 'Well, it was *meant to be* time off for Amber Best's funeral, but the Hawaiian tuck recovery just happens to take precisely three days.' ... '*Love* this issue, but that's Fallon isn't it?' ... 'Who *is* responsible for that bob, hasn't she got any friends?' ... 'Oh, forty-three if she's a day.' ... 'Great team, kill for it, I just don't think *she*, *personally*, has ever had it.' ... 'Forty-nine, Erica saw her passport at check-in.' ... 'Martin must be *seething*. Imagine, he gets the cover, and now that's the picture which is going to be on every front page, Amanda Worth wearing it like the mother of the bride.') 'And finally,' Amanda clasped the award to her chest, 'thank you to everyone in the industry who voted for us. We love you all' and the room erupted in a standing ovation.

Returning to the Bondi Sacs table Amanda deposited the award, sank her and her neighbour's glass of wine, and was turning to make her way back towards the sound system when she felt a restraining hand on her arm.

'Amanda,' it was Blumfeld, 'many congratulations. Number one yet again, always ahead of the game.' He was looking directly over her shoulder, while keeping a grip on her arm. 'And your friend, who I understand is nicknamed Rio – quite the toast of the evening. We could do with some of that energy on the third floor, don't you think?'

Out of the corner of her eye Amanda could see Moira Blumfeld, sitting bolt upright, trussed up in a corset-tight Christa jacket that made her own problems seem like a walk in the park.

'I think Martin rather has his heart set on her,' Amanda said, trying to look disappointed.

'Oh well,' Blumfeld's lips twitched, 'I'm sure Martin owes us a favour or two.'

'And' – there was nothing else for it – 'not that it makes any difference, of course, but she is a lesbian. An activated lesbian.'

Blumfeld's chin dipped and his shoulders drew back sharply. '*Activated*?'

'Yes. Very committed, you know. Goes to *meetings*.' Amanda grimaced.

'Are you quite sure?'

'Oh, yes.'

'Well, I must say I am very surprised to hear that.'

'Mmmmm . . . and she's not one of the photogenic, experimental dalliance sort, you know, more the other sort.' Blumfeld's eyebrows were steadily creeping up towards the lagoons. 'More the no pain no gain sort – I believe.'

'Really?'

'Mm hmm. Now, I absolutely must go and – sort a few things out.'

As Amanda swept past the table she noticed that Moira Blumfeld was stroking something in her lap, and when she glanced back she saw that it was her own hand, a big lavender-tinted thing that had no place at the end of those needle-thin arms.

Julie was waiting by the sound system when she got there, blowing smoke rings from a menthol cigarette ringed in mocha gloss.

'So, you was saying,' she folded her arms and slung her weight onto one hip, 'you ain't who I fink you are.'

'I just meant that I've – moved on. Not that there's anything wrong with that li— with your life. But it's not my life any more, that's all. This is my life, here, and' – Amanda glanced over her shoulder – 'I am a very different person now.'

Julie's hipbone twitched. 'Yer mean yer posh.'

'Not *posh*.' Amanda took a deep breath and closed her eyes as if drawing on hitherto untapped reserves of patience; when she opened them Julie was grinning.

'What jew call it then?'

'Look. I am the editor of *LaMode*.' Amanda punctuated this statement with an extravagant widening of the eyes. 'I have different priorities, different standards—'

'Different friends.'

'Yes, different friends.'

'So yer don't want me 'angin' arand to show you up. Funny, I thought your lot 'ad rather taken to me, or is that me missin' the point again?'

'Nooo.' Amanda gave Julie her generous-in-the-circumstances smile. 'No. Everyone is very taken with you, really . . . it's not that. I just don't—' Julie's eyes narrowed. 'Because of who I am, I can't afford . . . I mean it's one thing Martin taking a shine to you, but it's quite another if people find out who you really are – and make the connection.'

'You don't want 'em knowin' we was mates . . . you don't want 'em lookin' at me and thinkin' there goes Amanda, pre the makeover?'

'That is not it.' Amanda glanced over Julie's shoulder and saw Blumfeld making his way towards them, finger raised in the air to reinforce his intention. 'Yes it is! Yes it is! Shit! Look, Blumfeld thinks you're a make-up artist.' She grabbed Julie's hand. 'Please!'

'Well,' Blumfeld was on top of them, flexing his lips, 'I hope I'm not interrupting anything, girls . . .'

'Nah,' said Julie, 'just a teeny tiff.'

Blumfeld glanced at Amanda. 'Well . . . er . . . Amanda and I were just talking about you, my dear. I was hoping to coax you onto the winning team, but she informs me that you are . . . committed elsewhere.' Blumfeld didn't actually have a cigar and a white Burmese cat under one arm but he might as well have done. He placed a puffy tanned hand on Julie's bare upper arm. 'I must say though, I'm having to take her word on that, my instinct has never been wrong yet.' He gave Amanda a cautionary look, and tightened his grip. 'It seems to me that our editor may be trying to keep you all to herself?'

'She knows we can't work in the same place, too much 'istory init?' Julie flicked at a stray piece of hair snagged on her mascara-caked eyelashes. 'See, we go waaay back Mand— Amanda an' me. We was from very different backgrounds a course, totally separate, she was the uptown girl, I was the—'

'Make-up artist,' prompted Amanda.

'Egg-zackly. It's a miracle, a *miracle* we was ever, like, friends at all, but we 'ad fashion in common din' we? And what we 'ad back then, was somefink else. An' you know what they say – you can't repeat that kinda chemistry. I mean, I love 'er, but it's tricky for the both of us. Just wouldn' work.' Julie nodded emphatically and glanced at Amanda who was standing very still with her eyes shut.

'I see . . . Amanda didn't give me the full story obviously. So you too were – friends in the past.'

'Oh, definitely.' Julie grinned at Amanda. 'Only wiv me always very much in the subsurvient role an' 'er bein' the classy, superior one, if yer knowwotimean – more of a teacher-pupil relationship, if you can imagine.' Blumfeld's expression suggested that he could indeed, and had frequently paid good money to picture it that bit more clearly, with the aid of schoolgirl outfits and a couple of canes. He narrowed the already uncomfortably small space between himself and Amanda and breathed on her confidentially. 'I think you could have trusted me with your little secret, Amanda. We're not living in the dark ages you know. Well . . .' he straightened up and puffed out his chest, 'great shame.' And with one last, moist look at Julie's cleavage he made off in the direction of a group of young models.

Julie put an arm round Amanda's shoulders and gave her a squeeze. 'There yer go doll. Yer only 'ad to ask nicely. Now I'm off or I'm out of a job.'

'You're not going anywhere,' mumbled Amanda. 'I need a fucking big drink.'

Eleven

Transmission clock counts down the seconds.

A large woman in a tweed suit stands by a fireplace over which hangs a black and white photograph of a sprawling Gothic building. Caption reads: Miriam Irving, headmistress Northanger House 1969–1982. She is smiling as if under instruction to do so. 'I wouldn't say academic. She was very good at languages and fine art and, of course she was a popular choice for school plays, but I wouldn't say that studies were a priority.' Voice off: 'Was Amber perceived to be a bad influence?' Miss Irving shifts her hand from the mantelpiece. 'She was quite unruly, yes. We did have our run-ins. The only time the police were ever called to the school was as a result of an incident involving Amber. She had lost her mother, of course, and this undoubtedly had an impact on her behaviour. There was very little . . . supervision at home.' Voice off: 'How did you feel when you took the decision to expel her? What did you think the future held in store for Amber?' The headmistress's eyes fix on something high up on the wall to the right of the camera. 'I was anxious for the girl, naturally. But one has to make these decisions in the interest of the school as a whole.' Her attention is summoned back to the camera, she straightens her neck and clasps her hands in front of her waist. 'She was rushing at life, very impetuous and thoughtless. She wasn't prepared to look ahead or to deliberate the consequences of her actions. The truth is I feared it was never going to end happily . . .' Cut to cine-footage of the entrance porch of the house and a swarm of young teenage girls dressed in floppy hats and flares carrying trunks. They deposit the trunks in a pile at the foot of the steps, wave at the camera, embrace. Cat Stevens's 'Wild World' fades *up*. Camera settles on a group of the girls' arms linked, long stripey scarves tied together, high kicking their legs can-can style. Focus narrows in on Jack and Amber, freeze-framing the two girls' faces, mouths wide open, eyes shut, laughing.

'Hi, how's it going?' Sam was ringing from the van, Jack could hear the sound of the road through the hole in the floor by his feet.

'Fine.'

'Today's the day, isn't it?'

'Mm.'

'So, are you all set?' There was muffled giggling in the background, the sound of a female determined to advertise her presence in the passenger seat. Jack felt a lurch of irritation. In the first place she thought that it was somehow disloyal of Sam to ring her in the company of a strange woman, let alone bring up a subject that was so personal. Also it suggested that Sam, instead of going about his business, every now and then thinking about her on what was, arguably, the most important day of her life, was, in fact, concentrating all his energies on someone else altogether. And then, she could just picture the anonymous giggler, right down to her jumbly bag full of quirky, funky bits 'n' pieces: crystal-studded lighter, 3D fluoro-covered address book, giant hairbrush covered with stickers, candy cigarettes and a mobile phone (hologram cover only available in New York) that literally never stops ringing with calls from Xanthe and Manthe and Inigo offering weekends in Norfolk and parties in Hoxton and passes to secret gigs and the after after party VIP room. Now she was actually annoyed.

'Who's that?' she said.

'Who's what?'

Jack held the receiver away from her ear and gave it her most patronizing look. 'The other person in the van, Sam.' There was another reason why she was irritated. It sounded childish, but she didn't like the idea that someone was sitting in her place, in the van. (Forget sitting, actually, she'd be curled up – crazily shod feet perched up on the bench – or languidly sprawled, with the van blanket wrapped around her, like a California trust fund girl at a beach party.) Because it did feel like her place. No one else had occupied it as much as her. She had been there the day Sam had picked up the van from the man in Chigwell, she had been there when it had burst into flames on the M25, and she had been there every time he'd sold plants out of the back, in the market. It was – her place.

'Oh. A friend – ' now Sam was laughing ' – Hey, pack it in, you! Sorry, Jack, just having a bit of a problem with the crew . . . recovered the controls now.' Not only was he laughing, but in a special, throaty, sex-injected kind of way, that was supposed to suggest he was hot as hell in bed – she could hear it.

'Sam? Did you ring me just so that I could listen to you

showing off?' Jack held the mouthpiece under her chin to demonstrate her detachment from the situation.

'Nooo. I rang to find out how you were doing. The answer is bricking it, obviously.'

'I'm absolutely fine. Where are you off to, anyway?'

'Shopping. Flavia's going to help me choose some stuff for the flat.'

Oh, for fuck's sake, she wanted to scream, what a cliché. And we're going to bounce on the beds together in the furniture department, and then we'll go to the park and I'll wrap my coat around her and we'll chase each other and roll in the leaves like puppies, and lick ice cream off each other's noses, and then we'll go back to the empty flat and have a picnic on a rug on the bare board floor and then . . .

'Jack? You still there?'

'Yup.'

'So, yeah, that's what we're doing.'

'What about later?'

'Weeelll . . .' Sam paused, was he making rolling eyes at Flavia? Was he pointing at the mobile, mouthing, Sorry, can't get rid of her?

'I'm not that interested,' she said. 'I just . . . don't want to bump into you.' Jack jammed the mouthpiece further under her chin.

'Not much chance of that, I wouldn't have thought, you'll be going to Onu at the Stanbury or the Zen Bar . . .' Sam paused again, she could hear the trust-fund girl murmuring something in the background. 'That's about Simon's level, isn't it?'

'I don't know.' Her stomach was turning over like a

tumble drier. 'I can't think why you're suddenly such an expert.'

'Yeah. It'll definitely be one of those. Or maybe his club! Yeees, that's it. He'll rock up in the Lurve Porsche, tuck you into the front seat, neeeeyeeeeooooow Voom! Straight to – whatsit – Tricky Finns. "Hi there guys, any chance of a private room?" ' Sam's impersonation of Simon's voice – public school, crossed with Felix Cat with a bad case of laryngitis – was eerily convincing. ' "And . . . er . . . a boddle of your *best* champagne." '

'Very funny,' said Jack. 'Call me a privacy freak, but I don't much like you sharing the details of my personal life with anyone who happens to be listening, thanks.'

'She's got her Walkman on. Relax, will you? I'm starting to feel sorry for the guy.' Sam laughed, his normal yuk, yuk, yuk laugh; his take me as you find me, I'm not trying to seduce *you* laugh. 'Come on, Jack, it's going to be great. You're all set, nothing to worry about. Just remember your four Ss: sweet, sexy, serene, and . . . silent. Only kidding! It's sunny, of course! Watch the drink – bit of lubrication at the start, but don't overdo it. And you know that thing you do when you make me check your teeth for bits of food? Well don't try it at this stage.'

'Ha Ha.'

'You'll be fine! And remember it's scary for him too.' Jack pictured Simon in this month's *Herald* magazine, shot from above, standing in the middle of a circle of society girls arranged on the floor like the spokes of a wheel, their bare toes clustered together around his feet.

'Where are you going to go later, you and Flavia?'

'I have no idea, pub quiz at the Cock and Elves, I should think.'

The Cock and Elves was the nastiest pub for miles
around but suddenly it seemed like the most welcoming
place on earth. She had the same feeling now, talking to
Sam, that she used to have when she called home from the
pay phone in the Northanger House entrance hall. Amber
would be slouched beside her, the bottom of her flares
covered in mud, reeking of that distinctive mix of cigarettes masked by aerosol deodorant and Polos, feeding her
10ps as if they were purple hearts, while her father on the
end of the line delivered words of encouragement. 'Only a
couple more days and exams will all be over, and you'll be
home in your own bed.'

'Well . . . break a leg, Jack. Give us a call tomorrow.'
Sam sounded distracted, she could hear the giggler in the
background again, sense her pretty little fingers coaxing
their way into the buttonholes of his duffel coat.

'Don't let her make you get anything you can't take
back,' she said, and rang off.

Three hours later Jack was dressed and ready and almost
hyperventilating. 'I'm almost hyperventilating,' she whispered down the phone to Amanda. 'I'm so nervous I can't
sit up straight, I've sort of lost it from the waist up.'

Amanda sighed heavily on the end of the line.
'Honestly, Jack, has it ever occurred to you that you've
just got too much time on your hands? You shouldn't have
taken the day off.'

'You were the one who told me I had to rearrange my
flat to look like a knocking shop.'

Actually, looking round it now, it looked more like
a Moroccan riad meets Mongolian steppe dwelling.

Amanda had sent someone over from the *LaMode* living department with an armful of rugs covered in rows of shiny silver coins, some hairy lamb throws and an assortment of blood-red glasses. 'It's all from next month's sensual living special,' the girl had said in a tone that suggested Amanda had informed the whole office, by Tannoy, of Jack's romantic aspirations.

'Anyway, could you just please suggest something?' Jack was gripping her head with both hands, the receiver jammed between her shoulder and ear. 'At the moment I can't hold a glass steady. And I can't swallow. Nothing. All my food will have to be liquidized.'

'Are you serious?' Amanda sounded mildly worried now.

'Deadly . . . there's only two hours to go and if disintegration continues at this rate I'm going to be in nappies by the time he arrives.'

'All right, this calls for some Mandrax.' Hurrah! Mandrax was what Dr Magda gave her clients in the lead-up to her more invasive procedures, and her best clients for use at their own discretion. Amanda had, for example, been Mandraxed for Amber's memorial (half a tablet), Mandraxed for the funeral (one tablet) and one-third Mandraxed for the party Davina held, in London, during the week that Amanda took over at *LaMode*. That, Perzocan sleeping pills and two kinds of antibiotic (used as a prophylactic) were the staples of her health regimen. But Mandrax was the big one. To quote Amanda, 'An earthquake measuring nine on the Richter scale couldn't disturb your aura of absolute serenity.'

One Mandrax was summarily despatched in an envelope, by bike, and twenty minutes later Jack was swallowing the recommended half with a glass of red wine and settling back on the sofa to wait for the feelings of serenity to wash over her. Half an hour later nothing had happened, she was still failing the steady glass and the upright torso test, so, with just over an hour to go before Simon was due to pick her up, she took the other half. By 7 o'clock she was feeling much, much calmer, not catatonic by any means (Amanda's assessment when she'd rung at 6.50) though maybe just slightly too . . . laid back. Simon was due in half an hour and she'd definitely lost that bit of edge required to get you up off the sofa and out of the flat, so she did the only sensible thing, given the circumstances, and had a shot of tequila. And then another, tiny one. By 7.15 she was feeling really, really, good, serene in spades, liquid limbed. She practised a bit of liquid-limbed dancing in front of the mirror above the fireplace, and the gods were definitely smiling on her now. Her dancing, which was usually kind of jerky and messy, had been automatically upgraded and was now strikingly sensual and original, as if she'd been specially choreographed for each track, including 'The Birdie Song' (it was on the album and she couldn't be bothered to fast forward). Then, because she couldn't really see what her legs were doing, she pulled a kitchen chair over to the mirror, stood up on it quite easily after a couple of practice runs, and resumed dancing, in a semi-crouched position, so that she could get the full-length effect. This was also an ideal opportunity to check for cellulite so she hoiked up the dress, gripped the hem between her teeth and, to the accompaniment of 'White Wedding' (what was this tape?), did a few three-point turns while pinching the tops of her thighs and then, Bzzzzzzz. It was the entryphone buzzer. Not a problem. No problem whatsoever. She stepped very slowly off the chair, made her way across to the flickering black and white image of Simon's profile, waved, and lifted the receiver. Easy. 'Hey,' she said, and it turned out that the old synthetic serenity pills had worked miracles on her voice box too. Unbelievable. She sounded like she had blood-red lips a fox-fur stole and a monocle.

'Hello?' Simon was squinting into the camera eye.

Jack licked the miniature screen a few times. 'Hmmm?'

'Jack, are you coming down?'

'No!' That wasn't part of the plan *at all*. 'No, no, you've got to come up.' He had to see the silver coin rugs and the hairy throws and the completely empty draining board and the candles burning brightly and the two vases of fresh flowers (one with actual oasis fixture) and the CD collection and the vast collector's item book on Jimi Hendrix. It sounded peculiar, not that she had volunteered the information to anyone apart from Sam, but, although Simon had never actually been to her flat, there were quite a few things in it that had been bought with him in mind. She hadn't particularly wanted the Hendrix book, for example, it was too big to fit on any of her shelves, but she knew that if Simon were ever to see that she owned it, well, his estimation of her would hit the ceiling. She had even bought the odd item of clothing – oversize velvet jackets, chunky rockstar belts – that she half fantasized they might one day share, wandering the streets, thumbs in each other's back pockets. She'd be lying in a bath – one of those freestanding cast-iron ones in a room the size of an aircraft hangar – and he'd wander in wearing those jeans he had on at the Hinckleys' party, in 1974, and her candy-striped jacket that she bought in the market, and he'd say, 'Mind if I wear this, babe . . . mind if I—'

'Mind if I don't, babe? I've got some people down here in the car.'

Jack leapt away from the entryphone. *People? People.* The way he said the word told her everything she needed to know. Not only people, as in other unknown persons on their two-person date, but pee-pull, as in 'all my people' as in 'they're a really coolbunchapeepull' as in instant street-credibility assessors whose definition of 'worth bothering with' is someone who can provide access to something or someone they need, and who can detect and discard the detritus (anyone else) in 0.9 of a second. Jack doubled over and half crouched, half speed-walked to the window where she flattened herself against the wall and then very slowly poked her nose around the edge of the curtain.

It was quite a lot worse than she had imagined. Parked outside was an old-style American convertible and on the back seat were the people: two girls and one man, arranged in a floppy, bed-sharing way that suggested they were all sexually acquainted. The girls were the worst possible sort – fashionably ugly – the kind with beaky noses, jutting hipbones and vintage wardrobes, for whom the wearing of the right kind of belt is a substitute for looks, and who are, therefore, ruthlessly competitive. Jack could have blended in OK, on a normal day, but today she was, of course, wearing the fabulous vamp ensemble, and when those girls zeroed in with their cred counters she was going to register in the minus minus category. Naturally they were wearing jeans and woolly hats, not any old woolly hats but the woolly hats as worn in the last Christa show, probably. Bzzzzzzzzzz.

Whoops! Simon was still at the door. She skittered back to the entryphone. 'Hello?'

'What's going on up there?'

'Ah, nothing – I thought I might just quickly change.'

'No way, Jack. Get down here, we're late already.'

'Oh. OK.' She didn't have the right jeans anyway, hers were one shade behind in the denim finishes. Late for what though? Never mind, never mind, she was a liquid-limbed temptress. She turned off the CD, blew out the candles and took a swig from the neck of the tequila bottle.

'Hi.' Jack was on the pavement pressed up against the car fins. The two girls raised their hands in response, like cowboys meeting on a dirt track, their mouths twitched momentarily into smiles before they returned to examining each other's bracelets.

'Hey,' said the man. He was giving her one of those turbo-charged friendly expressions, all teeth and staring eyes, the kind which scared you and patronized you all at the same time because it was so patently obvious that the person giving it was unaccustomed to using those facial muscles, and that the only reason they were doing so now was because they had been led to believe you would crumple without it.

'Was that you, up on the chair?' he said.

'No,' said Jack, 'flatmate. We look very alike – I've borrowed her dress actually – since just now. I suddenly thought, "No. Off with the jeans and . . . er . . . top from the market, chiffon thing . . . and wham bam into the little black dress".'

The girls looked at her in that ultra-bored way that makes your neck bend in the middle.

'Looked pretty crazy to us,' said the man.

'Right!' Simon leant across from the driver's seat and flung open the passenger door. 'In yer get . . . Like it? I'm babysitting her for the winter. This is Mungo, and Rosa and CJ,' he gestured towards the back seat, 'and they know that they are very very lucky people to have been asked along on our big date,' he dived for her ear, 'only the first part, mind you.' Then he sprang back and flicked the car into drive. 'But I just happen to have five very hot tickets, courtesy of a certain very hot PR person – for *Corex*!' Mungo whooped, Simon hugged the wheel to his chest and grinned at her. 'Howzat sound?'

'Brilliant, brilliant.' Jack tried to smile. Corex. Corex. Were they the ones who wore the white biological warfare suits?

Rosa and CJ were muttering lyrics, 'Wasamatawasa-matawhichooo NUTHIN',' and at the Nuthin' part Mungo would slam his fist into the back of her seat.

'It's a private gig, five hundred tickets max.' Simon gave his fringe a quick downward rake in the wing mirror. 'But hey, I don't have to tell you, you probably knew all about it, right? Jack does fashion features and stuff for *LaMode*.' He flicked his chin over his shoulder to indicate that he expected a reaction from the back seat.

'Right,' said CJ, 'great.'

Jack smiled and nodded. Part of her was thinking she should try to get Sam on the mobile, so that he could tell her who Corex were, but another part of her just couldn't be bothered. A bit of her was wondering what to do about the very barstool-to-table-at-Onu outfit, but then the rest of her just wanted to curl up, right here, next to Simon, forget about the slimy dress, maybe just take the whole lot off. And he was looking so beautiful. He had a new kind of fluffy page-boy haircut, like Romeo's . . . and he smelt of vanilla . . . and he had these snakeskin trousers which . . .

'Babe . . . BABE.' Simon was jiggling her knee, which she had left provocatively exposed, as instructed. 'Jack? Babe are you OK? You were – snoring.'

The Corex secret private gig was quite a big affair, as it turned out, and every single person there was wearing ripped and torn clothing that had seen several previous owners. At one point, when she was making her way to the bar to get another shot of vodka (Corex turned out to be something called 'electro rappers', which was not a good match for the serenity or the languid limbs) a young boy asked her if she was with security.

'Do I look like I'm with security?' she snapped.

'Yeah,' he said, and, to be fair, she was still wearing her black coat, buttoned up to the neck. She had tried to get into the swing of it, but the Mandrax dictated a sort of dreamy, skirt-swishing interpretation of Corex's signature track and she happened to catch Rosa giving her a look that was hard to come back from. After that it just seemed easier to hover near the bar, from where she could watch, if she stood on tiptoe, Simon and Mungo, down at the front of the stage, dancing with their arms and spraying each other with fizzed-up beer.

'Hey.' Simon was standing next to her wiping the sweat from his face and chest with the shirt he'd been wearing earlier. He had one of those bodies that made you behave like a lascivious dowager: you felt the need of a fan to shelter your eyes as they fluttered here and there of their own accord. Looking at Simon she understood what a man must experience in the presence of a particularly tantalizing decolletage. 'Hey.' He reached for her hand and placed her forefinger over his heart. 'See?' Just above his left nipple the word Amber was tattooed in small capital letters. 'I had it done straight after the funeral. She'd have liked it, don't you think?'

'Yes.' All the fox had gone out of Jack's voice. She could see the portrait of Amber's mother, the one they had worshipped at as children, only now Amber was standing in the place where her mother had stood, reaching out to Simon, pointing to his heart, and as she pointed flames ignited on his chest, blue flames that fizzled out, like in a burger ad, to reveal her name, branded in sizzling black.

Simon was studying her. 'You don't like it.'

'No, I do . . . it's jus—'

'I know what you're thinking,' he said.

'It's jussabit forbin . . . forbidding. Course no one can replace her . . . but . . . is it really right to pro . . . pro . . . to give your heart t'her forever?'

Simon was smiling. He slipped the shirt on and pulled her towards him.

'We'll cover it with a plaster if it puts you off,' he said, 'and maybe I'll get your name done on the other side. How much have you had to drink by the way?'

'Liddle bid . . . iss fine . . .' Apparently this was the

point at which it was OK to lose Mungo and the hatchet girls.

'They're so great, CJ and Rosa. Didn't you think they were great?' said Simon, taking her arm and placing it around his waist, under the shirt, where it was bare.

'Mmmm,' said Jack, 'lovely,' and let her cheek rest for a moment against the cool front of his shirt.

'Whoa!' She peered up at him through confused bleary eyes. 'Jack, you're like a furnace, babe.' Simon put a hand to her cheek. 'Maybe you should take the coat off?'

The fact was that she had almost taken the coat off, about an hour into the gig when she reckoned everyone was beyond registering her appearance, but the mirror in the ladies' lavatories revealed that coat removal was not an option on account of the dark, oval-shaped sweat marks under both her arms. Luckily, there was one of those adjustable hand driers in the lavatory, so she aimed the nozzle, gave her left armpit the full two-minute blast, and the dress was returned to its normal state, but for a frilly white line like a rim of salt. A Jamaican girl in leather batty riders stared at her in the mirror, pursed her lips and pronounced, 'Sister, yo fucked.'

'What d'you think, if I rinse the whole dress and then dry it quickly?' said Jack brightly, as if they were in this together and she, for one, wasn't going to shirk the challenge. But the girl just stared back at her blank and bold and Jack felt just the way she saw her, like a daddy's girl who couldn't handle the heat.

•

When they got to Bradley's Hotel there were no tables left in the Sino-Pacific restaurant, Simon said, so he booked a room and ordered sushi and Bollinger to be sent up.

'An' also some unfizzy . . . coffee . . . please,' said Jack.

'Thank you, sir,' said the receptionist.

'I'm not aksherly a bloke,' said Jack, attempting a CJ style sneery expression and pushing her fringe out of her eyes in an effort to aim her glare more accurately.

'He's talking to me, Jack,' said Simon, handing over a gold credit card and signing the register with one long wormy line and a dot two inches above it.

'Oh, shorry . . .' she waved at the receptionist. 'Thank you very very much. Couldjew hurry with the coffee, anmakeit quadruple strength, virshally no water, jusa teeny bit – Tell you what though,' she said as Simon led her towards the lift. 'I don't feel remotely sick. So thassa result!'

'You can take the coat off now,' said Simon. They were in a room which exactly corresponded with Amanda's womb theory: it was dark, blood red with quite a bit of black and the lighting was such that you could only just make out the lacquer four-poster and the long black chaise longue at the foot of it.

'Brrrrrrrr,' said Jack, 'maybe in a minute . . . Have they got robes, dyouthink . . . in the bathroom?' Simon looked puzzled. He was gorgeous. Uniquely gorgeous. Unlike, say, Sam, whose face bounced in and out of elastic expressions as if he was auditioning for a mummer's show, Simon's range was tight and exquisite – a smooth trajectory from electric gorgeous, via effortless everyday gorgeous, to deep and brooding gorgeous. Right off the scale there was, of course, dirty dog gorgeous when his eyes narrowed into turquoise slits and his lips curled back from his teeth, as they were doing right now, in a smile not unlike the wolf's in the story of *The Three Little Pigs*. It was a smile that assumed you knew exactly what you were doing, probably that you were proficient to display standard.

'Jack,' he murmured, 'why don't you find a *robe*, then, if that's what you want? Go for it, let's not hang around.'

Suddenly the robe idea, that she'd only come up with to get her out of the soggy armpitted dress, had taken on a whole new, sulphur-tainted dimension. 'Find a robe, *find a robe*.' God, it was some code for spankers and hand-cuffers: Do you robe? We're robers, how about you? Do you want to do the full robe or without the nipple clamps?

'I've gone off robe,' she said with a shrug. Simon blinked very slowly. 'Think I'll juss get myself cosyina towel, you know.'

Jack headed off towards the bathroom, keeping one hand straight out in front of her and one on the wall, to guide her steps. Several minutes later she emerged wearing two towels, one wound around mummy fashion, from breastbone to mid calf, the other draped over her shoulders, like a cape. After the halogen lights of the bathroom the room looked even more like hell's kitchen and the cloven-footed snakeskin trousered one was lying on the altar at the far end in a pool of murky red light, waiting for her to do something diabolical to him.

'Come over here, babe, and we'll play some music, yeah?'

There was nothing for it. Jack penguin-shuffled over to the bed, levered her bottom onto the mattress, steadied herself and swung her legs up, clinging to the corners of the cape towel with one hand.

Simon had some kind of channel changer thing in his hand. 'What'll it be?' he said.

'Chopsticks level, please,' said Jack. 'I mean justo start with, if thasalright, moving on to swinging about stuff . . . later maybe . . . see how dizzy I get. Maybe should have one foot on the ground though . . . f'now . . . ifthas OK with you.'

'Well, I was thinking mellow.'

'Yep.'

'Like – Dylan, maybe?' She raised her head and stared at him, his hand with the channel changer thing was pointing at a sound system next to the bed. He was talking about *music*.

'Yes, yes,yes!' she said.

'That's more like it.' He leant over and kissed her hard on the mouth.

'I thought you had diabolical sex plan,' she murmured.

'I do,' he said.

She could see his teeth glinting in the dark and suddenly the swaddling towel started to feel rather restrictive.

'Isallcomin off right now, Simon. I juss need a quick glass of water firs,' she said, hopping off the bed and padding geisha-like towards the bottles of mineral water on the table by the window. 'Musadmit, have been . . . a tiny bit nervous . . . anyway thissisit . . .' She felt her way around the table, one hand sweeping for the bottle, the other discarding the towel. 'Yknowwot? Thossmarabou girls of yours?' She tried the other side of the table, sweeping in the opposite direction. 'They very cute an' all that, Im*shure* . . . but you havenseen anything yet . . . Oh, bugger it . . . lessforgetabout the water . . .' and with that she turned to run back to the bed, caught her foot in the phone flex, and flew through the dark until she felt a thud and the scratchy texture of carpet against her cheek.

'Jack? Babe?' A half-naked Simon was crouching beside her but even his decorative appearance wasn't enough to distract her from the throbbing in her ankle. ''Ave broken my ankle,' she muttered. 'Know cosiv done before. Fuckit.'

'Well, this is a first for me, babe, I can assure you,' said Simon, and that's the last thing she remembered before she passed out.

Twelve

'How did it go?' Mike was spread out on the cream sofa, hands behind his head, feet resting on Lydia's newly upholstered stool. Andrew stared at the feet, in their all-terrain lace-up boots, the heavy treaded heels digging into the Regency striped fabric, and then lifted his eyes to the doorway of the living room where Lydia stood, stroking the paintwork, languid as a flower child. He held his breath in anticipation; he couldn't wait to see Mike experience the full impact of his carelessness.

'Want a beer Mike?' Lydia had removed her fingers from the doorframe and was trailing them up and down her breastbone, deep into the V of her silk sweater.

Mike nodded his head slowly, still keeping his eyes fixed on Andrew's face. 'Yeah, Lyd. That'd be great.' They held each other's gaze as the clack of her mules gradually receded down the corridor.

Mike smiled. 'OK. Let's start from the top again shall we? So, how did it go?'

'You mean, how did we meet?'

'I mean what sort of relationship did you and Amber have?' The smile was steady, patient, determined, the smile of someone who knows he cannot lose. Mike folded his arms across his chest and cocked an eyebrow, making

Andrew feel like a very young au pair being interviewed by the master of the house.

'We were friends,' said Andrew.

'And how would you describe the friendship?' Mike's eyes flickered. 'Were you her confidant would you say – like a brother?'

'I suppose . . . a bit like a brother.'

'A bit like a brother. So you looked out for her, you were protective of her?'

'It worked both ways. She liked to have someone in the background who she could depend on. But then she was a lot worldlier than the rest of us so, in some respects, you looked to her for guidance.'

'What kind of respects?'

Andrew knitted his fingers in front of his mouth. 'Well, you know – women, relationships.' Mike widened his eyes in encouragement. 'Being a woman – living the kind of life she did – she . . . she had some useful insights.'

'Insights?'

'Yes. She'd tell you where to take a girl to dinner, what to buy her – that sort of thing. She used to joke about setting up a consultancy for men called What Women Want.'

'Really? So she advised you, about wooing Lydia?'

'No. Not exactly.'

Mike rubbed his chin. 'Would I be right in thinking that Amber was quite opinionated when it came to her friends' choice of partners?' Andrew said nothing. 'Would I be right in thinking that she was happy to show you the right moves so long as they were directed where she saw fit?' Andrew stared at his feet in their brown suede loafers.

Even though they were several sizes bigger than Mike's they looked considerably less powerful.

'Ha!' Lydia was clacking across the bare board floor brandishing a bottle of Budweiser. Bottled American beer was a new addition to the household grocery list since the start of filming, along with extra cases of wine, packets of bacon, bread rolls. 'I told you, Mike, you'd have a better chance of getting Thatcher to vote Labour than getting him to admit that she was a controlling—' Lydia smiled suddenly, and held out the bottle for Mike to take, swinging it lazily by the neck as if it were a suspender belt. She perched on the arm of the sofa next to him, and leant towards Andrew, mock ingratiatingly, twirling her red hair around her finger. 'I've told him everything, Andy, no point being coy now. He *knows* that you were Amber's trusty old Labrador. Well, he'd worked *that* out for himself.' Andrew was conscious of Mike's eyes boring into the side of his head, conscious that the muscle flickering in his jaw was being registered and filed. 'He knows how she manipulated all of you so that you were beholden to her, her little puppet army, signed up for life.' Andrew saw that Lydia was swaying slightly and Lydia saw him notice. 'Well, who wouldn't be a little bit – fortified in my position? We've had a bit of a false alarm you see, Mike.' Andrew lowered his eyes. 'Another little false alarm, haven't we, darling? It's one of those things, isn't it? One of those things that are sent to try you – punish, some might say.' She took a swig from her beer bottle. 'Oh, don't look so appalled, Andrew. I'm only doing my duty. It's all part of the documentary process. Making the story of someone's life involves the baring of souls, the excavation of secrets, doesn't it, Mike? And our story is *part* of her story, darling. Oh yes, it's all inextricably linked, wouldn't you say? Of course it is. Amber made sure that whatever happened she would always be a part of our lives.' She started to giggle, raising the bottle in a toast. 'God bless Channel X for giving me the chance to tell the world what it's like to live your marriage in the shadow of some perfect fucking dream girl – You know the thing about those girls? They bury the hook and then they skip away. But the hook's in there forever, isn't it? So you can forget about it for a while and then – ' Lydia made a jabbing movement with her hand like a fisherman twitching a line ' – tug tug tug, tug tug tug.' Andrew stretched an arm out towards her but she buckled away from it, slithering out of his reach and making for the door. 'It's all right. I'm going. You two can get sharing.' She turned and pointed a finger at Andrew. 'Don't you forget our appointment with Doctor Hayley. I'm not beaten – not quite yet.'

'I won't have you taking advantage of her,' said Andrew when they could hear the tread of Lydia's heels on the stairs. 'She isn't – she's in a very vulnerable state at the moment, you know that, and you're using it.'

'It may seem like that, Andrew.' Mike had substituted the smile for a concerned furrowed brow and praying hands, fingertips resting against the nub of stubble under the centre of his bottom lip. 'I can understand you feeling that. But, you know, your wife may need to talk – it could be that this process is doing her some good.'

'Please do *not* try to tell me that this in my wife's best interest. You're not a therapist, never mind the fact that this "process", as you put it, is going to be broadcast to millions.'

'Trust me, Andrew. We never start filming before we've gone over the ground, just as we're doing now, sorting out what should be said and what's better left unsaid.' Mike removed his feet from the stool and straightened up in his seat, momentarily relinquishing the role of the extortionist laying down his terms. 'Can I be straight with you, Andrew?' He leant forward and put his elbows on his knees, his face a picture of sincerity. 'The thing is – I'm confused. As far as I can see, you and your wife are both agreed that your role in Amber's life was that of the loyal, dependable friend, that's the way you would describe your relationship – ' Mike stretched his neck and ran his tongue around his teeth ' – but your wife's attitude has aroused my curiosity. What surprises me is the intensity of her feelings towards Amber. It suggests to me . . .' he pursed his lips and shook his head slowly from side to side, 'something else . . . something more.'

'Well, I'm sorry if that's confusing for you. We were friends. It does happen you know, even if it isn't good for ratings.'

'Right. Friends.' Mike drained the bottle of beer and placed it carefully on the side table. 'Friends in the way that Nicholas and Sam were her friends.' His eyes narrowed. 'Would that be the sort of friendship we're talking about?'

Andrew glanced at his watch. 'Look, Mike. Whatever you're insinuating, whatever muck you are trying to rake up, you'll have to look elsewhere I'm afraid. I am not your man. I have never been unfaithful to my wife. And I have no reason to believe that Amber was ever unfaithful to Dave.'

'Right.' Mike's head bobbed, he put his fingers to his

temples. 'That's what makes it so puzzling to me. The infidelity vibe, that scar that you glimpse every so often – the expectation of disappointment, the over-developed pride and self-sufficiency.' He pointed a finger at Andrew and then rested it against his chin. 'That's not what I'm getting here. Not exactly. And if it were just that, of course,' he raised his hands in a gesture of resignation, 'I'd be happy to let it go. More than happy to. But you see my problem? To me Lydia's behaviour implies some far greater hurt.' He gave a short, cracked laugh. 'If you were to tell me that Amber had stolen Lydia's child, now that would be in the ballpark.'

'My wife has no children to steal.' Andrew's voice was flat and low, the voice of a sleepwalker.

'Right. It's impossible, of course, but is there some reason why she should blame Amber for that – for your problems in that – area?' Mike was making small, soft tutting noises and staring into the distance. 'Clearly that would be illogical but . . . I dunno. Could it be that she felt Amber had come between you in the most fundamental sense? Preventing your – union – as it were. Am I sounding ridiculous now?' Mike stroked the nub of stubble with the tips of his fingers. He was watching Andrew, patiently, as if they'd been through all this before, many times, and they both knew exactly how it would end up. 'See, from my point of view, this isn't about catching anyone out.' He ran his thumbnail along the length of his bottom lip. 'It's about getting the pieces to fit. Imagine you were doing this job.' Andrew raised his eyebrows. 'Your job, then. You're a scientist, right? OK. You've done some research, and the results of your tests, they don't add up. Simple as that. You've done it all by the book, cross-checked the lot, and it's just slightly out. Now, this isn't a matter of life and death, it's the difference between, say, a pretty effective washing powder and an excellent washing powder. D'you see what I'm getting at? My job, like your job, is to get it right, so that I can say I have made the as near as damn it definitive life of Amber Best; not the fans' version, not the family-viewing version, but the real story. I just want the truth, Andrew.'

'Very convincing.' Andrew jiggled one leg impatiently. 'Until the truth gets a bit too ordinary for you, until old friends really do turn out to be just that. Look' – there was an exasperated edge to his voice now – 'my wife has had some disappointments to cope with, and sometimes she focused her disappointment on Amber. You see it all the time: people who are successful or celebrated are magnets for other people's insecurities, and Amber was no exception. That wasn't her fault. She took a lot of trouble not to let it – affect our friendship.'

'So, she felt responsible in some way for Lydia's unhappiness?'

'No! I—' Andrew ran his hands through his hair. 'The point is . . . if things had worked out differently for us, I really believe they could have been friends.' Mike was nodding, barely perceptibly, willing him on. 'But it just wasn't to be,' Andrew's voice was running dry, cracking at the edges, 'and I bitterly regret that. I bitterly regret that someone who was such a good and true friend to me, who went to such lengths to consider my – situation – my happiness – should have suffered for that.' Andrew wiped his sleeve across his eyes and gazed out of the window. 'You think by raking through our lives you're going to discover dirt that goes all the way to the bottom. What if

you dug and dug and only found gold? What if you dug
and found a bedrock of love? That would fuck up the
plan, wouldn't it?'

Keeping his eyes fixed on Andrew's face, Mike reached
one arm behind the sofa. 'If it's all right with you, I think
we might start now,' he said. 'Just a bit of Handicam to
begin with.' He paused and gave Andrew a slow smile. 'I
think you're ready.'

Upstairs, in the room above, Lydia lay sprawled on the
bed, naked under her oyster satin dressing gown, one
arm curled around a crochet-trimmed pillow, the other
cradling an ice bucket containing a bottle of something
from Andrew's top shelf. It was not quite midday but she
was already dozy with drink and enjoying the sense of her
own decadence. A murmur of voices drifted up through
the floorboards; she couldn't make out what they were
saying but then she didn't need to. Lydia pinned her chin
to her chest and addressed the pillow. 'Don't you know
my wife has a drink problem?' she said, in a deep, sombre
voice. 'Can't you see, she doesn't know what she's saying?'
Then she tilted her chin and pinched her pale, freckled
nose between forefinger and thumb. 'Hey, Andrew, mate,'
Lydia giggled at the flat, nasal sound of her voice, 'would
I stitch you up? Would I harm the group?' She released the
fingers and dropped her chin again. 'Exactly what has my
wife told you, Mike? I demaaaaaand to know?' 'Oh, only
everything, Andy.' She squeezed her nose tighter. 'Stuff
that I didn't need to know, to be frank, right the way back
to the night you first got it together. And I must say, even I
was impressed. She's quite some little schemer, your wife.'

Lydia slumped back against the pillows, eyes closed, the wine glass balanced on her stomach. She remembered lying, just like that, stretched out on the sofa in her Islington flat, a tumbler resting on her bare midriff, the night she'd decided that Andrew would have to do. That hadn't been the plan at all four hours earlier. Andrew had only been asked to the dinner as a cover, so that Jeremy, the one she had earmarked as the answer to everything, wouldn't feel quite so – singled out. And Andrew was always useful for demonstrating the level of devotion she was capable of inspiring in men.

He had been the first to arrive, of course, hovering on the doorstep, holding a bottle of sparkling white wine. Seeing Jeremy coming up the stairs behind him, she had clutched Andrew to her breast for a moment before pushing past him into the hall, adjusting her hair with the flat of her hand.

'Thank goodness you're here, Jeremy,' she said, linking her arm through his. 'I think I might have been eaten alive otherwise.' She gazed up into his small grey eyes as if she could never fully repay him.

Jeremy looked momentarily confused, and then twisted round to look over his shoulder, slipping out of her grasp as he did. 'You've met Angela, haven't you?' he said, and Lydia turned to see a small dark woman standing in the shadow of the hall, peeking cutely from behind a large bunch of flowers.

'Cooeee!' she squeaked. 'Jem's told me so much about you.'

The flowers took fifteen minutes to arrange, once she'd found the scissors and peeled off the leaves and trimmed the ends. Andrew leant against the cooker watching her with an amused smile.

'Angela not expected?' he said.

She paused, a delphinium in one hand and a bit of foliage in the other. 'What do you think? And how bloody rude is it to bring the whole herbaceous border with you so that your hostess is stuck in the kitchen arranging them for the entire bloody evening.'

'Give me those.' Andrew took the scissors from her. 'Never mind. I hear Jeremy's had a pretty bad year.' She looked at him sharply. 'Put it this way, he finds himself suddenly smitten with the daughter of his biggest investor.'

Lydia wiped her hands on the towel by the sink and paused for a moment to take stock. She wasn't going to let this opportunity be wasted. She'd spent £100 on this dinner party – not including the cost of the button-through Ultrasuede skirt – money that she didn't have since Richard had withdrawn his backing for Sixteen Minute Sandwiches a few hours after announcing that 'It wasn't working out.'

'What do you mean?' she'd said, even as her body was packing its bags, freeze-drying her mouth, keel-hauling her stomach, draining the blood from her features.

'We're just not in the same place, Lyd,' he'd said, 'you're crowding me. You want kids and stuff. I can hear you ticking from here.'

'Oooh, I do not,' she'd said, looking as appealingly petulant as she could manage, 'not *now* . . . I want to have a good time, just like you, Ricky – I wanna live it up.' She'd waggled her shoulders and clicked her fingers to indicate just how ready she was, realizing as she did that she looked like someone's mother auditioning for a Cliff Richard film.

'Listen,' he'd said, staring at her fingers. 'It's been great. I just think, maybe you should find someone – you know – a bit more your own age.'

She knew when she was beaten, but she had managed to summon up the energy to leave him a goodbye note.

Fat Pig

Your mother rang and I took the opportunity of explaining to her why your sister's old school uniform is tucked away in the back of your cupboard. Also, thanks so much, again, for last year's thirtieth birthday party. Wasn't it a blast? Especially since I was thirty-five.

PS. Don't worry about your little quick on the draw problem. Only Derek at your office knows, and I told him to keep it really quiet. Kiss Kiss, or in your case buckets of slobber, buckets of slobber.

There must be some way she could salvage the situation. Lydia squinted through the kitchen hatch at her guests. There was David and Annette – David was a painter who specialized in dog portraits, even the clothes on his back were paid for by Annette's father. Then there was Geoff, talking animatedly to Jeremy. Geoff – he was doing well, obviously. Molly's accessories budget had ballooned over the last year and Geoff himself had started wearing those special glove-leather loafers that signal the transition from corridor bashing to the thick-pile cushioned world of the senior partner. She narrowed her eyes and tried to remember something useful about Geoff.

Racing, that was it, very keen, owned half a horse. Used to go out with Belinda Big Tits. She shifted slightly to get a better view of Molly.

'Molly's pregnant – apparently they're over the moon.' Andrew was holding the vase of flowers at arm's length and making for the sitting room. 'Where do you want these, Lydia?'

'Down Angela's front would be nice,' she muttered as he disappeared through the door to join the bunch of ineligibles who were about to munch and drink their way through her safety net. She stayed in the kitchen for a minute or two, watching them all through the hatch, absentmindedly chewing her thumbnail, before taking a pencil to the seating plan, scoring a line through Jeremy, on her right, and putting Andrew in his place.

'Well,' said Andrew, he was standing in front of the fireplace, the stub of a cigar smouldering between his fingers. 'I suppose I should—'

'Oh, don't go yet,' said Lydia. 'I can't bear everyone rushing off at the same time. Have another cup of coffee. Put the kettle on.'

When he had disappeared to the kitchen she checked her position. Yanking her hair loose she let it fan out on the arm of the sofa and then undid three buttons on her skirt so that the split exposed, or would do from where he'd been standing, a centimetre of glossy stocking top. The sofa routine was automatic, she had arranged herself like this a hundred times for a hundred late stayers, but this time the presentation was for Andrew: Andrew the short-sighted boffin, the rugby-playing twitcher, the only man she knew who polished his shoes, religiously, every Sunday night. She pressed a hand to her temple and closed her eyes.

'Have you thought of ringing Andrew?' She could see Jack, standing at the bus stop, a few weeks before, shielding her eyes from the morning sun. 'I mean, if it's all off with ... er ... Richard.' Lydia had rolled her eyes. 'When will you lot give up? He's a nice boy, but I could no more – he's not man enough for me, all right? Let's just leave it at that.' Jack cocked her head inviting Lydia to elaborate. 'OK then, he's too straight, he's too clean, he's too predictable,' she was itemizing the list on the fingers of one hand, 'he's too *good*. His idea of living it up is a morning of DIY followed by an afternoon of rugby. Not to mention the fact that he clearly doesn't know one end of a woman from the other.'

'That's not what Anna says.'

'Anyway, what are you – his agent?'

Jack hauled up the collar of her coat and wriggled down inside it. 'No. It just seems a shame, if you haven't got anything more – pressing on the go.'

Lydia sighed and shuffled her feet like a penguin adjusting its egg. 'Look, I wish he was my type. I really do. I don't seem to be getting very far following my instincts. But I need someone with a bit of, you know, ambition. A bit of money, and influence—' She caught Jack's eye. 'All right, Richard was a mistake – but at least he was the sort who's going places.'

'Just because Andrew is a scientist and wears glasses doesn't make him a loser, Lydia. It's people like him who are making people like *Richard* obsolete. He's the future.' Jack blew on her hands. 'When did you last see him anyway?' Lydia shook her head and looked at her watch. 'It's just that Amber was saying he's really sort of – blossomed – recently, got a lot more confident.'

'Thanks, anyway,' Lydia said. 'I'd better get going – hope your bus turns up.'

She had been ten yards down the street when Jack called after her. 'You know Vigicom is being floated next month?'

Lydia frowned. 'So?' she'd mouthed, raising her palms to the sky.

'Well he invented it, didn't he? He's going to clean up. And, by the way,' Jack stood on tiptoe for the benefit of the onlookers in the queue, 'you don't deserve him.'

'What's on your mind?' Andrew was bending over her with a mug of steaming coffee. 'You look . . . I think conflicted is the word.'

'Do I?' Lydia smiled sheepishly. 'Oh, I won't have any, after all. Here, come and sit down beside me.'

'That's OK, I'll hover.' He wandered back to the fireplace and set the mug on the mantelpiece. 'You know, I could get a real fire going here, if you want, some time.'

'Could you, Andrew?' she said, and gave him the look she had wasted on Jeremy earlier. 'That's what I love about you, you're so . . . resourceful. Tell me, what's all this I hear about Vigicom.' She arched an eyebrow. 'Have you been terribly, terribly clever?'

'I didn't know you were interested in my work, Lydia.'

'Of course I am.' She pouted prettily. 'I'm just ignorant that's all. Just scared of making a fool of myself.'

'Well,' Andrew looked at his feet, 'er . . . well – Vigicom – it's a new kind of information technology, to do with microtec points.' He glanced up, Lydia was examining the ring that Richard had given her for her 'thirtieth' birthday. 'It will – in a nutshell it allows you to see through someone else's eyes . . . so . . .'

'And this is your – invention?'

'I had something to do with it.'

Lydia breathed in deeply, allowing the split in her skirt to drift ever so slightly. 'How wonderful,' she said.

'We do have great hopes for it.' Andrew grinned. 'It has enormous potential for educating people on the ground, in Third World countries. If you think of the possibilities in the area of something like irrigation, if you had one Vigicom in every village—'

'Sooo.' Lydia stretched her arms above her head as if the Vigicom effect were raining down on her there and then. 'I hope they're going to reward you for this . . . miracle?'

'Yes, I'll do well out of it,' he said, matter of factly. She blinked at him. The fringe would have to go, it made him look like a Scout leader, and the tweed jacket, and the hideous watch. 'It was a present from my mother,' he said, smiling. 'Not quite the business, is it?'

Lydia laughed, merrily. 'Oooohhh, I'm sorry, was I staring, Andrew? It's just, I'm seeing you in a new light, that's all. Sometimes you can know someone forever and never really appreciate their – value. Don't you agree?' She felt strangely nervous. He wasn't playing along according to plan. For a start he was still over by the fireplace, still looking her in the eye, as opposed to feasting on one of the other areas she was offering up on an Ultrasuede-coated plate. And it was almost as if he was deflecting her advances – though it was common knowledge he had dreamt of an opportunity like this since the day they first met – almost like there was something else he wanted from her. Oh God, she thought, I get it. It isn't going to work for him unless I pretend to be the girl he first fell in love with: the girl with the ponytail and the red duffel coat and the knapsack full of D.H. Lawrence.

'You know, I've still got that old duffel coat somewhere,' she said, scrunching up her nose. 'Funny, but even now there's nothing that feels quite so . . . me.'

Andrew glanced over at the coat rack, sprouting faux-fur jackets and picture hats; his mouth twitched.

'Let's dance,' she said, refusing to meet his eye. 'You always liked me dancing. Let's dance to something that brings it all *flooding* back. Mmmmm. We can imagine we're in your cottage at university, and it's a hot summer evening, and we've got all the time in the world and everything ahead of us.' She swung her legs off the sofa and made her way across the room in the direction of the stereo, swaying her hips rhythmically in anticipation.

'You don't have to do this, Lydia, not for me,' he said.

'Oh, but I do.' She peeked at him over her shoulder. 'Because I haven't always been as nice as I might have – But now we've got something to celebrate: your new success and my new . . . *awareness*.' She turned back to the stereo, closed her eyes and breathed deeply. How much was enough to make this worthwhile? What if the money was all tied up? What if the Vigicom fortune was all in Jack's head? Someone like Andrew's definition of 'do well out of it' could mean anything. It could mean time to wallpaper the bathroom or splash out on a barbecue. She thought of the bottle of sparkling white wine he had brought. 'Oooh dear, someone's Tombola winnings,'

Jeremy had whispered to Angela loud enough for them all to hear. 'Any plans then, Andrew?' Her back was still turned to him. 'I mean now that you're a whizz kid – a holiday or something?'

'I thought I'd take a couple of weeks.'

'Oh?'

'In Wales, do some walking.'

'Ahhhh.' Lydia pursed her lips and drummed her nails very lightly on the CD case in her hand.

'It's very beautiful now, good for bird watching.'

'Mmmm.' She closed her eyes and put her hand to her mouth in a stage yawn.

'And I want to buy my mother a house.'

'Really?' Lydia flipped the CD case shut and slammed it back on the shelf. This was never going to work. Not a chance. Even if he did make millions he was always going to spend it on somebody's mother, somebody's Third World problem, some pair of fucking binoculars. She might be desperate, she was desperate, but not so desperate that a scientist with a social conscience and a crush on her pre-adult self was going to make the difference. Lydia spun around and smiled sweetly at him. 'You know,' she said, 'I think the music might wake the neighbours after all, and it is late. Perhaps—'

'I've also made an offer on a house right on the edge of the common.' Andrew dumped the stub of his cigar in the ashtray. 'It needs a lot of work, but it's big, it's got a garden, bit of a stream even, and it could be really something – with the right person in charge of it.' He rubbed his hands together and plunged them into his pockets. 'Look, Lydia, I'm not going to mess around. I know I've never cut it in your eyes. But things are going pretty well for me now, and I've finally got the resources to make you happy. There's plenty there, you can see the statements if you want.' She was staring at him with an expression of curiosity and amazement. 'And, well, things have changed, for both of us. I've got something else to offer, besides my unconditional love' – he grinned – 'and I think – it seems like you might be more prepared to give me a chance.' Andrew paused while Lydia, who had edged her way back across the room without taking her eyes from his face, lowered herself onto the sofa as if it were made of glass. 'The thing is,' he knitted his hands in front of his mouth, 'I don't want to waste any more time. We've both done enough of that, in our separate ways. I know this is a bit direct, but I just wanted to skip the . . . preliminaries.' He crossed the floor and sat down beside her. 'I don't need to be seduced, Lydia. I've been crazy about you since I was nineteen, remember? And I don't want you to have to be that person with me either. You think that's what makes you desirable, but not to me. It's who you are – it's Lydia. The real Lydia.'

She wanted to ask him what he meant, who he meant, but instead she stretched out a hand and touched his hair lightly. 'So what happens now?' she said.

He laughed. 'Well, I hadn't got that far to be honest – but I think the proper thing would be to go to bed and talk details later, don't you?' She nodded, cautiously. 'And don't worry,' he said, 'I'll revert to Mr Predictable in the morning.'

*

'Lydia, wake up, darling.' Andrew was bending over her. The fringe had gone, the tweed jacket, the glasses, he was thinner in the face, a little grey around the temples and wearing a rather flattering chalk-blue shirt. 'I was day-dreaming,' she said, putting a hand up to shield her eyes, 'about the night you came to dinner and never left. D'you remember? The night you said that nothing else mattered so long as you had me.' She reached a drowsy hand up to touch his face. 'You were so sure, I think I almost believed you.'

Andrew straightened up and walked over to the window. He ran his hands through his hair and glanced at his watch. 'Look, do you want me to cancel Dr Hayley? We could always make it another day, if you're not feeling up to it.'

Lydia smiled. 'Ooooh no, no. I'm up to it.' She pushed herself up on the pillows and sat for a moment, her hair falling over her face, the satin dressing gown gaping open. 'What time is it?'

'Three o'clock. We've got half an hour to get to the hospital.'

'I can't think why you're even coming.' She reached for the cigarettes on the bedside table. 'You must have had a word with them in private, surely. You must have told them that *you* are the baby-making half of the couple, and *I* am the sad, bad, mad, dipsomaniac half. The one who's cocking the whole thing up, so to speak.'

'Lydia, please.' Andrew's back was to the bed, she could see the muscles in his neck tensing. 'You mustn't talk like that.'

'*Mustn't*. Why not? Why should I let you pretend that this is the same for you when we both know that it's all about humouring me?' She forced a hard bark of a laugh. 'As far as you're concerned a child would be a bonus, something to shut me up. But it's not a big deal to you, is it? *Is* it?' She banged her hand on the pillow, forcing him to turn around and look at her, 'because you've already got what you want, Andrew, *haven't you?*'

'Come on, Lydia.' His voice was gentle. 'We can still make it if we hurry. I'll get you a cup of tea.'

She watched him walk towards the door through the tangled curtain of her hair, his head was bowed as if he were hoping to find something he'd lost on the parchment carpet.

'Andrew . . .' her voice was barely audible.

'Yeah?' He turned around, he was smiling, ever hopeful.

'I'm sorry.' There were tears in her eyes. 'I'm sorry I let you marry me.'

Thirteen

'Mandi.' Lorraine addressed her in the mirror that ran the length of the salon. 'Your four o'clock's 'ere.' She blew a pink sticky bubble, keeping her eyes fixed on the mirror, poised for her boss's reaction.

'Ta.' Her eyes flicked up to meet the junior stylist's and back to the client's head. She picked up a section of hair and scrubbed at it with the teeth of the comb, getting it to stand in a stiff matted peak. In the background the radio was playing 10CC's 'I'm Not in Love'.

'And that's for all the girls at The Final Cut in Basildon,' said a creamy voiced Tony Blackburn, 'this week's *number one*. Fabulous song. Fabulous *echo*.'

'Oi, Mandi.' Julie was standing two stations along from her, waving a yellow Marigold-gloved hand in the air. She was wearing a short black skirt, a black waistcoat with the words 'Martin Anderwurst's Inspiration' etched across it in rhinestones and a name tag that read Julie Elder, Stylist and Colouring. ''Ere your Blumfeld's been on the blower,' Julie said, thrusting a tray of mango and passion fruit slices in her direction. ''E wants us for the cover of *Lar-Mode*. I said, "You'll 'ave to ask Mandi, she's the boss." He said, "Owdyoumean?" I said, "The Boss of The Salon, a course." He said, "But that isn't possible.

She's a senior Bondi Sacs employee!" I said, "Suit yerself, but I only get every other Saturday off, cover or no cover." '

Beyond Julie's shoulder Amanda could see Troy, beckoning frantically to her, and jabbing a finger in the direction of his newly arrived client. 'Take a look at my lady,' he hissed when they were huddled together by the tropical fish tank.

Amanda glanced over at the gunmetal bob and her stomach lurched. It was Davina.

'Quite,' said Troy, pursing his lips. 'What to do? She's already *done*. I thought maybe some frosting through the middle and then a bit of a flick up. She says to me, "Sounds raaarthar mid seventies, don't you think?" I says, "I should hope so, *modom*, it is bloody 1975." ' He rolled his eyes. 'Anyway, *it* wants a second opinion – specially requested you, Miss Mandi White.'

Her throat felt constricted, her mouth was dry and her head throbbed. 'No I can't,' she croaked. 'I know her – she's a magazine editor, my arch rival. It's a long story.'

Troy widened his eyes. 'I should think it is since the nearest you've got to magazine editing is ripping out pages of *Honey* in the ladies toilet.'

'Troy, please . . .' she moaned, pressing herself into the corner. 'You have to get me out of here. She can't see me like this.'

'Like what?' said Troy, giving her the brisk once over. 'All right, the perm's a bit limp, but—Oooh look, whatd'-youknow? She's talking to your fiancé, Gary.'

'Amanda!' Davina was waving gaily at her from across the room. 'Or can I call you Mandi now? How delightful it is to meet your other life, at long last. I just had to call up a few friends and tell them to come right over and take a look.'

'You should stay a bit, Mrs . . . er . . . Davina,' said Gary. 'Fridays there's a special offer on: bleach 'n' a Babycham.'

'Oh this is just *puuurfect*,' said Davina, 'just as I'd always pictured it – the suburban salon, the bad perm, the fiancé who works in a furniture warehouse.'

'World of Leather,' said Gary, plumping out the giant knot of his tie.

'Who have you rung, Davina?' Amanda said, unable to disguise the panic in her voice. 'Who's coming here to see my other life?'

'Mandi, love.' Gary stretched out a hand crenellated with gold plated rings. 'About the wedding – Darren says he can do us a special on the cake if it's mandarin and lime.'

'I was only eighteen,' she shouted, although no one was listening. 'I didn't marry him, did I? I got out, didn't I? I was only eighteen and I didn't know any better.'

'Oooh charmed, I'm sure,' said Troy. 'Pleasure to have known you too.'

'Now, now.' Davina stood up, and suddenly her waist was level with Gary's head. 'No bickering. Not when there are important people here to see you, Mandi.' Davina gestured with a blood-red fingernail towards the salon door where Amanda's mother-in-law, Bridget, was standing, arm in arm with Mark Blumfeld.

'Well,' said Bridget, 'so much for the fashun degree. Of course, *I* was never taken in, not for one *moment*.'

'Seems you're in denial about a lot of things, Amanda,' said Blumfeld, waggling a finger in her direction.

'There's more?' said Davina pressing her fingertips together. 'Oh, do tell!'

'Nicholas, darling, I think you should hear this.' Bridget marched over to the product store cupboard, flung open the bamboo doors, and out stepped Nicholas, brushing down his new Ogilvy & Harbourne grey flannel suit.

'Oh, for fuck's sake,' she said. 'You can't *all* be here. This is ridiculous.'

Bridget and Blumfeld glanced at each other and raised their eyebrows in unison.

'Vulgar,' said Bridget, 'they never lose it.'

Nicholas stared straight ahead, and adjusted his cuffs.

'Who gave you those cufflinks?' she shouted at him. '*She* gave you those cufflinks, didn't she, on our wedding day? They're inscribed with your pet initials, aren't they?'

Nicholas looked blank. 'Does sound familiar, Squidge,' he said. 'But aren't you thinking of someone else?'

'Who could blame him?' said Mark Blumfeld. 'Who could blame him for seeking solace from a woman who appreciates a *man*?'

'Who could blame him?' said Bridget. 'If he needed someone he could talk to. One of his own kind.'

'Shut up!' she shrieked. 'You make me sick. What are you all doing here in my old life, you *arseholes*.'

'Mummy?'

Amanda shot up in bed, gasping. Ludo was standing a few feet away from the bed wearing a white pith helmet and dark glasses.

'Ludie?' She clutched at her throat and blinked rapidly to check if she was really awake. 'Mummy was just having a bad dream, darling, that's all. Nothing to worry about . . .' Her eyes scanned the room for reference points. Martin Anderwurst dress hanging on back of bedroom door, good, good, though strange dipping at the hem; one half full tumbler of something . . . green . . . uurr; alarm clock reading . . . 10.30 a.m.! Fuck! 'How long have you been standing there, Ludie, sweetheart?'

'Hours,' said Ludo. 'One hour, probably.'

She peered at him from under her hand. 'Darling, take those glasses off, they're Mummy's.'

'So? Sharing.' Ludo continued to monitor her silently like a Guyanese traffic policeman.

'Not sharing *Gucci*.' Now that her heart had stopped racing the blows to the head were kicking in and the rolling high seas stomach. For a moment she thought the bed was moving. 'Ludie . . .'

'Nooooo, Mummy. I need them for bein' Dennis Finch Hat On.' Flying in the face of his peers, Ludo's current number-one video was *Out of Africa*, followed by *Gone With the Wind*. 'I just don't get it,' Nicholas would say. 'I mean you'd have to actually pay me to watch that rot, and he's five years old. Do you think he's spending enough time with boys his own age? Darling, I don't want you taking him to any more fashion shows.'

'All right, Ludie, just bring Mummy the waste-paper basket,' she said. 'And then go and get Riva.'

Riva appeared in the doorway of the bedroom, moments later, looking as if she'd won the lottery. 'Oh wow!' she said. 'I bet this hurtink. I have never see women drink like this.'

'Well, stick around,' croaked Amanda, 'and could you

please get me the bottle of pink stuff from the bathroom cupboard, now.'

'I harve it.' Riva waved the bottle at her and started to unscrew the top. 'Nicholas, he say "Leave them to it, Riva, they on a benter. You sleep in spare room tonight." '

'What was wrong with your own room?' Amanda was pressing her temples with as much force as she could muster.

'Nothink. Only you and uzer lady you come in an out, in an out. Lookink for cigarette, whisperink, knockink over, bangink – and playink music very loud. Here, open vide.' She parked a spoonful of Pepto Bismol up against Amanda's lips, Amanda did as she was told. 'You vish Alkar Seltzer also?'

'Everything,' said Amanda.

Riva retreated to the bathroom again, still talking over her shoulder. 'Nicholas say he never see this lady before. He say she must be ol' friend, from very history. An' you know viy he sink this?' Riva paused for effect, eyes wide. 'Because you get tosting sanvich maker,' she spoke very slowly and deliberately now, to emphasize the freakishness, the one in a million chance of this actually happening, 'old tosting sanvich maker, from out of garage cartboard box, and you making sanvich – lot of sanvich. Like – horrible. Vis jam, an pickle an egg an *Crispes*, all crunch up.'

'That's enough,' said Amanda, beckoning for the waste-paper basket which she nestled against the pillows next to her, like a favourite pet.

'Is incredible you no voamit. You have also green drink, vis cherry drink.' Riva folded her arms and snapped her head to one side. 'So, anyways, Nicholas, he take Cass to school, also rink office and say you come in late.' She paused and gave Amanda one of her penetrating 'not in my country' looks, her 'you may have the cash but boy you lot haven't even got off the blocks when it comes to class' looks. 'You know I nayver think you this kind of woman, Amandair,' she said, narrowing her eyes. 'Disco dance an' sinking an' everythink. Is surprise to me ack-sherley.'

'Well, that's the thing, Riva,' said Amanda, speaking into the waste-paper basket now. 'You just never know with people, do you? Now, how are you at fry-ups?'

Amanda was at her desk by 12.00, Gucci sunglasses clamped to her face, emanating an aura of detachment induced by prescription-strength painkillers. 'Martin, Christa, Tiziana,' – her assistant, Mitzi, was running through the flower arrangements dotted around the office, jabbing at each of the vases in turn with the point of a silver-plated pencil – 'cactus thing's from Peace, the roses are Lily Lister, big one's from Blumfeld.' Amanda waved a hand at her. 'Right.' Mitzi flipped open her leather jotter. 'I'll just keep a record of the cards then, and get any others distributed round the office as they arrive. Couple of phone calls this morning. Dr Magda, saw you on the telly last night, and thinks you should come in . . . er . . . make an earlier appointment to see her . . . um . . . Blumfeld wants to fix up a meeting as soon as. Cass's school rang. They want to have a word . . . and someone called Julie, says, "Thanks for last night and looking forward to the party and so is" I think she said, "*Troy*"—' Mitzi broke off to answer the phone on her desk, which was positioned like a checkpoint just outside the smoked-glass doors of Amanda's office. 'Martin for you,' she said.

Amanda made a beckoning motion with her fingers. 'Hello.' Her voice was now a gravelly whisper.

'HEL-LO number one editor!' She thought she could feel the earpiece vibrating. 'How does it feel to be the Queen of the Scene? Just wanted to say you rock, and can't wait for the pardee.'

'Party?'

'Ignacio is made up that you've asked him to DJ.'

There was a shuffling sound on the end of the line and Ignacio's falsetto pierced her consciousness like silver foil on metal fillings.

'A-Man-Dar – Oh . . . is *unspeakable*, really is like spectacule for me . . . weeeeee . . .' Ignacio's voice faded for a moment as he flung his arms in the air, or maybe whirled the phone around his head, lasso style '. . . Whoa!' There he was, back in range, clear as a whistle. 'Is fabulous vibe this party, really fabulous. I'm really like gonna push it.' More shuffling.

'It's like a real boost for him,' Martin was on again, sniffing, 'you know, after all these immigration hassles.'

'When is . . . when exactly did we say, for the party?' Amanda's eyes were screwed tight shut and her head was undulating slowly from side to side.

Martin snorted. 'Yeah right, the Editor of the Year doesn't know when she's having the party of the year – two weeks tomorrow, babe! An' everyone is gonna be there.'

'Why – why am I having it so soon?'

'Earth to editresssss! Becaaaaaause everyone is in town for . . . something, I forget.' A lot of banging and rattling

231

on the line suggested Ignacio had attempted to grab the receiver and been repelled, after which he resorted to shrieking in the background 'AM-AN-DAR, YOU HEAR? Maybe Martin is makin' you an' your Joooleee some *fabulous matching leather outfit* – really nasty, spiky, bitchin' . . . Ouch!'

'Whatever,' said Martin. 'But hey, by the way – respect – and we all understand your reasons for keeping it quiet until you were in a position to really do some good for the gay community. You know what though? I *always* knew.'

Amanda felt the need to put her head between her knees. 'You still there?' said Martin.

'No,' she said, 'I'll get back to you.'

Ten minutes and a litre of Evian later Mrs Elsworthy was on the line. 'Ah, Mrs Worth,' she said, in a tone that suggested she had wasted half her day chasing after Amanda. 'I'll get straight to the point, if I may. It's about Cassandra's history primer. It seems there has been a mix-up and Cassandra has come to school with another book.'

Jesus, thought Amanda, whatever happened to doubling up, £3,000 a term in school fees and they can't share a sodding history primer. 'Couldn't she have shared, Mrs Elsworthy?' she said, attempting to sound bright and resourceful before she was ambushed by a phlegmy coughing attack.

'That isn't really the issue.' Mrs Elsworthy pronounced the word iss-yew. 'No. It's the nature of the book that Sally, Cassandra's class teacher – ' ooooh definitely a hint of I'm-sure-you-won't-have-felt-it-necessary-to-commit-that-detail-to-memory-Mrs-Worth ' – that Sally felt she should bring to my attention.' Mrs Elsworthy paused. 'I believe the book is entitled, *Yes, He Is Having an Affair.*' Amanda felt her jaw swing open like a rusty coal hole. 'It has been covered in the same brown paper that we use to cover the children's text books so that, I'm assuming, explains the confusion. But since this situation has arisen, I felt it would be appropriate for us to meet and talk about the possible implications for Cassandra – Mrs Worth? Are you there?'

Amanda's whole face was scrunched up as if she was trying to reduce its surface area. 'Yes. Er . . . we're extracting from it. It's a self-help book that we – that I am considering running extracts from in *LaMode* – that's what it is.'

'Mrs Worth, the book incident is, in our opinion, merely confirmation—'

'You thought Nicholas was having an affair?'

'Confirmation, Mrs Worth, that all is not as well as we would hope in Cassandra's home life. Children do pick up the signs and then bring the problem to school with them – if not often this literally.'

Amanda made a sneery, clever-clever face at the receiver. 'Cass may be exceptional, Mrs Elsworthy,' she said, 'but she's not psychic. My husband doesn't even know that I know he's been having an affair, if indeed he was, if it's any of your business, which it isn't. She is only eight years old—'

'Seven.'

'Seven. And she is not listening at doors, Mrs Elsworthy. In fact—'

'Well, she seems to have been going through drawers,' Mrs Elsworthy hesitated, 'and she has found one or two things that have unsettled her. I do appreciate, Mrs Worth, that this is a very delicate—'

'What sort of things?'

'I think it would be best if—'

'What sort of things, Mrs Elsworthy?'

'Mrs Worth,' Mrs Elsworthy sighed deeply, 'may I suggest that you take the time to come in and see me.' She lowered her voice to a bedside murmur, 'I'm sure it will be the best solution all round. Shall we say this afternoon at four o'clock?'

'Thank you,' said Amanda. 'I'll pick up the book then, if that's convenient. I need to make my decision over the weekend.'

Mitzi was standing in the doorway of the office. She had restyled her hair, changed her shoes and added a canvas flower to her belt in the time Amanda had been on the phone. 'It's Davina for you,' she said, her eyes flicking from dipped to full beam, indicating that this call was, in her estimation, the one that proved Amanda had arrived.

'Put her through,' said Amanda, 'and then interrupt us in one minute exactly.'

'Amaaaanda.' Davina sounded close enough to make the hairs on Amanda's neck stand to attention. 'Terrific news. Thought I'd call, rather than let your florists over there screw up the order.'

'How thoughtful.'

'Jake tells me we're all invited to a *party*?' Amanda clawed frantically at the slurry obscuring her memory lens until a fuzzy image emerged of herself sitting on the lap of Jake Zimbalis, CEO Bondi Sacs, New York – wearing a hat. 'Jake and Rebecca, they were just *bowled over* by your – enthusiasm at the awards dinner. "What a girl that London editor is," they said.' Amanda could hear the note of amusement in Davina's voice, could picture Jake on the line from his suite at the Stanbury, relaying the night's events in his high-pitched Brooklyn whine: '. . . and that broad, Amanda Worth – Boy! Was she bombed! These Brits, they're like, "Forget the pint glasses, bring on the garden hose!" Jesus – and the teeth don't get any better. So, she says to Rebecca an' me – she's on my knee, at this point, and wearing Rebecca's *hat*, having yanked it right off of Rebecca's head, when it was like *sewn on* there – so she says, "Party! All come! To shelebrate. SSsssh not birthday . . . Noooo, just me top magazine person. Bring a friend! Bring a colleague! Bring the whole hundred and tenth floor of Bondi Sacs, New York, whydontcha?" So I say, "Whoa there Amanda. You mean Davina as well?" And she says – get this, "You can't shcare me, Mr Zimbalis. Davina may have been the toughest broad in the business, but things have changed, Misher Zimbalis, and I am, as of this moment, the hardest of hard-hearted, fashion bitches." ' At this point Amanda pictured Davina tilting her head back and giving one of her victory V laughs, more an expression of total control of her environment than actual amusement, before buzzing through to her secretary. 'Have Gillian change my ticket to London – I wouldn't miss this for the world.'

'Really Amanda – ' there was the sound of smoke being tightly exhaled on the end of the line ' – according to Jake, you were largesse itself.' Davina loitered on the first syllable of the word. 'And, of course, the date of your party is right after the big Letham's couture auction, so pretty much the whole team will be over in London anyway. It's just perfect.'

'Well,' said Amanda, 'I wouldn't go out of your way. It's just going to be a little, casual—'

'Oh, you! Everybody is talking about it – the scale of it, the celebrity count, the racy theme.'

Amanda was frantically scribbling notes on a ring-bound pad, ripping off the pages as she went and flinging them across the desk in the vague direction of Mitzi. The latest one read: Find out theme of my party, URGENT, and draw up guest list for 300 (crossed out) 400.

'What'll you wear?' She could hear the tip tap of Davina's cigarette holder, or was it the drumming of her nails.

'Oh, you know.' Off came another page: DRESS. Call Martin. NOW. Get Drawings sent.

'Say . . . Amanda?'

'Hmmm?'

'Is it true what they're saying?'

'No, absolutely not,' said Amanda. 'I'm not interested in women, never have been.'

There was silence on the end of the line and then a dry, strangled sort of laugh. 'Really? Well, well – and I was just going to ask you about Dr Magda screwing up Tiziana's facelift.'

'Excuse me for interrupting,' Mitzi's voice echoed on the line, 'I have an urgent call for Amanda on line two.'

'Of course you do.' Davina exhaled luxuriously. 'I look forward to hearing more on the big night. Goodbye for now, Amanda.'

'Byeee,' said Amanda. 'Fuck, fuck, fuck – FUCK!'

'Darling?'

'Nicholas?'

'Well, lucky for you, yes. What *is* the matter?'

'Among other things, other minor things like lives being destroyed, children's lives being torn apart.' – she

paused for breath. There was silence on the end of the line
– 'Among other things, Davina thinks I'm a closet lesbian,
and Blumfeld, and Martin – everyone.'

'Really?'

'Is that all you can say?'

'Well, I did warn you about that scary brown dress,
my darling, and there you go, I was right. Even fashion
people have their limit.' Amanda started knocking her
knuckles against her teeth. 'But Squidge, I wouldn't worry.
You'd have to be bi anyway, wouldn't you? Realistically,
because of the children and everything, unless they
think—'

'Nicholas—'

'Congratulations by the way, my little petal. You did
terribly, terribly well. I want to hear all about it later. Now
have you remembered—'

'Not much, but Riva filled me in.'

'No, I mean about mother coming down to the cottage
for the weekend.'

Amanda started scribbling furiously: Ring up Dr
Magda for repeat Mandrax. URGENT, Get Fludgate big
country pie in dish × 3. Buy WaxMac, my size, and twig
arrangements.

'Amanda?' Nicholas was sounding mildly anxious.

'Yes?'

'Have you got that? I know it's not ideal given your
condition, but we did make the plan months ago.'

'What will we do with her?' She was aware that her
voice was verging on the hysterical.

'Darling, we'll do what we do in the country. That's the
whole point of having a cottage with three spare rooms,
remember? We have people to stay, go for walks, go to the

pub – have a Channel X film crew tailing our every move.'
Amanda made a kind of trapped-mouse noise. 'Squidge,
you can't have forgotten *everything*? Dar-ling, they're
doing my slot this weekend, and then going over to do
some more of Milly, which is why you had to pick up my
new suit.'

Amanda's pen stabbed at the notepad: Send bike
URGENT Pick up Ogilvy & Harbourne grey flannel suit.

'Sweetheart, maybe you should come home and lie
down before we head off.'

'Please do not bully me, Nicholas, I am absolutely fine.
And, anyway, I've got lunch with Jack.'

'OK, good girl. Well, see you later.'

'Mitzi . . .' Amanda was waving the Send bike
URGENT message at the end of a rigid extended arm.
Mitzi appeared wearing a different cardigan and yellow
python court shoes. 'Did you get all the notes, Mitzi?'

'Apart from the twigs one. I didn't quite understand—'

'Uuurghhhh.' Amanda started scoring the pad with
wiggly dark lines. 'Like this. Like this. I need authentic
autumnalist arrangements. You know, berries and brown,
copper leaves, twiglets – things that look like they've come
out of the ground somewhere near bloody Avebury.' She
ripped the page out of the pad and handed the illustration
to Mitzi. 'There. When everything's here let me know. I
want to head off early.'

'Mmmm,' said Mitzi, dreamily. 'You lucky thing. A
weekend in the country, what bliss.'

'I know,' said Amanda. 'Lucky, lucky me. Now get me
a cab, I've got lunch at one thirty at the Rotunda.'

*

'It's a broken ankle,' hissed Jack, 'not a suppurating sore.'

Jack and Amanda were seated opposite each other at one of the tables lining the window side of the Rotunda, the ones that allowed you, counting pavement arrivals, a panoramic view of the clientele. Amanda pressed the sides of her sunglasses with French manicured fingertips. 'Well, it's offputting. If you won't swap places then at least put my bag in front of it.' Using the toe of her caramel leather slingback, Amanda guided her large quilted Chanel bag across the floor until it was just level with Jack's plaster boot. 'There. Now everyone's happier.' She gazed triumphantly around the restaurant as if fully expecting a burst of applause. 'When's it coming off, anyway?' Amanda raised the sunglasses, just far enough so that she could squint at the menu. 'Before your interview with Marcus Raven, I hope.'

'Yes, end of next week, but it's really itchy already.'

Amanda grimaced. 'So, has injury made the heart grow fonder?'

'Well, he has phoned, but he's been away, you see. That's what was so awful. He was shooting the Louis Louis campaign, the following day – only the biggest ad campaign of his career to date – and he spent the whole night in A & E, with me.' Jack sighed and rested her chin on the knuckles of one hand. 'He was sweet about it all though. He paid for the breakages and everything . . . the Chinese desk thing . . .' She fiddled absent-mindedly with the salt dish.

'The Chinese desk thing?'

Jack looked sheepish, mouthed the words 'free towzer round', and then shook her head distractedly.

'Free who?'

'Three thousand pounds,' hissed Jack. 'Three big ones. Anyway, I'm going to pay him back.'

'Don't be silly.' Amanda pushed the sunglasses back against the bridge of her nose. 'It's his fault for taking you to that sleaze pit in the first place. So, when are you seeing him again?'

'Tomorrow. He's taking me somewhere for the weekend.'

'Codrington House,' said Amanda, without missing a beat, Jack blinked, 'bound to be. Bluegrass Films are having a party there on Saturday night, so the young Brit Pack will be out in force. Well, don't look so dejected. You can do some networking on behalf of *LaMode*. Marcus will be there, I'm sure.'

Jack frowned and started drawing pictures on the table with her knife. 'Why couldn't he have taken me somewhere quiet and out of the way, where we could just be on our own, get to know each other.'

Amanda snorted. 'Jack, Simon is *hot*. You don't get hot in order to hide yourself away in some inglenook lounge of some nowhere country pub. If you want that sort of man you should be going out with Sam.' Jack rubbed the back of her neck hard and stared out of the window. 'Anyway, you think you've got problems.' Amanda raised her sunglasses, all the way up, and looked straight at Jack.

'Ooooh . . . allergy?' said Jack.

'Crème de menthe, cherry brandy and Michelob, apparently, on a Chablis base.'

Jack jerked her head back in astonishment. 'That's not like you. Editor's award go to your head then?'

'Sort of. It's a bit more complicated than that.'

Amanda took a gulp of her Bloody Mary. 'I was anxious about the award, of course, and then there was a bit of a misunderstanding with Blumfeld, which all got rather stressful . . . but' – she stretched her neck and tipped her chin up, glancing out of the window as if she scented danger – 'Jack, I think Nicholas has been having an affair.'

Jack stared at her.

'With Amber,' she said flatly, as if she had been rigorously coached to say the name without any inflection. Jack looked at her hands. 'It's not so implausible, is it? Not when you put two and two together.' Amanda kept staring out of the window. 'You know what's funny, is that even after everything we knew about her, it never occurred to me . . .' She pulled off her sunglasses and fumbled in her pocket for a handkerchief. 'I never dreamt she could do that to me. Pathetic isn't it really? The most desired woman in Britain, and I somehow imagined that being my friend would matter more than all that.' She slipped the glasses back on and held the handkerchief underneath the frames, to catch the tears that were now falling at quite a rate. 'Of course, Nicholas wouldn't have stood a chance once she set her sights on him. I don't imagine for a minute he could even see it coming,' she tried to smile, 'but how could she be so cruel? She knew what he meant to me. She didn't have to choose him.'

Jack reached across the table to grab her hands. 'I don't believe it,' she said. 'I just don't believe it. I mean I know there were some suspicious circumstances, but that's the part that doesn't add up. Your friendship. Amber wouldn't have risked it for anything.' Amanda shook her head, briskly. 'And she was so happy with Dave, and then there's Nicholas – I mean . . .' Jack waggled Amanda's hands between hers, ducking her head to force Amanda to look into her eyes, 'he's not exactly *obvious* affair material, is he? I don't mean that he's not – you know – but he's such a homey, contented sort of chap.'

'They don't divide up into shits and stayers,' said Amanda, gazing out of the window again, 'just ones who go looking for trouble and ones who wait until trouble finds them. And the ones who wait . . . it says in this book I've got that often men are unfaithful precisely because their wives and friends think they're incapable of it. It's called Pet Making. They start off thinking they're the hunter gatherer but then you treat them like the family hamster and the next thing you know . . .'

Jack wrinkled her nose in displeasure. 'It just doesn't ring true, Amanda. Nicholas is mad about you, he loves his life, he *likes* feeling like a hamster.' She picked up the knife and started drawing on the table again. 'Besides, Amber was sleeping with Sam.' Amanda sat back in her chair as if she'd been harpooned in the chest. 'Honestly, I saw them together. I'm pretty sure Lydia saw them too. And looking back on it, Channel X obviously knew – all those steamy glances over the compost heap, those innuendo-packed advertisements. I never said anything about it before because – I don't know, it seemed like an insult to Dave.' Jack took a deep breath. 'And, if I'm honest, I suppose I wanted to believe it was just a meaningless fling, for my sake too – selfish friend thing.' She looked up from the table and smiled at Amanda. 'Anyway, the truth is it must have been more than that. Neither of them would have risked it unless they were really in love, which is good news from your point of view because even Amber would have found juggling *three* men a little bit demanding.' Jack leant across the table and rested a hand on her friend's arm. Amanda looked exhausted, her skin was ash white against the black lacquer of her sunglasses.

'There's more,' said Amanda. 'If it were just an affair I think I could – Jack, he was seeing her even before we were married and,' – she hung her head – 'and Zelda is his child.'

Jack cupped her hands over her eyebrows as if trying to block out the thought. She shook her head from side to side. 'No,' she said. 'It's not possible.'

'That's what I thought at first.' Amanda's voice was lower, dragging under its burden. 'Even when I started to spot the physical similarities, I still held out some hope that I was wrong. But then I called Channel X, a few days after your dinner party, the one where Lydia was threatening to blow the lid on our sordid little secrets. I told them that they were to ease off, guessing that it was Nicholas she was onto.' Amanda attempted a chuckle. 'But they were ahead of me. Way, way ahead of me. They said, did I know anything about a wreath of flowers that had been sent to the church on the day of Amber's funeral? A wreath of wild flowers with a card that read, "To the best mother in the world", written in my husband's hand? Nicholas drew up the terms of agreement for the documentary, so they had a sample of his writing to compare it with. They must have been punching the air.' Amanda drained her drink and clasped the empty glass in both hands. 'Of course I told them that I would sue them to hell if they ever mentioned it again, and I have the card now, safe in a drawer. But you see there is no doubt. None whatsoever.' Amanda's mouth crumpled. 'The best mother in the world,' her voice was barely a whisper. 'That's quite something to have to see, from the father of your children.'

'But,' Jack searched Amanda's face for something to say, 'they can't have loved each other though. They can't have. Nicholas loves you.' She was aware that she sounded like a child, hopelessly at sea in an adults' game.

'No, Jack. He married me, that's quite a different thing.' Amanda raised a hand to attract the waiter's attention, making a squiggling motion in the air with her forefinger and thumb. 'I know you thought we were the original happy couple.' She smiled sheepishly. 'I did too, I suppose. But we're not so different from Lydia and Andrew, you see. Lydia thought Andrew could at least give her security and a family, and Nicholas . . . Nicholas thought I'd run his life smoothly for him. But that isn't enough to base a marriage on. And now look at us. Without children, they've got nothing, and without Amber, the person who made Nicholas's life with me bearable, we haven't got much more.'

'What are you going to do?' said Jack.

'I don't know. I've got this book, as I say, on how to save your marriage. I thought I'd keep on going and see what happens when I get to the end. Though of course they're assuming the affair started *after* you walked down the aisle, and there isn't a chapter on how to deal with his illegitimate children. There is one, however, on reconciling yourself with the other woman. Apparently it's pretty much always your best friend, either that or the girl at the office.' Amanda rubbed her wedding ring, examining it closely as if she hadn't seen it for a very long time. 'That's the other peculiar thing. I can't help feeling – only because she's dead of course – but I just can't help thinking that we could have sorted it out, somehow.' Jack nodded, tears gathered in her eyes and she wiped them roughly with the sleeve of her jean jacket. 'And it would have been nice to have had the chance to make Nicholas choose between us, finally, you know?' Amanda delved into her bag and handed Jack a tissue, and then another. 'Now for God's sake don't let yourself get all puffy, you've got quite a bit of ground to make up with Simon by the sounds of it.' Amanda eyed Jack's plaster boot.

'Well, maybe it's a kind of divine justice,' Jack grinned, 'as punishment for Amber never giving you the chance to have it out, her brother has to mix in the choicest circles with me and my boot.' She looked suddenly serious. 'What would she have thought of Simon and me, d'you think? Would she have approved?'

'God knows,' said Amanda. 'God knows what she thought about anything.'

Fourteen

Simon picked Jack up at 3.00 the following day in the American convertible. This time she was thoroughly prepared, wearing her navy peaked cap and carrying one small suitcase, purchased the day before as part of her strategy to become Together Woman – the kind who has a make-up roll, shoe bags and a manicure kit. Normally she would have embarked on a country weekend with a holdall, a plastic carrier containing her wash bag (damp), another one for her boots and trainers (muddy), and, finally, her rucksack-stroke-handbag.

'Hey,' said Simon, 'I like a girl who travels neat,' and kissed her on the lips, one sinewy hand cupping the back of her head, fingers hooked in her hair, so that she had to rifle in the rucksack for several seconds afterwards until the heat in her cheeks subsided. 'Missed you,' he said, slipping the car into drive. 'Wanna see the Polaroids from the shoot?' Keeping one finger on the steering wheel he reached behind him and grabbed a canvas bag, swinging it over the seats and depositing it on Jack's knee. 'Check the side pocket. Pick some music too, there's a load of CDs in there.'

The models were naked, body painted to look like logo-stamped robots, and wearing Louis Louis accessories in unlikely places: watches around throats, shoes on hands, bags balanced precariously on heads. At the back of the pocket were the obligatory snaps taken during the preparation for the shoot, the sort Simon would one day soon assemble in a book called *Access All Areas*, or *Backstage Bites*. There was one of Wanda, smudge-eyed, gazing into the lens cheek to cheek with a tiny, white chihuahua, another of Peace in a G-string, her naked breasts being spray-painted silver by a man with hip-length dreadlocks. In the picture her nipples were roughly level with her armpits. Jack's hand sneaked across to the equivalent place on her anatomy, and using her thumb as a measure, she started to mark out the distance to her own – one inch, two inches . . .

'Like 'em?' Simon's voice made her jump. 'Pretty hot, right?' He sparked up his Zippo lighter on the faded thigh of his jeans, flicking his head to get the fringe out of his eyes, and lit the cigarette that had been dangling between his fingers since he'd picked her up. 'Whassup?' The cigarette fingers stroked her wrist.

'Sorry.' She'd been staring again. 'You're . . . *they're* . . . Sorry, they are fabulous . . . Really. I love the body paint.' Simon drew hard on his cigarette, and nodded his head rhythmically as if appreciating a piece of unfamiliar music. 'I'll pick a CD, then,' she said, unzipping the bag and rifling purposefully through its contents. Corex was near the top, then there was something called Antarax, then something unidentifiable, just a plain red cover.

And then – she dipped her hand into the bag and pulled out a dull yellow album cover, slipped the record out of its cardboard sleeve and onto the turntable floating at arm's length in front of her, and the sun bounced off the shiny black vinyl and Simon's long black hair fluttered against the nicotine-coloured wool of his Afghan coat and she rested her denim platform boots up on the dashboard of the Jensen, felt her embroidered dungarees digging into her hipbones as the words of the song washed over them, '. . . I packed my bags last night, free flying, zero hour 9 a.m., and I'm gonna be highiiiiyiiy as a kite by then . . .' And then they were singing together, belting out the words into the warm wind rushing over the bonnet, '. . . and I think it's gonna be a long long time till touchdown brings you down it's much too fine . . .'

'Are you singing?' Simon's hand was on hers, on top of the bag. 'What were you singing, babe?'

'Um . . . nothing. I was . . .' His eyes were on the road, a fraction of glittering blue just visible if she turned her head to look at him. 'I was thinking, how different it was when – when there were just a few records that everyone had and everyone loved.'

Simon was chewing something, his arm trailed across the back of her seat. 'Like what?'

'Oh, I don't know – Honky Chateau, that kind of thing.'

'Yeah, right.' He chewed harder, checking his rhythm in the rearview mirror, his fingers just brushing the back of her neck. She could smell Eau Sauvage, mixed with the wet dog of his Afghan coat, see his lips mouthing, 'I'm not the man they think I am at home. Oh no, no, no . . .'

He flipped a CD out of the bag. 'Well this is on another level – you're gonna love this.'

With one hand he manoeuvred the disc out of the case and into the slot, teasing the volume control up to eight.

There was a sound like icepicks dragging on sheet metal, a wailing of sirens mixed with babies crying, and then he leant over, cupped her head in his hand, and kissed her. Jack closed her eyes and her head was filled with silver light and the sound of Elton John singing, 'I'm a rocket maaan. Rocket maaan . . .' just as she remembered it.

Codrington House was a Georgian country house that had been bought by an Internet millionaire in the late nineties, and turned into a hotel catering to the affluent Londoner looking for a change of scene, without any deviation from their lifestyle. The Codrington catch-phrase, for those few who were interested in reading the literature provided in the ostrich-leather folder, was High Style and Green Grass ('the de luxe metropolitan experi-ence transplanted to the depths of the Wiltshire countryside'). It had been a gamble, so Max, the manager, told them as he led the way up the bleached oak staircase to their first-floor room. 'But straight off we got the right clientele, and that's the whole battle in this business.' He turned to address Jack for the first time since they had arrived. 'Get a few players like Simon here, and the rest will follow like lemmings. Then again, we've got exactly what these boys are looking for, isn't that right, Si?' Max planted both hands on Simon's shoulders and started to knead them vigorously. 'All righty – Here we are.' He released his grip and flung open the double doors ahead of them. 'The Barcelona suite, best in the house, naturally. All mod cons. You've got your mood-sensitive lighting – ' Max flicked a lever causing the giant bed, on its buckskin-leather platform, to be bathed in a Steradent-pink light ' –

all colours for all eventualities. Your liquid screen. Seventy-eight channels. Hot tub on the terrace. Aaand' – he gestured with a flourish to the far end of the room – 'the roll-top bath. Or, alternatively, there's the double bath in the next room, if you're looking for that little bit more privacy.' His lips parted to reveal a millimetre of shiny capped teeth. 'Well, you know the ropes, Si, mate.' Max rubbed his hands together and raised his eyebrows in anticipation. 'Ask and ye shall receive.'

Simon wandered across the black varnished floor, stepped up onto the leather platform, and flopped backwards onto the bed, hands clasped behind his head.

'Tell you what . . .' Max took this as an invitation to offer some direction. 'If you're in the mood for a party there's a fantastic crowd in tonight. Big, big scene. All the Bluegrass guys, Marcus and Bea, the Brodie sisters, really great crowd. If you wanna join them – no problem whatsoever.' He paused for a reaction, Simon continued to lie staring up at the mirrored ceiling, his biker boots snagging the cashmere throw at the end of the bed. 'Right! Soooo.' Max glanced at Jack. 'Tell you what. Why don't you just go with the flow? We can fix you up with something to put you in the party mood, if you're interested. Baz is delivering early evening . . .'

Simon raised a hand in the air. 'Count me in for two – make it three,' he said, still gazing at the ceiling.

Max flicked a couple of thumbs in his direction. 'Consider it done, mate. All right then, I'll leave you to it. Anything you need just pick up the phone and ask for Vince, or myself.' Max gave an ironic bow and slipped out of the door into the corridor, smoothing down the sides of his hair with the heels of both hands as he went.

Jack checked that the door was closed behind him and then wandered over to the window. From here she could see guests arriving in their four-wheel drives, windscreen wipers thrashing at the light drizzle, and two couples making their way across the gravel towards the front door, directly beneath her. The women, both walking in a stiff, mechanical way that indicated they were wearing four-inch heels under their bootcut jeans, were escorted by a short man in a black Chinese-style suit, struggling to shield them with a golfing umbrella. The men, who followed a few steps behind, were squat and well fed by comparison, with cropped silver hair and laptop bags slung over their shoulders. 'Oh, fuck.' The woman wearing the rabbit gilet spun around to address the stockier of the two men. 'I can't fucking believe it – I've left my yoga stuff behind.' The man paused and furrowed his brow, as if he knew from experience to dignify this type of observation with serious consideration. 'That's OK, babe,' he said, after a lengthy pause, 'we'll get you some more here, from the spa.' The other woman glanced at her friend to check if this was an acceptable reaction and then looked at her thumbnail. Rabbit gilet ran a hand through her creamy highlights, and threw her head back, appealing to the black skies above. 'You just do not get it, do you?' she said, the rock on her ring finger glinting in the light from the porch. 'You haven't got a fucking clue, have you?' Jack craned her neck to see the man's expression but was distracted by the sound of car doors slamming, out of view, and the scuffling of feet on gravel as two more black suits raced out to meet the new arrivals.

'Welcome, Mr Raven,' she heard one say. 'Pleasure to have you back, Mr Raven.'

'Well, thank you, Martin.' Marcus Raven's silky, measured voice, the voice animators had matched with a wise golden eagle and an organized-crime-proficient Burmese cat, drifted towards the house and, seconds later, the man himself wandered into view. He was a little shorter than she had imagined, a vision of de luxe casual in stone moleskin and biscuit cashmere, his glossy brown Eton crop bouncing at the roots as he walked. Clinging to his upper arm, as if they were on the deck of a foundering yacht, was Bea Lyle, fellow Young Brit actor and his girlfriend of six years. She was wearing a fur hat and a scarf covering her mouth and nose, but you could tell it was her by the legs in the leather trousers, legs that had been featured on the cover of *Time* magazine on account of her lower limb to body ratio being 1.5 times greater than the average. At the end of his other arm was a long lead attached to a big, grey, woolly-looking Dulux dog. As they approached the front door, the light from the windows caught the copper highlights in his hair; he glanced up at the house for a moment, breathed in the crisp night air, and flung his lead arm wide causing the dog to let out a yelp. 'The English countryside, nothing like it,' he murmured. 'What a relief to be out of those Hollywood hills, and back in the real world, you know?'

Martin nodded earnestly, raising the umbrella a foot or so to give Marcus more room for self-expression.

Bea hunched her shoulders and shifted from one foot to the other, despite the beaver fur jacket. 'Do they do in-room treatments here?' she said, addressing Marcus in the voice that evoked images of girls in gymslips and boaters and, of course, Freyburton Hot Chocolate. 'I really feel like I need a Salvador Special before the party.' She jiggled up and down on Marcus's arm making his hair dance and the muscles in his neck visibly tense. Behind them, their overnight bags were being loaded onto luggage trolleys: five suitcases, all of them monogrammed Louis Louis, two sets of golf clubs, two vanity cases and a giant leather dog basket stamped with the distinctive double LL logo.

Jack turned back to the bed where Simon was now lying propped up on one elbow, apparently editing film on a miniature camera. 'Do you think I need a Salvador,' she said, 'before the party?'

'What's a Salvador?' said Simon, without looking up from the viewfinder.

'You know – beauty thing.'

'Sure, go for it.' He slipped a hand into his back pocket, produced a credit-card-shaped piece of plastic and held it aloft, his eyes still fixed on the camera. 'Take the room card. Get your nails done too.'

Jack whipped the fingernail she'd been chewing out of her mouth and stuffed her hands in her pockets. 'No, that's OK,' she said, shuffling across the floor towards the door. 'I'll manage.'

'Hey! Simon lifted his eyes to meet hers, as she turned the handle. 'Glad you're here, babe.'

Jack nodded and waved cheerily, as if she were about to board a school train. 'Thanks,' she said, giving him the thumbs-up as she slipped out into the corridor. 'See you, then.' Once safely in the hall, with the door closed behind her, she stood very still for a moment, eyes screwed shut, fists clenched, pummelling the sides of her head. 'What are you *doing*?' she hissed under her breath 'Grow *up*. Be sexy. Be mysterious. What are you doing? That could have been it! And you . . . *uurgh*! What was the thumb thing? You are such a—'

'Excuse me, madam.' It was one of the Chinese suits. 'Sorry to interrupt . . . Shall I put this in the room for you now?' Jack looked down at his feet and saw her suitcase, her new black suitcase, with the black zip, which was now white along most of one side.

'Shit! Shit!' Jack pointed at the case, the Chinese suit's eyes flickered. 'Toothpaste! Look!' She bent over, ran her finger along the white portion of zip and then sniffed it. 'Yuurk! No! Bloody moisturizer! I don't believe it! Oh, my God. Right, er . . . just leave it here please.'

'Here, in the corridor, madam?'

'Yes, please. No, wait a minute.' Jack crouched down awkwardly, her plaster boot trailing out behind her like a rudder, dragged the suitcase onto the floor beside her and gingerly started to unzip it. 'OOOOhh shit. Shit!' She lifted the lid just far enough for them both to have a clear view of the pool of white fluid surrounded by red chiffon. 'Look at that! It's gone straight for the dress! Can you believe it?'

The Chinese suit shook his head a few times before surreptitiously glancing at his watch.

Jack looked up at him imploringly. 'We'll have to . . . it will have to be emergency cleaned,' she said, grabbing his sleeve for emphasis. 'At once. By your cleaning department,' she added when the suit failed to register that this had anything to do with him.

'I don't think we offer an express service,' he said, his eyes widening.

'Oh, fuck.' Jack started to bang her head on the lid of the case.

'You didn't have an alternative outfit?' His tone suggested this was an oversight on a par with, say, the queen forgetting her handbag. 'I was travelling neat,' said Jack. 'Look – are you going to help me out here or just gloat? What's your name?'

'Vince,' said the suit.

'Well, Vince, I am here to write a review of Colling . . . Coll . . . Codrington House, and this crisis is actually quite fortuitous, in one sense, because it gives me the chance to test your resourcefulness.' Vince's eyes skittered to left and right as if he was checking for an escape route. 'After all, that's what five-star service is all about in the end, isn't it? Going the extra distance.' Jack folded her arms across her chest. 'So, let's see what you're made of shall—'

'Whooooomph. There was a rush of warm air, the faint aroma of meat and a dog fell out of the sky, thwump into the middle of Jack's suitcase, where it lay panting, a G-string snagged in its collar.

'JeeeeeSus!' It was Bea, standing at the top of the stairs, still wrapped in the pashmina and now pressing it to her mouth as if they were under gas attack. 'Jesus, Marcus,' she shrieked over her shoulder. 'The frigging dog!'

'All right, darling.' Marcus swung into view and jogged past her over to the suitcase, marking time for a second before squatting down to Jack's level. 'Come on Santa, old boy,' he said, extending a smooth caramel hand towards the dog's collar. Santa bared his teeth and started to growl.

'Oh, Jesus.' Bea rested her forehead against the corridor wall. 'I told you, Marcus. That dog is an *animal*. Look at the state of her.' She flapped a hand in Jack's direction.

Marcus Raven removed a silk handkerchief from his trouser pocket, not unlike that moment in the scene on the verandah in *The Willoughby Legacy*, and proceeded to gently dab at Jack's cheekbone which had, apparently, been grazed by an airborne toenail.

'Forgive me,' he said, extending the caramel hand to Jack and fixing her with what had been described by one reviewer as his 'naughty patrician' gaze. 'Marcus Raven, I don't believe we've met.' Jack paused, convinced that he was going to kiss her hand. 'Er, Jack Farmer,' she said, 'and this is Vince.'

'Jack. How charming. I've always wanted to meet a girl called Jack.' Marcus let his hand linger on hers for a moment and then found he needed it to rearrange the droop of his half fringe. 'I am really terribly sorry about this. Our little dog is rather overexcited at being let loose in the country. Like me he misses it so very, very much.' A small strangled sound emanated from behind the pashmina.

'Oh, don't worry,' said Jack, struggling to get to her feet. 'I'm fine . . . the foot was done before. Don't worry, honestly.'

'But wait! Oh, my goodness!' Vince, who had been skulking on the sidelines since the dog incident, had stepped forward and was addressing them all in the over-enunciated monotone favoured by children in nativity plays. 'Just look at what damage the dog has done to the *dress*,' he said, pointing at the suitcase.

'The dress?' said Marcus, furrowing his brow fetchingly.

'Yes. Underneath the dog.' Vince gave Santa a shove with his foot, revealing a corner of moisturized chiffon.

'But—' Jack started to speak.

'Exactly!' Vince roared. 'Now madam's dress is ruined.' Marcus dutifully leant over the case for a closer inspection of the damage and Vince took the opportunity to give Jack a giant wink. 'Whatever is madam going to wear now?' he said, warming to his role and tossing in a bit of pantomime camp for good measure. 'Who on earth would have a spare outfit at this short notice?'

Marcus straightened up and snatched a nervous glance in Bea's direction. 'My darling,' he said, after a moment's hesitation. 'Bea, my love, may I have a word?'

The couple retreated a few paces down the corridor, Bea violently shrugging off Marcus's attempts to take her arm, and then stood in a huddle, their backs turned to Vince and Jack. It was impossible to hear what they were saying, though Jack thought she caught the words, 'If she sues . . .' which was confirmed by a sharp dig in the ribs from Vince, and then Bea said, quite clearly, 'this is the fucking limit . . .'. Marcus kept leaning into her, offering up his palms like plates and at one point he drew his finger across his throat, a gesture which prompted Bea to look up at the ceiling and tap her foot.

After what felt like several minutes, just as things were starting to look bad for the Vince plan, Marcus spun around and wandered casually back to the suitcase, hands deep in his trouser pockets. 'I'm so sorry. Just trying to work out the best way to . . . er . . . if there's anything we can do to make amends.' Marcus sucked in his lips and placed his palms together in front of them, just the way Dr Magnus Scott had when he was defending the serum, in front of all the doctors who didn't rate the serum, in *The Test*. 'Beatrice, my girlfriend,' he smiled, by way of acknowledgement that Bea clearly needed no introduction, 'is . . . um . . . would be very happy to sort you out with something wonderful from her own wardrobe.' Bea cleared her throat. 'Within certain limits,' he added, 'naturally'. Marcus leant towards Jack and lowered his voice. 'She has to be a bit careful, you understand. *Advertisers*.'

'Let's just get this over with.' There was something in Bea's voice that made Jack want to curl up in the suitcase, under the dog.

Marcus placed a reassuring hand on her arm. 'The thing is Bea can't *bear* to see people put out,' he said. 'She's one of those "let me fix it *right now*" people.' He bunched up his fist and tapped his sternum with it a few times. 'So, shall we adjourn, then, to our suite?'

'Five minutes,' said Bea, flicking past them. 'I've got a party to get ready for.'

As they reached the door of the suite two Chinese suits were just leaving, having distributed the contents of the Louis Louis cases in the fitted wardrobes lining either end of the main room.

'This is the Tiffany suite,' said Marcus, 'silver and blue, Bea's favourites – not to mention diamonds, of course.' Bea glared at him as if a condition of their pre-cohabition agreement had been no mention of diamonds under any circumstances. Then she sauntered over to her stretch of cupboards and prodded one of the doors which sprang open at her touch to reveal yards of gleaming clothing nestling on tissue-padded hangers. She stepped back, one hand planted on a thrust-out hip, the other holding the scarf in place over her mouth, and sighed heavily.

'What about the gold knitted thing, my angel?' Marcus

slipped an arm around her shoulders and gave them a supportive squeeze. 'That would fit the bill, wouldn't it?'

Bea closed her eyes very, very slowly by way of an answer and when she opened them, several seconds later, raised a finger to indicate that the selection had been made. 'Here,' she said, yanking a pair of trousers and a corset off one hanger and a whisp of chiffon off another and tossing them at Jack, 'these are the most . . . versatile.'

'But I'm . . .' Jack held the bustier up against her to demonstrate the shortfall. 'I'm so much—'

'Oh, you are soooo skinny,' shouted Bea. 'Don't be ridiculous.' She snatched the corset back and pressed it to her chest, striking a showgirl pose, one pointed foot resting on the other, to demonstrate how it was meant to look, if you were a size eight. 'And anyway, it stretches.' She dropped the corset into Jack's hands. 'All her stuff does – that's what's so fabulous about it.' As if the word fabulous had triggered her poster-girl persona Bea suddenly flashed Jack a photocall smile, all mouth and wrinkled nose. 'Really you should have one, they just accommodate all those extra lumps and bumps.'

'Well, I – I just wonder if there's any point,' said Jack, peering at the tiny amount of chiffon. 'Is this . . . ?'

'It's a dress, of course! Oh you! Now how many people do you know who'd turn down the chance to rifle through Bea Lyle's wardrobe? Darling?' She swivelled her head in Marcus's direction, keeping her eyes on Jack.

'None!' Marcus obliged. 'Maybe my parents.' Bea laughed delightedly. 'If you're not sure which to go for' – Marcus gestured to the adjoining room – 'why don't you pop them on next door. Won't take a minute.'

Jack headed obediently for the second bedroom,

pursued by Santa, who appeared to be deaf to Marcus's clicking fingers and thigh slapping. She closed the door behind her, placed the clothes on a side table, and then sank into the nearest chair.

'This is crazy,' she said out loud, 'I should just go back to the room and tell Simon what happened and – and he'd probably think it was hilarious.' Santa rested his head on Jack's knee and looked up at her dolefully. 'I bet he couldn't care less if I've got nothing to wear. "All the better," he'll say.' She sat there tweaking Santa's ear absent-mindedly and suddenly she had a vision of Rosa and CJ at the Corex concert and Simon holding CJ by the hips, at arm's length, absorbing the unbelievable rightness of her belt (was it the belt or the trousers, or the two-inch gap between her thighs?).

'Jesus Christ!' Bea's voice floated in, crystal clear through the open window – she must have been standing right by their window just a few feet away on the other side of the wall. 'I mean, *Jesus Christ*! What are you going to ask me to do next – adopt a refugee?'

'All right.' Marcus's voice was more distant. 'The dog can go at the end of the month.'

There was a crashing sound and the floor underneath Jack's feet vibrated.

'End of the month! End of the fucking weekend more like.' The boater had been substituted for an oily fishwife's headscarf.

'I've told you, Bea.' Marcus had moved nearer the window. 'The dog is good for business. We have got to scotch the no sex rumours, and Tristan says this is the easiest way.' Bea snorted. 'It's called associative something or other, apparently a dog is one step removed from a baby in terms of creating the right impression. It's all in that doctor thingummy – Franklin book.'

'Oh, bullshit.'

'Plus, it's good for my earthy image.'

'Good God! Who the hell believes you're earthy?'

'Women who shop at Kenop. The English Tourist Board, no less. I'll have you know *The Willoughby Legacy* increased tourism to west Dorset by twenty per cent last year. I am also the face of Waxmac, the country gentleman's coat of choice—'

'Oh, shut up. May I remind you the agreement was to carry on as we are, nice and cosy, for another eighteen months, during which time, and I quote, we would both "assist" and "enhance" *each other's* public image, in particular on the Hollywood and fashion party circuit. Well, this year I've done three freezing weekends with your lightweight schoolfriends, one Highland Games, two bloody miserable country weddings, a celebrity *golf* tournament in bloody Scotland, and what have you managed? A couple of fashion shows, and the tribute to Fanny Oppenheimer at the Met. Geoff says you're cramping my style, darling. He says you'd better buck up or we're in the market for a replacement Marcus. Who knows, maybe one who can combine a glamorous profile with the normal functions of a boyfriend?'

'Sweetheart, since there are only a couple of days in the year when you're not off games due to some surgical intervention or other—'

'Christ! I almost forgot. I've got to get Jilly to patch this mess up . . .' there was the sound of a mobile phone dialling, 'and go and check out the lighting downstairs, will you Marcus. I need pitch dark. Diffused candlelight, no more. I'm serious! I'll lose the bloody Roccome contract if this gets out.'

'Let's have a proper look at the damage then. Take off the scarf – come on . . . Tsssss! Ouch!' Marcus sounded genuinely pained. 'They look like a couple of bits of liver. What do they feel like?'

'Hot concrete.'

'Oooow . . . and those little spot things under the eyes, or are they blisters?'

'Just go and— Jilly? Hi. I need you to make that detour here.' Bea's voice was once again oozing daddy's money. 'Total . . . I don't know whether it was the Moxot or the acid peel, or the . . . well, the lot! Spots, discolouration, swelling . . . I couldn't hold a straw between them, put it like that . . . OK. OK. See you.' There was the clunk of a mobile being snapped shut. 'I mean it, Marcus' – Bea had moved slightly away from the window forcing Jack to drag her chair nearer the door – 'they, *we*, think I could do with a real man on my arm rather than Mr Anyone For Tennis.' Marcus made a spluttering noise in the background. 'Well, what was all that Cary Grant routine on the stairs? The old silk-handkerchief number. I mean give me a break. The posh charmer thing is over, Marcus. I need macho and street cred and hard and bloody sexy not a grammar school boy posing as a toff.'

'When you couldn't get within a mile of those people, I was the poseur who got you through the front door, let's not forget that shall we, "ligger Lyle"?'

'Oh, please.' Bea gave a trilling stage laugh. 'Before I came on the scene you couldn't make it through the front door, you were always out the back with your trousers round your ankles looking for the waiters.'

There was silence and then the phwump of a fridge door closing and the rattle of ice against glass.

'So, go on,' Marcus's voice was wheedling, 'who's the lucky bit of rough going to be then? Make my day.'

'Actually we've got our eye on Sam Curtis.'

Jack froze, she could hear the muffled sound of Marcus cackling, as if he were face down on a bed, or clutching a pillow to his mouth. 'Oh dear, oh dear, not that hairy gardener? You'll have trouble getting him scrubbed up for the shows.'

'I wouldn't expect you to get it, darling. That's exactly my point.'

'Go on, go on, I'm all ears. Channel X presenter, yeees – and?'

'He's the man, simple as that. Since that garden programme he did with Amber Best, he is *everywhere*. You can make all the faces you like, Marcus, Sam Curtis has got what everyone wants – the look, the easy-going natural style, the spiritual thing.'

'*Spiritual*? I think you mean organic, sweetheart. It isn't quite the same.'

'You don't need a house in Belgravia and a fleet of Filipino maids to be big time these days, Marcus. It isn't about *cufflinks* and *handmade shoes* and your own personal blend of *aftershave*.'

'Oh, do me a favour! He's done one lousy television lifestyle programme, got very lucky on the back of someone who did have a bit of class – a situation that exactly mirrors our own as a matter of fact.'

'Well, I think he's divine – and, sweetheart, he'll be in

the place of honour on the Bluegrass table, right next to
Jez, you wait and see.'

'Have Garden Boy. Be my guest. Just not before the
premiere of *Glass Ceiling*. The deal holds, as agreed, until
then – Bea? You know how important that is . . .'

'Doesn't stop me making a start, though, does it
darling?'

'While we're at it,' – Marcus was on the move again,
his voice was growing fainter – 'I got snapped in a bar, last
night – with an urchin.'

There was a clunk that sounded like Bea slamming
something down on the mirrored dressing-table top.

'Don't fuss, Beatrice. Tris has got it all under control.
The story is I'm helping him with his drug problem. Just
hope it doesn't bugger up my thing with Alice, though, she
is *that* close to casting me.'

'Congratulations. Didn't think you had it in you.'

'Don't! She's *covered* in hair, like a centaur. Furry
shorts, to the knee pretty much. I tell you, it's been the
toughest test of my ambition to date. At least you're depil-
ated to within an inch of your life.'

'Oh God! The Salvador Special! I completely forgot.
Quickly, ring down for me. And I need my hair blown out
– and check if Jill's arrived, Marcus, we've only got an
hour.'

There was a pause, Jack heard the muffled sounds of
Marcus talking to a third party. She looked at her watch.
She'd been in there for ten minutes.

'Wonder what's taking her so long?' Marcus was back
by the window, she could see his hand wrapped around a
tumbler, resting on the sill. 'You are a bitch, giving her the
Perucci fluff dress. Even I know that was thrown in for

the benefit of the unpackers. Tinkerbell couldn't carry it off.'

Bea laughed lazily. 'The trousers are going to be just a little long too. Still, I'm sure they'll do for supper in the brasserie.'

Jack picked up the clothes, holding them at arm's length for a moment, one eye closed. Then she hobbled over to the dressing table, opening the drawers one by one until she found the complimentary scissors and a notepad and pencil. First she scribbled a note on the pad: 'Do Not Disturb Under Any Circumstances', nipped out into the corridor and stuck it on the main door of the suite. Then she tried on the trousers, managing to just get them over her hips, though not done up, and the chiffon dress which was far too short but at least had potential.

'Nothing for it. We'll have to operate,' she said, perching on the end of the bed in her bra and pants and making the first incision four inches above the hem of one trouser leg. As she worked she kept Santa abreast of developments. 'So I've shortened those – that's that – and they should stay up with a bit of string and some safety pins. And now I'm cutting a little bit off the dress... like... sooo – making it just long enough to disguise the top of the trousers – see? That's pretty good, isn't it?'

Santa stared up at her, tongue lolling, tail thumping on the carpet, the saliva-drenched remnants clamped under his paws.

'Are you all right in there?' Marcus was drumming his fingers on the adjoining door. 'Anything I can help with?'

'No thanks, almost done!'

'Really, you mustn't keep us in suspense.' He was

sounding peeved now. 'We're absolutely champing at the
bit to see how it's worked out – open up.'

'I'll just be a minute. 'Jack wrapped herself in a towel,
grabbed her clothes and her new, customized outfit, and
tiptoed across the room and out into the corridor, Santa
following close behind with a mouthful of Perucci print
chiffon.

Simon was in the bath when she got back to their room,
not the bath in the bathroom but the on-view, centre-stage
bath. His head lolled over the back and his elbows rested
on the sides, like a cowboy taking a soak in a tin tub over
some saloon bar. When he heard the door close he shifted
his head just enough to catch her out of the corner of one
eye and raised a hand in greeting.

'Hey,' he said, 'you've got yourself a dog.'

'Yes, this is Santa.'

'Swopped him for your clothes?'

'No, ha! No, actually – you'll never guess what's happened. Guess whose room I've been . . .'

'Sssshhh.' Simon put a finger to his lips. 'Come over
here,' he whispered, stretching out his hand, palm up, and
curling in the finger like a scorpion's tail. His fringe was
slicked down over his eyes like he'd come in from driving
cattle over a swollen river on a wild, godforsaken night.

'Erm . . .' Jack tucked over the top of the towel. 'Can't
I tell you what happened first? It started with me getting
toothpaste – well, moisturizer – on my dress and I was so
worried, you see, that—'

'Baaabe. Forget about it. I'm not interested. Come
over here. I need that towel, right now.'

'Would you have been OK about it though? The dress I mean. That's what I've been wondering. I just feel a bit—'

'Jack,' he was leaning over the side of the bath now, shoulders hunched and glistening, 'this room is costing me fifty pounds an hour. You wanna talk about your dress, we could have done that on the phone.'

'You're right.' She took a few paces towards him. This was it, this was really it, with all the lights on, with the remnants of an oat bar clinging to her teeth, a grazed face, a plaster cast on her right foot – the moment she'd imagined for twenty years – though usually she'd pictured it in the velvet-shrouded semi-darkness and always on dry land. She took a deep breath, pulled in her stomach, and stumbled the last few steps across the room like a drunk in a storm. As she reached the side of the bath she closed her eyes and felt his arms fold around her like wet cables and her feet lifting off the floor. She was floating in a eucalyptus-scented haze, her lips buried in the sticky hollow of his neck, the towel sliding off her in slow motion. And then, from beyond the haze there was a sound like a roar, and a high-pitched cry, and Jack was suddenly toppling backwards onto the floor from where, when she opened her eyes a moment later, she had a baseline view of Simon, stark naked, wrestling Santa in the bath.

Fifteen

Amanda's departure for the country had gone remarkably smoothly, all things considered. When she arrived home at 5.30, bearing her new outdoor clothing, autumnal foliage, etc., the children were dressed in their country best, as prearranged with Riva, and already packed into the four-wheel drive, along with the weekend equipment. Now she only had the three-hour journey, getting the logs from the local village and where to fit the hamster's travel box to worry about.

To be fair, Nicholas had warned her it would be like this. It was only a year since she'd insisted on them buying the cottage, not that particular cottage, but anything detached, beyond comfortable driving distance from London, with at least two open fires, exuding 'a sense of your own history', as described by Zuleika Pritchett Evans in that month's *Herald*. The article was entitled 'The New Posh' and there was Amanda, consigned to a pink-tinted sidebar headed, New Pretenders. Zuleika had written.

'New Pretenders' are affluent and socially ambitious but lack the depth of experience required to move up a rung and join the ranks of the New Posh. While Pretenders may have many of the trappings of New Poshness they are fundamentally urban in their tastes and distinguished by their preoccupation with comfort and hygiene, stealth status purchases (cashmere blankets, rare-wood flooring, scented candles) and maintaining a glossy, ordered appearance.

Amanda had caught her breath at this point and, although she was in the hairdresser, under a hotlamp, cast a furtive glance over both shoulders to check if her reaction had been spotted. She read on:

Unlike the New Posh, whose priority is to emulate the life of their Old Posh antecedents, creating wild, romantic gardens and shabbily grand houses, Pretenders instinctively dislike the countryside and have no experience of those habits and hobbies that continue to define Posh (horses, dogs, gardens, livestock, fruit and vegetable husbandry, walking, cooking on Agas, etc.).

Amanda had bent the spine of the *Herald* more tightly to the point where the page was starting to come away.

It is not city dwelling, per se, that separates the Pretender from the New Posh. Plenty of scions of the New Posh are city dwellers (see New Posh in the City) but, crucially, they have either access to family homes in the country or their own weekend houses. Note: the most desirable and glamorous element of the New Posh are increasingly identifiable by their capacity to move between the two environments with consummate ease, taking advantage of the continuing vogue for bohemian, ragged-edged style.

There were arrows from the New Pretenders sidebar to a green box, further down the page, headed New Posh Essentials, and underneath 'animals (as opposed to pets) including horses, dogs, bantams, ducks, guinea fowl, rabbits' was listed 'house in the country', and various specifications including the counties that qualified. Dorset, Devon, Cornwall and Norfolk got a double star rating.

'We have to get a cottage in Dorset, or Cornwall, or Norfolk,' Amanda had announced as they got ready for bed that night.

Nicholas, who was already tucked up with a bridge book, had closed his eyes very slowly and made a trumpet mouth while Amanda continued to apply Crème Opalesce to her eye area in front of the dressing-table mirror.

'Darling,' Nicholas's eyes were still closed, 'who have you been talking to?'

Amanda replaced the lid on the Opalesce and opened the jar of Pour Les Nuits Extremes.

'No one,' she said, applying the cream in circular upwards movements and then slapping her throat like a seal. 'I just think the children are getting to that age when they would really benefit from a place in the country.' Nicholas raised his head off the pillow and adopted the expression that he used on the children when they had, for instance, pretended to lose the TV remote control. 'Mmmm.' She worked another drop of cream into her top lip. 'Sshhhtthink of all the pleasshherr it would give us, youbbbuub could grow things an I ceerrd keep animals, such as ducks and banhams—'

'And what?' said Nicholas

'*Banhams*,' said Amanda. 'Really, I'm surprised at you, Nicholas, what with you being brought up on a farm and everything. We're missing out on the good things in life, the real things.' On went the lid of the Extreme, off came the top of Dr Magda's silicone booster gel.

'Amanda?'

'Yes?'

'Who have you been talking to?'

'What? I couldn't have thought of it on my own, when everyone we know is buying a house in the country; when half of them live there *all the time*? Wiltshire will do, if the others are too far.'

'You hate the bloody country. What are you up to? It's a fashion-shoot thing, isn't it? They've cut your budgets and you need a bolthole with *retro* wallpaper—'

'Nicholas, you are behaving as if I'd suggested buying a bunker in Kazak .. somewhere. This is what people do, at our time of life, they find a place with ... a sense of their own history.' She rummaged around in the Dr Magda bag for a moment so as not to have to meet his eyes in the mirror.

'Squiiiidgeee, who have you been talking to?'

'Tell me one thing you've got against it.'

'Oh, let me think. There's the cost, the upkeep, the long wet drive every Friday night, the damp, musty house that takes two days to warm up, by which time you're packing the car for the long haul back, the leaking roof, the dry rot, the immersion heater that gives you half a hot bath every three hours, the things that have to be done to the garden but you never have enough time, the neighbours who know every detail of your comings and goings and resent all of them, the interminable journeys in the car, trying to make the most of those two special days. Off to the sea. Off to drinks.'

'I thought you'd be pleased. You'd like it, wouldn't you? You'd like to have animals and vegetables and—'

'Who is going to look after them, Squidge? It doesn't just happen the way it looks in the pictures, you know. Someone has to build the tree house, someone has to feed the ponies, walk the dog, get the wood to light the fire, grow the lovely flowers for the lovely flower arrangements, make all the picturesque jam in the little spongeware bowls.' Amanda swivelled round on the stool and blinked at him. 'Squidgy, my darling – it just isn't you.'

'Amanda shall I putink jam also?' Riva was standing behind the Land-Rover holding up two pots of homemade jam, complete with handwritten labels, that had been given to Amanda by one of Cass's schoolfriends.

'Brilliant, Riva!' Amanda waved at her in the rearview mirror. 'And then I think that'll do it.' She craned her neck out of the window to check there was nothing left on the pavement. 'OK, shut us in then. Wave goodbye to Riva now, darlings.'

There was a general shuffling and squeaking in the back as Ludo, Cass and Poppy attempted to twist round in their seats despite their new navy oilskins. 'Byeeee.' Amanda swivelled a hand in the air, as if changing a lightbulb, they pulled away from the kerb and she relaxed back in the throne of the driving seat.

'All right?' she said.

There was silence.

'Pleasemayhave Teletubbies?' said Poppy.

'No,' said Ludo. 'It's the television.'

'Aeoh.' Poppy sounded terrifically posh these days. It was the influence of her new nursery school, which had finally accepted her this term, after Amanda and Nicholas had been interviewed on two separate occasions, supplied a small illustrated album detailing their reasons for wanting Poppy to attend Hearst Lodge, and donated a king-size trampoline to the mini gym. Recently Poppy had taken to saying rarely, as in, 'Mummy and Daddy are going out tonight' – 'Rarely?' and pefer, as in, 'I'd pefer not to go to the park.' It was a bit like having a very vertically challenged royal guest in the house.

'Mummy?'

'Yes, Ludo?'

'Tomorrow, can I go to Valleria's and play ballet?'

'No, darling. Your granny Bridget will want to see you, won't she?'

'Can Valleria come and play ballet with us?'

'Why not ask Rufus over and play gladiators or something like that?' Amanda angled the rearview mirror so that she could check her son's expression. He was pouting. 'Why don't we make a castle, or a camp in the garden. Wouldn't that be fun?' Ludo kept pouting. She noticed that he'd pulled up the collar of his tartan Viyella shirt, giving a certain dash to the otherwise conservative ensemble. 'No, Ludy, no Valleria this weekend.'

'What is vagina?' Cass was gazing at her in the mirror.

'Valleria's friend,' said Ludo authoritatively.

'That's *Regina*,' said Amanda. 'Cass, are you going to make a habit of this?'

'This what?'

'This asking . . . words – you know what I mean.'

'Mrs Elsworthy says: Ask away. Ask every day, questions light the learning way. Ask, ask every daaay and you shaaall know your world. Ask—'

'Oh, do stop it, Cassandra. There's to be absolutely *no* asking this weekend, all right? If I catch anyone asking—'

'Or playing with Valleria.' Ludo had his hand up.

'Or playing with Valleria.'

'Or doing London stuff, like computer games or TV.' Cass craned her neck to make sure her mother could see her clearly.

'Yes.'

'Or wearing any clothes 'cept for scratchy ones that come in the post.' Ludo grinned revealing a slot between his teeth wide enough to fit a pound coin, which was indeed one of his favourite tricks.

'Exactly. You are all very clever.'

'Mummy, if we do very well,' Cass was leaning forward in her seat, 'can we have a dog in the country?'

Ludo and Poppy started whooping and clapping as if she'd just performed a marvellous magic trick.

'Maybe,' said Amanda, and there was more cheering.

'Maybe is yes,' Cass hissed to the others, in what she imagined was a whisper.

'Will doggy go in the spare room?' Poppy shouted, a tiny hand sandwiched either side of her mouth.

'No. Because Daddy's problee going to live there now,' said Ludo, 'until Mummy lets him back again.'

Cass froze, she sat rigidly back in the seat and stared out of the window, her cheek pressed flat against the upholstery, her hands clamped together in the lap of her junior kilt.

Vince, as it turned out, was an ex-air steward, qualified in first aid, so he was selected to sort out the situation in the Barcelona suite.

'Hello there,' he said, standing in the doorway of the room, holding the red and white box squarely in front of him, like the chancellor on budget day.

'Hello, Vince,' said Jack. 'Come in.'

She was kneeling on the platform beside the bed, still wrapped in a towel, winding a length of loo paper round and round one of Simon's hands. Simon raised his head a few inches off the pillow, glanced between them and then lay back groaning.

'So what seems to be the problem?' Vince bustled over to the bed, snapped open the clasps of the case and then waited, poised, hands on hips.

'Dog attack, man!' Simon gestured with the loo-paper hand to his bare nutmeg chest, now scored with scratch marks. 'I've been *bitten*, in my own room.'

Vince swooped round to the side of the bed and fluttered over the scratches. 'Oooh, deary me, we have been in the wars, sir. Still,' he widened his eyes at Jack, 'nothing that it won't be a Per-leasure to put right for you, Mr Best. Now then.' He held up a miniature bottle of surgical spirit for their approval. 'I'm thinking a little bit of this on some cotton wool, clean it all up nicely, spot of the old Savlon,' the tube of ointment was duly displayed, 'and then some lovely tight bandages around the chest.' Vince blew on his fingers like a snooker player warming up for the crucial shot.

'What about rabies?' said Simon. 'I mean the dog was foaming.'

'Oh, I don't think so.' Vince's eyes bulged. 'It's Marcus Raven's dog.' He paused as if this should have been sufficient information to put Simon's mind at rest. 'He's well known to be terribly fastidious, isn't he? It's got a Louis Louis basket.' Simon narrowed his eyes and slumped back on the pillow again. 'Soooo.' Vince drew in his chin and pursed his lips. 'May one ask how it happened?'

'He just sort of ended up coming back to the room with me,' Jack glanced in the direction of Santa who was lying with his head on his paws in the corner, 'and then, Mr Best was trying to . . . um . . . show me something and he went—'

'It went for me,' shouted Simon. 'Attacked me, in the bath, for Chrissake.'

'I think he misunderstood,' said Jack. 'I think he thought Mr Best might be going to harm me, rather than, you know . . .'

'Tsch!' Vince placed a soothing wet wipe on Simon's brow. 'Well, you can see how it could happen. The poor dog wouldn't have been exposed to much of that sort of thing. Boys and girls together all of a sudden must have upset his sense of the natural order of things.'

'I don't care about the dog's *motives*' – Simon was being hauled up under his golden armpits by Vince who was rolling his eyes ecstatically at Jack and mouthing, 'Divine' – 'I just want to know why the thing is still *here*.'

'It won't happen again,' said Jack. 'He's used to you

now. And we can't send him back, or Bea will have him put down.'

'Best thing for it – Aaaaarggh!' Simon flinched as Vince stretched the first strip of bandage across his lower ribs. 'It's not staying here, all right? That's it. I just wanna get through a weekend, with you, without paying a visit to A & E. OK?'

Jack nodded.

'There we go.' Vince tucked in the last corner of bandage and stepped back to admire his work. 'All ready for the party. Would sir like me to help him dress? One could find it a little tricky.'

'I think we'll manage,' said Simon, levering himself up off the bed. 'I'm going to have a slash and when I get back I want the dog to have disappeared.'

Vince and Jack watched him hobble across the carpet, strapped up in his cream bandage corset, his modesty preserved by a badly chewed hand towel.

'And, hey,' he turned to look over his shoulder, 'I don't want this getting out. I've got a reputation to think of.'

'Well,' said Vince, when the bathroom door had closed. 'Aren't you the lucky one?' He gave a little shiver to demonstrate Simon's impact on his constitution, which was wasted on Jack who was gazing intently at the dog.

'Vince, you have to keep Santa for me. Please,' she said. 'Just until I think of a way out of this.'

Vince raised an eyebrow. 'Is madam seriously prepared to jeopardize her chances with Mr Exquisitely Gorgeous Man The Like of Which I Have Never Seen for the sake of a motheaten old dog with a misplaced sense of loyalty? Is madam thinking quite clearly?'

'I don't know,' said Jack. 'But if you look after him,

overnight, I'll persuade Mr Best he needs his bandages redoing in the morning.'

'Done.' Vince crossed his hands over his chest, and mouthed something at the ceiling. 'And if I might offer a word of advice, don't look for obstacles, madam. It can be hard when all you've ever wanted is right there for the taking. Grasp the bull by the horns. Trust me.' And with that he scooped up the first-aid box, snapped his fingers and breezed out of the door with Santa at his heels.

It was after nine by the time they drew up at the cottage, what with Ludo having been sick and the hamster escaping at Losley Services. As Amanda killed the lights the front door swung open and there was Bridget, arms extended, wearing the exaggerated expression of relief tinged with sadness with which she liked to remind Amanda that, as far as she was concerned, her grandchildren were little prisoners of an unnatural life.

'Aaaaah. Poor little things,' she said, as they shambled through the door, trailing teddies and knapsacks. 'Are you frifully tired?' And then, glancing back over her shoulder, 'You are brave, dear, driving them down on a Friday after a long week at school. Now' – she turned to examine the three children in the light of the hall – 'goodness, aren't we smart? Anyone would think you'd been having tea with the queen . . . and what's this?'

Poppy opened her hand to reveal a soggy piece of tuna sushi. 'Soochi,' said Poppy. 'Wis too much hot on it.'

Bridget smiled brightly. 'Well, granny's got proper supper for you, so you don't have to worry yourself with that any longer.' She pocketed the sushi and placed a healing hand on Poppy's head.

'They love it actually.' Amanda was tugging at the zip of her new WaxMac. 'It's a bit of an extravagance, but what the heck, it's so easy, isn't it?' The zip was jammed tight now, she could see a bit of the lining wedged between the teeth.

'I'm sure it is,' said Bridget, smiling so brightly that only her daughter-in-law could have sensed the accusatory subtext.

'Darling!' Nicholas was staggering through the door behind her. He'd obviously come out to meet them through the kitchen. 'What on earth is all this I've found in the back of the car?'

Amanda glanced down at his feet and there were the bags that she had planned to retrieve later, when the coast was clear. On top of the biggest was one of the Fludgate pies in its pottery dish, complete with little pastry leaf cut out; there, clearly on view, was the Floribunda autumnal arrangement, wrapped up in a cone of silver paper and tied with a red velvet ribbon, jostling up against the jars of homemade jam.

'Has one heard of the expression coals to Newcastle, my angel? What have we here?' Nicholas dived into one of the bags, pulling out a branch of holly and waving it triumphantly. 'Holly! What's our address, my sweet?' He winked at Bridget.

Amanda said nothing.

'Holly Lane!' Nicholas hooted with laughter. 'Back to the front door, four paces forward, three paces left, what've you got? Holly hedge!'

'Now, Nicholas.' Bridget was puffed up like a cock-
erel. 'You know Manda is triffickly busy.'

'Of course.' Nicholas gave Amanda's shoulders a
squeeze.

'And she's not going to want to scrabble around in
some horrid hedge, is she, silly? Not with that 'spensive
manicure. Talking of which,' Bridget placed a nice but
firm hand on her daughter-in-law's arm, 'I took the liberty
of organizing some ponies for the children tomorrow, was
no trouble, and really they should be having reglar lessons
by now. Greatfriendamine organizes the local pony-club
so you're all right for next summer.'

'Who can say where we'll all be by then?' said
Amanda, glaring at Nicholas.

'And,' Bridget leant towards her confidentially, 'I'm
giving Ludy a gun for Christmas, so we thought a few
lessons, here at the Churdwell school, to get him started
orf. Didn't we, Nicky?'

'I don't like firearms.' Ludo was standing between
them, still wearing his oilskin, his head tilted back to try
and glimpse his mother's expression.

Bridget laughed gaily and patted his shoulder. 'Not
firearms darling, air rifle. All little boys your age have one.
For shooting nasty squirrels.'

Ludo shambled off, casting soulful looks over his
shoulder at Amanda.

'I don't think he's interested, Bridget. He's not that
sort of boy,' said Amanda.

'Nonsense, dear. It's an important part of his ejcation.
He's only picking up on your prejdices. Now, shall we eat?
I've done a stew.'

Nicholas went ahead of them into the kitchen, dragging the carrier bags as if they were as heavy as wet lead and chortling wildly.

'Manda, there was just one more little thing, before I f-get.' Bridget hovered at Amanda's shoulder indicating that this thing was of a slightly more personal nature. 'Hope you don't mind me poking my nose in, but I did notice that in the downstairs lav-try there was one of those fluffy *mats* round the base of the loo. I think with the lovely flagstones it's such a pity. I mentioned it to Nicky, but he said to have a word with you, 'cause it was your part-ment. Just one of those things that one picks up, but you *ab-slutely* couldn't be expected to know.'

'Sorry? I don't quite . . .' Amanda squinted up at Bridget, who seemed to grow taller every time she saw her.

'The lav-try mat, dear. I've got rid of it. Well, put it to one side, in case one of – someone else can find a use for it. It's just not very . . . *country*, you know.' She patted Amanda's arm reassuringly. 'Don't you worry, I'll keep an eye out.'

'All right! It's Mr Simon Best and the lovely Jacqueline!'

Max the manager stood at the bottom of the staircase, clapping his hands in the air and thrusting his chin rhythmically. All the guests gathered in the hall turned their heads to watch as Simon and Jack descended the stairs. Simon walked slightly ahead, shaking out his legs with each step, one thumb hooked in the belt of his butterfly embroidered leather trousers, while Jack clung to the bannister and let her plaster boot lead her down like the weight on the end of a line. When they reached the bottom step, he slipped an arm around her waist and pulled her close to him.

'I think they like us,' he growled in her ear, 'and you have totally ruined Bea Lyle's evening.'

Jack looked across the hall and saw Bea standing stiffly at Marcus's side, one pinched white hand gripping her throat, the other digging claw-like into his arm. Marcus looked distinctly puzzled. He glanced from Simon to Jack and back, raised a finger as if to attract Simon's attention, and then, with a wince, apparently thought better of it.

'You never told me where you got the outfit,' Simon murmured into her hair. 'It's so original. You make all these actresses in their cocktail frocks look like blowsy old matrons. Hey!' He squeezed her tight against his hip bone. 'How do I look?'

'Oh, great.'

'Enough?' He flicked a thumb in the direction of his open-necked shirt. 'I'd usually wear this more open but like, with the bandages . .'

'No, no.' Jack found her eyes wandering around the hall. 'No, that's – perfect.'

She noticed that Bea had moved over to the fireplace with Marcus and was plucking nervously at the straps of her floral chiffon dress with one hand while shielding the lower part of her face with the other. Next to them a couple of young women were casting hungry looks in Simon's direction, and playing with each other's fingers with increasing agitation.

'You guys!' Max was coiling and uncoiling at Simon's side. 'Come and meet somea the team. Sooooo, Mr Jez Hoffman, head of Bluegrass Films, and the lovely Anna Jacks, I think you already know. This is Simon Best, the new Ralph, if I can say that,' Max widened his hands to indicate he was at the mercy of his plain speaking nature, 'and, er . . . his lady, Jacqueline.'

They all shook hands, except for Simon and Anna who pressed hips, and swayed in unison, adjusting each other's hair.

'God, I want you to photograph me again,' said Anna, looking straight at Jack. 'I mean, this *man*.' She touched Jez Hoffman's arm. 'Baby, you should let him do you. He is a *genius*.'

Jez was somewhere in his fifties, bald headed with the neck girth of a heavyweight boxer and wearing a large plaid suit. 'Fortunately there is no reason whatsoever for me to get the wrong side of a camera.' He laughed good-naturedly and the suit rose up and down. 'Ever think about the movies, Simon? Ever tempted to come and visit us in California? You should, you know – you've got the face for it.' Simon fingered his collarbone and thrust his lips into fourth gear. Jez gave Jack a look that she couldn't quite interpret and then he winked, 'Guess he's pretty high maintenance right, Jacqueline? Show me a star who isn't. Well . . .' he raised his eyes to look over Simon's shoulder, 'if it isn't my old friend Marcus Raven.'

'Jez, old boy.' Marcus was scrambling through the narrow space between Simon and Anna. 'You are a bloody genius, Jez. *Esther the Firegirl* . . . absolutely out of this world.' He put a hand to his mouth and lowered his voice to a stage whisper. 'Tell me, what did Ian have to do for you to give him the part of a lifetime?'

Both men smiled hard at each other for several seconds until Jez ended the stand-off by placing a cigar between his teeth.

'Darling!' Bea was right behind Marcus, clawing at Jez's arm like he was allocating seats on the last lifeboat. 'My God, it's been ages, where have you *been*?' She pushed herself into the middle of the circle, adjusting her position so that her back was turned squarely to Jack. 'Do say we're sitting next to each other at dinner. I've got so much to *tell*.'

Jez patted the hand hooked firmly through the crook of his arm. 'Well, sweetheart, there's a kid here that I have to talk business with. But I figured you'd be happy to sit on his other side and keep him amused for me.'

Bea shook out her hair and looked up at him through fibre-enhanced eyelashes. 'Well he'd better be de-vine to make up for the disappointment.' She straightened Jez's collar. 'What's his name?'

'Sam something – Curtis? Onea these garden boys you Brits are so crazy about.'

'Aeeeow.' Bea shot Marcus a triumphant look. 'How thrilling!' Her hand hovered at her mouth as she spoke and when Jack glanced at her a moment later she was discreetly fanning her upper lip.

'Sam Curtis – he's one of yours, isn't he?' Simon was looking down at Jack, and for the first time she noticed his eyes were outlined with kohl with a faint dusting of silver on the lids. 'Man, I always hated that programme – What's up? You don't look too happy.' He cocked his head, and then tipped his chin back suddenly. 'Aaaah . . . I get it. You haven't told the gang that you're seeing Amber's *baaad* brother.' Jack shook her head but he was looking somewhere else. '. . . You're scared the "Family" won't approve, right? Hang on a minute. Here – Baz.' Simon beckoned to a man lurking on the edges of the group, stretched out his palm and the man clasped it for a split second, then both of them put their hands in their pockets and turned their backs on each other.

'What was all that about?' said Jack, staring after Baz who was shaking hands again with someone equally uninterested in making conversation.

'Nothing.' Simon stroked the back of her neck absentmindedly. 'Let's go and see where we're sitting. Come on.'

Simon laced his fingers through hers and led her across the room, the crowd reluctantly making way, clinging onto their last chance of a close-up. The men jutted their chins as they passed as if some insult had reached their ears simultaneously; the women ran their eyes over Simon feverishly, and then fixed Jack with looks of naked hostility. She felt him tighten his grip on her hand and had the strangest sensation of elation and disappointment all at the same time.

Dinner was set up in a private room next to the bar, with leather-covered dining chairs and black-tulip flower arrangements. They found Jack's place name at the far end of the table, in between Marcus Raven's and someone who was, according to Simon, Jez's boyfriend. Simon was on the opposite side, next to a Bluegrass producer and the illustrious author and Fletcher book prize-winner, Pat Ayres.

Jack gasped when she saw the name card. 'Oh! She's my heroine, how brilliant.'

Simon stared at her and then let his head hang back for a moment while he contemplated the ceiling. 'Jack, she's like sixty years old, and built like a brick shit house. I am not watching her fill her face for four courses – and the producer's on the way out.' He picked up his place card, sauntered along the edge of the table, turning it over and over in his fingers and then lit on a name. 'Right, mate. Off you go. You get the old bat.' Simon tossed the stranger's card into the gap where his had been. 'There we are. And I get that little minx, Jez's daughter. That's more like it. Lovely swap. Awwww, come on, Jack, why the face? Don't be jealous, babe. This is our night, but you don't want me to die of boredom before we get to the best part, do you? Do you?' He waggled her hips between his hands.

'But . . .' Jack found herself pulling away, 'but it's Pat Ayres. I can't believe you'd rather sit next to a fifteen-year-old than Pat *Ayres*.'

'Sweetheart,' Simon ran his fingers through his hair, sizing up the effect for a split second in the window behind her, 'you are living on another planet. Men like interesting, we like funny,' – he chucked her under the chin – 'so long as it comes in the right package, you know? And I've gotta tell you, I didn't bring you down here for the weekend to find out about your taste in literature.' The liquorice teeth glinted in the candlelight. Jack smiled weakly, she tried closing one eye and looking at him through the other. 'And, Jack, too much of the weird faces. You're a pretty girl, you don't need that stuff.'

'Sorry,' she said. 'I was just trying to see . . . something.' Behind them the Bluegrass party was starting to filter into the room, Jez leading the way, fanning them through.

'But, hey.' He pushed her hair off her neck and brushed his lips against her ear. 'It's true I like the way you're hot and you don't know it. I've always liked that.'

'When?' Jack almost shouted. 'When did you first notice me?'

She pictured herself standing on the front steps of Northanger House, waving to Amber as she stepped into the waiting Jensen. She was wearing a brown cord wrap-over jacket with quarterback padded shoulders, a Biba cloche and pale-blue corduroy loons. Even her underwear, a matching set of Smiley bra and knickers, was borrowed. It had taken her an hour to get dressed for this fifty-second opportunity to catch Simon's eye, not including make-up and nail-varnish. 'Go in, quick. It's freezing,' Amber had shouted, cupping her hands around her mouth. 'Simon says go in and get warm.'

'I'm fine,' she'd shouted back. 'Have a lovely time.' Then she'd stood there in the biting wind, sucking in her cheeks, pulling back her shoulders, waiting for him to look again, willing him to see how right she was, how easy-going and cool, and how perfectly suited they were, their taste and hopes and everything they wanted out of life. He threw the car into reverse, passed Amber the cigarette between his lips, raised a hand in the air above his head and within seconds the car had disappeared down the drive.

'I dunno.' Simon traced his finger along her collarbone. 'Way back . . . maybe even when you were still at school.'

Jack thought of the night he'd kissed her on the dance floor, when she was fourteen, how she'd gone home and lain on her bed in her candlewick dressing gown with her five-year diary open on the pillow.

'We love each other so much,' she'd written. 'Sasha says how can I tell it's love, rather than fancying, but it's because I know what he's thinking and he knows what I'm thinking. Things happen all the time that prove it, like tonight when they played "Rocket Man" and he knew exactly what it meant. And it's so cool that he doesn't feel he has to talk to me particularly, because we have this understanding. It's like we're on a higher plane and he'll go out with other girls, but he knows that we're different.'

'Do you remember?' Jack said. 'Do you remember, Simon, the party, when you first kissed me?'

Simon smiled and looped his arms around her waist. 'You bet,' he said, pulling her closer.

'D'you remember Susie was right beside us?' Jack was arching her back so that she could watch his face.

'Susie?'

'Susie Harcourt . . . your girlfriend. And you had those painkillers they'd given you for a knee injury and you were selling them to all the other boys on the dance-floor. Remember?'

'Sure.' He tightened his grip.

'But then you said, "That's enough, this is our song and we don't want to be interrupted." And I just couldn't believe it, because I always thought of you when it was playing and there was no way you could have known that.'

Simon gave her a long, slow wink. 'Chemistry, babe.'

'I know. That's when I really . . . that's when I started to believe that it could happen . . . that this might happen. You know in the car, today?'

'Hmmm?'

'When you kissed me, "Rocket Man" was playing in my head again, I could hear it just as if we were back there, on the dance-floor, under the glitter ball.'

'Right.' Simon gave a chuckle. ' "Rocket Man".'

'You do remember.' Jack was holding him by the lapels now. 'We went outside, and you lent me your jacket, and you told me all about London and all the clubs and the restaurants and you said, "The day you leave Northanger I'm going to drive you straight up to Poons and show you the best night of your life." '

'And did I?' Simon glanced over his shoulder at the guests settling down around the table.

Jack's smile faltered for a second and then she pushed him away playfully. 'No! You know you didn't. You were in California. But you sent me that 3D postcard.'

'Right. Well . . . that's nice.' He smiled and bent over to kiss her. 'Guess we should sit down now, babe. But listen. I'll come and rescue you if I can see you're bored. I can read your mind.'

Bridget served the stew straight off the Aga, letting it splosh and spit onto the hot plates that Amanda liked to keep spotless as new, occasionally even glossing up the blue enamel covers with Windowlene. Nicholas was already hunched over his plate, the elbows of his checked Viyella shirt poking through a favourite old jumper that had long since been banned from London. 'Delicious, mother. One of your best,' he said, gesticulating with a piece of her legendary soda bread.

Bridget took this as a cue to ladle more onto his plate, pausing to pluck out some string and toss it onto the Aga where it sizzled quietly, emitting a thin plume of black smoke.

'Pass the bread to Mummy, darling.' Nicholas was

addressing Ludo who looked incredulous but nonetheless did as he was told. 'Amanda, I don't know what possessed you to bring down all those pies and whatnot when we've got Mother staying.' Nicholas said 'mother' as if it were the universally recognized word for culinary miracle. 'You know you can't keep her out of the kitchen.'

'Well, I thought it might be nice to try.' Amanda pushed the bread to the other side of the table. 'And the children particularly like the leek and potato.'

'I'm vegetarian,' said Cass, staring hard at her mother, as if this show of loyalty was not uncomplicated for her.

Bridget caught Nicholas's eye. 'Well Cassy, you're in the country now, darling,' she said, covering Cass's hand with her own, 'and we're eating Granny's lamb because that's how we live in the country, isn't it? We have the eggs from the chickies for breakfast, ham from Mr Pig for lunch and that's only being polite to the animals, isn't it?'

Amanda uncorked a third bottle of red wine.

'Oh?' Bridget paused, a laden fork quivering milli-metres from her mouth.

'Something the matter?' said Amanda. 'Not with the stew surely?'

'Just . . . I'm not drinking, dear.'

'Oh well, all the more for me then.'

Bridget looked mildly uncomfortable, maintaining her expression of concern for the time it took for Nicholas to look up from his plate and register it. Amanda topped up her glass and took another, long swig.

This was what it was going to be like when they were divorced, Amanda thought. Nicholas would keep the cottage, and every other weekend she would be obliged to deliver the children down here, into the arms of his gloating mother. 'Thank you, Amanda, I'll see to them from here,' Bridget would say, rubbing her flour-coated hands on her pinny as she closed the door of the cottage behind them. And then one day the door would be opened by a fresh-faced woman wearing those corduroy stretch jodhpurs and a handkerchief knotted at her throat and she'd smile at the children. 'Want to see the puppies everyone?' she'd say – and they'd all race out of sight without so much as a backward glance. The woman would have nut-brown hands, and there would be geranium pots in the porch where there had been none before and over her shoulder Amanda would be able to see discarded wellington boots, abandoned teatowels and woolly socks, the casual evidence of this woman's life with Nicholas, more painful to witness than the two of them locked in each other's embrace.

'Oh, Milly rang, darling,' said Nicholas, reaching for another slab of soda bread. 'Channel X are coming here, to do me, first thing tomorrow, and then they want to meet her at Hedlands and get her snooping around the house a bit. She wondered if you'd go over there and give her some moral support.'

'How pecu-ler,' said Bridget. 'A woman like Milly needing her hand held – by Manda.'

'Well, Milly knows Amanda won't stand any nonsense from them, Mother, she's onto all their sneaky little tricks. Aren't you, darling?'

'Oh yes, sneaky little tricks are my new special subject.' Amanda shot Nicholas her best killer look, he winked back.

'That's my fierce mouse,' he said.

She stared at him for a moment and then filled her

glass and slowly, steadily, drained it while Bridget fluttered the tips of her fingers together and gazed fixedly out of the window.

'It's all right, Bridget.' Amanda waggled her empty glass. 'I shan't be operating any machinery in the next few hours, not counting things with batteries, obviously.'

'What with batteries?' said Ludo, 'Gameboy?'

'Those poor children.' Bridget continued to stare out of the window. 'You don't get over losing a mother like that, you know. She was an inspiration. Really, one of a kind.'

'Hear, hear,' said Nicholas.

'Well,' Amanda pushed her chair away from the table, 'before we get into the two minutes' silence, I think I'll head for bed with the children. I've got some reading to do.'

'Daaaarling,' Nicholas waved a spoon at her, 'what did we say about no work at the cottage?'

'This is different,' said Amanda. 'It's just the end of a chapter, and after that I'm sure my bringing work home isn't going to be an issue any more.'

Once he realized that Jack was the journalist scheduled to interview him the following week, Marcus Raven cheered up considerably. 'Terrific,' he said, pulling his chair closer to hers. 'After all, what can you really get in forty minutes in some stale old hotel suite? Let's start now, make this the definitive Marcus Raven interview, why don't we? I like *LaMode*, I like that funny little editor . . .'

'Amanda Worth.'

'Yes. Sweet. She's always been rather good to us.'

'But I don't want to ruin your evening,' said Jack. 'You're supposed to be off duty.'

Marcus gave a little chuckle and cupped his hand over hers. 'Darling, there is nothing, *nothing* an actor likes more than talking about himself, and I like it a lot more than most. Besides, I think I owe you one.'

'Really? I thought you might be angry with me.' Jack toyed nervously with the neckline of the Perucci dress, 'what with the . . . er . . . alterations.'

Marcus glanced in Bea's direction and shifted slightly so that his shoulder was turned towards her. 'On the contrary, I have to say I rather admire your initiative.' He leant a bit closer. "A little competition never did anyone any harm. She's positively glinty-eyed now. I only hope Garden Boy is up to the challenge.'

They both looked down the table to where Bea was wiping traces of lipstick from Sam's cheek with a long, pale thumb. He inclined his ear towards her whispering mouth for a moment and then threw back his head and roared with laughter. He could do that, now that he had contact lenses and not those round spectacles with the taped-up arm. It worked with the new hair, too, which flopped backwards and forwards in one silky, ringleted mass, whereas before a sudden gesture like that could have marooned a section of curls on top of his head or left the whole lot hanging in a clump on one side. How they laughed, both of them now, watching each other's eyes, mutual appreciation ricocheting between them like lasers, while Jez looked on, beaming in a 'you guys, what a team!' kind of way.

'Who knows . . .' Marcus spooned the caviar off the top of his bellini and pushed the rest to one side, 'the way things are going in the film industry a garden special could be just the thing Bea needs. You look sceptical? Oooh no, perhaps not. Irritated, maybe?'

'Don't you mind?' said Jack, keeping her eyes on Bea. 'Mind what?'

'That,' Jack flicked her head towards the far end of the table, 'the way she's behaving.'

Marcus gave a trilling, girlish laugh. '*That* is a crucial part of the job, my dear. This is show business, darling. It doesn't stop just because the cameras aren't rolling. Oh, no.' Marcus dabbed at his mouth with his napkin. 'This is where the real auditions take place, around the dining tables of the people who count. You can have all the talent in the world but if you haven't got lots of lovely contacts, and the wherewithal to work them, you're going to be in rep in Cheshire for the rest of your days. What little Bea is busy doing now is no different in her mind to voice exercises or a Pilates class. It's part of what keeps her in the running. May I?' He poked at Jack's untouched caviar with the tip of his fork while his eyes roved around the table.

'Well, I think she's wasting her time with Sam.' Jack rearranged her cutlery making sure that it was lined up precisely against the mat. 'He's not really part of all this.' Marcus sucked on the fork, watching her vaguely through heavy lids. 'I mean, yes, he's getting a name for himself but he just wants to be good at what he does. He won't be interested in playing games.'

'Really?' Marcus licked his lips. 'What makes you think that?'

'He's an old friend.' Marcus raised a finely defined eyebrow by way of encouragement. 'I've known him for years. And he's just not that sort—' The eyebrow flickered in anticipation. 'Besides, he's seeing someone.'

This time the trilling laugh was almost a squeal. 'We're all *seeing* someone, darling, some of us are seeing several, not counting our therapists. But needs must. Sex is, next to money, what fuels this entire industry.' Marcus lowered his voice. 'Of course one wouldn't normally include *Tee Vee* celebrities.' He swilled champagne around his mouth as if the words had the power to contaminate. 'But, like it or not, it looks like Jez has big plans for your Garden Boy. And if Jez decides that he and Bea are the perfect fit, well then that is exactly what they are.' He patted her hand reassuringly. 'It's just the way it goes. No point taking it personally.'

Jack craned her neck so that she could get a clear view of them over Marcus's shoulder. She couldn't see their faces, only Sam's hand tracing voluptuous shapes in the air and Bea's fingers raking through her hair from root to tip, her head lolling back as the fingers slipped through the blunt cut ends. Jez was nodding, the stump of a cigar clenched between his teeth, his eyes tightly scrunched, as if sizing them both up through a loupe.

'I don't accept that just because you're famous you lose all sense of values.' Jack focused on her thumbnails. 'You don't all just blindly trot down the same path, sleeping with whoever's necessary for the next project.'

Marcus ducked to allow a waiter to remove his plate and replace it with a fish arranged on a bed of flowers. 'Well, there's always a first time I suppose, but it's not going to be Garden Boy who bucks the trend, is it? It's common knowledge that he was sleeping with Amber Best on that *House, Garden* whatever it was programme.'

'That had nothing to do with promoting himself. That was . . .' Jack paused, Marcus craned forward and made an ear trumpet of his hand, waggling the fingers impatiently, 'that was love,' said Jack very softly.

'Love! Well, I dare say he can find it in his heart to *love* another influential woman on the scene. I'm sorry, Jacqueline, but he's off swimming with the big fish now, and there's no getting him back. None of us thank our old friends for sticking around to remind us that we were once ordinary mortals. All this stuff about wanting to keep your feet on the ground, treasuring the ones who know the real you – forget it. When your star is rising, the last thing you want is your old pals holding onto your ankles, making sure you don't get "above yourself". You want to fly! You want fawning adulation. You want to be treated like a god and you want gods' perks – including women that other men desire. Your entry level, so to speak, is the measure of your star rating.' Marcus held a toothpick up to the candle in front of him. 'Of course, Garden Boy could get himself a hot little going-places number.' He swivelled in his chair to line the toothpick up with one of the model twins, the Brodie sisters, on the opposite side of the table. 'But then the older, established type has the advantage of the big C word.' He swung the toothpick back until it was level with Bea. 'Contacts, not to mention clout. She may not be in Amber's league, but it's surprising how good they can look when you know they're your ticket to the Other Place.'

Jack felt hot. 'Sam is different. He doesn't think like that. He doesn't even really notice those girls.' She glanced across the table to where the Brodie twin had risen from her seat and was catwalking her way slowly towards the door at the other end of the room. As she drew level with Sam's chair she drummed her fingertips lightly on his shoulder and he spun around, did a hammy double take and leapt up to kiss her on both cheeks. Jack's face was burning now, she could feel Marcus watching her. 'It's so hot, isn't it?' she said.

'Apparently so.' He sat back in his chair and folded his arms, gazing at her as if he'd only just noticed she was female. 'Sooo .. Garden Boy. Well, well. I rather thought you were with the leather prince.'

'I am.' Jack stared straight ahead at Simon, who raised his head for a moment from where it hung, directly over the fifteen-year-old's plate, and winked at her. With as much of a flourish as she could muster, she blew him a kiss, her eyes flickering in Sam's direction. His back was turned towards her, a long pale hand rested confidently on the shoulder of his perfectly fitted cashmere jacket.

Marcus sighed heavily. 'Why not try and think of it as . . . a job investment. One of those things that's necessary for the advancement of his career. Anyway,' Marcus slipped an arm round the back of her chair, 'what do you want with some scruffy old Garden Boy with his mop of hair and labourer's paws, when you've got that gorgeous hunk of a photographer.'

'Gosh, that reminds me.' Jack folded her napkin and put it beside her plate. 'There's someone I have to check on.'

Marcus reached in his pocket for a cigarette. 'Well, don't be long, sweetie. We haven't even started talking about me yet and there's so *much* to get through. Get the tape recorder, why don't you? No one will notice, and it'll save me repeating myself.'

'OK,' said Jack and slipped quietly away from the table.

Up in the bedroom, Amanda removed *Yes, He Is Having an Affair* from her fur-lined tote, pulled back the Calvin Country Collection duvet and got into bed. There was no way of telling that the book had enjoyed a day out at Pinton Prep until you opened it and saw that the title page had been defaced with a turquoise crayon, and the words 'Yes He Is' scored through with several darker colours to the point where the 'Is' was almost obliterated. Mrs Elsworthy had returned the book that afternoon, in her office, with the 'one or two things' she had mentioned on the phone slipped inside the cover in an envelope. She had gestured for Amanda to sit down in one of the visiting parents' chairs, pushed the book across her desk with the tips of her fingers, and then settled back with her hands clasped against her mouth, while Amanda removed the envelope and unfolded its contents.

'What is this?' Amanda had said, already too flustered to properly identify the sheets of typed paper and the cardboard wallet.

'The deeds to a property in New York and two aeroplane reservations in the names of Mr and Mrs Worth.' Mrs Elsworthy leant forward in her chair and placed her palms flat on the leather-topped desk. 'It seems that someone has been planning an imminent move to the United States.'

A white light exploded in Amanda's head and there were Amber and Nicholas in saturated colour: her blue-black hair, his sugar-almond yellow shirt, silhouetted against a clapboard house, a stars and stripes licking the turquoise sky and, crouched in the foreground, Ralph in his trademark bandana, motordrive hissing . . .

'Cassandra found them in a drawer in the spare room, I believe, and naturally was very distressed.' Mrs Elsworthy's voice sounded far away. Amanda felt too tired to look at her, too tired to hold herself upright in the chair. 'Could I please have a glass of water?' she said, and Mrs Elsworthy buzzed through to her secretary adding 'immediately' to the request. Even after the water Amanda found it necessary to lie down on the headmistress's sofa before she could focus on this new development.

'Mrs Worth.' Mrs Elsworthy drew up a chair next to the sofa. 'I'm so sorry. I had assumed, given the book – given the title of the book – that you must have known about this.'

Amanda stared at her, watching her lips move, her head shaking apologetically from side to side, noticing the grooves where the comb had raked her steel-grey hair into a shiny chignon. And then she was standing in the long, treacle-dark corridor of an apartment watching Amber as she ran out of the shadows into a room with a view of Central Park, her skirt flying up as she danced across the polished floor to where Nicholas was leaning against some packing crates, arms outstretched, laughing . . .

'As a matter of fact, Cassandra was convinced that it was you who was planning a new life in New York.' Mrs Elsworthy removed her spectacles as if to concede they were no help when it came to seeing the truth. 'Given that your work already takes you there so frequently. And – well, I must say Mr Worth doesn't seem at all the sort of—'

'Of course.' Amanda was staring up at the ceiling, her

arms stiff at her sides. 'I'd have thought the same in your position. Nicholas Worth, steady as a rock. English to the core. And if there's one thing I felt sure I knew about my husband, it was that nothing would persuade him to live in America. I wanted to, you see, at one point. They were going to offer me the editorship of US *LaMode*.' She glanced at the headmistress to see whether or not it was necessary to elaborate on the significance of this. Mrs Elsworthy nodded appreciatively. 'But I didn't feel I could ask him to make that sacrifice. Like you, I was convinced that a man like Nicholas could never feel at home anywhere but here.' Mrs Elsworthy picked up the spectacles on the chain around her neck and replaced them on the end of her nose. 'That's why this is a double shock, you see, Mrs Elsworthy. I'd accepted that he was having an affair, of course. But I hadn't . . . it's another thing altogether, isn't it? Actually having decided to leave your family and go off, to the other side of the world – to make a new life?' She reached out a hand for the tissue that Mrs Elsworthy was offering and blew her nose loudly. 'The thing is – the reason I bought the book in the first place – is I assumed there must be a part of him that regretted it, or at least wanted to make a go of it. For the sake of the children. But this changes everything. I should have been reading, *Yes, It's Over Get Used to It*, shouldn't I?'

Mrs Elsworthy stared at Amanda intently. 'Well, what's to stop you putting up a fight, now,' she said, quietly, 'finding out where this woman lives and going round there and seeing her off?'

'She's dead.'

'That's the spirit, Mrs Worth.'

'No. She really is dead. Dead under the ground dead. My husband's lover was Amber Best. You know, the—'

'Yes, yes,' Mrs Elsworthy looked sideways at Amanda, 'but she passed away several months ago, if I'm not mistaken?'

Amanda nodded. 'Yes. Well. I suppose it might seem odd, that we haven't – resolved it. Or even spoken about it, as a matter of fact. But it's impossible when the other woman was your closest friend, not to mention dead. Nothing is straightforward. We're both mourning her, you see, both of us. And then you can't be sure what you feel. I don't know how to separate the pain of discovering my husband's infidelity, from the pain of losing her, from my anger at her betrayal, and then – I still miss her, which is pretty confusing.' Amanda turned her head to look at Mrs Elsworthy, she blew her nose again. 'So you see, I haven't arrived at the state of "hopeful acceptance" that you're expected to have achieved by this stage in the book. Anyway,' she twisted the paper handkerchief in her hands, 'there's no point in any of that now. Not now we know that if it hadn't been for Amber's illness they'd be there, ensconced in their Manhattan apartment, picking out curtain fabrics.'

'Well, not quite.' Mrs Elsworthy nodded in the direction of the documents. 'I happened to notice the aeroplane tickets were dated the twenty-third of December, just two days before Christmas.' A look of panic crossed Amanda's face, she was getting rapid-fire images of Nicholas and Amber skating on the Rockefeller Center ice rink; spinning out through the doors of Tiffany's, arm in arm, swinging their acqua carrier bags; Amber balanced on a stepladder tying bows to the branches of a Christmas tree. And then

Nicholas, at home in London, impatiently brushing the tendrils of a homemade ceiling decoration out of his face as he pored over documents at the kitchen table; staring bemused at her choice of coat for church on Christmas day and, finally, asking her to change it. 'What a time of year to have picked.' Mrs Elsworthy scrunched up her eyes in empathy. 'Really most cruel.'

'Well, you know what they say about Christmas.' Amanda fumbled for a cigarette. 'It concentrates the mind on all those irritations you can just about tolerate for the other fifty-one weeks. This was my year to do it all, you see, and last year we were at Hedlands – Amber's house. He probably just couldn't face the thought of my low-fat brandy butter.'

Mrs Elsworthy folded her hands in her lap, pulled back her shoulders and tipped up her chin. 'Come along now, Mrs Worth. From what I know of you, you are not so easily beaten. Why give up now?'

'Because I'm tired of being second best.' Amanda closed her eyes and dragged deeply on the cigarette. 'Can you imagine, Mrs Elsworthy, if the Board of Governors were to tell you that they'd found a new headmistress for the school, someone who was so superior to you in every way that you could hardly resent their decision to replace you?' Mrs Elsworthy's eyebrow twitched. 'And then this replacement disappears. Well, you've got your job back, but it's never going to be the same again. You'll always know that she was the one they wanted and you are the one they had to settle for.'

'Well,' Mrs Elsworthy smiled, 'I take your point. But we are all the products of our self-belief, Mrs Worth. Others are only better than us if that is what we decide.

Amber Best is gone. And you have your children's futures to think of.'

Amanda lifted herself very slowly to an upright position on the sofa and smoothed down the back of her hair. 'You're right, of course. I'll try. I'll finish the book, as planned.' Mrs Elsworthy gave her an encouraging nod. 'Then, with any luck, I'll be able to talk to him about the future, rationally. That's all I can promise for now.'

'You don't have to promise me anything, Mrs Worth.' Mrs Elsworthy shook her head slowly. 'Personally I think he deserves to be kicked out on his ear wearing a placard reading "Unfit Husband and Father".' Amanda looked startled. 'Oh yes, indeed, without question. But then he may be more useful to you at home with your family. That's for you to decide.'

'Thank you, Mrs Elsworthy.' Amanda rose to her feet. 'It's a long time since I've been given a talking to in the headmistress's office. I feel rather foolish.'

'Good heavens, don't. We've had them all on that sofa: Marcia Gay, the television presenter, Mr Felix Ash's ex-wife. I keep a little bottle of brandy in my bottom drawer for just such eventualities.' Mrs Elsworthy extended her hand to Amanda. 'It's all part of the service, Mrs Worth.'

It took Jack several minutes to find Santa in the bowels of the back kitchens. The dog was lying with his head on his paws, ear cocked, listening to the radio which Vince had positioned at a convenient distance from his pile of blankets ('He loves pop,' Vince had said, when he bumped into Jack on the stairs. 'Adores the theme tune from *Dynasty*, and I've got him sucking peppermints.') Jack hunkered down on the floor beside the blankets and looped an arm round Santa's neck. 'I just came to see how you were,' she said. Santa waggled appreciatively and tried to lick her ear. 'It's all right out here, isn't it? I mean it may not be the Tiffany suite but you've got everything you need.' The dog waggled more violently, and threw his head back a few times to flex his barking muscles. Jack gathered up a handful of his fringe and started twiddling it into a topknot. 'We'll sort it out, don't you worry,' she said absent-mindedly. 'Despite the trouble you've caused me, you're my kind of dog – bit scruffy, not particularly house-trained and not exactly good-looking but affectionate and loyal. And who wants best in show when you can have a dog with a heart.'

'So . . .' Sam was standing in the entrance to the kitchen, one shoulder propped up against a fridge. He could have been there the whole time for all she knew. 'Character wins out over looks and pedigree, does it?'

Jack glanced at Santa, then at her shoes, and finally half looked at Sam, focusing on his nose rather than his eyes. 'I was just explaining – to Santa – that I'm not going to let him go.'

Sam nodded. 'I think I got that. Are you enjoying the party?'

'Yees.' She paddled her feet on the floor. 'Really getting into the swing of it!'

'Seems like it,' he said.

'How's Bea?'

The way she pronounced the name, like a sting, made Sam smile. 'We're getting along famously,' he said.

'Funny you should say that. And what happened to Flavia?'

'Tucked up in bed, I should think. She wasn't feeling well.'

Jack sucked in her cheeks and widened her eyes. 'Well,' she said, 'didn't take you long, did it, to turn into the stud for hire? Maybe the Brodie twins come as pair, so you can keep one in London, take the other one on location, and keep Bea for special occasions, like, you know – opening the Harrod's sale.'

'Oh dear. Aren't you having a good time, with Slime-on?' Sam's eyebrow twitched.

'Ha!' Jack gave a small, smug if-only-you-knew laugh, the eyebrow twitched again and this time stayed in the raised quizzical position. 'I'm having an unbelievable time, Sam. That is not the issue here, believe me.'

'So what is the issue?'

'Oh, what do you care? You're on your way to the Other Place, you're in bed with Jez Hoffman and, by the way, you might find that turns out to be more than a figure of speech, given his proclivities and your . . . boundless ambition.'

'I think you're being a little bit unfair, Jack.'

'Liddle! Uh, oh! Liddle bid unfair am I? God, doesn't it happen just like that!' She snapped her fingers. 'What next? Liddle house in Belgravia, liddle hacienda in the Hollywood Hills with liddle penis-shaped pool?' Sam looked at his watch. 'I'm sorry.' Jack hugged her knees, and rocked backwards and forwards. 'I just don't recognize you any more, Sam.' She looked up at him, he was staring at her, eyes narrowed, arms folded. 'You know, You've got a smart new haircut and contact lenses, and all these . . . trendy clothes and suddenly you're . . . you're this package, this desirable package, the kind of person that women like Bea have earmarked as a heart starter for their flagging careers. I mean where are you? Where have you gone? I don't want any more of my friends taken away, Sam. That's all.'

'But *you* can take up with the ultimate "package" man, swan down here for a dirty weekend and that's different? We can't all hang around being your safety net, Jack, while you do exactly as you please.' Sam closed his eyes for a moment and pinched the bridge of his nose. 'Look. It'll be OK. You've got what you've always wanted. That . . . that's pretty scary, I imagine.'

'Well, haven't you?' Jack hauled Santa closer to her, making him growl softly.

'Not quite,' said Sam, and he gave her a tight smile, turned and let the kitchen door swing closed behind him.

Jack sat in the dark for a while, then clambered to her feet, licked a finger, ran it under both eyes and took a deep breath. 'Well, curtain up,' she whispered. 'Second Act: Jacqueline cuts the umbilical cord and begins a new chapter of her life – how does that sound?' Santa stared at her, unblinking, and then after a few seconds, collapsed on his paws, defeated. 'Oh, come on, you'll grow to love Simon,' she said brightly. 'I know you will. Sometimes these things take time, that's all. You just have to really, really want them.'

Crossing the floor of the bar on her way to the dining room, Jack saw, through the open door, that Simon's place was empty. His neighbours were each resting a palm on the seat of the vacant chair, nodding and hair flicking and engaging in throat-baring laughter for the benefit of anyone who might be placing bets as to who was in the lead. On the opposite side of the table, Marcus had moved along one into her seat, and was in the process of describing something to Jez's boyfriend that required clasping his head between both hands and manoeuvring it slowly from side to side. She paused in the middle of the floor, deciding what to do, and suddenly, *poooof*, there, floating like Tinkerbell in the gloaming, was a pocket-sized but ferocious-looking Amanda.

'Don't prevaricate, take the initiative,' she said, pointing a miniature red fingernail straight at Jack. She was wearing the Prada tweed suit, a little pillbox hat and a surprising amount of make-up. 'Simon is looking for you or he's gone for a little freshen up. Either way, now is your moment. Go get him, girl.'

'But . . . I'm meant to be interviewing Marcus, now . . . for you.'

'So? Plenty of time for everything. Besides, that gives you the perfect excuse for running after him. You need to get your tape recorder from the bedroom, don't you?'

'Oh yes.'

'Oh yes. Take control. Seize the moment.'

Out in the hall again, Jack fluffed herself up in the giant Venetian glass mirror, yanked down the front of the chiffon dress, checked her teeth for debris and then shimmied up the main stairs. 'It's no use just being *on* when people are looking,' said the Amanda fairy, hovering a few feet ahead of her. 'You have to be the sex kitten for real. You have to live it like it's second nature, you've got to think hot, hot, hot even when you're out of range. Chest out, hips swivelling. That's it – do it now! Go on.' 'Hot, hot, hot,' muttered Jack making fish pouts with her mouth and letting her knees slide across each other as if her thighs were tied together. At the top of the stairs, and just a few yards from the door to their suite, she paused for breath. He was definitely in there, the light was on and she could hear music. He'd have the windows open onto the balcony. He'd be lying on the bed, stripped to the waist, strapped up like Clint Eastwood in *The Beguiled*. He'd say, 'Hey, I was hoping you'd turn up,' and she'd say, 'Dim the lights to red, Simon. I'm ready to go.' No, it would have to be, 'Dim the lights to green, I'm—' Oh, God. She put her hand on the doorknob and turned.

It took her eyes a moment to adjust to the blue light of the room and then she saw that Simon was on the bed, kneeling up on all fours, his face pressed flat against the white sheets as if he was smelling them. She started to move towards the bed, keeping her thighs bound at the top, wondering if she should say something, and then the sheets started to shift and she saw that they weren't sheets at all but a girl, naked except for a layer of white dust that stretched from her collarbone to the top of her thighs.

'Hey.' Simon sat back on his haunches and pointed a rolled-up note at her. 'Come and join in the fun, babe.'

She could feel her mouth hanging open but couldn't summon the will to close it. 'Is that . . .?' She wasn't sure what she wanted to say.

'We're just having a bit of fun.' Simon scratched at his bandaged chest; besides the bandages he appeared to be wearing a pair of leopard-print Y-fronts. 'Angela volunteered to provide the de luxe experience: it's called Skin and Snow.' They both sniggered. 'You've met Angela Brodie, right?' Angela raised her arm. 'Hi,' she said. 'Great room.'

'I just came up for my tape recorder,' said Jack, groping

on the dressing table, without taking her eyes from the bed.

Simon made a sound like a bull trying to clear its sinuses, threw back his head and shook out his hair. 'Get over here,' he said, 'you don't know what you're missing.'

'No, really,' said Jack, edging out of the door. 'I've got to interview Marcus Raven.'

'Oh, cool,' said Angela. 'I love Marcus Raven. Will you tell him I said hi?'

The last chapter of *Yes, He Is Having an Affair*, 'What Happens Next?', was starting to look rather well-thumbed. Amanda turned to the page where she had left off, which was subheaded 'Time to Talk'. She sighed heavily, adjusted the pillows behind her head and started to read:

You have prepared the ground, erected the sandbags to minimize the damage caused, now you must plan the controlled explosion. You will need:

- Several Hours – when neither you nor your partner are hurried, tired, or distracted by other concerns. Avoid the end of the day.
- A Place – where you can be alone without fear of being overheard, ideally far removed from family and friends.
- Neutral Space – avoid the kitchen and, at all costs, the bedroom.
- Plenty of Tea – on no account light the touchpaper when either of you has been drinking.

Practise broaching the subject. Remember from Chapter Three, 'Are You Communicating?' that the way in which you phrase a sentence will often determine the answer. I know about you and Jenny/ I want to talk about you and Jenny/ I think we should talk about you and Jenny. These are all fairly neutral statements but the first is more aggressive than the last and, most importantly, does not suggest the possibility of conciliation.

Approach the confrontation in two stages:

- One – set out the issues you wish to discuss. It is important at this very early stage to limit discussion to those areas that are strictly necessary for building your 'recovery base' (see Chapter Four). For example, it may be important for you to know when the affair started in order to ring-fence the extent of the betrayal in your mind, but do not be tempted to ask more at this stage. Begin to work towards a positive outcome, by asking questions framed in a positive way ('do you want to stay?').

Note: Here we are establishing the framework for our recovery *not* pointing the finger of blame.

- Two – probe for change. Attempt to discover what is necessary for the recovery of your relationship. Avoid use of the word, why? Why is a guilting word (see Chapter Three). Probes for change questions might include: 'when did you start to feel unhappy?'

Note: Here we are asking for answers to help each other, we are not seeking justice for ourselves.

Try mapping out three or four possible questions or statements in your mind before you turn to the section on confrontation. Do not skip this exercise, it is crucial for you to accept and understand the principles before proceeding.

Amanda lay back on the pillows, eyes closed, her lips silently framing the positive questions and the probes for change, pausing in between to memorize each of them. Once she half opened an eye and squinted at the page, shut it almost at once and resumed the mumbling.

'Mummy?' The door opened a few inches and there was a crackle of oilskin. The top of Ludo's head appeared round the door, then his eyes and nose.

'Ludo, you can take your coat off now, sweetie.'

'You haven't taken *yours* off.'

'No, well, Mummy's got stuck in hers, it's not on purpose . . . what's the matter?'

'There's a woman in the kitchen who says she's the housekeeper for the weeken', an Granny Bridget's *furios*.'

'What's Granny Bridget got to be furious about?'

'She said—'

There was a thudding noise in the corridor and a ruddy-cheeked Cass flew past Ludo into the bedroom.

'She said,' Cass was panting, 'shhhhush, Ludo. I am telling her – I AM – she said you really must put your feet down, Nicholas, this is a cott— This is a four-bedroom cottage not . . . somewhere . . . I dunno. An that money should bein – beinves—'

'Invested,' said Ludo.

'I *know*! Be invested for your children.' Cass paused to push the hair off her forehead. 'She said Wot is that woman playing at?' She waited for a reaction. 'That's you, Mummy.'

'What's happened to the other woman?' said Amanda, wearily. 'The housekeeper woman. Don't tell me she's gone?'

'Yep,' said Cass. 'She has *gone*. She said, "sort it out, an' let me know." She had a Luigi e Luna handbag.'

'I don't think so.'

'What's *wrong* about the handbag? Granny Bridget was *furious* when I said about it.'

'Nothing. Your grandmother just doesn't approve of you being quite so . . . good at spotting labels.'

'Daddy's coming now.' Ludo hissed at them through the keyhole as if he'd been told to keep a look out and Cass and Amanda were about to be caught redhanded drinking gin out of paper cups.

'Darling.' Nicholas flung open the bedroom door, not noticing that Ludo was still attached to the handle. He looked hot. 'A woman has just been here offering her services as a housekeeper.' Amanda raised her eyebrows. 'I've sent her away.'

'Why?' Why is a guilting word, said a voice in her head.

'Well, Mother seemed to think she was unnecessary, more than unnecessary – an extravagance. And I took her point.'

'Why?'

'Why? Because perhaps we should be less – she has observed that the children are becoming very M-A-T-E-R-I-A—'

'Oh, for God's sake.'

'Darlings, go away now.' Nicholas flapped his hands at

the children. 'Mummy and Daddy are having an argument about your upbringing.'

'We know,' said Cass. 'We can spell, actually.' Neither of them moved.

'Coffee,' Bridget bellowed from downstairs.

Nicholas didn't flinch.

'Run along,' said Amanda. 'She might smash the cafetière if you're not quick, on the basis that it's too indulgent, and we should be mulching our grounds through old farmer's knickers. I'm surprised coffee's allowed at all, come to think of it. Surely we could make some marvellous peaty concoction from the land, boil up a few roots?'

The children giggled hysterically.

'Daaarling. I think she does have a small point. I mean Ludo, I see, has got a *Christa* jacket.'

Amanda rolled her eyes, Ludo grimaced.

'It was in the sales, Daddy,' he said, tugging at Nicholas's jumper.

'I wouldn't be at all surprised if he were to tell me it was "classic with a twist",' Nicholas ruffled Ludo's hair, 'or "this season's must have". I mean, darling, is that what we really want?'

'Which *we* do you mean exactly, Nicholas? Is that the we, you and me, or is it another we altogether? The real we, in fact. The we that's been the we in your life since before we two became one. Would that be the we? I think so. That *we* would never have been so vulgar, wouldn't you say?'

'Right,' said Nicholas. 'Bed, all of you.'

'Awwww,' there was a general moaning.

'Can't we stay an' watch?' said Ludo.

'Carn we harve *Teletubbies* then?' said Poppy, who had somehow infiltrated herself between Ludo and the door.

'And what's all that about?' said Nicholas, jerking a thumb in Poppy's direction. 'Lady Bracknell I presume? Right, bed. Now. All of you. And no funny business. Mummy isn't feeling well.'

The children filed out politely and Nicholas closed the door behind them. 'Now,' he rubbed his hands together, 'what's all—'

'I know the whole fucking lot, you bloody bastard.' Amanda raised the book above her head with both hands and threw it as hard as she could at Nicholas, missing by several feet and dislodging a watercolour on the wall. 'I know when. Before we even got fucking married. I know why. Why why why?' She flicked two fingers at the book lying sprawled on the floor. 'It's obvious, isn't it? What gutless, limp-wristed reptile wouldn't have been tempted? In the beginning you weren't sure if you could cope, full time, were you? Then, as the years went by, you got a bit more confident and thought, "What the hell! You've only got one life, haven't you? Why compromise the total satisfaction of golden fat boy." You big bloody pig. I hate your guts. I hate you for conning me into thinking we were happy. I hate you for using me. I hate you for criticizing Ludo's jacket when what you really want to say is, "I married a girl from Basildon and it makes me ashamed." You won't have it, will you, your lot? You just can't quite get your head around it unless it's been to the right fucking school and knows the whole bloody bog mats, blah, blah, blah – and that isn't quite *right* and we're not quite *sure* about them and we don't really do it like *that*. I never had a sodding hope, did I?' Amanda fumbled on the bedside table for another missile, her fingers closed round a glass paperweight. 'Did you laugh about me, did you? My shop-girl legs, my funny little ways? Is the way I make love common? A bit all over the place, not holding that little something back. No mystique. A bit *vulgar*. "What you see is what you get with Amanda." Is that what you used to say? "She tries soo hard but she just hasn't quite got it, poor thing? How could she have hoped to ever compare. Oh dear, oh dear, how she tries though. Ha, ha, ha!" ' She lifted the paperweight in the air and as she drew back her arm to take aim, Nicholas flicked up the latch of the bedroom door and bolted.

Behind him there was a loud thud and the sound of the paperweight rolling across the sloping bedroom floor. 'Take that aeroplane and fuck off for all I care,' she shrieked through the closed door. Then there was silence. Nicholas waited in the shadows at the top of the stairs, breathing heavily, his hands tucked under his armpits.

'Hello,' she said, after several minutes.

'Darling?' Nicholas shuffled gingerly towards the door.

'Make sure you're at the party,' her voice was hoarse, 'I don't want to give Davina the satisfaction of thinking I'm manless on my special night. Even if you are, in fact, not a man but a bloody bastard pig.'

Jack walked back down the stairs, the tape recorder clasped tightly in front of her. When she got to the bottom she stood in the hall gazing in the Venetian glass mirror until one of the Bluegrass guests brought her back to the party with a jolt.

'We've moved into the club room,' he said. 'Come on through – everyone's dancing. Listen, aren't you here with Simon Best?'

Jack turned her head to look at the man. She wanted to be left alone but he was too flushed with alcohol and proximity to fame to register her discomfort.

'We were at school together,' he said, giving his legs a bit of a shake out. 'Really great bloke. Really, really talented. Is he around? Love to catch up with him.'

'He's upstairs,' said Jack, 'taking drugs off a naked Brodie twin.'

The man pursed his lips for a second and then convulsed with laughter, nodding his head wildly in knowing appreciation. 'Wouldn't be adall surprised,' he said. 'Quite a guy, Simon. Quite a guy. So! What about a turn around the dance floor while you're waiting!'

The turn consisted of Jack swaying listlessly, while the man sprang around in front of her like a GI on an assault course. Occasionally their eyes would meet, she would give him a weak smile of commiseration, and he would nod back and then resume his pounding performance with even more enthusiasm, like a competitive gym goer who spotted his boss during a workout. At one point she thought he was going to punch her, a desperate ploy to shock her feet into action, but it turned out to be part of a turn and spin routine.

'That was great,' he said, the second the music changed. 'Well . . . er . . . can I get you a drink?'

'No thanks,' she said. 'But could you get me Sam, Sam Curtis? I just need to have a quick word with him.'

'Whatsup?' She was jammed up against one end of a sofa on the edge of the dance floor, like a sheep sheltering in a snowdrift. Sam hovered for a moment and then sat down beside her. 'I thought you might be angling for a dance,' he said.

'I don't feel like dancing,' she said. Her voice was thick and barely audible above the sound of the disco.

'Well . . .' he leant forward with his elbows on his knees, 'actually it wasn't so much a dance that I had in mind as a long, full-length, remedial hug.'

She didn't move. She knew if she moved she would cry. Her hands were clenched in fists on her lap, her teeth sunk firmly into her bottom lip.

He rubbed the leg of his trousers once or twice and stared up at the ceiling. 'Come on,' he said. 'Let's give it a go, you'll feel better.' He took her hands and pulled her gently to her feet. They stood awkwardly for a moment, half shuffling to the music, and then he put his arm around her and she let her head rest against his shoulder. It was several minutes before she could speak.

'I've made such a mess of everything,' she said, her voice juddering as if she were being shaken from inside. 'You wouldn't believe, Sam, what a mess I've made. There's a girl upstairs in my bed, and Simon's snorting cocaine off her. But that's not it . . .' She shook her head violently, rejecting the sympathy in his embrace. 'That's not why I feel such a fool. It's the whole thing – I've just been clinging to this . . . to this idea of someone, this person that doesn't exist! It's not as if he even remembers – anything.' She was sobbing, wiping her nose clumsily on the back of her hand. 'It's not as if *any* of it was ever – *real*. You knew that. Why didn't I? Why couldn't I see?'

'I'm sorry,' said Sam. 'I'm really sorry.'

'No! I don't want you to be! It's a good thing. It is. I needed this, I just – I – I've had so many chances to see what was right in front of me and now it's too late. Everyone else has got a life, found what they want, and I don't have anything. Because mine was all . . . imaginary.'

He tightened his arm across her back and she flopped against him like a baby in a sling, eyes closed, letting the tears fall, saltily, as they swayed together. 'You've got me, Jack,' he whispered. 'I'm real.'

She opened her eyes and lifted her head to look at him. He smiled and pushed a strand of wet hair off her cheek, and then she flinched as if someone had prodded her between the shoulder blades. 'No, Sam,' she said, drawing away from him. 'You're not babysitting me any more. You're so right about the safety-net thing. I've been a selfish cow. But that's it.' She extricated herself gently from his grip, patting his hand briskly to show how recovered she was. 'You've got your own life and . . . and it's *great* what's happening. I'm really happy for you.' Her lip trembled slightly, she rubbed the back of her wrist across her eyes and then smiled as brightly as she could manage. 'Sorry.'

Sam shook his head. 'Don't be.'

'Friends again?' She took a step back.

'Sure . . .' he paused and summoned up a smile every bit as convincing as hers. 'Always . . . hello.' He tipped his head in the direction of the edge of the dance floor. 'Looks like Marcus Raven's got some urgent business with you.'

Jack followed Sam's eyeline to where Marcus was jigging up and down, pointing to his watch and mouthing something.

'Oh, the interview!' Jack clutched her head. 'The tape recorder!' She spun around. It was still where she had left it, tucked into the side of the sofa. 'I'd better go. He's been waiting ages. Thanks again.' She flung her arms round Sam's neck and kissed him hard on the cheek, and when she moved away he saw that she was blushing.

'Andrew, hi there. It's Nick.'

'All right mate? How's it going?' Andrew paused. 'You sound a bit fuzzy.'

'I'm in the garden. In Wiltshire.'

'Oh, right. Everything all right?'

'Er, well . . . not really. Amanda's gone a bit—'

'I saw her on the telly, by the way, she looked great! Bit what?'

'Mad.'

'Howdyoumean?' Nicholas could hear Andrew channel-hopping in the background.

'I'm serious, Andrew. You know the PMT thing she gets, well, she's . . . I've never seen her like this. I've never seen anyone like this, including Linda Blair, just before they sent for the exorcist.'

'What's she doing?'

'Ranting and throwing things . . . shouting stuff about me being a pig and using her and me thinking she has bad legs and no . . . mystique, I think. It was very hard to make any sense of it at all . . . something about before we were even fucking married. A heck of a lot of swearing.'

'Sounds a bit like a fat crisis.'

'A what?'

'You know, when they go ballistic because they haven't

got anything to wear and it all spirals into this self-hate hysteria and the next thing you know they're accusing you of not loving them.'

'Oh, no. No this was different.'

'Has she been taking anything?'

'We'd both had quite a bit to drink.'

'No, for the PMT, I mean.'

'Oh. Well, she has this cream she keeps in the fridge that she's meant to rub in. But, Andrew, it's gone beyond PMT if you ask me. I mean she was chucking things at me. And she's wearing a WaxMac for God's sake – in bed.'

Andrew snorted. 'Oooh, very last season. That *is* worrying.'

'Andrew. Would I be phoning you in the middle of the night, from my garden, if this was a joke?'

'No. How did it start then?'

'Well, it was to do with me taking my mother's side over this – something – and then I criticized her for splashing out on the children and – Bingo!'

'Fsssss.' Andrew made a teeth sucking noise. 'Could be that. They can take siding with the mother very badly indeed.'

'I know, I know, but there's got to be more to it – I just wonder – There have been one or two other things. For instance on the phone, today, she was going on about children's lives being torn apart. She'd obviously read something in the paper, but she was reacting as if it affected her, personally. And over the last couple of weeks – I can't quite put my finger on it, but it's as if, when she's talking to me, she's addressing someone else, someone she . . . detests. That's what it feels like. Could it be – I know it's not exactly your area – but it doesn't sound to you like some sort of paranoid delusion, does it? What if the stress of Amber's death had triggered something, some chemical imbalance, on top of the PMT I mean?'

There was silence on the end of the line.

'What d'you think. Andrew? Are you still there?'

'Has she mentioned Amber?' Andrew's voice had dropped to a murmur.

'No, why?'

'It's just occurred to me that there's another possible explanation.'

'Yes?'

'She thinks there was something going on.'

'I'm not with you.'

'Between you and Amber.'

'What between me and Amber?'

'An affair, Nicholas.'

'Good grief.'

'I just think – it might be that. I'm pretty sure it is that.'

'I see. Well . . . that would certainly explain – Poor Amanda.'

'I should have twigged earlier. It's what . . . some people were saying, around the time of Amber's death, and it's possible Amanda got wind of it.'

'Why didn't you tell me this was going on?' Nicholas's voice was suddenly husky, dry as a bone.

'Because I thought it would blow over and neither of you need ever know about it.' Andrew's tone brightened. 'Anyway, it's probably a good thing it's out in the open. Now you know what the problem is you can just go in there and tell her it's all a vicious rumour.'

'It's not that simple.' The line was bad now, Nicholas sounded as if he were on the other side of the world and the distance had given his voice a flat, mechanical resonance.

'Why not?'

'She's kicked me out for one thing.' He laughed a small, tinny laugh. 'Doesn't want to see me until the party.'

'Well, not now she doesn't, but you can put her straight in a second.'

'I can't, Andrew.' There was a long pause. 'I hope I can explain myself, my behaviour, when we all meet up for the will reading.'

'At Hedlands? But that's not for three weeks. Why wait until then, if things are this bad?'

'Because . . . because I'm not in a position to put her mind at rest, Andrew.'

The line fizzled.

'Nick?' The silence felt like dark outer space. Andrew pictured his friend standing on the lawn in front of the cottage, staring up at the stars, rubbing his knuckles up and down his temple, and as the silence gave way to more static he saw him bow his head, eyes tight shut, willing Andrew to give him a sign that he understood, that he would at least try to understand. 'Nick . . . I don't know what to say, mate. I'm sorry – It just never occurred – Christ! It makes me think we don't really know each other at all. I mean any of us.'

'I think I'd better go,' said Nicholas. 'I've got to make up the sofa.'

Sixteen

In the end, Jack had interviewed Marcus Raven in the front of Sam's van, because there was nowhere else they could escape the music. And afterwards she got into Sam's sleeping bag, stretched out on the bench seat and slept, until the birds woke her in the early hours of Sunday morning. It had frozen overnight, the windows were iced up and outside everything glowed white. Jack wriggled upright in the bag, cleared a patch on the windscreen and peered out at the frosty lawn and, standing in the middle of it, Angela Brodie, moving her limbs through the crisp air like a slow-motion swimmer.

She wound down the window and poked her head out. 'Morning,' she said.

'Hi,' said Angela, keeping her gaze fixed on the horizon. She was wearing a short leopard-skin coat and green glittery wellington boots. 'You never came back . . . to your room.' Her Californian accent was as slow and dreamy as her underwater movements.

'I don't do drugs,' said Jack, by way of explanation.

'Neither do I.' Angela's long Norwegian blonde hair hung stiff as straw in the cold, one arm drifted out weightlessly in front of her. 'But I do sex. Simon said you don't do sex.'

'Of course I do.' Jack tried to sound indignant. 'I do. I just haven't – lately. I have a bad foot.'

Angela nodded. 'Right, your foot.' She stopped in mid flow, brought her hands together in front of her chest and turned her head in the direction of the van. 'You wanna lift back to London?' she said. 'I always like to leave before the morning after.'

'OK,' said Jack, 'I'll just say my goodbyes.'

Vince was polishing shoes at a table when she walked into the back kitchen.

'Oh my,' he said, 'after all that trouble she hasn't so much as removed an earring.'

'Sorry, Vince.' Jack shrugged. 'There was someone else in my bed when I got there.'

Vince pressed his fingertips to his lips, evidently thrilled, then remembered himself and grimaced. 'Horror,' he said. 'So we've come for a bit of a cheer up?'

'Actually, I've come to get Santa,' Jack said. 'Sam says he'll take him back to London if I smuggle him into the van before they wake up. It's only a precaution. I've got full permission from Marcus.'

'And what's madam going to do?'

'I'm getting a lift with the woman who slept with my date – it's been that kind of weekend.'

'Hasn't it just!' Vince raised his hands to the ceiling. 'And won't it seem quiet without you.' He gave her one of his for-the-benefit-of-the-back-row winks. 'However, the work must go on! So what time does madam think Mr Best will be wanting his bandages done?'

'I think,' said Jack, 'that you'll need to see to him on

the hour. Tell him a Dr Farmer recommends it. And thanks, Vince, for everything.'

'Not a bit.' Vince clasped her hand. 'It's been my pleasure.'

Once Jack had stowed Santa safely in the back of Sam's van she helped Angela to load up the Mini with hatboxes. 'They're my regular luggage,' said Angela. 'I don't like edges. What about you?'

'I don't mind them.'

'Your luggage, I mean.' All that Jack was carrying was her rucksack, which she had left overnight in Simon's car. 'Didn't you have a suitcase?'

'Oh, that's fine,' said Jack. 'I don't think I need any of those things any more.'

Angela blinked very slowly as if receiving an electronic message direct to her frontal lobe. 'End of a chapter?'

'Sort of,' said Jack. 'It's not a big deal though.'

Angela blinked again and turned the key in the door of the Mini. For a second Jack wondered if the blinking rate was safe for driving but then the pale fingers snaked over to open the passenger door and it was too late to reconsider.

'So, was it fun?' Jack bunched her legs up as they swept out of the gates just missing a stone urn. 'Your evening I mean.'

'Do you mean was the sex good, or did we connect?' Angela looked at her like seals look at their clubbers in PETA ads, her hair was bone white, like an albino's.

'Er, either,' said Jack.

'I'd say he was a seven,' said Angela, 'but with issues.

So, more like a five. He's a little messed up about his sister. You knew her?'

'She was my best friend.'

Angela nodded. 'Right. So you both got to hang on to a piece of her.'

'No.' Jack stared at her. 'It was something we both . . .' she hesitated. 'Well, something I'd wanted – for years.'

They sat in silence for a moment.

'But now you don't want it any more, right?' Angela glanced over at Jack, though the effect was more like the slow steady sweep of a searchlight.

'No. Actually I've realized I'd been deluding myself.' Jack pronounced deluding in a silly voice and regretted it at once, hurrying on to make up for the lapse. 'I've done that a lot, building people up in my mind, making them out to be extraordinary when really they're . . .' she tailed off and turned her head to look out of the window.

'So, is Sam Curtis one of the fallen idols?'

'Oh no, Sam's my rock.' Jack smoothed down the front of her trousers. 'We've been friends for years. We look out for each other.'

Angela turned the seal eyes on her. 'He was sure looking out for you last night. And this morning. He was sitting on a bench in the garden at five a.m. when I came down.'

'Well, he's got a lot on his mind. And last night I was upset and, well, he was just being Sam – Wooaaaaa.' Jack clutched at the dashboard as the car lurched suddenly to the right causing the Indian charms strung along the top of the windscreen to dance and jangle.

'We have to make a detour to Avebury.' Angela pointed at a road sign to indicate the need for sudden action. 'We have to walk among the stones, feel the pulse of the earth, breathe in the air. I think you need to get in touch with your instincts.'

'OK,' said Jack.

Twenty minutes later, Angela and Jack were standing on either side of a standing stone, faces turned sideways to the freezing rock, arms linked.

'This is pointless,' said Jack. Angela closed her eyes and snuggled closer to the rock. 'Six months ago, maybe things could have been different, but now too much has changed.' She scrunched up her forehead. 'OK since Amber died, I have . . . felt a bit different about Sam. First I found out he and Amber were having an affair and now – now he's this completely different person, who has women throwing themselves at him, and film producers chasing after him, and it's made me . . . notice him, I suppose. It's made me see him *differently*.' They stood there, in silence, Jack blinking in the piercing wind, her eyelashes brushing against the rock. 'And then, last night . . . I couldn't avoid it any longer. I realized that I didn't want to be there with anyone else . . . and I didn't want him to be with anyone but me. It was just that simple.' Jack sighed and flipped around so that her back was to the stone, her hands clenched under the armpits of her Afghan coat. 'But now it's too late. I could make him feel sorry for me. I could go crying to him and say I'd made a terrible mistake. Last night I almost did. He'd probably even give it a try, knowing Sam, because he'd pretty much do anything to cheer me up.' She laughed, and her eyes watered in the wind. 'But his heart wouldn't be in it. To him I'm just a stupid girl who's never really grown up.'

She dug her teeth into her bottom lip and pushed her hands deeper into the armpits of her coat.

'Don't you think you should give him the choice?' Angela sounded half asleep, it was the first thing she'd said in over an hour.

'What? Just . . . come out with it?'

'That's right.'

'But . . . I can't. It would be such a . . . shock to him. He doesn't think of me like that and I don't think I could bear to hear him say it.'

'Say what?'

'Jack . . .' there was a long pause '. . . I don't love you.'

'You really think he could say that?' Angela peered round the side of the stone to where Jack was staring up into the sky, a strange look of peace and puzzlement passing across her face as if she had only just noticed that the clouds moved. 'Come on,' said Angela and she started walking back towards the Mini, her bare legs now flamingo pink under her leopard-skin coat, 'I think we're done here.' She turned her slow motion head towards Jack and gave her what was very nearly a smile.

Seventeen

Amanda arrived at Hedlands earlier than planned but there were already Channel X vans parked in the drive, and cables snaking across the flagstones in the hall. Lady Milly was up a ladder, laying branches of holly across the top of a portrait of Amber.

'Thank God you've come!' She flung her arms wide. 'I can't tell you the battles we've been having. They were just gaily going to start filming, without having thought to dress up the poor house and make it look respectable. Amber would have had a fit! I made them drum up a load of holly and ivy and I've been frenziedly doing the old pictures and banisters routine. What d'you think?'

'It looks lovely,' said Amanda, pressing her sunglasses closer to her face. Milly arched her back to get a better look at her handiwork. 'Apparently they're getting a tree and the whole works for the dinner, whenever it is. The big finale.' She shuddered and started reversing down the ladder. 'Sounds ghastly to me. What exactly do they want from us?'

'It's the night of the will reading.' Amanda shrugged. 'We agreed they could turn up afterwards, on condition they left us alone at the memorial. I think the idea is to get all the beneficiaries reminiscing around her table – saying our thank yous and goodbyes, that sort of thing.'

'Toasting absent friends.' Milly wrinkled her nose and shuddered. 'Can't wait. Well, you can expect tantrums from me if she hasn't left me her *entire* shoe collection. The bags I'm prepared to share.' She winked and hooked her arm through Amanda's. 'What will you be getting, darling, to remember her by?'

'Oh, I'll be getting a divorce.' Amanda smiled stiffly at Milly who dropped her arm and took a step back. 'They were having an affair, my husband and Amber. I'm surprised you didn't know.'

'No!' Milly spoke from under the hand clamped to her mouth.

'Unfortunately, yes. Anyway, don't say anything, please. I don't want it to affect the programme.'

'Bugger the programme, darling.' Milly tucked her arm round Amanda's shoulders. 'This calls for a stiff drink – Jeff . . .' she waved over her shoulder to a man wearing blue overalls, 'can you carry on with the holly, something's come up.'

While Milly rifled in the larder for the sherry, Amanda's phone went. It was Mitzi. 'Yes? Yes it's me. I've got a cold. Yes . . . well what is the theme? . . . Go on . . . go . . . *What*? . . . I beg your— Who? . . . *Julie Elder*? . . . Yes, I know she was there but . . . Martin . . . Anderwurst? . . . But she isn't *a party organizer*, she's a *waitress* . . . I don't care what Martin says, they are not *teaming up* for my— Ironic? . . . I'll give you *ironic*. It's not the bloody cure-all prefix you know . . . I don't care . . . Well, tell him to ring me then. Now.' Amanda slumped at the kitchen table, cheek pressed against the scrubbed oak surface, fists clenched either side of her head. Milly uncurled one of her hands and placed a small tumbler of sherry in it. 'Perhaps I'm going mad,' whispered Amanda, raising her head a few inches and tipping the glass into her mouth. 'I must be. Or was that really my assistant calling to tell me that the theme of the party which I am throwing in two weeks' time is Winter Wonderland?' She took another slurp of the sherry. 'Which means three hundred, or so, of the cream of the fashion world and international party A list are going to be treated to a Holiday on Ice experience in my back garden in Shepherd's Bush. I'm never going to live it down. Never.' The phone went again. Amanda put it to her ear without moving her head from the table. 'Martin . . . I *don't* think it's a good idea.'

Martin's voice was clearly audible on the other end of the line. 'Of course it is! I think it's inspired – a bit kitsch, a bit Gothic. It's *perfect*. I can see it all now – ice sculptures, a carpet of snow. *Feathers* – white feathers, silver and white, glass and fur, thick *polar* fur, like *skins draping*. I'm gonna handle the whole concept, with your fabulous Julie—'

'No, Martin. Julie isn't—'

'Amanda, baby. I've gotta say I think you have to move on. Really. In this business you cannot let your personal feelings get in the way of your creative responsibilities. Let it go, LIG. Because where Julie is coming from is the future and you *know* that, better than anyone.'

'Martin, I am not having—'

'It'll be like a fabulous show, with you, Amanda Worth, as the girl of the hour. Come on! I'm gonna do you like a snow queen dress, sort of medieval cyber, but veeery cool, veeery restrained, very corseted. Who else is gonna make it so fabulous?'

'Just . . .' Amanda closed her eyes. 'No one. I'll speak to you later.'

'Well, that's that, then.' Lady Milly was perched on the table in her pressed Levi's, white suede loafers balanced on a kitchen stool. 'One less thing to worry about.' She rattled her gold bracelet, with its acorn-sized charms, and tipped the rim of her glass against her lips, like a nymph blowing a horn. Amanda hauled herself up on her elbows and removed her sunglasses. 'Did she ever talk to you, Milly, about it?'

'No, darling, she didn't. And you amaze me.' Milly swung her knees around so they were pointing at Amanda. 'There couldn't be any mistake, could there?'

'None. They were going to run away together, to New York. I've got the tickets.'

'Heavens! It all sounds so unlikely, like something out of a film. Amber never cared for New York, as far as I know.'

'Did you . . .' Amanda rubbed at a wine stain on the table top. 'Did you see them together?'

'Yes, of course, but not in any – compromising sense.' Milly tilted her head to one side as if reassessing her memory of those occasions. 'I mean he was here a lot, wasn't he, Nicholas, towards the end? But so was Dave – and I was around, and Roger – I never saw anything that—'

'I think about the sex all the time.' Amanda held her hands flat either side of her eyes, like blinkers. 'I picture them in the meditation room downstairs . . . with candles. Nicholas is always wearing a headband, I don't know why.

He's massaging her with oil. I thought he hated all that sort of thing, you see.'

Milly nodded solemnly. 'I know the feeling, my first husband went off with a yoga teacher. You feel such a – lump. But, if it's any consolation, they'd been doing up the meditation room. No one's been down there in months.' She sloshed some more sherry into Amanda's glass. 'If it helps, I never got the impression she was particularly *keen* on all that. I mean she looked like she lived for nothing else, but she said to me once, she'd rather have a glass of bubbly and a lovely hot bath. She joked about it.'

Milly leant over and touched Amanda's arm.

'What should I do, Milly?' Amanda's voice was a whisper, the blinker hands had closed over her eyes.

'Get a lawyer, darling. Drop a stone before the party, get yourself looking sinfully good, and make him hurt.'

'All right, girls.' Mike was standing in the doorway of the kitchen brandishing a crackling walkie-talkie. 'We're all set up and ready when you are, Lady Milly.'

Milly raised a hand. 'With you in a tick, Mike, just got to touch up the old face paint.' She slipped off the table and bent to whisper in Amanda's ear. 'Life's all a front, darling, of one sort or another. It's just a question of degree really, isn't it?'

Eighteen

'Hello, Miriam speaking.' Sam's mobile calls were being redirected to his newly appointed personal assistant, based, presumably, in his newly acquired office.

'Oh, Miriam, it's Jack.'

'I'm sorry?'

'Jack Farmer, Sam's friend.'

'Oh yes, of course. What can I do for you?'

'Well, I was looking for Sam.'

'He's not in the country just at the moment.'

'Really?'

'Mmmm. He had a bit of good news on the work front, so he thought he'd take a quick break while the going was good. Oh, you'll be wondering about the doggie. I understand he tried to get hold of you, but it was all a bit of a rush, so in the end they dropped him off with Flavia's mother, on the way to the airport. She has her own Pekingese, I believe.'

There was a pause during which Jack was supposed to speak.

'Is there something else I can do for you?'

'What's the job news, then?' Jack waited. 'Is he off to Hollywood!'

'I'm afraid I can't reveal that.' Miriam cleared her

throat delicately. Jack pictured her homemade Philadel-
phia-based lunch snack waiting on a napkin next to the
telephone. 'If you have an urgent message, I will be
speaking to him today. Otherwise they'll be back on Saturday, this time next week.'

'If you could tell him I called,' said Jack. 'It's an
emergency.'

'He isn't back till the night of the party.'

Jack was slumped on a pink suede beanbag in
Amanda's kitchen gazing up at the table where Amanda
stood motionless, like a silver sculpture, being chiselled
away at by Martin and a couple of his androgynes.

'Never mind.' Amanda breathed in hard, pressing
her palms flat against her ribs as Martin yanked on the
metallic-finish corset, playing the laces like a Ben-Hur
charioteer. 'It's waited twenty years, I daresay it can wait
another ten days.'

Jack wriggled down in the bag and glared at her mobile
phone. 'Is she coming to the party?'

'Yes, Jack. *She* is his girlfriend. And as far as she's
concerned you are his old chum who is having a thing with
a fashion photographer. Now, come on,' Amanda shook
out the silver satin skirt. 'You're meant to be giving me
moral support not lolling about feeling sorry for yourself.
Go and get a couple of yards of that snow camouflage.
You and Lydia are in charge of stitching on the stars.'

'Lydia! What are you doing asking *her* here?'

'I've asked them both actually.' Amanda clutched at
the assistant's hands to steady herself as Martin gave a
final tug and secured the silver ribbon laces with a clasp.

'Jack. She was right! Lydia was right about a lot of things, it turns out. She could have been more tactful, granted, but I'm not letting this tear us all apart. This is between me and Nicholas, and I don't want any more casualties, thank you.' Amanda placed her hands on her hips and arched her back as she turned to look in the mirror balanced on the dresser. 'You don't think it's a bit . . .?' She glanced at Martin's face, reflected in the mirror, and thought better of it. 'A bit tight?'

'Of course!' Martin gazed heavenwards. 'But we've got a week to go and the way you're guzzling those Effulox, you'll have dropped another two sizes.'

'Amanda!' Jack scowled at her.

'Oh, for heaven's sake. When can you risk a bit of organ failure, if not before the biggest party of your life and your first social engagement as a single person in God knows how many years?'

'I think it's *fabulous*.' Martin was running his eyes up and down the dress like a greedy tongue. 'You should've left him before the Glamour and Style Awards, and I wouldn't have had to put that extra panel in the chocolate jersey.' He hopped off the table and sidled off before Amanda could catch him with her whiplash look.

'So how much have you lost?' Jack was watching her through narrowed eyes.

'Seven pounds. And Annie Ketchenberg is cutting my hair tomorrow.' They both did the open-mouthed salute and wiggle. 'Yes, the bob is going, signature or not! The bob is old Amanda, and the size twelve with feather shag, is the new, go faster, unstoppable *moi*.'

'Oh God,' Jack clapped her hands over her eyes, 'is *everyone* getting a makeover?'

'Nah, you must be jokin'!' They both turned to see Julie, standing at the back door wearing a short denim shirt dress and white knee boots. She glanced up at Amanda who was staring with barely disguised astonishment at the bare sandalwood tinted thighs. 'Just cos you feel the cold, Mand. No need to begrudge the rest of us wiv superior circulation.' Julie winked in Jack's direction. 'You muss be Jack. Pleased ta meet yer.'

'Hello, Julie.' Jack waved from the beanbag. 'I hear you're chief party organizer.' Out of the corner of her eye she could see Amanda give an impatient snap of her head. 'How's it all going then?'

'Fabulous.' Julie waggled a white pearlized fingernail in the direction of the garden. 'Out there is gonna be all sorta ice-world tents. The lounge is gonna 'ave, like, snow camouflage on the walls. You won't believe it when you see it. 'Ere – Martin's talkin' about us recreatin' the same sorta fing for 'is spring show.'

Amanda closed her eyes and sucked in her cheeks. 'For the last time, Julie, you are not a stylist,' she said, almost without moving her lips. 'And this . . . charade ends the moment the party's over.'

Julie raised her eyebrows at Jack. 'I've not said a fing 'ave I? You know what you are, Mand? You're paranoid. Anyway, I better get on, got two tons of fevvers to unload.' With a nod to Jack she disappeared back out through the door.

'She seems great!' said Jack, hoiking a thumb in the direction of the garden.

'Oh *please*. Don't you start.' Amanda flattened her hands over her ears. 'Hasn't anyone met a Basildon girl before? You'd think she was bloody Judy Garland the way this lot are carrying on— Lydia! Hello! I didn't see you there! Come on in.'

Lydia was standing framed in the door of the kitchen trussed up in a belted mac and high-heeled boots.

Andrew hovered behind her, one arm raised in the air. 'Hello there, door was open.' His voice seemed slightly louder than usual. 'Sorry we're a bit late.'

'But we've got a veeeery good excuse, haven't we?' Lydia flashed her eyes at them the way starlets do in films before brandishing the prize rock on the third finger. 'We're going to have a baby!'

'Well . . .' Andrew placed a restraining hand on her shoulder.

'Well, as good as definitely.' She was smiling tightly, her face was flushed. 'They say there's a fifty-five per cent chance of success with this new procedure.' Andrew glanced at Amanda, then at Jack. 'A bit less among our age group, maybe. But they said – Dr Hayley told me, in private – that I am exceptionally fit, you know, as compared to some thirty-year-old who never looks after herself. So!' Lydia turned her head and gazed up into Andrew's eyes. 'We're over the moon, aren't we, Andy?'

Andrew smiled. 'We're certainly hopeful,' he said.

'And the bad news is – we've been encouraged to talk about it!' She clutched at Andrew's hand, her knuckles were white. 'So, I'm afraid you lot are going to be the ones to suffer.'

'Oh, that is *wonderful* news.' Amanda hitched up her skirts and descended from the table, planting one jewel-encrusted sling-back on a kitchen stool and from there stepping down onto an upended milk crate. 'I am pleased that—' she caught Andrew's eye, 'that it's all looking so positive.'

'That's right,' said Andrew hastily, stepping forward and clasping Amanda's hands between his. 'But more importantly we are so sorry to hear your news.'

Lydia bowed her head, 'I hope it's not—'

'I fear it might be.' Amanda gently extricated herself and took a sharp gulp of air. 'But we're not even going to think about that until I've got this party out of the way, and the Hedlands dinner – that's the deal.' She pointed a finger at each of them, as if to seal her words. 'While we're on the subject, have you all finished your filming slots? Happy with them? Any problems?'

Lydia blushed and started to say something.

'We've scheduled a reshoot for tomorrow,' Andrew cut in, 'to go over some of our stuff. Bit of self-editing required, as you predicted. Lucky you wrote that into the agreement.'

'So long as we're still a united front, more or less. Now' – Amanda tapped her fingertips together – 'Lydia, you and Jack are on camouflage duty, if that's all right, and Andrew, I need you to help shift stalactites. Don't look so alarmed, you can't have an ice grotto without stalactites.'

'I know I haven't endeared myself to you, Jack.' Lydia and Jack were sitting on the floor of Amanda's drawing room, stapling stars onto billowing drifts of snow camouflage. 'Particularly recently.' Lydia pushed her hair out of her eyes. 'I know I've been a bad person to be around. But things will be different now, with the baby. I'll be different.' Jack reached for another silver star, she glanced at Lydia and then back to the camouflage. 'It's hard to explain what it's been like.' Lydia had stopped stapling and was craning her neck forward, willing Jack to look at her. 'I wish I could begin to tell you how important it is – how much of a difference it would make to us, if we could just have our own child. You see, I do care about Andrew – I know you think it's all about me, but I do desperately want to be able to give him this one thing.'

Jack looked up for a moment and nodded. 'I understand,' she said, reaching for another star. 'I can see, from the way he is with Zelda, and the others, what a terrific father he'd make.' Lydia's mouth trembled, she closed her eyes. 'I'm sorry . . .' Jack leant across and touched her hand. 'I didn't mean – I know you want it just as much. And it'll happen, I'm sure it will.'

Lydia hung her head and scrunched up a handful of camouflage in her fist. 'You all think he's the one who has suffered,' she said. 'You don't know what it's been like for me. You don't know how wretched I've felt. How angry.'

Jack was staring at her, she looked at the stapler in her hands and shook her head. 'I just didn't think. I'm sorry. All that stuff about Amber, I should have realized there was more to it.'

Lydia smiled at her, the tense-eyed smile of someone in pain. 'Yes,' she said. 'There was more to it. I just wanted you to know that really.'

'Look . . .' Jack dropped the stapler and clambered to her feet. 'Why don't I get us both a cup of tea. Or maybe something stronger. Would that be a good idea?'

'Tea would be lovely,' said Lydia.

*

Jack's mobile rang as she was making her way towards the kitchen. She pulled the phone out of her jacket pocket, saw the name of the caller on the display, and scrambled at speed down the corridor and into the downstairs bathroom. Once perched on the goldfish embossed lid of the loo seat she pressed the answer button.

'Hello,' she said.

'Hi. It's Sam.'

She tried to picture where he was. Beside a pool? On the balcony of a cliff-face hotel, with a cigar in one hand and a Buck's Fizz in the other, Flavia stretched out on a sun lounger wearing a visor and gold Manolo Blahniks? 'Where are you?' Ooooh . . . too demanding. 'Somewhere lovely, I hope . . . good for you.' Better, but weird.

'Italy. I got a message saying you needed to speak to me, urgently.'

Was that cross, or just anxious? 'Oh. Well, not sooo urgently. Just, I was a bit worried about Santa.'

'He's with Flavia's mum.'

'Right! Gosh. She must . . .' think she's in loco mother-in-law, '. . . be a very kind woman.'

'Yes. Anything else?'

That was a sigh. He sighed. 'Oh. I'm sorry, I didn't realize you were in a rush.' He can't wait to get off the line.

'Well, we're just going for dinner.'

Dinner . . . engagement ring in the soufflé. 'Dinner? It's a bit early for dinner, isn't it?' Interfering, envious, spinstery.

'Time difference, Jack. Besides it's one of those places where you have to get there early and, you know, they give you the whole works.'

Oh God, this is it, he's really going to do it. 'You know what they say; dine early, repent at leisure!'

'Sorry?'

'Nothing. Er . . . your . . . Miriam mentioned a job, a new job, sounded *very* exciting.' Prying, suffocating, slightly reproachful.

'Yeah, there's a couple of possibilities.'

'Great!' He's not going to tell me, he's actually not going to tell me. 'Still, doesn't mean you need to make any sudden decisions, does it? They always say wait until you've got things in perspective. You know, give it a week or two, or three even. I think three is the recommended number—'

'Can this wait, Jack?'

Shit. 'Of course, of course it can – till Amanda's party.' Say something else quick, quick, sound not like friend but potential – 'I am really, really looking forward to seeing you at the party. I wanted you to know that.'

'Great . . . see you then.'

'Don't— I mean . . . remember I am here – for you, that is. If you need me.' Heeelp!

'OK. Gotta go.'

'Sam?'

'What?'

'Have I ever told you how much—'

'OK. Tell him we'll be right there – two seconds. Jack? I've got to ring off now. We've got a car waiting. Bye.'

'Bye.' Jack turned off her phone and placed it on the bathroom floor. Then she stood up and jumped up and down on top of that Nokia as if she was going for trampolining gold.

Nineteen

On the night of the party you could see number 26 Belstone Road from three streets away. The house was draped in a curtain of pea-lights, and a cylinder on top of the roof was belching tiny silver stars into the night sky, covering windowsills, hedge tops and parked cars in a thin layer of glitter. Jack stood for a moment in front of the house, breathing the real air, before clutching her white rabbit cape around her shoulders and making her way up the path to the door.

The two security men who took her name were wearing silver three-piece suits, silver gloves and silver headsets. Beyond them was a tunnel of bronzed boys with frosted hair and eyebrows, dressed in swansdown shorts and carrying cocktails on trays of smoking dried ice. Once past them you were in what had been the drawing room – now a winter wonderland cave – lined with the star-spangled snow camouflage and dotted with white velvet chaises longues and the occasional clear perspex gnome. The entire ground floor, from the front door to the French windows leading into the garden – now the stalactite grotto tent – was two inches deep in white goose feathers.

Amanda appeared round a corner and flung out her arms to embrace Jack. 'Could it be more camp?' She moaned, spitting a feather out of the corner of her mouth. 'And these fucking things, they're everywhere! Ludy's had to be locked in an upstairs room strapped to his Ventolin.'

'You look great. Fabulous Ketchenberg hair!' Jack held her friend at arm's length and admired the full effect. The dress was peculiar but flattering, and the shorter, feathered cut, streaked with silver for the occasion, made her look unexpectedly fragile.

'Oh thanks, Jack – I *feel* terrible.' Amanda put a hand to her ribs. 'What with the Effulox, and the restricted breathing – not to mention the anticipation of seeing my estranged husband for the first time in weeks. Mind you,' she bent towards Jack's ear, 'I am quite looking forward to it in one sense. Martin offered to provide him with an *outfit*, so that he didn't destroy the ambience by turning up in his pinstripe suit.' Amanda made an ecstatic face. 'Can you *imagine*? Of course Nicholas didn't *dare* say no for fear of making me even angrier. Isn't it too good to be true?' They both dissolved into giggles. Amanda suddenly gripped Jack's forearm and flicked her head in the direction of the front door.

Jack turned around to see Nicholas, dressed in a white sealskin belted suit with a strawberry-pink scarf at the neck, carefully removing a white raccoon hat and handing it to one of the swansdown boys.

'No, no.' Amanda was at his side quick as a flash. 'I think you're meant to keep that on'.

Nicholas stood with his shoulders bunched up as if expecting to get his ears boxed at any moment. 'Really?' he said, his expression suggesting that his shoes were pinching badly. 'And the hunting horn thing as well?'

'Oh yes,' said Amanda, 'definitely the hunting horn. Yes, *and* the scarf. It's all part of the look.'

'Won't I get rather hot?' Nicholas was already looking more than usually ruddy cheeked.

'Not at all. Now, Nicholas,' Amanda turned her back to the room and lowered her voice, 'I need you to keep my family as far away as possible from the guests. It's your fault they heard about this in the first place, and you're the only one who knows who everyone is.'

Nicholas wrinkled his brow and ran a finger under the rim of the hat. 'The thing is Sq— um . . . Amanda, I haven't seen half of them since our wedding day. Who's coming?'

'The whole bloody lot it looks like. My parents, Troy, Julie of course – Ah, Davina! Good. You know Nicholas, my husband.'

'Yes. Hello Nicholas. It's been an age.' Amanda could have sworn that Davina winked at him, but fortunately, in Chapter Six of *Yes, He Is Having an Affair*, they had warned of exactly this scenario: '. . . the common experience of Bluebeard Syndrome. Many women find that no sooner have they accepted their husband's infidelity, than they are convinced that he is having an affair with every woman of their acquaintance, no matter how unlikely . . .'

'Let me . . . er . . . show you around,' said Nicholas, offering an arm to Davina and giving Amanda a gentle nudge in the ribs with his free hand. 'What would Davina like to see first, do you think, darling?'

'Oh, I think straight through into the stalactite grotto, my love. There are two bars, Davina, cocktails on the left, champagne on the right, a little sort of polar area, for sitting soft, and the dancing is right down at the bottom of the garden in the round tent.'

Davina smiled lazily. 'How . . . co-ordinated,' she said, taking Nicholas's arm and moving off in the direction of the tent. 'Oh, and Amanda,' she paused and looked back over her wolf-trimmed shoulder, 'Jake Zimbalis is right behind me. I just thought I'd mention it, in case you didn't quite recall meeting him.'

There, indeed, was Jake Zimbalis, CEO of Bondi Sacs, with Rebecca of the non-removable headwear, and another three or four, vaguely familiar looking members of the US *LaMode* team.

'Hello! Great you could make it!' Amanda embraced the first three and then waved encouragingly to those bringing up the rear. 'Jake! We meet again!'

'Fabulous theme,' said Jake, who had opted for the winter pimp look: white leather suit over a white sheer silk T-shirt.

'Well . . . and fabulous outfit.' Amanda was trying not to stare at his diamond-encrusted double L belt buckle. 'How about a drink? Frozen daiquiri, blue arctic – which is gin and something, I think—'

'Great. Love to. But first off – can I cut to the chase, Amanda?' Jake had his arm around Amanda's shoulders and was steering her across the room, in the direction of the tent. 'You're single right? I hear that—'

'Separated – separating rather, for tonight I'm—'

'Whatever. Rebecca,' he hitched a thumb back over his shoulder, 'Rebecca De Manga, recently appointed deputy editor *LaMode*, terrific girl. Very talented. She likes you.'

Amanda smiled politely. 'No hard feelings about the hat thing then . . . I'm afraid I was a little bit—'

'On the contrary, seems to have hit the spot.' Jake was now staring at her intently, as if waiting for her to own up to some misdemeanour before he had to bring it to her attention. 'Listen. I'm gay, so I know what it's like when you're new on the block. It's hard to know what's out there for you. I just wanted to give you a little push in the right direction. Take it or leave it. So . . .' he plucked a Martini off a passing tray, 'what can you do for me?' Jake stared at her expectantly, his top lip resting on the rim of the glass.

'Um . . .' Amanda lifted a finger in the air, as if testing the wind direction. 'If you could just excuse me for one moment,' she said, 'I'll be right back,' and she turned and hurled herself down the steps into the stalactite grotto.

The grotto was bathed in an Optrex-coloured ultra-violet light, at Martin's insistence, so that you could see everyone's underwear, including Gloria Westbrook's, *LaMode*'s distinguished septuagenarian publisher. Amanda pushed her way through the crowds of white, silver and occasionally eau-de-nil clad party A-list, waving and shrieking at the appropriate moments, and finally made it to the bar.

'What can I get you, Mrs Worth?' said the barman.

'What's the one they gave that woman when they had to amputate in mid-air?' She gestured towards the curaçao. 'I want one of them . . . only make it blue.'

'Innit un-ber-leevable?' Amanda turned around to find Julie doing a kind of pole dance, using her as the pole, wiggling up and down and clicking her fingers behind Amanda's head. 'Free cheers for the team!'

'Go away!' Amanda flapped a hand at her, stretching out the other one for a passing martini, to tide her over. 'Don't come anywhere near me, Julie. I mean it.'

'Aw, Mand!' Julie let her hands drop to the hips of her

white leather-fringed mini-dress and pushed her Statue of Liberty crown to the back of her head. 'They all love me! I'm doin' your reputation no 'arm whatsoever. An' 'ere,' she gave Amanda a quick prod with her silver-booted foot, 'we done a lovely job, you 'ave got to admit. Few too many naked boys maybe,' she grinned, 'but ever so tasteful on the whole. The mini arctic-rolls was my idea and they're goin' down a treat. Oh look! There's your mum 'n' dad.'

Shuffling across the floor towards them were two round red spheres, with red arms and legs protruding in the appropriate places, red-painted faces and pointed green hoods.

'Sweet Jesus,' said Amanda. 'Where's Nicholas?'

''Allo Viv, 'allo Jim.' Julie gathered in the pair, one under each armpit. 'Don't they look terrific, Mand? Yeah. Wot are you eggsakly, Viv? Sort of sprites or summink?'

'That's it, Julie. Hello, Mandy darlin'.' Viv raised a red stocking-covered hand to her daughter, and waddled across to where Amanda had frozen, her eyes darting to left and right. 'Oh, I'm ever so sorry, Mandy,' she whispered, 'there was a mix up at the costume shop and the lads opening the new pizza place got our winter elf suits. Lovely they were too. Don't mention it to your father though cos he hasn't suspected a thing.'

Amanda glanced over to where Jim was standing. He doffed his pointy green hat at her and returned to his conversation with Roger Marsh. 'It's an elf suit y'see,' she heard him say. 'This is how they do 'em these days, fatter in the body – and red.'

Roger appeared to be concentrating very hard on the costume. 'Isn't it a tomato?' he said suddenly, grabbing

Jim by the collar. 'Yeah . . . look at that, you've got the glue where the green petal bits were around the neck' – Viv put a hand up to her eyes – 'and then your green hood is your stalk, comin' out of the top. It's quite good, actually.'

'Amanda.' It was Davina, fortunately still chaperoned by Nicholas but nonetheless eyeballing Viv like a python sizing up a gerbil. 'And this would be?'

As Viv opened her mouth to speak, Nicholas, now almost the same shade of red as Viv, swooped, cupped Viv under the elbow, and spun her off in the direction of the bar.

'That was one of the . . . tomato canapé waitresses,' babbled Amanda. 'Actually they do all the vegetarian eats, not only tomato-based things. It just makes it so much easier to see what's what. I simply couldn't go back now to the old one-waitress-fits-all system.'

Davina looked at Amanda as if from the top of a very long slide, her eyes flickered for a moment and then widened as they lit on Julie's name necklace. 'Aaaah, so this is *the* Julie, British *LaMode*'s new discovery.' She licked her teeth. 'And a very old friend of the editor's I hear.'

Amanda drained the blue cocktail and wedged herself firmly into the small space separating Davina and Julie, just as Jim pottered up to join the group.

'There's some bloke over there thinks this is a tomato,' he said, patting his round sides with his red stocking arms, and searching their faces for suitable expressions of incredulity.

Amanda rolled her eyes at Davina. 'Good!' she said. 'I should hope so!' Jim blinked at her as if she were emanating strong light. 'Now Julie, here, is going to show you where everything is – *in the kitchen.*'

'We ate before,' said Jim, scratching his tomato tummy. 'Cos Viv said it would be all coos coos and raw fish.'

'Kitchen! Kitchen!' Amanda waved her hand wildly at Julie. 'Kitchen! Thank-you! Ah, Martin! Just who we were looking for.' She pulled Martin Anderwurst into the circle, presented him to Davina and then curled an arm round Julie and Jim, sweeping them off in the direction of the house. 'Keep him there for half an hour,' she hissed in Julie's ear, 'the names will have gone by then.'

'Oh, it's a shame.' Julie shrugged her off. 'He's yer own father, an' 'e's lovely. What's 'appened to you?'

'Not now.' Amanda smiled her maximum stretch with teeth at a passing designer. 'He is dressed as a tomato – Jerry! Hulloooo.' She peeled off to embrace the managing director of Olevar cosmetics as if he were her own flesh and blood.

Jack had positioned herself right at the entrance to the grotto so she had a clear view of the front door and anyone arriving.

'So who's the lucky boy?' said Marcus Raven, when she'd glanced over his shoulder for the fifth time.

'I'm waiting for Sam,' said Jack, checking her watch. 'Sam and Santa.'

'Of course! Garden Boy and Wild Thing. How could I forget? So, what's the plan?'

'Sex kitten.' Jack pulled the rabbit cape around her

shoulders and folded her arms tightly. 'Not too much, just enough to change his perception of me.'

'Hmmmm.' Marcus lit a cigarette and contemplated her through one scrunched-up eye. 'You don't think he might have noticed your . . . er . . . potential already?'

Jack shook her head briskly. 'He thinks of me like a sister. I told you, he even advised me on how to snare Simon.' She looked suddenly depressed. 'And he's bringing his girlfriend.'

'So, what does sex kitten Jacqueline do, exactly, that good old Jack didn't? Saucy heels I see, rather than plaster boot – that's a start.'

'Yes, and then I've— Oh God! They're here.'

Marcus turned his head slowly. 'So they are,' he said, taking a long drag on his cigarette. 'But where's the girl-friend?'

Sam and Santa were making a swift path towards them, feathers churning in their wake.

'Flavia is at home with her mother,' said Jack in a trancelike monotone. 'When they went to pick up Santa, they told her about the engagement, about the ring in the soufflé and the million-course dinner, and then they decided that Flavia might as well stay at home and start drawing up lists. After all, the wedding has to be pretty soon, what with Sam's new job, and their imminent move to LA.'

'Hi.' Sam was extending a hand to Marcus. 'Got a bit held up.'

'Hi.' Jack pecked him on the cheek and crouched down to stroke Santa.

'I hear you've been away.' Marcus lit another cigarette. 'Got good weather, obviously.'

'Yep, beautiful.' Sam plucked a drink off a passing tray. 'Aaaah, just what I needed.'

'No Flavia?' Jack straightened up, and became engrossed smoothing down her skirt.

'No.' Sam's eyes wandered round the room, he took another gulp of his drink. 'She decided to stay with her mother.'

'Hoh!' Jack's hand leapt to her chest.

'Yeah, well. It seemed like the best idea, all things considered.'

There was a pause.

Marcus stared hard at Jack, then at Sam. 'Jacqueline!' He nudged her foot with the toe of his hand-tooled nubuck loafer, 'Well! I must say I am seeing you in *quite* a different light tonight! Lucky you came along when you did, Sam, or . . .' they both looked at him expectantly, 'I'd have been eaten alive! Grrrroooooowww . . .' He waggled his eyebrows. 'No doubt about it.'

'Yep, you don't want to get into an argument with Jack, she'll have your guts for garters.' Sam raised his glass to a passing guest who took this as a cue to rush over and latch onto him like a chimp.

'Sammy! We have *got* to dance to this,' shrieked chimp girl. 'We have *got* to!' She hooked a wiry finger in his waistband and started dragging him towards the dance tent.

Bea was seconds behind her. 'Oh well,' she said, looking straight at Jack, 'you'll have to do then, I suppose,' and gave a tug on Marcus's silver tie.

Jack watched the four of them as they disappeared into the far tent, Marcus fluttering his fingers at her apologetically, Sam carrying the chimp on his back.

'Jack? Jack, are you all right?' It was Lydia, wearing a white velvet catsuit and whiskery mask.

Jack shook her head. 'No,' she said. 'I've blown it.'

'First things first. Julie's just told me Amanda needs our assistance – she's in the downstairs bathroom. And it's an emergency.'

They found Amanda slumped against the towel rail breathing heavily and gesticulating to her back.

'What?' said Jack, twisting her around. 'I can't see anything.'

'Undo,' said Amanda hoarsely. 'Hurry!' Jack released the sliver clasp and started to tug at the laces, while Lydia hauled on the edges of the corset. 'Careful.' Amanda clenched her teeth. 'I've got to get the bloody thing back on.'

Seconds later the corset was dangling from her waist and they were examining the livid purple indentations on her naked torso. Lydia extended a tentative finger and prodded a scarlet patch, just below her right breast. 'Is that a blood blister – Oooh.' Jack applied cold cream. 'There. Now, maybe if we put something over the top.'

'What about my camisole? That might help.' Lydia unzipped the front of her catsuit to reveal said camisole.

'Yep,' said Jack. 'We'll have that – get it off.'

When they noticed Blumfeld standing in the doorway of the bathroom, his gaze flicking from Amanda's breasts to Lydia's, and back, only Jack was fully clad. 'Please don't let me interrupt, ladies.' His nicotine-tinted eyes swivelled round the bathroom. 'Very nice indeed . . . but no Rio?'

Amanda grabbed a handtowel and pressed it to her

chest. 'Do you mind? We're dressing,' she said, pointing to the corridor.

'Ah yes. Dressing.' Blumfeld winked at Lydia. 'You ladies think some of us live in the dark ages, I fear. Though I must confess,' he gave a little hop of his eyebrows, 'I never appreciated quite how many of you there were. Well, mum's the word.' He reversed out into the hall, popping his head back around the door just as it was about to close. 'Quickly wanted to mention, Amanda, we've been given the chance to front those publications I memo-ed you about.' He tapped the side of his nose. 'I think you know the ones I mean. I have put your name forward this very week, for senior consultant.' Amanda placed both hands against the door and pushed. 'You know you have a responsibility now my dear.' His voice was rising and growing fainter as the gap narrowed. 'There's a big new audience out there, Amanda, and it needs your input. What do we always say: "a fear faced becomes an advantage".'

The door clunked shut. Amanda leant against it and let out a long low moan.

'Who's Rio?' said Lydia, pulling on her catsuit in no particular hurry.

'Never mind.' Amanda beckoned to the corset. 'Now, let's do it again in reverse please.'

'Viv, short for Vivien, like Vivien Leigh?' Davina was sitting side-saddle on the arm of a Mongolian-lamb-covered sofa while Viv perched on the edge of the seat, her handbag clasped between her knees.

'No, actually, my name's Doris. But Jim's nan was

called Doris. So when Doris come to live with us, when Mandy was – oooh, musta been eighteen, I just become Viv.'

'How wonderful. And what year was that exactly?' Davina's fingers were toying lazily with the wool cover, coiling the curls round and round.

'Now, let me see, nineteen seventy . . . six . . . no . . . seventy-five.'

'Reeeealllly.' Davina flexed her feet. 'Isn't that interesting?'

'And that was the year that madam joined Us.' Troy arranged himself behind the sofa, pushing up the cuffs of his leather shirt so that his new bracelet watch was on display. 'Perms 'n' party specials, that was Mand in seventy-five. She did a lovely fluffy perm *threaded* with plastic Babies' Breath . . .'

'Oh, those were the days,' said Davina, sounding like a foreign language student in possession of an untried phrase.

'Were they!' Troy gave a little toss of his head. 'Fifty cans of hairspray on a weekend! Forty bottlesa setting lotion! Twenty boys a night.' He gave Davina a playful push. 'Only kidding! Oh, but it was a laugh wasnit, Viv?' Viv nodded vigorously. 'I used to do Viv on Fridays, didn't I? Shampoo, rinse 'n' set, an' a little something special for Mand's engagement party – remember?' Viv shrieked and covered her eyes with her tomato hands.

'Oh, Christ.' Nicholas, craning his neck over the crowd, had caught sight of the group on the Mongolian-lamb sofa. 'Andrew! We've got to get over there. She's got Viv and the other chap.'

'So?' Andrew took a sip of his margarita and gazed benevolently around the room.

'So we'll be in deep trouble if Amanda sees them . . . fraternizing. Come on.' Nicholas strode out across the room, the drinks he had been sent to get by Davina extended at arm's length in front of him.

'Oh you are a dear,' she said as he burst through the wall of bodies and waggled a glass in front of her, the lion tamer distracting his charge, 'but isn't it awful? I don't think I'm in the mood any more. I should really be going.'

'Fine,' said Nicholas, 'er . . . if you must.'

Davina slipped off the sofa arm and jostled her wolf pelts into position. '*Such* an original party.' She planted a fingernail on Nicholas's forearm, and tilted her head to indicate that he might kiss her. 'It's all set,' she murmured as he pecked her awkwardly on the cheek. 'I'll be waiting for you at the airport on the twenty-third.' Then she stepped back on her four-inch heels, quivering like a skittish pony, tapped the side of her wraparound sunglasses and turned into the crowd.

'What did she mean, Nick?' said Andrew as they watched her pick her way across the room, brittle and exposed as a glass figurine out of its packaging.

'Oh, who knows?' Nicholas pushed the raccoon hat back on his head and fanned his damp matted hair. 'What are you looking at me like that for?'

'You're not still going to do a runner?' Andrew followed Nicholas's eyes as they travelled nervously around the room. 'Talk to me, Nick. Is that what you're doing, running off to New York?'

'Oh, God! Jim's out, I'll have to cut him off at the gnome.'

'Nick you can't do that to her – not after everything she's been through recently.'

'Oh, bugger. Sorry, Andrew, he's almost reached Blumfeld. It's more than my life's worth.'

'Well you're a bloody cool customer, I must say. I'd like to see you sweating a bit more over this.'

'My dear chap, I couldn't be sweating more if I were wearing an Anthrax suit in a Turkish bath, now do me a favour, get rid of this.' He stuffed the damp raccoon hat into Andrew's hands. 'And shut up.'

'Excuse me.' Jack turned to address the young woman standing next to Sam at the bar. 'I'm sorry to interrupt, but there's something I need to discuss with my friend, privately.'

The girl pouted and looked at Sam for confirmation. He shrugged, and returned to his drink.

'That's very understanding, thank you.' Jack hooked her arm through his and pulled him away in the direction of the dance tent, a pint of beer still sloshing around in his other hand.

'If you wanted to dance so badly, you only had to say,' mumbled Sam, trying to get his lips to the glass.

'I don't want a dance . . . Besides, I haven't seen you all night.' She stopped dead in the middle of the floor, and adjusted him, like a wing mirror, so that she was looking straight into his eyes.

'Is this the spot?' Sam glanced around. 'Private enough, I suppose.'

'Sam.' She took a step towards him, he raised his eyebrows expectantly. 'Sam?'

'Yes, Jack.'

'Isn't there something you have to tell me about Flavia?'

'I thought that could wait actually.'

'Well, I have to say what I'm going to say anyway.'

'OK.'

'I wanted to prepare the ground a bit, but you've made that impossible. So I'm just going to come straight out with it. And – will you pay attention, please?' Sam was giving the thumbs-up to a tall man on the other side of the tent. He took a sip of his pint and looked at her sternly. 'Thank you. Now, Sam, I have . . . I don't expect . . . I know this might come as a bit of a shock . . . but I feel that I have . . .' She closed her eyes and jabbed at her cheekbones with her thumbs. 'The thing is, it's very simple really. I love you.' She opened her eyes and Sam was looking at his watch. 'Sam?'

'Yep?'

'Did you hear what I said?'

'Sorry, missed it.' He cupped his hand behind his ear and swivelled it in her direction. 'Bit of a racket.'

'I said I love you.' There was a roar of laughter from the group next to them, Sam waggled the hand and scrunched up his eyes to demonstrate that, this time, he was going to try and lip read as well. She took a step towards him and then another, put her hands on either side of his head, pulled his face towards hers and kissed him. She was breathless from kissing him, her fingers buried up to the knuckles in his tangled mop of hair, tears melting from the corners of her eyes, when Sam finally said, 'I definitely got that.'

Twenty

'So, what happened, then?' Sam was propped up in bed with a plate of toast, a mug of tea and a sweatshirt wrapped around his bare shoulders.

'Then that American in the see-through shirt . . .' Andrew paused on the end of the line for Sam to fill in the blank.

'I know, the gay one.'

'Exactly, him, and the Bondi Sacs boss . . .'

'Blumfeld.'

'Yeah. They were sharing some kind of – observation about Amanda.'

'Like what?'

'Like all comers welcome, knickers off any time any place was the general gist. Anyway, Nicholas swung at Blumfeld. And knocked him out cold.'

'Hurray!' Sam rattled the mug on the plate in appreciation.

'And then he said . . . to the American bloke.'

'Jake . . . Zimbalis.'

'That's it. He said, "If there is one thing I detest it's people who get their facts wrong and couldn't give a damn how much harm they might be doing as a result. And if there's another thing I will not tolerate, *let alone under my own bloody roof*, it is people besmirching the reputations of women I love.'

'*Women*, plural.'

'Yes. And then he sort of gathered up Amanda and gave her this fantastic Hollywood-style, backbender of a kiss. Unlike anything I've seen at a party since – oooh – since you and Jack going at it forty-five minutes earlier.'

'Shut up.'

'Well?'

'Well?'

'Come *on*! After all this time, what did it take?'

'She cracked. She convinced herself I'd got engaged to Flavia and it prompted – a declaration you might say.'

'Fantastic! Is she there, can I have a word?'

'Piss off.'

'So, what has happened to Flavia?'

'We were driving back from the airport, perfectly happy, thought I'd put on some music. Picked up a tape lying around in the front of the van, shoved it on, and it was Jack interviewing Marcus Raven – that weekend we were down at Codrington. Naturally I was going to take it straight off, but she said, "No I want to listen, Marcus Raven is my hero." So we listen and listen and listen and then the interview winds up and they're just chatting, off the record, and he says how he's in this sham relationship with Bea, which is more like a brother–sister thing, and he doesn't know who he is – is he the bloke in *The Willoughby Legacy* or is he – you know.'

'Yeah. Yeah.'

'And she says, "I've been in love with someone who doesn't *exist*, which is even more frightening." And then out it all comes. How she'd wasted all these years thinking she was in love with Slime-on, and never given anyone else a chance because she was so determined he was the one – not consummated, by the way, her and Slime.'

'Really?'

'Yeah, never got round to it apparently – and how she'd had her suspicions, but that night – the night of the Bluegrass party – it had all come to a head and she had realized – she's pretty emotional at this point – that all the time the one she really wanted was *me*.'

'Yes!'

'Yeah. So I was a bit chuffed at this point or, as Flavia put it, "Grinning like a fucking maniac", and then Marcus asked Jack what she was going to do, so I turned up the volume, which did not go down at all well. And then Jack said, "It's hopeless. I think he's happy with this girlfriend of his – despite the *fat ankles*." And Flavia says, "She's never even met me. Where did she get that from, *Samuel*?" '

'Ooops!'

'Right. And I was still grinning, apparently, and that was more or less it. I picked up the dog and she stayed behind with the mother, who turned out to have a pretty foul mouth on her.'

'Heartbreaker!'

'Don't mention the tape to Jack, will you, Andrew? She thinks I was completely in the dark about her feelings, and I haven't exactly disabused her . . . But listen, what about Amanda and Nicholas – did that look at all hopeful? After the fisticuffs?'

'Hard to say. Earlier in the evening I'd have said definitely not. He's been planning to leave her, you know.'

'Shit. Maybe he changed his mind, when he saw her being insulted.'

'Maybe. I dunno. Who knows what's going on in his head, he refuses to talk to me about it. Anyway he seems to think he can explain himself, one way or the other, when we meet on Friday.'

'Right. The dreaded dinner finale. One more reel to go. Well, ring me if you hear any more. Otherwise, see you there, mate.'

Sam rang off and lay back against the pillows for a few moments reflecting on what it felt like to have Jack floating in his bath on a Sunday morning, with the door wide open, so that he could wander past and have a look whenever he felt the inclination. He had dreamt of this moment, of Jack cluttering his chest of drawers with rings and things, Jack padding about in his boxer shorts, stretched out in front of his electric fire reading aloud his TV reviews, a day of sex and TV and listening to music and sex stretching ahead of them.

'Sam.' It was her, drowsy voiced from half an hour of soaking. 'I can't stay here again, this place is a disgusting tip.'

Twenty-One

Transmission clock counts down the seconds.

Camera focuses in on the broad back of a man with cropped silver hair, gazing out across a lake. Voiceover: 'I suppose my original fantasy was that the house would be a stage for outrageous parties, y'know, but 'course, I was pretty much retired when we moved down here . . . off the booze an' all that . . . and Amber was getting into gardening so, in reality, it became this sort of bucolic haven where all our friends could come and just chill out.' Caption bottom of screen reads: Dave Cross. 'I can't tell you the work that went into it. We 'ad the lake drained. I mean years and years of hard slog. And then later on there was the programme, and the Amber Best organic stuff – it never stopped. In the weeks before she died she was planning, planning, y'know, for the house's future as well as everything else.' Cut to Dave Cross walking through the empty gardens. Voiceover: 'Yeah, well. There was a lot of talk about why she kept it a secret – she 'ad Aids, she 'ad this, she 'ad that, she was fiddling her life insurance . . . But in the end that was just a decision we reached – a difficult decision but one that she never regretted. And Amber let her friends know how she felt about them injythe will.' Music fades up, Carly Simon's *We Have No*

Secrets.' Cut to shot of Dave greeting Nicholas at the front door of Hedlands. Nicholas is carrying a briefcase. There is a Christmas wreath on the door. Music fades.

Nicholas and Amanda arrived separately at Hedlands on the Friday, some hours before the others were due. The agreement was that Nicholas would prepare the stage for the reading of the will at 5.00 p.m. and Amanda would supervise the Channel X team and get a full briefing on their plans for filming the dinner that night.

'She's happy to come down a bit early, is she?' Nicholas had said to Sam, on the phone that morning.

'Yep. She'll be there at two.' Sam had cleared his throat. 'She says – sorry Nick – but she says she'll keep Channel X under control on condition that you stay out of her way. And she wants you to do the placement for dinner, bearing that in mind.'

On the way down, Amanda had stopped off at a bookshop and purchased the third in the 'Good Relationship' series, *So You're Getting a Divorce (How to Let Go with Love)*, which she wedged, cover facing outwards, against the side of her sheer tortoiseshell handbag. Back in the car she called directory enquiries, on the hands free, and requested the number of Noble publishing.

'This is Amanda Worth,' she said, when she was put through to the editor of the 'Good Relationship' series, 'and I'm thinking of writing a self-help book for women – one, with respect, that does actually help. What you need is a book about how to get back at him and get back on your feet at the same time, life strategy plus makeover . . . lots of stuff on diet and dress. I mean "framing questions in a positive way" just isn't going to do it for your average wife of a philandering bastard.'

After she'd dealt with Angela at Noble she rang Mitzi to check that her hairdresser was on the way to Hedlands ('and I'm going to need a Doctor Magda top-up, ask her if she can do a kitchen job, on Sunday'), followed by Luigi e Luna, to check that her dress was on a bike to Jack's flat. ('No, no mistake Giancarlo, that's the size all right. Hmm? No, no, not medical advice, just stress. Was she really concerned? Aaaah, bless her, well tell her, no more than I am about her flying with those ten-year old implants.') Then she called Jack. 'It's me. You owe me. I've booked Simon to do a last-minute cover try for the March issue . . .' There was silence on the end of the line. 'Well, think about it, Jack. Otherwise he'd have been at the will reading, wouldn't he? And that might have been ever so slightly awkward for some people.'

'Oh yes.'

'Oh yes. How is it all?'

'Lovely.'

'And don't forget my dress, it'll be with you in half an hour.'

'What is it?'

'The Sicilian widow number that in the end was a little too vamp for the memorial but now I think will be just the ticket.'

'You sound very – punchy.'

'I've got to be, haven't I? This is it, the final chapter: Amber's last will and testament, the end of filming, and my last outing as Mrs Nicholas Worth. It's probably, come to think of it, the last time I'll see Hedlands. Tomorrow morning it'll all be over and we'll begin our new post-

Amber lives. God,' her voice went out of shape as she lit a cigarette, 'you know I honestly can't remember what we were even like four months ago.'

Thanks to Milly's intervention, the front hall of Hedlands was festooned with holly and ivy and a cloud of mistletoe crowned the central wooden chandelier. In the dining room, off to the right, a couple of production assistants were overseeing the decoration of a ten-foot-high tree and Judy, the housekeeper, was in the process of laying the long oak table, burying beeswax candles at intervals along a central bed of black roses and camellia leaves.

'Oh, Mrs Worth!' Judy leapt back from the table when she saw Amanda, wiping her fingers on her apron. 'Your husband said you'd be coming to help us out.' She clasped Amanda's outstretched hands and glanced furtively in the direction of the assistants. 'They were after the gold goblets and that,' she whispered. 'Wanted the whole table all gold and dark and all covered in *grapes*.' Her shoulders bunched up around her ears to indicate the level of her excruciation. 'I said, "She'd never 'ave 'ad that, not in a million years." So Lady Milly, she sorted them out. And now we've got the Christmas table like it should be. Oh . . .' Judy squeezed Amanda's hands more tightly, 'but it's not the same, is it, Mrs Worth? Nothing's the same, is it?'

'There now, Judy.' Amanda gave her a paper handker-chief and dabbed her own eyes with the silk one she'd been using in the car. 'You've done a lovely job. She'd have been very, very pleased.'

'That's what Mr Worth said.' Judy blew her nose and

crammed the remains of the handkerchief up her sleeve.
' "Judy," he said, "no one had style like her and now
you've got it too." He's a lovely man, always got the right
words. Oh, there! Talk of the devil.'

Nicholas was hovering in the doorway brandishing his
right hand which was bandaged into the shape of a small
rugby ball. 'Blumfeld's chin!' he said, waving the hand in
the air like a foam thumbs-up in a crowd. 'Still, worth the
trouble!'

Amanda gestured to Nicholas to retrace his steps and
followed him into the middle of the hall, heels clacking on
the stone flags. 'Right,' she said, when they were at a
suitable distance from the dining room. 'I want you out of
wherever it is they've put us before I get up there.'

'Ah . . . right.' Nicholas glanced at his watch. 'Only
can it wait until after the will reading? We're not supposed
to go to our rooms until later. It's one of her conditions.'

Amanda considered this for a second, looking him up
and down as if she could only gauge the legitimacy of his
request from the cut of his suit. 'All right,' she said, 'but
straight after. What do you need me to do now?'

'Maybe you could have a word with . . . er . . . Mike. I
thought we might insist on keeping the filming of dinner
pretty brief. I think we've all just about had enough,
haven't we?'

'Oh yes, just about.' Amanda was addressing the end
of her fingernails.

'Exactly . . . so the less we have to do of that, the
quicker we can get on with really celebrating Amber's life
and generosity.' Nicholas met her eyes for a second and
then quickly switched his attention to the rugby-ball hand,
making it swoop from side to side like a model aeroplane.

'I'll see what I can do,' said Amanda, and swept past him taking care to elbow the bandaged hand as she went.

'No bedroom allocation? It's most peculiar, isn't it? What have you all done about freshening up?' Lady Milly was leaning against the fireplace in the library, pointing her cigarette at each of the occupants of the sofa in turn.

'Oh, I expect it's to do with us always being late,' said Andrew. 'I think Nicholas just wanted to get this over and done with, as soon as everyone arrived.'

'Well, I don't know.' Milly took a long drag and tossed the stub into the fire. 'Are we all here then? No Simon?'

'No,' Amanda glanced at Sam, 'he's on a job for us.'

'Shaaame.' Milly winked at Jack. 'So *gorgeous*.' She chewed on the word as if it were double cream toffee. 'Nothing like a dazzling photographer to liven up a will reading, I say. Roger isn't going to make it either – trouble with his foot.' She lowered her voice to a stage whisper. '*Gout*, though naturally we're not allowed to call it that, for fear of him sounding like the crusty old buffer he's rapidly becoming. Please,' Milly threw her arms wide, like a TV evangelist, 'whatever any of you do, *never, ever* move to the country.' She sagged theatrically and then lit another cigarette, inhaling as if the smoke were the elixir of life. 'Whatever you try – throw money at the heating, ask all your fastest friends to stay, get Harvey Nics to deliver – you'll still deteriorate three times quicker than your average urban dweller. I mean you just don't get gout in Chelsea.'

The clock on the mantelpiece struck five and, right on cue, the double doors swung open and there was Nicholas, gesturing with the rugby ball. 'Do come through,' he said. 'We're all set up for you.'

Behind him, the sun room curtains were drawn and the room was lit with lamps. In the middle was a table, surrounded by chairs, and at one end a large television set which Dave was seated next to. He waved at them as they approached and then returned to polishing the smudges from the screen with his handkerchief.

'OK.' Nicholas took up the place at the opposite end of the table and made a sweeping motion with his arm. 'Everyone sit down please, anywhere you like. That's it. Now – We are gathered, as you all know, to hear the last will and testament of Amber Eve Irene Best, and I am here in my capacity as chief executor. My client specified that the contents of the will should not be disclosed until today, at five o'clock, exactly four months after her death. It was her belief that this represented a suitable period of mourning and her fervent hope that the lapse of time would create the distance necessary to allow each of us to enjoy the benefits of her . . . passing, without regret. The confidence vested in me has meant that I have been unable to discuss any matters relating to Amber's affairs, or the nature of my involvement therein, at any stage.' He glanced across the table at Amanda and cleared his throat. 'So I, for one, am very relieved that this moment has arrived. This is an unconventional will reading, involving, as it does, the deceased delivering the conditions herself, via a video recording made in the weeks preceding her death.' Nicholas indicated the television with the rugby-ball hand and a murmur went round the table. 'Everything that is outlined in the video you are about to see is ready to be acted upon, subject to your consent. I have drafted these papers for each beneficiary to sign – should you so wish.' He held a sheaf of papers aloft and passed them to Lydia, on his right, for distribution. 'It is also unusual in the sense that this –' Nicholas rotated the bandaged hand as he searched for the appropriate word, 'visual document is not solely concerned with the apportioning of material assets. It was Amber's will that it should be a record of her wishes, that is those things she most desired for her friends and family, after she had gone.' Nicholas's lip quivered and he raised the bandaged hand to cover his mouth before continuing. 'The division of her possessions she has handled separately and that is explained in letters which are waiting for each of you in your bedrooms. Likewise there are aspects of her will that she wanted us all to share in, and others that she felt we might prefer were kept private; these are also dealt with in the letters. It only remains for me to say that this has been a unique experience for me . . .' the hand hovered at his mouth again, 'and it was an honour. Now, if you're ready, Dave. Press the start button, please.'

You couldn't see her clearly. She had propped the video camera on a table to the left of the wing-backed chair in the library, so that the picture was mostly chair, and her profile moving in and out of view, though never quite in focus. Once or twice, as she adjusted the camera position, her face loomed towards the lens, rising up as if through cloudy water and breaking the surface for a split second before submerging into the murky depths again. But her voice was unmistakable, that girlish, husky murmur that had been the theme tune of their lives. 'Sorry,' she said, 'you *know* I'm no good at these things – Now! Thank you all for coming, I've been looking forward to this, believe it or not.' She made it sound like this was going to be fun, like one of the parties she used to spontaneously announce by hurling dressing-up clothes over the banisters until there was a glittering mound of them piled high in the middle of the hall. Jack started to cry. 'As my executor will have informed you' – Amber leant forward in the chair and turned her head to the camera for a moment – 'that's you, Nick, Nick . . .' she waggled her fingers at the screen, 'we decided that the whole division of spoils thing was raaaather vulgar, so we've kept that separate. This video will is dedicated to me, telling you what I want for all of you, years down the line, when I won't be around. You see' – her voice softened and dropped so that Dave had to lean across and turn up the sound – 'in the normal course of events I'd probably have let you all get on with it. But it's true what they say: when you're in my position you start to see things very clearly. The right thing to do seems breathtakingly obvious. And you're impatient, of course. Suddenly the wasted energy, the time spent in the wrong places, with the wrong people, all seems utterly unnecessary. So you'll forgive me if this whole exercise seems like a bit of a liberty. It takes quite a nerve to meddle so brazenly in one's friends' lives, I realize that. But it's the prerogative of the dying, frankly, and I think the least you can do in the circumstances is *indulge* me.' There was a murmur off camera, a flash of white as Amber threw back her head and smiled. 'Dave says, "What do I mean *in the circumstances*" anyway . . .' her voice faded for a moment as she picked up a glass from the floor. 'I like to think that our friendship is strong enough to take it, and special enough to warrant it – I wrote that bit down, quite good, don't you think?' She flapped a piece of paper at the lens.

'And about not telling you all. That I was ill. Well . . .' There was a pause, she sank back in the chair and put the glass up to her cheek, 'I thought I had lots of good reasons . . . but the truth is, I just couldn't face it. For me it was better to have you as friends to the end than as mourners. I'm sorry if that seems selfish now. You can blame Dave, he was all the support I could want.'

Everyone round the table glanced in Dave's direction, wondering what this must be like for him, watching his dead wife talking from the next-door room. He smiled in acknowledgement, keeping his eyes fixed on the screen.

'All right then, let's start.' Amber sat up straight in the chair again and raised a finger in the air. 'First of all, Jack. It is my wish that you should use the old summer house by the lake as a writing retreat and hurry up and write a book, about me, about all of us, or anything at all. You are better than you think (no offence, Amanda).' Amanda looked confused, and then smiled brightly. 'Also I wanted to say I love you, I loved all the times we had together. It's a wonderful gift to have known someone for as long as we have known each other. But forget about me now. I think you'll know what I mean by that. Don't dream it, be it. OK?' Jack blew her nose and nodded her head.

'Now, Sam.' Sam leaned into the table and rested his chin on his fingertips. 'I'm leaving you the business, because I trust you to make it work. I also want you to be in charge of the garden, and don't let all our hard work go to waste.' Sam glanced at Dave, who nodded back. 'Channel X are going ahead with the next series, same deal, here at Hedlands, only this time you're in charge. That should just have been confirmed, if everything's gone according to plan. They wanted you to carry on, we just had to arrange permission for the house and all that. I'm going to miss our TV lives, and I'm going to miss you terribly.' She gave a little shake of her head. 'But it makes all the difference knowing that you'll still be doing it for both of us. That's about it for you, I think. Oh, one more thing. Don't *ever* trade those specs for contact lenses, please.'

Sam pulled his spectacles out of the breast pocket of his jacket and waved them at the screen, before wiping his eyes on his sleeve. 'You bet,' he whispered. 'Whatever you say.'

'Andrew. Most of what I have to say to you and Lydia I've put in a letter, because . . . well, I feel like we had more to sort out.' Amber sighed and hung her head against the side of the chair. 'All of you know Lydia and I didn't always see eye to eye. But I want you to understand it was my fault, I take the blame for all the bad feeling there's been and I want this to mark a new stage for Andrew and Lydia.' Andrew's eyes were closed, Lydia was staring at the screen with a strange half smile. 'I'm saying this in front of the whole group because everyone needs to forgive and forget and help them move on. Lydia, I hope that it's not too late for us to make up. Just because I'm not around doesn't mean it isn't worth it. And Andrew . . . all I want for you is that you should start to take advantage of everything you have going for you, and stop apologizing. This is a chance to turn your luck around, and that's my dearest wish.

'Now to Amanda. I know you'll be on tenterhooks so . . . just for you and Milly I'll make an exception. The bags are all yours and Milly gets the shoes . . . Darling Milly, and all my Ossie Clarkes, naturally.' Milly winked at Amanda, pushed back her chair and went to stand by the window, drawing her pashmina tightly around her and digging her fingers into her upper arms. 'As for the main business . . . well, Nicholas and I have been hatching a bit of a plot behind your back.' Amber laughed, and then lowered her voice adopting a mock serious tone. 'It is raaather interfering of us . . . but we know you too well, Amanda; we know how stubborn you are . . .' she paused to take a sip from her glass, 'and we also know your secret dreams. You cut a very fine figure as the editor of *LaMode*, of course, but the editorship of US *LaMode* is the one you've always wanted. And that is where we think you should be. Hold on – what do I do now, Dave?' Her voice faded as her head turned away from the camera. 'What? This one? OK.' She spun around again and stretched out a hand towards the lens. 'Now for something completely unexpected.' Amber's aquamarine engagement ring loomed like a fuzzy green iceberg, the picture quivered, and then there on the screen, silhouetted against the New York skyline, wearing a starched white trenchcoat and sunglasses not much smaller than diving goggles, was Davina.

'Hello, Amanda,' she said, the thin pencil line of her lips curling slightly at the ends. 'As you can see, I'm on the 110th floor of Bondi Sacs New York, the *LaMode* editor's suite . . . and, as of January, your new office.' Amanda's chin was creeping slowly down her chest, her eyes stared unblinking at the screen. 'Funny how things turn out, isn't it?' Davina placed her hands on the back of what looked like a glass swivel chair. 'You knew that my time here was almost up, and that you would have been first choice to succeed me – that is if you hadn't made it abundantly clear that leaving sunny England was not an option. Well, it would seem that . . . eccentric position has been overruled. Apparently your friend Amber made a few calls, explained that it was a misplaced sense of *wifely duty* that had prevented you from applying for the job,' the pencil lips twitched, 'and the boys on the top floor took the bait. They even went along with holding off meeting you and making it official, on the understanding that you needed to pick up your awards before the rumours of defection started. Well . . .' She paused, her face a picture of frozen composure. 'You won't be surprised to discover that my co-operation in this little scheme was not – how shall I put it – unconditional. Amber generously offered me her final photo shoot, of course, plus she has sweetly bequeathed me that London mews apartment and, as a thank you for keeping this all to myself, a few bits of – memorabilia, I guess you could call them.' Davina stroked the pearl choker around her neck. 'Oh . . . and I get to keep the corporate country club membership. I explained to the board it wasn't really your sort of thing.' She flicked a lazy hand in the direction of the view. 'So, a new life awaits you here. No one likes surprises at your age – but, who knows, you might enjoy this one. I'm meeting you both at JFK in' – she checked the tiny silver watch on her wrist – 'exactly one week's time. Also part of the deal. Au revoir until then, Amanda.' The film flickered and then the screen went black.

Amanda ducked her head violently as if she'd suddenly become hypersensitive to the light, flung back her chair, and, her chin still firmly cemented to her chest, half walked half ran to where Nicholas was seated. Without saying a word she fell into his lap, burying her head in his shoulder and smothering his face with her hands, as if he too was at risk from the dim lamp light.

'There, there, Squidge,' he mumbled through her fingers. 'Everything's all right now. Everything's all right.'

'Ooops, hang on,' Amber's voice quivered in the dark, and then the picture returned, only now Dave was visible in the background, stretched out on the sofa, with a terrier perched on his chest. 'OK, we're back.' Amber took another sip from the glass. 'I hope you took that all right, Amanda. Please forgive us for the subterfuge, but it seemed like the right thing to do at the time.' She shrugged her shoulders and raised her glass to the screen. 'America is where you should be. We love you, I love you, and I want you to be yourself, not to have to fit some mould that's made for people more limited than you.' There was a gulping, strangled noise from the end of the table and Nicholas gestured to Jack to pass the tissues. 'Now for my co-conspirator, Nicholas.' Amber was leaning into the camera again, shaking her head gently. 'Oh, Nick. What can I say? You've given me so much support and advice. So much time, when you should have been with your family. I couldn't have begun to do this without you. And, in a way, these have been some of the happiest times of my life, plotting the ending to our story. Thank you. As for wishes, you have everything you want in Amanda, and your family. So my wish for you . . . is that you stay just exactly as you are, an example to us all of how it's possible to get it absolutely right.

'And lastly, Simon. My lovely brother. Everything I have to say to you is in the letter, because there's lots of stuff I needed to get straight – family stuff. So I haven't got much to add, except that I want you to keep in touch with this lot. They're your family now and I know that they'll be there for you, looking out for you, now that I can't.' Sam took hold of Jack's hand and gave it a squeeze. 'And Dave . . . my rock.' Her voice was shaky now, Dave got up from the sofa and came to stand behind her chair. 'Dave doesn't want to stay here at Hedlands any more, everyone. It's too much for him on his own.' She reached an arm up to him and he took her hand. 'Which is why we're giving the run of the gardens to Sam, and putting the house in trust for all of you. Now you'll never have an excuse not to meet up and be together, and I'll know that my beloved Hedlands isn't going to be carved up into some conference centre. Milly and Rog have already said that Dave and the children can move in with them, until such time as Milly kicks him out . . . or he finds another *lady*.' Dave rocked the hand against his chest and turned away from the camera. There was a pause, he muttered something inaudible, and then in a sing-song voice she said, 'OK. Time to go to your rooms now. Until we meet again.'

The picture went out like a light, leaving the screen grey and empty.

Twenty-Two

It had been one of those nights, one of those nights that happened maybe twice a year, when Amber would ring, always lateish, after he had started to cook something for his supper. 'It's me,' she'd say, 'looking for trouble.' Just the sound of her voice made him smile, husky, mischievous. 'What are you doing?' she'd say. 'You haven't eaten, have you?'

And he'd say, 'No, of course not, what d'you want to do?'

'I want to see you,' she'd say, 'and talk, and drink Martinis.'

So he drove over to her flat, the ground-floor mews flat that she'd had since she was seventeen, a place that was, as she said, 'a terrible advertisement for the owner's domestic skills – I wouldn't let any man but you come here, Andrew. They'd never call again.' You walked straight off the street into a room furnished with a partially destroyed velvet sofa, a tungsten lamp complete with silver umbrella, left behind after some shoot, years before, and eight clothes rails, heaving with enough sartorial bric-a-brac – Sergeant Pepper's military jackets, fur coats, lamé catsuits – to give the impression that she was holding her own exotic charity sale.

'I did once bring a man back here,' she said, casting a lazy eye over the brimming ashtrays and half-full champagne glasses, the mantelpiece cluttered with gleaming lipstick cases and bottles of scent, 'and, darling, he thought the place had been ransacked! He frogmarched me straight to the police station! Fortunately I managed to catch the constable's eye, and they were marvellous about it.'

He had brought with him a bottle of chilled vodka and some olives and, after rummaging for a moment in the purple darkness of her bedroom, Amber produced two sparkling Martini glasses.

'They're a wedding present,' she said, 'but they'll never know, not unless you nibble the rim of yours.'

He hadn't seen her for six months or so. She was a little thinner in the face and her hair was twice as long, almost down to her waist.

'Oh, don't,' she said, when he commented on its extraordinary rate of growth. 'They knot it in, piece by piece, hour after hour. The *lengths* you have to go to, to please these rock legends.'

Andrew had heard that she was seeing Dave from The Perfect Fixture.

'Some would say stalking.' She winked at him and took a long, triumphant drag of her cigarette.

'Since when have you needed to chase anyone?' he said.

Her head was tilted on one side, her top lip, a dark dewy rose colour, hovering on the rim of the Martini glass. 'Maybe since I've realized what I want; maybe since I can suddenly picture the end of the story.' She laughed and stretched her legs out along the floor. She was wearing an emerald-green velvet jacket and gold lurex stockings.

'Funny how it makes it so difficult when you actually care,' she chinked her glass against his, 'but I'll pull it off, Andy, if I proceed with caution, because he likes me all right.' She flashed her best smile, unique in its blend of worldly wise seduction and schoolgirl euphoria. It was that smile that exactly summed up how Andrew felt about her: lustful and protective, wary and enchanted.

'*Likes* you?' he said. 'Oh, and he was always going to be a tough one to crack – PF frontman spurns attentions of the most celebrated rock 'n' roll muse of the late twentieth century – I don't think so.'

She laughed but her smile was different, more guarded. 'It's trickier than you might think, Andy, being a girl like me . . .' The velvet jacket came to the level of a pair of hotpants, her legs were honey brown under the mesh of the lurex stockings. 'A girl like me who's in love with a man like Dave, who, *naturally*, has had it up to here with girls like me.' She waved her cigarette high in the air, and let her head hang back against the seat of the sofa so that he could stare openly, for a few whole seconds, at the long, sparkling legs, the milky-brown arch of her throat. 'When they give up the booze and the drugs it's imperative, you see, that they sever all contact with the good-time element. Their counsellors insist upon it.' She sat bolt upright and drew her knees up under her chin. 'They are so terribly *formulaic* about it all – ' her shoulders drooped to indicate her exhaustion with the process ' – only teetotal girls with good credit will do for their boys. Soo . . .' she flapped her eyelashes, 'that is why you find me scurrying along to AA meetings, every other minute, scrubbed and repentant. I agonized over which would be the proper addiction for the would-be wife of a reformed rock legend, and I came up with sex – ' Andrew stared at her, lips poised to take a sip from his glass – 'but it did seem a bit too good to be true.' She grinned. 'So I settled for drink of course. My downfall was strong shandy.' She squealed with laughter. 'I can tell Dave thinks it's quite sweet, as addictions go. There's some horrible hippy who's been sidling up to him all month, but her tipple was crème de menthe, which is just too revolting to contemplate.' She flicked her ash vaguely in the direction of the fireplace. 'Anyway, just so long as he doesn't think I'm a girl like me.'

'There's no one like you,' he said.

'Well, you and I know that, but as far as Dave's concerned I could be another Gloria . . .' her emerald eyes flashed under the thick fringe of lashes, 'Gloria the groupie, they were married for ten years.' She twirled the stem of the Martini glass between her fingers, gazing into the swirling pyramid of oily vodka. 'They were so in love, only Gloria was very bad for Dave and Dave was very bad for Gloria. I know all about it, darling. We talk about it endlessly in group, their co-dependency, his little cocaine thing, her little food thing . . .' She shivered theatrically. 'Which is how I know that now he needs serenity and security and a hardheaded woman, so that the rest of his life will be blest. And I am that woman. I want to be.' She smiled, almost shyly, and held out the glass for a refill. 'I feel quite silly about him, you see.' She started to laugh. 'Isn't it ridiculous, the trouble we go to, to make ourselves fit other people's dreams, when we know we're perfect for them just as we are?'

Andrew nodded slowly. 'Only some of us can't begin to match up,' he said. It sounded sadder than he'd meant it to.

She blinked at him and drew back her shoulders. 'Well then, Andy. Whose dream would you like to be in?'

'Oh, you know – the usual.'

'Aaah . . .' Amber cocked her head as if trying to hear a distant bell. 'Let's do it then . . . let's make you the answer to Lydia's dreams.'

'We can't,' said Andrew. 'It won't work.'

'Darling,' she said. 'Women change. When they're young they have all these high-minded ideas about who will do and who won't, you just need to remind her how wonderful you are.' Amber tucked a stray piece of hair behind her ear, it shone in the light like wet liquorice. 'We'll just have to make her look at you from here . . .' she stretched her hands out towards opposite walls, 'instead of here.' The strand of hair came loose and fell across her face.

'It's no use. I know I could make her happy, but I just haven't got that . . .' He reached for a stray spent match lying on the rug and crushed it between his fingers, rubbing the charcoal smear roughly on the leg of his jeans. Suddenly he felt that he might cry, overwhelmed by his third Martini, by the smooth, slippery movements of Amber's legs against the polished floor. 'The trouble is, she's right,' he said, keeping his eyes fixed on the charcoal stain. 'I'm just not confident . . . in that way.' He drained the last inch of vodka in the glass.

'And then I just said it . . .' Andrew knelt in front of Lydia, squeezing her hands tightly between his as she sat, stiff and motionless, on the edge of the bed. 'I said, "Amber, will you sleep with me?" I asked her, like a favour, like a practical request. I thought if I could carry that off, then I could do anything.' Lydia gazed at him as if their eye contact was all that was keeping her from falling into the abyss that lay just beyond his shoulder. 'You would never let me explain before, that it was like – like a rite of passage.' Andrew scrunched up his eyes, struggling to extract the appropriate words. 'I felt that if I could – just once – then I'd be free. I'd be – empowered.' He rubbed Lydia's hands between his, as if trying to revive her; her complexion was pale, bloodless. 'Afterwards she made us drink to my new-found confidence. And then I felt ashamed . . . that I'd asked that of her.'

Lydia had stopped staring and was looking over his head out of the window into the black trees on the other side of the lake. Someone was lighting flares in the garden, Judy was rattling pans in the kitchen below. At the far end of the corridor they could hear Dave calling to the children. Andrew put a hand to her chin and tipped her head, forcing her to look into his eyes.

'It was all for *you*, Lydia. She knew how I felt about you, that's why she didn't tell me when she found out she was pregnant. She didn't want it to get in the way . . . of us. You think that having Zelda was all part of her plan. But neither of us would ever have known if she'd had her way.' Lydia closed her eyes tight, but the tears still leaked out, fat and hot; he tried to wipe them away and she ducked her head to prevent him. 'It wasn't meant to happen, Lydia, but I'm not sorry it did. Zelda is part of me.' Andrew stretched out his hand again to touch her face. 'Zelda is my child, we both have to accept that.'

Lydia stared at him for a moment and then lashed out suddenly with her arm, knocking aside his hand and catching his cheek with her fist, her hair trailing in her mouth, her eyes bloodshot. 'Why?' she shouted. 'Why? Why should she be so good, so *generous*, all so that you can live happily ever after with . . .' she clutched at the front of her dressing gown, 'with this *shell*, this – *nothing*.'

Andrew got to his feet and cautiously lowered himself onto the bed next to her, gently placing an arm around her shoulders and settling it there as if preparing for a long, long wait. After a few minutes she let herself sink into him, her damp cheek resting against his shirt, her pale violet eyelids fluttering slightly as if she were dreaming.

'I didn't love you,' she said softly. 'I didn't even see you. To me you were just my last chance to get all those things that were owed to me. And then, when you found out about Zelda, I actually thought it was a bonus, something I could use against you, as a bargaining tool.' She lay limply like a doll in his arms, breathing heavily. 'But gradually something changed. It didn't feel like love, or not any love I'd ever known.' She smiled weakly. 'It took a while . . . but then I realized all I wanted was to make you proud of me. To make you happy. I wanted to give you something back, for making me feel the way I did . . . only the one thing you wanted, I couldn't manage.' She looked up at him, her eyes were swollen. 'And then I realized . . . that this was to be my punishment. To watch you and Amber share something I could never be a part of. To live with the knowledge that she was always going to be the mother of your only child.' Lydia plucked at his hand, spreading the palm in her lap and nodding her head up and down, distractedly. 'She came to see me once, you know. She turned up at the house. "I'm no threat to you, Lydia," she said. "You're the only woman Andrew has ever loved, you know that." She said she wanted us to see more of Zelda. "It'll be better for everyone," she said. I slammed the door in her face.' Lydia's hand quivered as she pushed a damp lick of hair out of her eyes. 'I thought, "You bitch . . . you have everything, I have nothing. How dare you tell me how I should feel?" Then I went upstairs and destroyed every photograph I could find of you and her – every picture of Zelda. And when I'd finished I came downstairs, went to the drinks cupboard, and poured myself the first of many stiff painkillers.' She reached a hand up to the side of Andrew's face, tentatively tracing the outline of his jaw, as if checking to see if it matched with that of the man she had married. Her lips were trembling. 'I always thought I wasn't good enough you see. It was the only thing I had to give – the only way I could have redeemed myself. And she'd taken it away from me.'

'How did she know to put us in the same room?' Jack stretched out on the china-blue cover of the four-poster bed that she and Sam would be sharing. 'I mean that is *very* weird, isn't it?'

'Hmm?' Sam was leaning against the window shutters, watching the children playing on the lawn in the light of the flares. 'No. I expect Nicholas put Judy straight at the last minute. Just a matter of switching me with Slime-on. You'd have been in here with him if this had happened a few weeks earlier.'

Jack lay back on the bed and stared up at the yellow canopy, her face suddenly sombre. 'She'd have liked that, wouldn't she? I mean Amber would have liked to know that someone was taking care of him.'

Sam raised an eyebrow and sauntered over to his suitcase which sat propped open on the stool at the end of the bed. 'I dunno.' He flipped open the lid. 'I thought she had rather a soft spot for me as a matter of fact.'

'I don't mind about that, you know.' Jack propped herself up on one elbow and kicked off her shoes, narrowing her right eye slightly as if she were assessing the flaws in a stone. 'I mean I did feel a bit funny about it . . . at one point.' Sam continued to pick through the contents of his suitcase, occasionally holding up a shirt collar to the light. She pulled herself up on the bed and crossed her legs. 'All right then, what was it like?'

'Fantastic.' Sam made whirling shapes around his head with a pair of socks. 'Fantastical is the word. Who's first in the bath then?'

'Fantastic?' Jack looked pale. 'Howdyoumean? Is it fantastic with me?'

'No . . .' Sam was foraging in the suitcase again, 'eeeruggh toothpaste, *your* toothpaste.' He waved a washbag smeared with white in her direction. 'No, with you it's not so much fantastic, as really real, really *true*, you know?'

Jack frowned.

'Didn't you ever wonder about Simon?' she said, her jaw sliding forward a fraction.

'Of course I wondered about Simon!' Sam tossed a dressing gown onto the floor, followed by a pair of Jack's shoes. 'I had him down as batting for the other team for a start. Did you ever find out?'

'Ha!' Jack lay back on the pillows, throwing her arms

behind her head. 'Did I . . .?' She peered at him through the narrowed eye. 'You don't seem exactly bothered.'

'Well, jealousy just isn't my thing, Jack. You know that. Besides, I'm the better man. So, was it out of this world?'

'Yes, actually.' She gazed up at the canopy, a small private smile flickering on her lips. 'Incredible.'

'Great! Now, you first or me? I'm dirtier, you'll be longer.'

Jack stared at him.

'You,' she said. 'I've got to get my handbag from downstairs . . . um . . . Sam?'

'Hmm?' He had wandered into the adjoining bathroom, leaving the door open behind him.

'D'you think that was our first tiff?'

'No,' said Sam, grinning at himself in the mirror, 'that was just us talking honestly, like lovers, instead of friends.'

'Darling.' Nicholas was standing in the middle of the green bedroom with Amanda clinging on round his neck, sobbing quietly into his shirt front. 'Darling, come on, Squidge, this is going to be way beyond the frozen eye-pack's capabilities.'

Amanda glanced up at his face for a moment, and then tried to burrow her whole head into his chest. 'I can't believe what a poof can do,' she bawled.

'Oh Squidge, that was nothing. I've worn humiliating clothes before, none quite so hot, admittedly.'

'No!' Amanda turned her head to the side for a second, like a crawl swimmer taking a breath. 'I can't believe What I've Put You Through.' She tightened her grip around his neck. 'And all the time you were thinking of me. Planning to uproot your whole life, just for me.' Her head shot back as if someone had yanked on her hair. 'What about the children's schools?'

'Mrs Elsworthy has dealt with the whole thing . . . Pinton Prep is twinned with some frightfully expensive establishment near the Park.'

'Aaaaaawwww, Mrs Elsworthy!' She collapsed on his chest again. Then the hair yanker gave another sharp tug. 'What about the cottage?'

'On the market.'

'Aaooooweee.' Amanda let out a wail and then stopped abruptly. 'God, what a relief.' She grasped Nicholas by the shoulders. 'But what about you . . . and your shooting and riding and . . . everything . . .' Nicholas raised an eyebrow. 'You can't just leave all that – it's your whole – it's your *heritage*.'

'Darling, Squidge. It may be my "heritage", but I can take it or leave it. It's you, my angel, who imagines that all these things are so terribly crucial to my happiness.'

'But your . . . *racing*. What about the racing?'

Nicholas shrugged. 'We're not going to Papua New Guinea.'

'You *hate* New York. You hate it. All those accents and the noise . . . the bottled beer, the brown paper bags. Remember how you hated the brown paper bags.'

'Amanda—'

'Where will we live?'

'For the time being in a rather large apartment, four blocks from the small-fortune school.'

'And work? What about Blumfeld?'

'Ah. That was the fun bit. They got the big compulsory

purchase order from New York yesterday, the morning after the party. Nothing they could do. Not a thing.'

Amanda's arms slipped down his chest, coming to rest around his hips. 'What about us?' she whispered. 'I've destroyed it, haven't I? I've poisoned it.'

'Not at all.' Nicholas rested his chin on the top of her head. 'I should have guessed what was going on inside here.' They stood like that for a moment, Amanda gripping him determinedly, like a tosser with her caber. 'Then again,' said Nicholas, wriggling an arm free so he could look at his watch. 'I think that would have been asking a bit much.'

Amanda nestled closer. 'Is there anything I can do for you?' she said. 'Anything.'

He paused, rubbing his chin absent-mindedly against her forehead. 'Hmmm . . . there is something actually. Could you eat a lot between now and next week and put on your Utterly Butterly bits again – I hate it when you've got bones.'

The sun room was pitch dark now and Jack had to fumble under the shade of one of the lamps next to the door to find the switch. When the light came on there was the sound of mechanical whirring which, for a moment, she couldn't place and then she caught sight of the green eye of the video recorder and realized the tape was rewinding. Her bag was a few feet away, marooned in the middle of the floor, under the table.

'Oh Miss Jack!' she spun around with a start to see Judy, standing in the doorway behind her, clutching a pile of kindling. 'I didn't mean to make you jump – I was just going to lay the fire, but if you're busy . . .' she glanced in the direction of the television, 'I'll come back later.'

'No, I . . .' Jack hesitated and then nodded. 'Well, OK – if that's all right, Judy, I'll only be a minute.' She hovered by the television, and when the whirring stopped, pressed the play button and stood in the shadows, waiting for that first glimpse of Amber's profile. The screen crackled like white gunfire in the night sky and then there was the lake at Hedlands, glaring like flame in the light of the sun. Jack glanced over her shoulder and then back at the screen. This must be the remains of some earlier footage of Otis's that Amber had taped over. The camera panned left, and then abruptly came to rest on a group of people – Dave and Amber, and Sam – lolling on the newly mown lawn, outside the library.

'Otis please, darling.' Amber flapped a hand at the camera. 'Go and film something interesting, we're just talking, it's boring.'

It must have been June, around the time she'd had her fringe cut very short.

'Forget it' – the picture focused in on Dave, stretched out on a wooden lounger, hands behind his head – 'that's not gonna put 'im off. He's got an hour's footage of me washing the Roller this afternoon.'

'Well I give in.'

Otis pulled back the focus so that Sam and Amber were in the frame again.

'Oh don't give in, Sam!' Amber laughed. 'We're getting there, I'm sure we are, aren't we, Dave?'

'No,' said Dave. 'Nothing like.'

'She hasn't even noticed.' Sam ripped up a handful of grass and let it fall through his fingers. 'She's oblivious. I mean,' he lowered his voice and glanced at the camera, which instantly zoomed in on his face, 'the fact is she could catch us both naked in the jacuzzi and she'd think we were looking for a contact lens.'

'No offence, mate,' Dave's voice was faint out of shot, 'but has anyone considered she might have better sense than to think a lout like you had a hope in hell with a beautiful creature like AB. It's just totally effing implausible. Not to mention the likelihood of you bloody well daring.'

'I know.' The camera pulled back, Sam wedged his knees into his armpits. 'I know, it was a stupid idea. Sorry Ambs. I know you meant well. But Dave's right, she was never going to fall for it.'

'It's a good idea.' Amber's voice sounded sleepy. 'We just haven't gone far enough, that's all.'

There was the sound of moaning off camera, and the picture jumped right to rest on Dave who was holding his head and shaking it from side to side. 'Oh give it up, Amber! It's been three years since you 'atched this little scheme. I mean Lydia's got you both canoodling on bloody video.'

'Yes, well obviously we'll have to stage something she can't miss.' Amber's voice was mock peevish. 'Look, do we want her to notice him or not?'

'I don't think' – the camera swung back to Sam – 'she *can* notice anyone, apart from – ' He put a hand up to the side of his mouth.

'Weell, maybe we have to do something about *that* too.' Amber leant into the frame, her wide-brimmed straw hat, obscuring her face from view. 'Let's try the shock tactics first, Sam. This weekend, when you're all down here, she can catch us . . . fooling around. And if that doesn't do it, I'll just tell Simon he's got to give it a go.'

'Great! That's all I need.'

'It'll never *work*, silly. They're totally unsuited. But maybe she needs to find that out for herself.'

'Tiny bit of a risk, don't you think?' Sam was rubbing his hands together as if trying to rid them of something sticky. 'Setting her up with her ideal man! Mr Perfect.'

'You've got nothing to lose, have you?' Amber reached over and patted him on the leg. 'You're never going to get anywhere if she's carrying a torch for him. Besides, men like my brother are a bit like chocolates. Better left to the imagination.'

'I don't know. It's a bit radical.' Sam was kneading his temples now. 'Christ! Imagine if she found out! She'd never forgive us, ever.'

'Well,' Amber glanced at Dave, and smiled, 'that's something I, for one, am prepared to live with. Come on, you know it's wor—' The screen went black for a split second and the scene on the lawn was replaced by a blurry Amber in the half light of the library, swooping towards the lens. 'Sorry,' she said, her arm looming into shot, 'you *know* I'm no good at these things – Now! Thank you all for coming, I've been looking forward to this, believe it—'

A loud knocking drowned out her words and Jack turned to see Judy's head poking around the door.

'Oh don't go,' she said, jabbing the Stop button of the recorder.

Judy edged into the room and stood there smiling at Jack, sympathetically. 'Must be unsettling, was it?' she said. 'Looking back like that.' Jack nodded. 'I don't like the things meself.' She was bustling across the room now in the direction of the fireplace. 'Home movies an' that – you always think, was that what we were really like?' She knelt down by the wood basket and spread a sheet of newspaper in front of the grate. 'It's never quite like you remember it, is it?'

Amanda was sitting at the dressing table by the window. Her hairdresser had just left in a snit ('Anyone would think you were the professional hairdresser, Mrs Worth, with all the instructions you dish out'), and now she was examining the results in the three angles afforded by the dressing-table mirror, plus the compact she was manoeuvring behind her head.

'Read it out again, Nicholas,' she said, and Nicholas, without raising his head from the pillow, stretched out a hand and plucked a piece of writing paper off the bedside table.

'From the top?' he said.

She nodded and smiled at him in the mirror.

'Very well:

My darling Worthies. Look in the bathroom and you'll find a bottle of bubbly which I insist that you open and toast my health without further ado. Amanda, I'm leaving you my bags (as you already know), my fur coats (perfect for the New York winter, darling) and some of your favourite jewellery (see dressing table), plus all those fashion shots which are rotting in the drawers of the planning chest in the library. Dear Nick, you get my art books, and the set of architectural prints in the kitchen corridor. I know you always admired them. Soppy though it may seem I want you to know that yours is the only marriage I have ever truly admired, and, on occasions, even envied. You are the mummy and daddy of the group now, like it or not, and I hope you'll come back often to keep an eye on your brood.

Love you both always,
Amber

Nicholas replaced the piece of paper on the side table and cupped his hands under his head. Amanda watched him for a while in the mirror, absent-mindedly stroking her earlobe and the diamond stud the size of a pea, given to Amber by a certain member of the royal family on the occasion of her twenty-first.

'I didn't know you liked those prints,' she said eventually, taking a sip from her champagne glass. Nicholas tipped his head up so that he could see her face in the mirror and then, as if reassured that she was really talking to him, let it drop back onto the pillow. 'You never mentioned them,' she said, pinching the stud between her thumb and finger and squeezing, 'to me, I mean.'

'Squiiidge.' Nicholas shifted on the bed, doubling the pillow under his head so that he could see her from where he was lying. 'Noow.'

'Oh I know, I'm sorry, Nicholas.' She spun round on the stool to face him, pulling her dressing gown tight around her. 'I know it's ridiculous, only it isn't just since the summer that I was worried about you and Amber. There are things – little things that have troubled me over the years, and then everything sort of snowballed and seemed to fit.'

'Aaah.' Nicholas raised a limp arm in the air like a wounded man begging for assistance. 'Right – I give in. You've got five minutes. Last chance to get it all off your chest.'

Amanda caught her breath and sat up smartly, the bright girl in class who has finally caught the teacher's attention. 'All right,' she said. 'Well, for a start, I thought that Zelda was yours—' There was a snort of disbelief from the bed followed by uncontrollable chuckling. 'It all added up. The dates worked.'

'Darling, what d'you mean the *dates* worked? When exactly had you got it narrowed down to?'

'Tuscany.'

'Tuscany? On the sickie holiday? Good Lord!'

'You were on your own, together, all the time.'

'Not through choice, my darling. You and Dave were *ill*.'

'All right then – I saw you. Before that. At our wedding. I saw you kiss her.'

'Yeeess – and everyone else, several times.'

'This was different – I overheard you – you said, "You know what's right for *us*." You said you were "the luckiest man in the world".'

Nicholas looked up at the ceiling for a moment and then clapped a hand over his eyes in mock horror. 'I was thanking her – I'd forgotten to buy a present to give you on the day, so I rang her in a flap, and she said she'd find something that would look just like I'd chosen it, and sure enough she did, and I was beside myself with gratitude.' Amanda put a hand to her wrist and stroked the tiny turquoise watch engraved with her and Nicholas's initials and the date of their wedding, 18 April 1993. She glanced over at the bed, Nicholas was waggling his eyebrows at her. 'Anything else?' he said. 'You've still got a minute and a half.'

'Yes,' she said, almost inaudibly. 'The note. The note "to the best mother in the world".' Nicholas looked perplexed. 'With the flowers at the funeral, it was in your handwriting.'

'Ah.' Nicholas nodded quickly and then hauled himself up on his elbows as if this one was in an altogether more reasonable league. 'Oh, what the heck.' He ruffled his hair with his hands. 'They'll tell us all sooner or later. The fact is, my darling – Zelda is Andrew's child.'

Amanda's eyes widened in disbelief. 'Andrew's?'

'A one-night stand, apparently. He only found out himself a couple of years ago, poor sod. It was when Zelda needed that blood transfusion. They discovered she was one of those rare blood types, Amber wasn't a match so they needed Andrew before they could operate. He didn't have the first idea until he got that phone call from the hospital.' Nicholas pursed his lips and widened his eyes as if discovering this information for the first time. 'That was the main reason Amber employed me in the first place – to set up an arrangement whereby Andrew could get actively involved in Zelda's upbringing. Amber was convinced that with her out of the way it wouldn't be such an issue for Lydia any more.' Amanda shook her head hard, as if trying to scramble her mental filing system. 'Yep,' Nicholas slumped back on the pillows, 'makes everything fall into place, doesn't it – all that hatred. She was eaten up by the fact that Amber had given Andrew a child. That's why I wrote the note on the flowers. Lydia had forbidden him to send any message, and he was desperate – so desperate, he had to confide in me. Though, of course, I knew it all by then.'

'Oh, Nicholas.' Amanda's face crumpled.

'Ah . . . Squidgeee, come here.' She shuffled obediently over to the bed, head hanging, a tissue clamped to her nose. 'Now, no more of that.' Nicholas pulled her onto the mattress beside him and hugged her tightly. 'I'm going to tell you something, my darling. The week before she died, Amber told me that she knew you were sometimes jealous of her.' Amanda stiffened in his arms. 'She said that was one of the reasons she loved you so much: for rising above it, for being her friend in spite of your anxieties. She said she'd come to accept that she could do nothing about it. And you know why?' Nicholas paused and drew back his head so that he could look into Amanda's face. ' "Because," she said, "it only has a tiny bit to do with me and a lot to do with being Amanda." And you know what I said?' Amanda lay there perfectly still. 'Squidge?' She shook her head. 'I said true love is loving someone despite the pain they cause you.'

'She wants us to play a real part in Zelda's life.' Andrew turned away from the window and held the piece of paper out towards Lydia, who was crouched up against the bedpost like a wastrel in a shipwreck. She didn't move. 'All right, I'll read it. She says,' he tipped the paper up to the light:

As you know, Dave has been saintly about it and has only ever wanted what was best for Zelda. He always said you should have been involved right from the start, right from when she was born – and I think that in trying to protect you and you, in turn, trying to do what was best for Lydia, we both made a mistake. Well, it's not too late, and Dave and I feel that now is the obvious time for you to start to play a significant role in her life, and her in yours. Zelda loves you very much, I know she already senses her bond with you, and we want her to know that you are her father and to have the time to get to know you better. Darling Nicholas has set up a sort of trust (I think!) which would give you a bit towards her upkeep (she has very expensive tastes, naturally) and allows you a say in any decisions about her future. It'll be so much better for everyone. Dave could do with the help, and Zelda needs a mother figure now.

Andrew put the letter in his pocket. 'I want us to forgive each other, Lydia,' he said. 'I've had enough. I want to do this. For Zelda and for Amber.'

'How can you be sure?' Her voice was faint and phlegmy. 'How can you be sure we can make it work?'

'I'm not,' he said. 'I only know that this is our last chance.'

Lydia sat in silence, knees pulled up under her chin, her cheek pressed against the bedpost. After a while she uncurled her legs, slipped off the bed and crossed the room to where Andrew was standing looking out across the lawn. Outside the children were still building a snowman in the light of the flares. She leant across him and opened the window a few inches, letting in an icy blast of wind that made her catch her breath. 'Zelda,' she called, through the narrow gap and all the children looked up at the house and waved.

'Daddy said I couldn't come and see you yet,' shouted Zelda, jumping up and down. 'He said you were *busy*.'

'Come up and see us now, darling.' Lydia was shivering. 'All of you need to come in, right away, it's getting much too cold.' The children slumped where they stood as if they'd been abruptly unplugged and then started padding obediently towards the house. Lydia closed the window, and stood for a moment in silence, watching the trees swaying in the wind. 'I want you to know,' she said, 'that I never slept with any of them.'

'I know that,' Andrew said.

On the other side of the door they could hear the squeak and flap of small wellington boots running along the corridor. 'I will have that champagne now, I think,' she said, turning to draw the curtains. 'Just the one glass.'

When Jack flung open their bedroom door she was breathless, having run without stopping from the sun room. Sam was bent over the suitcase again, a towel wrapped around his waist.

'Jack, have you seen my *Hits of the Seventies*?' he said, without looking up. 'You should get a move on, you know. We've only got half an hour before we're on parade.' Jack didn't answer him. She stood in the doorway, one hand rising and falling on her chest. 'I thought the purple velvet.' Sam slung a jacket over the back of the case. 'Bit tight though, to be honest, *or*,' he did a little fandango step, 'the moleskin with a hint of a print, whatdyouthink?' He looked up and smiled at her. 'You should take a bit more exercise, lady.' He waggled his eyebrows Groucho Marx style. 'Maybe I can be of some assistance?' She opened her mouth to speak. 'Come on then, Jack, the purple or the moley – how do you want me?'

'What about your cord suit?' she said. 'Have you got that?'

'Yeess,' he answered tentatively as if it might be a trick question.

'Wear that,' she said, 'and your specs, will you? You don't look like you without your specs.'

He grinned. 'OK then.'

She walked over to the lacquer chest, picked up the envelope that was lying on top of it, and made her way towards the bathroom.

'I left the water in,' shouted Sam, over his shoulder. 'It wasn't too bad in the end.'

She pulled off her jeans and jersey in two easy movements, slipped off her shoes, and stepped into the bath, holding both arms above her head to keep the envelope out of splash range. It took a moment to find her balance, her toes just making contact with the end, then she pulled the note out of the envelope, opened it up and let herself sink deeper into the soapy water.

My darling Jack,

You're not interested in any of my stuff, not really, but I've left you a ring or two (couldn't resist) and I want you to have my record collection because no one else will appreciate it quite as much, plus the portrait of my mother (that's the thing in brown paper). It has kind of happy memories for you, I think, but none for Simon. I know that you will be the happiest of everyone, if you only aim to see the world in shades of grey, rather than black and white, and remember that none of us can ever be as perfect as you want us to be.

At the bottom, in a different ink, with crude shooting stars and grinning moons dancing around the words, she had scrawled, 'You can't always get what you want, but, with a little help from your friends, you can bet you'll get what you need. Love always, A.'

Twenty-Three

Tracking shot, camera moves swiftly across the brightly lit hall at Hedlands and in through the open door of the dining room. The walls glow a deep red in the firelight, candles flicker, the faces round the table are flushed and animated, apparently unaware of being watched. Camera tracks down one side of the table, taking in the piled-high hair and soft bare necks, the hands resting on the backs of neighbouring chairs.

Cut to close-up of Dave Cross, rising from the head of the table, his glass raised in his right hand. 'Here's to the best wife, mother, friend and muse that anyone could hope for. Amber Best. Long may she continue to be a force for good in our lives.'

Everyone round the table stands, their glasses raised to the ceiling, their heads flung back and a cry of, 'Amber!' rings out like a chorus.

The camera pans to a portrait of Amber, Dave and the children over the fireplace and The Rolling Stones' 'Angie' fades up with the credits. The channel X symbol and the date float across the bottom of the screen.

Voiceover: 'That was a repeat of a programme that was first broadcast in January. Donations to the Amber

Best blood disorders research fund should be sent to
ABBDR, PO Box 409.'

Sam flicked the remote control to Off and stretched out on
the floor of the sun room.

'Well I liked "Angie" for the closing credits, rather
than "Simply the Best",' he said, reaching out a hand to
Jack. 'Definitely an improvement.'

She laughed and let her head rest back on Santa's
prone, hot body. 'I liked it *all* better,' she said. 'Ten months
on it seemed to have settled down a bit somehow, didn't
you think?'

Amanda glanced up from the colour supplement open
on her lap and held out her empty wine-glass for Andrew
to fill. 'Mmmm. We did a pretty good job in the end. No
regrets, apart from wearing Luigi e Luna for the dinner
finale, of course. Martin still hasn't forgiven me. Oh, I do
miss these things – Sundays just aren't the same without
the papers, are they, Nicholas?'

Nicholas shook his head solemnly and nuzzled up to
her on the sofa. 'No darling, it's horrid for us. Mind you,'
he winked at Andrew, 'the driver and the house in the
Hamptons somewhat make up for the disappointment.'

'Yes.' Andrew cleared a space next to the fire for the
bottle of claret. 'We hear you had Jim and Viv staying for
the summer.'

'*Had . . .*' Amanda shuddered. 'They're still with us –
living in what was supposed to be our "entertainment
cottage". It has the most divine outdoor eating area which
Jim, how can I put this, has turned into an *allotment*.' She
raised her eyes from the magazine and smiled.

'And she's got Julie over there too.' Jack gave Amanda an affectionate prod with her toe. 'Isn't that right?'

Amanda flicked faster through the pages of the supplement. 'By the time I arrived she was practically part of the package. "Jewleee from Lundun".' She pinched her nose affecting a Brooklyn whine. ' "We gotta see this Jewlee!" What can you do? And, besides, I had to have someone to keep Rebecca *De Manga* off my back – so to speak.'

'Darling?' Lydia poked her head round the door. She was carrying a baby tucked into the crook of her arm. 'Andrew – aren't we meant to be picking up Zelda?'

'No, Milly said she'd drop her back later.' Andrew glanced at his watch. 'Come and sit down here with us for a minute.' Lydia propped the baby over her shoulder and came to perch beside him on the sofa.

'How's Amber?' Jack stretched out a hand to jiggle one of the tiny sheepskin-booted feet.

'Oh, you know, won't go to bed, doesn't want to miss anything.' Lydia smiled blearily. 'The usual.'

'I'll go and get Zelda, if you like.' Simon jabbed at the fire with the poker. 'I've got to go over there some time anyway – check up on them all.' He kicked at a log with the toe of his biker boot, sending a shower of sparks onto the hearth and prompting Andrew to leap up and move the bottle.

'Very good of you, mate.' Andrew patted Simon affectionately on the shoulders. 'Great idea. Wouldn't have anything to do with Roger's niece staying with them, would it?' He winked at the room and they obliged with a collective murmur of interest. Simon continued to riddle the fire, shaking his head, but when he turned to get another log from the basket he was grinning. 'By the way.' Andrew waved his diary aloft. 'We need to get all your possible dates for Amber's christening. Let's start with you, Amanda, you're always the trickiest.'

'The rest of the year is impossible.' Amanda fished in the bag at her feet, dragging out a leather-bound book not much smaller than a Bible. 'And January's out, I'm afraid.'

'First weekend of Feb?' Andrew licked his finger and turned over another page. 'Everyone all right for that?'

'Let's see – Eeeeurgh. No.' Amanda stabbed at the book with her pencil. 'That's when we're putting together the issue on New Model Talent. I'll either be personally plying Tiziana with prescription drugs or in the hospital.' She covered her eyes with both hands. 'He wants to do the whole shoot in a giant flotation tank, with all the girls in mermaid tails. Can you imagine? If only you hadn't been busy, Simon, it would all have been so easy.'

'Who's your one to watch, then?' Jack hugged her knees and gazed up at Amanda who hesitated and then continued to flick purposefully through the month of February. 'Oh . . . er . . . someone called Lucille Demoins,' she said, without looking up. 'Little Texan thing, looks like the young Mia Farrow. We're convinced she's going to be huge. Well – you know . . .' a muscle flickered in her upper lip, she stopped turning the pages and her eyes met Jack's for a moment, 'good enough, anyway.'